WOMEN
OF THE
POST

WOMEN
OF THE
POST

JOSHUNDA SANDERS

PARK
ROW
BOOKS

PARK
ROW
BOOKS™

Recycling programs
for this product may
not exist in your area.

ISBN-13: 978-0-7783-3407-1

Women of the Post

Park Row Books
22 Adelaide St. West, 41st Floor
Toronto, Ontario M5H 4E3, Canada
ParkRowBooks.com
BookClubbish.com

Printed in U.S.A.

For General Harriet Tubman and every single
Black woman veteran, past, present and future.

WOMEN
OF THE
POST

PART . ONE

ONE

JUDY

From Judy to *The Crisis*

Thursday, 14 April 1944

Dear Ms. Ella Baker and Marvel Cooke,
My name is Judy Washington, and I am one of the women you
write about in your work on the Bronx Slave Market over on
Simpson Street. My husband, Herbert, is serving in the war, so
busy it has been months since I heard word from him. It is the
fight of his life—of our lives—to defend our country and maybe
it will show white people that we can also belong to and defend
this place. We built it too, after all. It is as much our country
to defend as anyone else's.

All I thought was really missing from your articles was a fix
for us, us meaning Negro women. We are still in the shadow of
the Great Depression now, but the war has made it so that some

girls have been picked up by unions, in factories and such. Maybe you could ask the mayor or somebody to set us up with different work. Something that pays and helps our boys/men overseas, but doesn't keep us sweating over pails of steaming laundry for thirty cents an hour or less. Seems like everyone but the Negro woman has found a way to contribute to the war and also put food on the table. It's hard not to feel left behind or overlooked.

Thank you for telling the truth about the lives we have to live now, even if it is hard to see. Eventually, I pray, we will have a different story to tell. My mother always says she brought us up here to lay our burdens down, not to pick up new ones. But somehow, even if we don't go to war, we still have battles to fight just to live with a little dignity.

I've gone on too long now. Thank you for your service.
Respectfully,
Judy Washington

Since the men went to war, there was never enough of anything for Judy and her mother, Margaret, which is how they came to be free Negro women relegated to one of the dozens of so-called slave markets for domestic workers in New York City. For about two years now, her husband, Herbert, had been overseas. He was one half of a twin, her best friend from high school, and her first and only love, if you could call it that.

Judy had moved with her parents from the overcrowded Harlem tenements to the South Bronx midway through her sophomore year of high school. She was an only child. Her father, James, doted on her in part because he and Margaret had tried and tried when they were back home in the South for a baby, but Judy was the only one who made it, stayed alive. He treasured her, called her a miracle. Margaret would cut her eyes at him, complain that he was making her soft.

The warmth Judy felt at home was in stark contrast to the

way she felt at school, where she often sat alone during lunch. When they were called upon in classes to work in groups of two or three, she excused herself and asked for the wooden bathroom pass, so that she often worked alone instead of facing the humiliation of not being chosen.

She had not grown up with friends nor had Margaret, so it almost felt normal to live mostly inside herself this way. There were girls from the block who looked at her with what she read as pity. "Nice skirt," one would say, almost reluctantly.

"Thanks," she'd say, a little shy to be noticed. "Mother made it."

Small talk was more painful than silence. How had the other Negro girls managed to move with such ease here, after living almost exclusively with other Negroes down in Harlem? Someone up here was as likely to have a brogue accent as a Spanish one. She didn't mind the mingling of the races, it was just new: a shock to the system, both in the streets she walked to go to school and to the market but also in the halls of Morris High School.

Judy had been eating an apple, her back pressed against the cafeteria wall when she saw Herbert. He was long faced with a square jaw and round, black W.E.B. Du Bois glasses.

"That's all you're having for lunch, it's no wonder you're so slim," he said, like he was continuing a conversation they had been having for a while. Rich coming from him, with his lanky gait, his knobby knees pressing against his slacks.

A pile of assorted foods rose from his blue tray, tantalizing her. A sandwich thick with meat and cheese and lettuce, potato chips off to the side, a sweating bottle of Coke beside that. For years, they had all lived so lean that it had become a shock to suddenly see some people making up for lost time with their food. Judy finished chewing her apple and gathered her skirt closer to her. "You offering to share your lunch with me?"

Herbert gave her a slight smile. "Surely you didn't think all this was for me?"

They were fast friends after that. It was easy for her to make room for a man who looked at her without pity. There had always been room in her life for someone like him: one who saw, who comforted, who provided. Her father, James, grumbled disapproval when Herbert asked to court, but Herbert came with sunflowers and his father's moonshine.

"What kind of man do you take me for?" James asked, eyeing Herbert's neat, slim tie and sniffing sharply to inhale the obnoxious musk of too much aftershave.

"A man who wants his daughter to be loved completely," Herbert said. "The way that I love her."

Their courting began. Judy had no other offers and didn't want any. That they had James's blessing before he died from a heart attack and just as they were getting ready to graduate from high school only softened the blow of his loss a little. As demure and to herself as she usually was, burying her father turned Judy more inward than Herbert expected. In his death, she seemed to retreat into herself the way that she had been when he approached her that lunch hour. To draw her out, to bring her back, he proposed marriage.

She balked. "Can I belong to someone else?" Judy asked Margaret, telling her that Herbert asked for her hand. "I hardly feel like I belong to myself."

"This is what women do," Margaret said immediately.

The ceremony was small, with a reception that hummed with nosy neighbors stopping over to bring slim envelopes of money to gift to the bride and her mother. The older Negro women in the neighborhood, who wore the same faded floral housedresses as Margaret except for today, when she put one of her two special dresses—a radiant sky blue that made her amber eyes look surrounded in gold light—visited her without much to say, just dollar bills folded in their pockets, slipped into her grateful hands. They were not exactly her friends; she worked too much to allow herself leisure. But some of them were widows, too. Like her, they had survived much to stand proudly on special days like this.

They settled into the plans they made for their life together. He joined the reserves and, in the meantime, became a Pullman porter. Judy began work as a seamstress at the local dry cleaner. Whatever money they didn't have, they could make up with rent parties until the babies came.

Now all of that was on hold, her life suspended by the announcement at the movies that the US was now at war. The news was hard enough to process, but Herbert's status in the reserves meant that this was his time to exit. She braced herself when he stood up to leave the theater and report for duty, kissing her goodbye with a rushed press of his mouth to her forehead.

Judy and Margaret had been left to fend for themselves. There had been some money from Herbert in the first year, but then his letters—and the money—slowed to a halt. Judy and Margaret received some relief from the city, but Judy thought it an ironic word to use, since a few dollars to stretch and apply to food and rent was not anything like a relief. It meant she was always on edge, doing what needed doing to keep them from freezing to death or joining the tent cities down along the river.

Her hours at the dry cleaner were cut, so she and Margaret reluctantly joined what an article in *The Crisis* described as the "paper bag brigade" at the Bronx Slave Market. The market was made up of Negro women, faces heavy for want of sleep. They made their way to the corners and storefronts before dawn, rain or shine, carrying thick brown paper bags filled with gloves, assorted used work clothes to change into, rolled over themselves and softened with age in their hands. A few of them were lucky enough to have a roll with butter, in the unlikely event of a lunch break.

Judy and Margaret stood for hours if the boxes or milk crates were occupied, while they waited for cars to approach. White women drivers looked them over and called out to their demands: wash my windows and linens and curtains. Clean my kitchen. A dollar for the day, maybe two, plus carfare.

The lists were always longer than the day. The rate was always offensively low. Margaret had been on the market for longer than Judy; she knew how to negotiate. Judy did not want to barter her time. She resented being an object for sale.

"You can't start too low, even when you're new," Margaret warned Judy when her daughter joined her at Simpson Avenue and 170th Street. "Aim higher first. They'll get you to some low amount anyhow. But it's always going to be more than what you're offered."

Everything about the Bronx Slave Market, this congregation of Negro women looking for low-paying cleaning work, was a futile negotiation. An open-air free-for-all, where white women in gleaming Buicks and Fords felt just fine offering pennies on the hour for several hours of hard labor. Sometimes the work was so much, the women ended up spending the night, only to wake up in the morning and be asked to do more work—this time for free.

Judy and Margaret could not afford to work for free. Six days a week, in biting winter cold that made their knees numb or sweltering heat rising from the pavement baking the arches of their feet, they wandered to the same spot. After these painful experiences, day after day all week, Judy and Margaret gathered at the kitchen table on Sundays after church to count up the change that could cover some of the gas and a little of the rent. It was due in two days, and they were two dollars short. Unless they could make a dollar each, they would not make rent.

Rent was sometimes hard to come up with, even when James was alive, but when he died, their income became even more unreliable. They didn't even have money enough for a decent funeral. He was buried in a pine box in the Hart Island potter's field. James was the only love of Margaret's life, and still, when he was gone, all she said to Judy was, "There's still so much to do."

Judy's deepest wish for Margaret was for her to rest and enjoy a few small pleasures. What she overheard between her parents as a child were snippets and pieces of painful memories. Negroes lynched over rumors. Girls taken by men to do whatever they wanted. "We don't need a lot," she heard Margaret say once, "just enough to leave this place and start over."

Margaret's family, like James's, had only known the South. Some had survived the end of slavery by some miracle, but the Reconstruction era was a different kind of terror. Margaret was the eldest of five children, James was the middle child of eight. A younger sibling left for Harlem first, and sent letters glowing about how free she felt in the North. So, even once Margaret convinced James they needed to take Judy someplace like that, it felt to Judy that she always had her family in the South and the way they had to work to survive on her mind.

Judy fantasized about rest for herself and for her mother. How nice it would be to plan a day centered around tea, folding their own napkins, ironing a treasured store-bought dress for a night out. A day when she could stand up straight, like a flower basking in the sun, instead of hunched over work.

Other people noticed that they worked harder and more than they should as women, as human beings. Judy thought Margaret maybe didn't realize another way to be was possible. So she tried to talk about the Bronx Slave Market article in

The Crisis with her mother. Margaret refused to read a word or even hear about it. "No need reading about my life in no papers," she said.

Refusing to know how they were being exploited didn't keep it from being a problem. But once Judy knew, she couldn't keep herself from wanting more. Maybe that was why Margaret didn't want to hear it. She didn't want to want more than what was in front of her.

Herbert's companionship had fed her this kind of ambition and hope. His warm laughter, the way she could depend on him to talk her into hooky once in a while, to crash a rowdy rent party and dance until the sun came up, even if it got her grounded and lectured, was—especially when James died—the only escape hatch she could find from the box her mother was determined to fit her future inside. So, when Herbert surprised her at a little traveling show in Saint Mary's Park, down on one knee with his grandmother's plain wedding band, she only hesitated inside when she said yes. It wasn't the time to try and explain that there was something in her yawning open, looking for something else, but maybe she could find that something with Herbert. Her mother told her to stop wasting her time dreaming and to settle down.

At least marrying her high school buddy meant she could move on from under Margaret's constant, disapproving gaze. They had been saving up for new digs when Herbert was drafted—but now that was all put on hold.

The dream had been delicious while it felt like it was coming true. Judy and Herbert were both outsiders, insiders within their universe of two. Herbert was the only rule follower in a bustling house full of lawbreaking men and boys; Judy, the only child of a shocked widow who found her purpose in bone-tiring work. Poverty pressed in on them from every corner of the

Bronx, and neither Judy nor Herbert felt they belonged there. But they did belong to each other, and that wasn't nothing.

Sometimes Judy thought of the ocean when she looked over the Bronx. Her neighborhood was situated on some of the city's steepest rolling hills. They rippled slightly in some places but dove deep down in others—it made parts of the Bronx appear like they were ebbing and flowing under the heavens. There on the ground, newspapers carried by the wind wandered in the street. In the distance, drills and metal hammered on as the men building the Triborough Bridge seemed to be always at work.

A handful of Negro women were already standing on the street when Judy and Margaret arrived, barely a few feet apart, many of them coffee colored, their hair pressed and pulled back into severe ponytails or left to sit in tight curls over their foreheads and eyes. The prostitutes who still lingered from the night before wore too much makeup and showed their gartered thighs. Moving her attention to the women around her made Judy curious to know how they managed to keep the garters' loops from ripping into the fabric. A delicate detail in a hard edged life.

By the time the sun was rising in the sky, brightly colored Fords started to pull in. Margaret jutted her chin toward a blonde woman in a turquoise station wagon.

The woman's cutting, brown eyes scanned them, her gloved hand on the steering wheel as she stared. Judy could not look away from the stranger's appraisal, so when they locked eyes and the woman yelled "Come here," it was obvious who she was summoning. Margaret whispered, "Go on."

As she walked hesitantly toward the car, Judy looked quickly at her mother for further reassurance. Every step she took toward the frowning woman and the air of disdain around her,

Judy thought about the money they needed for rent, for food, to keep the lights on. The chorus *We need the money, we need the money*, repeated in her head.

By way of introduction, when Judy reached the partially rolled-down window, the blonde said, "Thirty cents for four hours."

Addition wasn't Judy's thing, but she could surely divide, and the offer was less than ten cents an hour. "Ma'am, may I ask what kind of work it is?"

As soon as the question left her mouth, Judy tasted its stupidity. All work recognized as real labor was men's work, except that Negro women had always worked together with their men. They knew how to do both kinds of labor.

White women like this one, however, were newly initiated into the juggle that working within and beyond home required. She laughed bitterly. "Girl, I have a house to run on my own. I have no time to barter." Her eyes narrowed like she was trying to see into Judy's spirit. "I need the windows cleaned, the chandelier dusted, the silver polished and toilets cleaned. Forty cents for five hours."

The reminder of just how far that number was from the rent she needed made Judy hold her breath. "Fifty," Judy said, exhaling after a beat.

The woman paused. She took a gloved hand off the wheel and studied the road in front of her windshield for long minute, as if another answer waited beyond the traffic light.

"Fine," the woman said.

Relieved, briefly, then anxious, Judy turned back to give Margaret a slight wave. Margaret motioned for Judy to get in the car, making a fast-sweeping gesture with her hand. The woman reached over to open the passenger side door as Judy tried to get in the backseat.

"Girl, get up here. I am no chauffeur for Negro girls."

The last thing Judy wanted was to get inside the car, especially hearing the loud laughter of the other women on the market behind her. Feeling their eyes, including her mother's, her cheeks went hot with shame, and Judy reluctantly crawled into the front seat, hands flat on her thighs, her paper bag crushed between her forearms like it was the only thing keeping her from flying away.

Sunlight filled the sky for their drive north. The black-and-red fire escapes and lonely tenements in the city changed to suburbs, leafy sweet gum and maple trees in neat, round tufts growing in perfect rows, their canopies protecting the big white houses behind them.

It gave Judy time to reflect on how a job like this was even possible for a Negro girl. The truth was that there was a shortage of white help in New York and America since Adolf Hitler and Mussolini came to power and began antagonizing the US. That was what had triggered Secretary of State Henry Stimson's closing off immigration from abroad, cutting off the flow of the preferred European maids. A similar stipulation had been in place two decades before the second world war, but cultivating American labor, even in the private sphere of homes and apartments, picked up in popularity a generation later.

All around them, in morning news headlines, the electronic ticker that wrapped around the *New York Times* building near Times Square, at the movie house in ten-minute newsreels, in radio bulletins and Roosevelt's fireside chats, was a steady stream of unrelenting anxiety. The world was on fire, and it would never be right again. One exception to this lapse in their normal way of life would be for their husbands, sons and brothers to come on home. As it was, no one knew how long the men would be gone—or if many of them would make it back. A day at a time, the women had to keep leading their lives.

As the woman parked, she said, "Let's get you started on those six hours."

Judy's stomach sank. "Ma'am," she said, carefully.

The woman's tone was droll, almost daring. She was, Judy noted, a practiced bully. "If the extra hour will put you out, perhaps you can find a trolley home?"

Judy knew a trolley ride back home meant failure to herself but, more importantly, to Margaret. It would also take an hour and a half, at least, possibly longer, to get back, where there was no guarantee she'd find more work. She also didn't have the extra money to spend on a ride home.

"No, ma'am," Judy said, relenting to the pressure. She could see Margaret now, huddled and cold on one of those crates, waiting for her as she had to walk the miles back home as the sun set. "Six hours will be fine." Her teeth gritted lightly before she smiled without teeth.

"I figured as much." The woman sniffed.

The woman's house was small enough, with a black roof and matching shutters. The windows *were* filthy, and Judy wondered how many years of storms and wildlife had gone by since this lady decided to do something about them. Inside, clutter congregated in every corner. The kitchen was especially chaotic: empty boxes felled by disuse, dishes caked over with flour, cloudy water with various dishes floating in a grayish, filmed river. When she could tear her attention away from the disaster, Judy tilted her head to glance at the chandelier, a once-regal object that had not sparkled in many months.

But the toilets—well. They had streaks of yellowish brown on their covers, below the porcelain bowls. Someone had missed the mark by quite a bit. It smelled like exploded bowels, a steamy, salty stench that brought the bile from Judy's throat onto her tongue. She swallowed quickly and breathed from her mouth. Judy fought the urge to spit at the woman, to run out of the house and start the long walk back home.

But even if fifty cents would not allow her to pay all her bills, it was better than nothing. Judy hung her purse on the bathroom door in defeat as the woman directed her to the paltry cleaning supplies. "These are for you."

It was a small kindness but a kindness nonetheless; the gloves in her bag were torn. She was happy to have these intact ones for the work ahead, even if they were moist. From what, she didn't even want to guess. She and Margaret had learned the hard way that Blue Mondays in their line of work—the laundry domestics were required to do with ice-cold water which turned their palms a deathly blue—was another preventable danger. There were so many things like this, working in the homes of others. Judy yearned for a job where the expectations were not only clear and the duties paid well, but the work also carried stability and meaning. A job, any job, that would not leave her worse for wear. She wanted to leave her mark, not the other way around.

On her knees in the partial dark, the smell of strangers' bowels in her nostrils, Judy let her mind turn over the idea of leaving the market and the city. She was proud that Herbert was a part of the war effort—so few Negroes were chosen to fight and the military told them it was a privilege for them to be selected to die for this country. Herbert was doing a noble thing.

And Judy wanted the same thing for herself. Margaret would shake her head whenever Judy said so aloud. "Nobility is for rich folk, for men. For white people," her mother said. "Just stick to making an honest living. No shame in that. It makes a difference, whether you see it or not."

Judy did not. She did not believe the day was coming when

she would. This was not a way she could live or survive for much longer. Every moment on her knees brought forward a fresh despair, the sensation that she might be stuck groveling for pennies for eternity.

Judy scrubbed the outside of the toilet, then cleaned the sponge in warm water from the tub. She lathered soap in the sponge until the water she squeezed from it ran clear. She got up and, walking out of the bathroom, turned her attention to the windows, clouded over by time and neglect.

Looking at them, trying to see through them, Judy thought of how she took windows in the Bronx tenements she grew up in for granted. The windows in those buildings were set off from the brick facades, their smallness emphasized from a distance, like a row of unblinking, bruised black eyes. From rare trips to the Bronx Zoo and to the amusement park, Judy saw that the closer one got to Westchester, the wider the windows opened up. As if having more money meant seeing more of the world. As if the more of a place you saw, the easier it was to be a part of it, to be in it, not just swept up in it.

Wiping the grime and film from the windows was more satisfying than the toilet work. She could breathe, at least. And there was a noticeable gleam to the panes now, and that was because of her.

When she moved on to the kitchen, her sights set on the chandelier, she couldn't help but notice a pile of bills on the corner of a nearby table. Most were addressed to a Sergeant William McIntosh and had the familiar red stamp PAST DUE. She felt a momentary wave of pity for the woman who seemed intent on paying her next to nothing. Despite this big house and the bad attitude, perhaps she was struggling, too. Maybe, Judy wondered, she had not heard from her husband either. Maybe her husband was also missing, silent.

"My, you move quickly," the woman said, startling Judy.

She felt like she had somehow conjured the lady and had been caught. "Attend to the chandelier next," she demanded.

Judy's brief empathy scattered like the dust around her. For this was another part of these arrangements. Doing what the woman ordered was only the first step. To do it in the manner and order in which she said it was the next. It made her feel tired and impatient in her bones, which she struggled not to show when she answered with all the brightness she could muster, "Yes, ma'am."

The woman lifted her chin in the direction of an old ladder. "You'll need to use that."

The old chipped thing looked the way she felt: like the slightest additional weight would make her cave in on herself. The obstacle course of servitude continued, and Judy felt powerless to do anything but bear it. In these moments, she could feel the lives her grandparents had endured in her body. Hunched over, hiding their hearts from the probing eyes of masters and overseers, picking cotton until their hands bled, hoeing the earth as their backs curved into the weight of everything they could not produce. She thanked God the South was a place and a predicament she had been born free of, no matter how long its shadow. But in some way, this experience of servitude brought home what she only knew through Margaret and James's stories: the barren place of dirt roads, bodies swaying from branches, missing limbs, crowded one-room churches where they all went to pray for salvation and deliverance.

The North was supposed to be a Negro paradise; that was how her parents saw it. Their chance for a taste of freedom and a little bit of joy might be slim to none, but they jumped in on the first wave of the Great Migration to make a different life possible for Judy.

Times like this, when Judy was covered in the grit and

grime of someone else's life, she wondered if their sacrifice was worth it. The filth felt permanently singed in her nostrils, like the stink was now a part of her. She climbed the ladder, one hand wiping off the first layer of dust, her hand maneuvering around the delicate pieces, the other wielding a cloth damp with lemon and water.

She did have one privilege, she mused, finishing up this menial task. Wherever her body might be, no matter what it did, she could escape in her mind and thoughts. Her mother thought it dangerous to read too much, to dream beyond one's station in life. The rare occasion Margaret discussed the news with Judy was after the Tulsa race riot. "Those Negroes had too much, that's what happened," Margaret said, warning Judy. "It's okay to have things, but it's a risk. You could lose your life showing off in front of white folks."

It made Judy feel more alive believing in the impossible. Where else might she see an example of who she most wanted to become but books? There weren't any Negro heroines, in Greek myths like *The Odyssey*, so in her imagination, she made their skin match hers, the giant, courageous goddesses like Athena or Artemis or Hera. Names and stories as poetry. Her mind was as expansive as her world was small, too small to fit her big dreams. Almost.

"I have to be getting home, ma'am," Judy said, approaching the woman. Judy had not eaten all day, and her stomach gurgled its protest loudly in the silence. The woman placed the coins delicately in Judy's hand while giving her a look Judy did not understand.

"Of course. Here you are, girl."

"Thank you," Judy said, feeling the ache of the day's work in her thighs, her calves, between her shoulders. And there was still the mile or so she had to walk to the trolley to return to the South Bronx, four flights of stairs to climb at home before bed. At least another two hours before she could really rest. Meditating on her exhaustion put her in a daze, and she started toward the door.

"Don't forget, you left your purse hanging upstairs."

Judy turned her chin first, then her whole body, to look in the woman's direction. Only uppity Negroes looked white people in the eye, and it was generally fatal. Judy wondered if it was the fatigue that gave her a funny feeling or the woman's tone. All of this clutter and chaos in her house, and she still managed to note Judy's purse hanging on the door?

Turning back after a solemn nod, Judy gathered her purse upstairs. She lifted the long brown strap up off the edge of the door. She remembered the fifty cents she had before, the two quarters she'd left in the small top pocket. Now she had a whole dollar. She awaited the sound of the quarters clinking together; the way change clanged brought her deep satisfaction, as much gratification as one could feel knowing there just was never enough.

She glanced inside to see her navy blue handkerchief had been nudged aside, her compact untouched but leaning against the front. Two quarters were missing. The woman had taken her money and given it back to her! Judy didn't want it to be true. She rummaged through her few things, looked at the ground around her for them.

After a few moments of searching the empty, now clean floors, her hand went limp inside her purse, the two lonely coins in her hand. The heat of shame and disappointment settled in her chest like heartburn rising.

"You did find it, didn't you?" the woman called from below.

Rage and disgust spread in Judy's chest. She felt like she could throw up. All that time wasted, all that dirt she waded through—for nothing. What could she do against this thieving white woman but smile and refuse to give in to the bait, refuse to beg?

At that moment, through a wave of anger, Judy realized she would have to stop working at the market.

"I did. I'm coming now," Judy said. As she hurried down the stairs, her footfall slowed long enough for her to see what looked like a twinkle in the woman's eye. Judy did not smile, or frown. She kept her mouth in a straight line, grabbed the center of her coat to her like a shawl, so that it bunched up in the middle, and left, humiliated, not letting the tears fall until she was out the door.

TWO

JUDY

From Judy to Herbert

Saturday, 16 April 1944

My dearest Herbert,
Where is the 366th Infantry Regiment these days? It has been
too many months now. I know you have other things to consider,
but please do write and let me know how you are. I miss your
bad jokes and your kind encouragement, especially when it comes
to Mama and her old-fashioned ways. You always did know
the right way to handle her. I am not as good as you at that.
    Speaking of Mama, she and I are in dire straits. The radio
addresses and news bulletins all seem to echo the feelings we have
at home, that we want to "End the War in '44" and with sol-
diers all over the world, that seems even more possible and gives
us hope that you will be home in no time. Still, our relief and

rationing stamps combined with the pennies on the market make it hard to get by without the money you used to send.

But money aside, please just write and let me know how you are. After so much time, you'd figure my mind might be able to wrap itself around you being gone. But I miss how you fill up most of the bed, sleeping like you've never shared anything a day in your life.

I am always looking for mention of your regiment. Seems like the only soldiers whose names make it in the paper are the ones who have passed, and... Herbert, if you don't make it home alive, I swear I'll kill you.

Forgive the bad humor. I just miss you very much. Send a few lines.

Love to you,
Judy

In the months that had passed since Judy last received a letter from Herbert, she began to feel that something was not right. The stress of the market made it hard for her to trust herself, to trust that feeling. Maybe it was just her being tired from the work, from worrying about herself and Margaret. Surviving in a world bent on victory pushed out all the other thoughts.

She had not made time to write as consistently as when they were first separated. After high school, he yearned for college, mainly to join the Reserve Officers Training Corps, but there were none in New York for Negroes. Then Pearl Harbor thrust the US into conflict again. By then, in 1941, he had settled for the janitorial work available to him, before he tried for the Pullman porter work, which meant that he could at least travel.

But as the war spread in the Pacific then throughout Europe as Hitler expanded his power, and the Germans felled thousands of US troops, suddenly, in 1942 to 1943, the army started posting notices offering Negro men "the privilege" to die for their country in select combat roles.

"This is my chance," Herbert had said to Judy when he returned home from the office where he mopped floors on Kingsbridge Road.

"Your chance for what?" Judy was making dinner after a day of chores then, split between caring for Herbert and her things and those of her mother.

"To show this country we belong," he said. "That we can fight."

She was half-listening, because she had heard him go on and on about wanting to serve. He always wanted to prove to himself, maybe, that he could do more than what this country said Negro men could—shine shoes, make babies, be menacing. Maybe it was selfish, or she was just jealous, but Judy tried to keep her hard feelings about this to herself. She had been told all her life that there was a limit to what a Negro could do, rules about how far they could go, almost zero chance in any lifetime they would be able to escape the stories of the lives that had been written for them. She tried not to pass on this boxed-in way to Herbert.

"Maybe so" is all she said, announcing dinner was ready and inviting a change to the conversation. But Herbert had the same look on his face that he'd had when he chose her at Morris High School. He had decided. He was already enlisted in his heart, even if Judy didn't yet believe.

In the first year of Herbert's service, when mail was flowing freely and fast, Herbert's letters came monthly, sometimes two at once, with twenty or fifteen dollars combined with stories from boot camp, weapons training, the segregated barracks. Still stateside, it almost felt like nothing much had changed. She made a victory garden on their fire escape. As long as the tomato plants could survive, they were set. But then, they entered the second year, and the bloodshed and lives lost abroad meant the strategy had to shift. The boys were going abroad; they were needed on the Rhine, in Italy, on the borders of Germany to get Hitler and those Germans under control.

Herbert had warned in a letter his long silence might be coming. "No word yet exactly where we are headed, but these are secret operations, so I couldn't say one way or the other," he wrote. "You know it's bad if they are shipping us out there on warships, though. We call them monsters. So big, Judy—Germans have sank 'em by the hundreds like little sailboats, but they weigh hundreds of tons. Carrying thousands of us and bombs and everything. Gone, just like that."

That was December, 1943. No word since then, but that didn't stop Judy from checking the mail constantly. She needed to hold out hope for relief.

She would have even settled for the single sheet of Victory Mail—the military's answer to saving cargo space by taking pictures of a single page of a written letter, sometimes whole sentences blacked out by censors with the word *Free* written in the upper right-hand corner.

If only she could talk to Herbert, get his advice on what to do for work. She didn't want to tell Margaret about that white woman paying her with her own money. The longer she kept it to herself, the more she just could not believe she had been robbed. The nerve of that woman! Judy had even felt sorry for her, briefly.

But the real problem as she saw it was that there was no other line of work available for a Negro woman who could not pass for white. Even the menial, backbreaking jobs men used to do before being sent overseas were closed doors: factory work was hard and dangerous. Rosie was cute, but riveting inflexible ship metal or handling ammunition or welding—those were jobs white women took. Textiles and dry cleaning weren't easy either. The rare light-skinned girl who might pass could get work sitting in a secretarial pool. But there had to be something open to Negro women.

When Margaret returned home, her eyes dragged over Judy in a slow, almost mournful way. Her child looked exhausted, and she was spent. Pale yellow curtains hung down behind the tangerine couch in the living room, next to what had been her father's favorite chair. The hallway to her bedroom and the one she used to share with Herbert were dark, to save money on the electric.

"How was the day?" Margaret asked, putting her paper bag on the floor and pulling off her heels.

"I think I'm through," Judy said, careful not to lie.

"Some days are like that," Margaret said.

"No, Mama. I mean I don't think I can do any more work on the market. Not after what happened today."

Margaret sucked her teeth. She plopped down into a kitchen chair and looked at Judy for a long moment, like the girl hadn't said anything. Then she lifted up a napkin Judy had set there next to the bowl. "You ate?"

"Not all day."

"Closed mouths don't get fed."

"Didn't get to eat on that job either."

Margaret tied on a white half apron she had sewed by hand, even though she was reheating stew from the icebox. "You should have said something."

The anger Judy still felt rose in her and made her tremble. "That woman stole the money out my purse and gave it right back to me."

Margaret made a face. For a split moment, Judy thought it might have scandalized her, been the rare something Margaret couldn't fathom. Then she snorted, "You're sure?"

It felt like all the blood in Judy's body rose to her face. She knew Margaret would take the white woman's side. A sense of betrayal lingered in the air between them. "Are you taking her side, Mama?"

Margaret turned sharply, wincing. "You can be forgetful."

"I know what I had, and she took it."

"Have some," Margaret said, putting the bowl down in front of Judy, who couldn't resist food after waiting for so long to eat. "Thinking some lady stole from you is no reason to give up paying work. And you can't just go around saying things like that about white folk. We raised you better than that."

"It's just us, Mama," Judy said after a bite. "Besides, she took my money after making me do the worst things. I won't go back."

"You should have asked for half of it up front," Margaret reasoned. "I made two dollars today like that. Half when I got there. Even when they try to barter, you have to hold your ground. Me and your Daddy figured it would be different up here, but then the Depression hit and Negroes everywhere have to just keep working like this. The way I see it, we need to just be glad for the work, since some people don't even have that."

The cold air hitting her teeth made Judy realize her mouth was open until she closed it firmly, her teeth clicking into place like marbles crowded in a corner. "I am nobody's slave, Mama. And fifty cents or even a dollar is not worth how it makes me feel to wipe shit from a toilet that ain't been clean in who knows how long. I won't do it."

Margaret had given herself less than half their leftover meal so Judy could have more. She always gave as much as she could. She rubbed her temples and kept her eyes closed. "You could at least try and make it work. Tell those people to feed you something. Or bring your own—"

"What was the woman who hired you eating while you

worked like a dog?" Judy's voice broke. Her heart was in her throat.

The tone made Margaret quiet again. The years of her life had taught her that her anger did not matter, so her ire was never visible, not even to those closest to her. She simply took a beat for herself, as she did in that moment, collecting her empty bowl even if she was still hungry and carrying it to the sink. "A little meat and some potatoes," she said, her voice like an old, mournful record. "But I ate, too. And that's all I'm trying to tell you. Make sure you eat. And if you find it can't happen after you've fought for it, then I suppose you can come on in here and starve yourself in protest. But you give it one more try. Don't be so quick to give up."

Judy wanted to scream. The unfairness of white women was not her fault. She could not make them fairer through patience. As if Margaret could hear her unspoken thoughts, she said, "Just don't sass me about this, now. I mean it. We have enough trouble of our own. We don't need to go borrow none. I won't have you acting high-and-mighty. You do what I say."

"Well, I'm your child and I know it, but I will do what I want. I'm still a grown, married woman. I'm going to find another job."

"Good luck with that."

And Judy knew that she would need luck. So many Negroes wanted to work, and President Roosevelt had even passed a law to help, Executive Order 8802. The problem was nobody wanted Negroes having good pay and benefits. As soon as the president's Fair Practices in Employment went into effect, white workers from Oakland to Atlanta to Brooklyn protested with violence, screamed and howled about forced integration.

"You spend all your time with your head in those papers, so I know you know that just because that order dropped doesn't mean white folks will pick it up," Margaret said. "One way or the other, the way the world was set up, you end up cleaning up behind white folks. Some Negroes just do it in fancier clothes."

There was no use arguing, as Judy saw it. "We'll never agree."

Margaret shook her head. "Stubborn child. Just like your father. I'll save you a crate back at the market just the same."

Judy was determined to find work elsewhere and prove her mother wrong. She had been keeping track of job advertisements in the papers while she stayed up-to-date on the war and word of changing the slave markets. So when she rose the next day with Margaret, as they usually did before dawn, she knew she wanted to answer ads for a butcher in Little Italy and another at the Estey Piano & Organ Company. Both said they needed help with cleaning. Even though the ads were general and didn't say what they paid, they did announce things like steady work, eight thirty to five thirty, age eighteen to thirty-five, men and women.

Much of what a woman needed to be presentable was being rationed during the war, including nylons, which were a rare, expensive luxury, and bobby pins. She decided on her simple blue dress with pumps, leaving her legs bare. Margaret looked aghast and just shook her head as they parted ways—Margaret to the market and Judy to the butcher.

The trolley north, headed toward Belmont Avenue and Fordham, was filled with businessmen and a few ladies seated in the front. She boarded the back of the trolley and made her way to the Colored section, seated herself all the way at the back, her purse safely in her lap. She'd come to appreciate sitting in the worst possible seat on the trolley because at least she had a window, that is if it wasn't crowded and she'd have to relinquish her seat to a white person. She could just watch the Bronx as she rode; observing the white people around her

WOMEN OF THE POST

also let her study and observe other ways of being, options and possibilities she felt she would never have.

Rides like this also reminded her of the difference between the worn tenements in her neighborhood and the broad, Art Deco designs of the buildings on the Grand Concourse, modeled after Parisian plazas. These were occupied by flourishing white immigrants. They made Judy wonder if Margaret wasn't right about her taking in too much of the news, all the promises Roosevelt made about making things more fair. Maybe she was naive to think the promise of the Four Freedoms Roosevelt spoke about—freedom from want, from fear, freedom of speech, freedom to worship—were also meant for Negroes. The difference between her and her mother, though, was that she was willing to at least find out. Margaret seemed to just know. Judy wanted to investigate.

On Arthur Avenue and 183rd Street, Judy pushed from the back door of the trolley, while the white passengers emerged from the front. Below neat rows of three- and four-story brick buildings, grocers displayed boxes of cantaloupe, oranges, grapefruit and other fruits and vegetables under navy blue tents in front of their stores. She maneuvered sideways as she passed the abundant offerings.

She walked farther along the block into Antonio's, the butcher shop, in the middle of the street, where the black-and-white Help Wanted sign she had been thinking about all night still leaned against the gleaming glass of the storefront.

A loud bell announced her entrance. Customers in line turned to look, to see if a neighbor had joined them. Whether they saw her, or just her skin, it registered to each of them simultaneously that she was a Negro girl. They immediately returned to their waiting, their backs to her.

The reaction made Judy's stomach sink. Maybe she had miscalculated. In her neighborhood, the butcher was friendly

37

enough to Negroes that during the Depression he sometimes offered them pork chops or skirt steak on credit. But she left her block precisely to avoid seeing any of Herbert's family or Margaret's church friends. They would be sure to ask why she was cleaning up after a butcher instead of working alongside her mother or even teaching or nursing. One of the great impositions of poverty was that people never wanted others to know how in need they were of help. Perhaps the only benefit to slave market work was, that beyond the public waiting stage, it was invisible.

Judy could tell this butcher would not offer credit to anyone, Negro or white. The air felt forbidding. Despite the messy, bloody business in the back, the white counters in the front beneath a chalkboard listing meats for sale were spotless.

She stood in line, her eyes darting around like she was casing the place. As she got closer to the frowning cashier, she lost her nerve and walked out, gulping air. She had been breathing just fine until she inhaled the smell of flesh and bone, then she felt nauseous and held her breath. Judy realized if she couldn't even stand to wait in line, she couldn't fit there, not even to chop meat or clean the place. It would be one thing to don an apron imprinted with blood and bits all day. It was something else altogether to realize she might not be deemed worthy of even something as undesirable as that.

She walked back to the trolley stop now, thinking through this next part of her plan. It was still early in the day, around eight o'clock. She did not want to give Margaret the satisfaction of being right. Maybe the piano factory would hire her, and she was just being a pessimist.

She tried to feel hopeful as she made her way to the piano factory's red brick building. The entrance was wide as a barn door without hinges. It led to a spacious showroom featuring a single, finished Steinway piano, evidence of the work that made the place run.

A man with a broom-handle mustache passed her, preoccupied with a small notebook in his hand, writing and walking fast. Before he could scurry away, she said, "Excuse me, sir? Do you work here?"

He looked up from his writing with a confused expression. "Who's asking?"

"My name is Judy Washington," she said, standing straight, her hands firmly gripping her purse handle. "I live a few blocks from here and saw in the papers you were looking for help, sir."

"Not hiring," he said, walking away.

Judy was about to protest, but her shoulders were already starting to slump. By the time she thought of what to say in response, the man had disappeared into one of the building's cavernous rooms. Surely someone more authoritative in this place might have a better answer. She turned away from the door, studying a wrought iron staircase leading to the second floor.

She was steeling herself to climb the staircase when someone shouted "Coming through!" and before she could move, two men hauling a huge piece of an unfinished piano frame nearly knocked her down. It was much more than an omen, she thought. She looked up again, but decided it was better just to leave.

Judy braced herself as she walked back to the market and the possibility of facing her mother empty-handed. Sometimes the mornings were slow, and there were always more women looking to clean than those looking to hire. Her streak of bad luck continued, as Margaret was one of a dozen women still waiting on the crates and boxes on Simpson Avenue when Judy arrived around 11:30 a.m.

"Look who finally joined us," Margaret said with a smirk. "Long time no see."

"Oh, it wasn't so long," Judy said. It was the usual scene but for a voice carrying behind them, surrounded by a small group of women. "What's that all about?"

Margaret looked over her shoulder. "Some Negro says she's with the women's army. Did you find the work you were looking for?"

Judy shook her head. "You were right about it, okay, Mama?"

She was sore to admit she was wrong. She turned her face to the crowd.

"Some kind of apology that is," Margaret said, calling after Judy as she wandered over to where the women gathered. It was the first time all week she felt a jolt of curiosity instead of despair.

As she got closer, a khaki-colored cap atop the head of a tall, brown-skinned woman with a full moon-shaped face came into view. She was wearing a khaki military uniform in the same unflattering brown—a jacket and skirt with fresh, matching nylons and chocolate brown regulation pumps. Her brown eyes sparkled black under the cap as she looked confidently into the faces of those around her.

"My name is Captain Charity Edna Adams," the woman was saying. "I am recruiting smart women like yourselves to help free men up from support services so they can fight. We help with switchboards and driving and other supports. The work we do is crucial for helping your husbands and sons come home victorious, and sooner," Captain Adams said.

Judy and the women around her looked at one another as they let the words sink in. The more Captain Adams talked, the more hope swelled in her to solve the two greatest dilem-

mas in her life—to have Herbert home and to find meaningful work that also paid her what she was worth.

"I'm from South Carolina, originally," Captain Adams continued. "I was teaching math after college in Ohio when I
was recruited for Officer Candidate School, which is the only
part of the military that is currently integrated. Negro officers
train alongside whites, but our living quarters are still separate. I am currently stationed with about forty other Negro
enlisted in Fort Des Moines, Iowa."

"Iowa?" Judy wondered aloud. She couldn't even conceive
of such a place, though she knew it was west of New York.
She imagined cows and grass, and an endless number of white
people. If there were forty Negro women there, how big was
the town?

"Yes, Iowa," Captain Adams answered, shuffling the bro-
chures onto a clipboard. She tucked them into one elbow so
she could extend her long arm with the other. "Your name
is...?"

"Judy Washington," Judy said, pumping Captain Adams's
hand with a firm grip. "You're saying Negro women are in
the army now?"

"Yes, and we're looking for more to join us. Our units don't
handle weapons, but we train in almost all the same ways as
the men."

Judy was hooked now. She wanted to tell Captain Adams
she didn't need any further convincing, but the captain continued, "Congress approved the creation of the Women's Army
Auxiliary Corps in May, 1942. Both Negro and white together, there are thirty-five thousand of us."

The number sounded enormous to Judy. She was about to
begin imagining herself in a uniform just like Captain Adams's when she heard her mother shouting her name. She
turned with a start.

"I'm headed out," Margaret said, pointing toward an impatient woman in a car a few feet from her.

"Okay, Mama," Judy said, ready to turn back to Captain Adams.

"You best be doing the same!" Margaret warned, hurrying to the car.

Judy pretended not to hear. "May I ask how much the pay is?"

"Fifty dollars a month to start," Captain Adams answered, with a sound in her voice like she wished it was more. But Judy's mind was going now. From the looks of this Captain Adams, she wouldn't know the first thing about having to bow down for money.

"You seem like a good candidate, and we need more women like you. Smart, hardworking," Captain Adams observed. She folded an application in thirds and placed the brochure on top. "Just give it some thought. You can say I recommended you, here in New York. I head back to Iowa tomorrow, but I'll keep an eye out for your application."

Judy nodded, looking at the paper but not really seeing it. She was already drafting her application letter in her mind.

THREE

JUDY

Saturday, 16 April 1944

To Whom It May Concern,
My name is Judith Anne Washington, and I am applying
with great enthusiasm (and at the recommendation of Captain
Charity Adams) to join the Women's Army Corps. First and
foremost, I want to serve my country. But I also want to be
a part of bringing my husband, Herbert Washington, home
sooner, maybe finding his unit.

I have been doing day work on the Bronx Slave Market
for more than a year since he left. Without his support, we
are having a hard time, my mother and me. That has trained
me to do just about any kind of work you need done in the
Women's Army. I look forward to your prompt reply. Thank
you for your consideration.
Respectfully,
Judith Washington

Judy had read and reread the brochure Captain Charity Adams had given her so much she practically had it memorized. It read:

Women Wanted
18 to 35
All-Inclusive
$50 to $75 month
Based on experience or skills
Free A Man Up for War!
Secretarial Postal Administrative
Support Duties
We Aim to End the War in '44
Help Us Achieve Victory for Our Boys
Apply Today
Box 86-5

Surely everything had aligned for her to have this brochure and application after the morning she'd had. She had walked the few blocks home so fast it felt like she was jogging. She had immediately written her letter and filled out the application in an inspired frenzy.

In her mind, she was already training for the WAC. From the minute she took that brochure, a vision of herself in uniform had embedded itself within her and hadn't left. She already had plans for the money they needed that she felt sure would come from the WAC. And she would have money left over! The application was sent, and Judy was making dinner when her mother came home from the market. Margaret was in a mood, her brow furrowed. Judy was humming, filling a pot with water and salt.

"How did it turn out with that woman?" Margaret's voice was soft, shaking a little like she was shy to ask the question.

"I sent in my application for the women's army. Pays much better than the market. Fifty, seventy-five dollars a month. And there could be bonuses, too. Means I can send you some and you can stop working yourself to the bone."

Margaret paused before saying, "Money isn't everything."

Judy tilted her head toward her mother, trying to understand. Money was the core of their lives—the lack of it, the want of it, the worry about it. She did not often mistrust her mother, but in this moment, she understood what she was hearing was a lie. "How could you say that? Money shapes our every waking moment."

Margaret looked at Judy, her eyes mournful. Then she shifted her eyes to the small window, which faced a brick wall. "Some days you sound just like your father, you know. And it makes me sad and glad at once. Because I miss him every hour. I guess we made you, and you're his gift to me now, is how I see it. It's hard enough making it through the day and you're right here with me. How am I supposed to manage if you're gone, too?"

Clicking off the stove, steam climbing in white ribbons above the pot, Judy turned to face Margaret now and put her hand on her mother's shoulder. "Oh, Mama. I'm sorry about Daddy. I miss him, too. So many men for us to always be missing. It is a heavy burden to carry alone. But I didn't apply to the women's army to abandon you. I can see how you might feel that way. I'm doing it so we can have more. So you can have a better life. The life you deserve."

"That sounds nice and all, baby. But work for Negro women is just the same as it was in slave times. Any money you make in the white man's army is the same work, different uniform. They pay you more so you don't complain too loud when there's more to endure.

"And I know girls your age think it's some shame in that

45

work at the market. Up here, Negroes act like they too good for the work their mamas and daddies did. Say they left the South so they could get up off their knees. Stand in freedom. But we all do what we have to do in order to live. The sooner you make peace with that, the happier you'll be."

Judy was not sure how she felt about her happiness. What did it mean to be happy—was it the way she felt when Herbert stood close and she smelled the spice of his aftershave? How she felt protected, loved, safe because he was so near? Was it the thrill of a new adventure with new people in a different city? Maybe it was just knowing that she could find happiness doing something else. Something with meaning and purpose.

"The thought that I could make more and help with the war makes me feel good, I suppose," Judy said, hesitating. "I don't want you to feel left behind. Or that I feel too good for the market. But I think we are, Mama. I don't think we were made to be the help forever and always. I don't know why we can't agree on that."

"Maybe it's because I gave birth to you, Judith Anne. I'm older than you. Not by that much," Margaret said, letting herself smile. "But no matter where we go, coming over here as property means anybody who looks at us sees servitude in our faces, in our skin. And that's out of our hands."

Judy shook her head, but she knew it was a lost cause arguing with Margaret now. "I just don't think that's true, Mama. But there's only one way to find out."

FOUR

CHARITY

From Charity Edna Adams to Abbie Noel Campbell

Monday, 18 April 1944

Dearest Abbie,
Well, my first trip of preliminary recruiting duty is behind me.
I declare New York City is crowded and filthy. That said, I
think I made the case for our outfit, even though it's hard to
know exactly what we're recruiting for since we're fresh out of
Officer Candidate School ourselves. I hope you had as much
success on the ground in Iowa as I did here.

The goal according to Lieutenant Colonel Barrows was to
find as many Negro women as possible and persuade them to join
us. At the Bronx Slave Market, a kind of open-air day work
site where women make hardly any money at all, I found sev-
eral eager recruits. They'd have much more stable income in the
army and no combat to contend with to boot. Making it known

that at the very most, they'd be cleaning weapons or assembling parts seemed to help reassure some of the more hesitant ladies.

You know I'm not that skilled a liar, but I tried not to give away my boredom with some of the classes we had to take. I may not be great at operating switchboards, but these ladies may find it much more rewarding and dignified.

You've known me since we were teenagers, and I trust you'd tell me if it were otherwise, but I imagine I'm not that convincing. I have to hope that the mission we're working toward is convincing enough.

No one asked, so I felt it better to keep the matter of public opinion out of our discussions. That ugly talk about us spreading disease as a distraction for lonely soldiers stateside. Maybe the girls work so much they wouldn't know the first thing about this kind of talk, anyway.

I'm headed home for a few days to Columbia before being back on post. I can't wait to see you soon and hear how you fared. Better than me, I'm sure of it. It's always been so.
Fondly,
Charity Edna

Charity Adams was called Edna by fast friends she'd made in high school, like her best friend Abbie Noel Campbell and by her family. The two taller-than-average girls were different in temperament and ambition from the other girls in Columbia, South Carolina, and it didn't take them long to discover they were both the same kind of outsider.

Charity was a little stiff and clumsy at times, evidenced by her embarrassing fumbling about during dodgeball or the way she flailed during any sport and tripped on nothing. In contrast, Abbie was a graceful athlete who caught every pass, made most shots she took and was generally at home with her body, which was round in all the places Charity's was slim and angular.

Before the Campbells had moved to town, Charity's main companions had been her brother, Avery, and his toy soldiers, although she was chided for abandoning her dolls. Her first memory of being unlike most of the girls she knew was pulling out the black yarn of her doll's hair, which made her mother wince. Why did the doll need hair anyway? The better question to Charity was why she couldn't make a leader of her hairless doll to get those toy soldiers in line.

"They're all over," she would say to her little brother. "Line them up right."

"Toy soldiers are for boys, not girls," Avery protested. "Girls don't fight. Too soft for war."

"Nuh-uh," Charity corrected, although, when she thought about it, when she went through the images in her mind, maybe her brother was right. She had never seen women in any of the newspapers or in any newsreel. The radio addresses never mentioned women doing anything but being good hostesses and keeping up the house.

Only Abbie knew about her obsession with the toy soldiers—a confession she made as they changed out of their gym uniforms senior year, and Charity tried not to peek at Abbie's perfect skin.

Abbie was the color of yellow cake, with glossy, jet-black hair that she wore pressed and curled so that she resembled a Colored Betty Page. She favored full-skirted dresses, whereas Charity would have been completely satisfied to wear pantsuits if her mother had allowed her to.

"Heavens, people will start to think you're unnatural, dear," her mother, Edna, had said to her when they went downtown to shop at the Negro department store and, when given the chance to select an outfit, Charity decided on a plain white blouse and stiff dungarees.

Edna responded by holding up a poodle skirt in an elegant navy blue.

"But I would feel more comfortable—" Charity muttered as her mother took away the offensive manly items and thrust the skirt into Charity's hands instead. There would be no discussion.

Charity recounted these things to Abbie because her friend wondered aloud often about Charity's quirks. "You're so strong," Abbie said. "But you seem skittish in gym. Have you always been like this?"

"I'm sure I don't know what you mean."

Abbie giggled and Charity felt two things at once: that Abbie's voice was even, light and tingling in the air like a bell. It was addicting. When Abbie laughed, part of Charity ached to immediately hear it again.

The second feeling was shame: for being the subject of that laughter, for knowing the beginning of what she wanted with Abbie and for the long list of ways she was forbidden to be but could not help.

"All right, I'll say it plainly. You can be so direct and tough and you're as tall as me, but you're so removed at the same time," Abbie said. "You're confident and shy all at once."

"So, you're insulting me, Abigail?"

"Ugh, only my mother calls me that, and usually when I'm in trouble."

"You're in trouble now," Charity said, pulling her shirt over her head and trying not to stare as Abbie did the same. But there was, in fact, never trouble between them, even when Charity's inclinations and desires for Abbie began to grow.

It was just as impossible for her to really imagine being the leader of an army as it was for her to imagine being with Abbie freely. Her father, Rev. E. A. Adams, and her mother, made it a point to introduce her to a range of vetted male suitors. Charity was as polite as she could be, knowing her mother knew her daughter and knew how improbable a marriage prospect for Charity truly was.

"You'll know the one when you see them," Edna reassured her once, and Charity only nodded. She felt they understood one another without having to say too much.

The closest Abbie and Charity got to real trouble had to do with how popular Abbie was and her parents' determination to marry their pretty girl off to someone like her brother, one of the first Negro doctors in the country, or her father, who'd moved them to Columbia because successful Negroes had been driven out of their native Tulsa and were looking to find enclaves where more Negro families remained. The special, close-knit clubs they created for the nascent Negro middle class gave Abbie the opportunity to meet their kind of people in safe balls and cotillions they could just barely afford. Abbie enjoyed getting dolled up, with ribbons in her hair, adorned with her mother's sapphire brooch on her ample bosom.

Charity knew she was in love when she saw Abbie at one such dance before they parted ways and Abbie went to Hampton University, while Charity attended her father's alma mater, Wilberforce University in Ohio. The farewell graduation party took place at a Masonic lodge behind her father's church, a sanctuary in a modest building set off the road so as not to attract attention from the indignant, poor white people who, of course, had already sized it up and were waiting for the best time to destroy it.

Charity wore a tangerine taffeta dress—her mother had insisted—with crinoline in the full skirt which gathered in a flattering line at her waist. Edna had also pinned her curls and set them so that her full face was framed nicely by a crown of slick ovals. When Charity saw Abbie, her friend and crush was talking to a tall, square-jawed man who shared not only her striking features but the similar skin tone of almond flesh. They would have some good-looking babies with good hair, Charity had to admit. She watched Abbie's parents salivate at this prospect, and she felt fidgety and warm suddenly, even though the ceiling fan was working hard and there was a breeze from it to match the outdoors. She pulled a silk fan from her clutch, borrowed like the dress, to cover her frowning mouth.

It also gave her a little cover as she took in Abbie in her pink lace dress with pink satin heels, like a ballerina. Her long neck looked even more elegant in pearls, which her hands flirted with at her throat, just lightly stroking them as she placed the other hand briefly, flirtatiously on the young man's shoulder before she spotted Charity.

"Oh, Edna, come here! Aren't you a vision in that dress?"

Charity stopped fluttering her fan, then, pulling her shoulders back from up by her ears. She smiled shyly, walking over, all too happy to interrupt. "You look lovely, too, Abbie. Truly."

The gentleman cleared his throat. Charity tried not to give him a wilting stare. She was all too aware of what she was interrupting, and she was glad for it.

Abbie gave her a knowing smile while grabbing Charity's wrist to pull her closer. "This is my dearest friend, Charity Edna Adams, Johnny. Edna, this is Jonathan Crews, Jr. The Crews are relatively new to town. I'm afraid Johnny is soon to be off to war."

Charity was glad to meet this would-be suitor who would be soon out of their way. At that, she was able to smile and say without lying, "Pleased to meet you." But now she had even more envy for this man, going to serve. At that time, in

1941, the US military only allowed women in support roles, to be nurses, volunteers with the Red Cross, the YMCA or the YWCA.

"And you, Charity," he said. "Abbie has said nothing but wonderful things. In fact, I don't know if she's spoken of much else."

Charity ignored what seemed like a dig. "What will you be doing over there?"

"I'm to help with a mobile laundry unit in Germany," Johnny responded with an air of dignity Charity found distinctly humorous, given the assignment. She shot Abbie a mildly amused look, all but scoffing. She was annoyed with herself that she'd felt somehow threatened by a man whose future consisted of becoming a full-time launderer.

"I suppose someone's got to clean the clothes at the front if we've all been left behind without weapons," Charity replied.

"No job is too small for the brave," Abbie said coyly. Charity nodded even though she fumed before Abbie continued, "Not everyone can be a math whiz like you."

"So you have better talents than berating men?" Johnny asked with a tight smile.

"Charity is just sore because we'll be splitting up for college is all," Abbie interjected for fear of what her moody friend might say next. "But we'll of course write to each other and keep each other close, no matter where we end up after."

The word *college* seemed to unnerve the gentleman and he excused himself. When he was out of earshot, Charity leaned closer to Abbie and said, "Smart thinking, bringing up school. You know these men would rather not have a bookish wife."

"Or a woman who can write and speak for herself."

"Their loss," Charity said, looking down at her punch.

Abbie nodded, her eyes sparkling with pride and, Charity thought, a little sadness. Though Hampton University was as well regarded as Wilberforce, they might as well have been in different countries for the distance they put between the close friends. But Charity's father had attended Wilberforce, the country's oldest private school for Negroes, founded in 1856, and there was no way she could break tradition. It also happened to be one of the first three schools in the US that offered the Reserve Officers' Training Corps to Negroes.

For those four years, Charity and Abbie exchanged missives and observations about adjusting to academia, then planning their lives without it. Charity was set to become a math teacher in those final years, spending half her days explaining equations and beginning algebra at a local Colored school and Abbie was learning shorthand and typing. She wanted to be a leader, an assistant to a boss, a CEO or some other important person. She was preternaturally organized, and she knew her skills were meant for a greater purpose beyond keeping house.

They exchanged letters, too, about the creation of the Women's Auxiliary Army Corps, created to assist the war effort because the military was losing many more men than they had expected they would. It was Abbie who sent one of the flyers to Charity, recalling her childhood dream to lead an army, which Abbie had to admit sounded like a good opportunity for them both.

Charity had stared at the notice, a call for Negroes to apply for the new Officer Candidate School in Iowa. And then, the headmaster at Wilberforce encouraged her to apply, in case she needed another sign from the heavens that her little-girl dream was becoming possible now that she was grown.

So it was that Charity submitted her application to the OCS in 1942. Abbie said she did the same. What were the chances they both would get in? There were just a few thousand spots for Negroes.

Charity assured her they were among the best recruits the

military was likely to find. She was not worried. That turned out to be wise: they were both accepted swiftly into the first class of Negro officer candidates to be stationed in Fort Des Moines, Iowa.

As delightful as it was to be reunited, Charity and Abbie were startled by the adjustments they had to make. Reveille starting at 0600 hours, inspections, falling in and out, their hands to rest just so at the seams of their uniform skirts. Even if integration was not perfect at Fort Des Moines, there was an effort, and it was the effort that impressed Charity, at least initially.

It did not take long for them to encounter placards in the mess hall, placed there by white enlisted, reading Colored, for the tables where they felt the Negro enlisted should sit. After their allotted swim time one afternoon, Charity was astounded to learn that they drained the pool, believing it had been contaminated.

Moments like that had led to Abbie's perpetual watchfulness and pushed Charity to be the best she could at their trainings.

"I've decided to become much better at drill than anyone else," Charity announced one day.

Abbie shook her head. "You can never compete with others. Only yourself."

"They teach you that at Hampton?"

"Indeed. It's served me well."

"I'm not so certain it has, since you're here with me," Charity said.

"That's true. I'm not behind a hot stove waiting on my rich, handsome husband."

Charity stiffened at the mention of a married Abbie. She awkwardly changed the subject. "My point is that close-order drill and formation are the most significant aspects of how we move on post and outside of it. It's important to get it right."

"If you say so, Edna," Abbie said, her tone a little teasing.

But Charity was determined to show Abbie that she was a woman of her word and would practice what didn't come easy to her.

Between meals and inspections, Charity muttered the commands under her breath. *Attention. Fall in. Fall out. Rest. March.* They became a mantra.

After years of separation, they became each other's shadows now. At Fort Des Moines, their commanding officers sometimes confused them for one another, even though they looked nothing alike. That made it easy to make the growing seed of intimate friendship flourish as an open secret, under the guise of sisterhood.

When Charity needed to learn how to effectively give commands in a way others could hear, Abbie gave up her teasing and decided to be helpful. She and Charity were nearing the end of their time in Officer Candidate School. It was 1942, and the war was still going, spreading throughout countries they'd never even heard of before. Who knew what they would need their voices for?

The platoon leader, Lieutenant Colonel P. E. Barrows, an intense, reedy man from Ohio, kept his face emotionless and drawn like shades against sunny dispositions. He was the taxing, impressive leader Charity hoped she might someday become. But at first, he tormented her as she struggled not to squeak during a close-order drill. "Use your outside voice," he said. "That's an order."

Correction from her superiors stung because Charity wanted to be the best, to be perfect. She knew her ambitions were big and grandiose for a Negro woman, but she had been born with the drive to win lodged in her bones and she couldn't shake it. She cleared her throat in response, lifted her chin and said, "Attention!"

"Adams, did you say something?" Barrows pretended to be sweet. Charity would have blushed deep red if she had been fair skinned. The commander shouted, "At ease, ladies. Fall out!"

Before she had a chance to defend herself, Barrows walked away. He was joined by a tiny fellow officer, General J. G. Nash. He was squarely five feet five inches tall. He walked with his nose lifted to give the air of being taller. Word in the barracks was that he liked mountains and whiskey with his war plans. Girls on the younger side of legal. He did not, being from North Carolina, like Negroes. He also had no trouble at all being heard.

"I don't know why you even try with these people," Nash said loud enough for Charity to hear.

"General, you watch your tone," Barrows growled.

Charity was pleased with the correction from Barrows. She shot them both a look, because she couldn't help it, before looking quickly away. They were still in America, in Jim Crow America. A look like that could get her killed.

Abbie tugged discreetly at Charity's elbow. "Don't be so sore you get kicked out or worse. You just need more practice is all."

They just had two weeks left before they were done. And then, they didn't know what their fate would be after, which was up to the Barrows and Nashes of the world. "Why do you help me so much? You could just focus on your own skills. I bet it would make your time more enjoyable."

"I happen to be skilled at everything already," Abbie boasted. "We've got to correct that little warble of yours.

Let's give it some more practice. It's not like you to let anything get you down. C'mon—let's go to the field and practice."

"I've had to yell at Avery before," Charity said, somewhat sheepishly, standing several feet apart from Abbie, who was walking farther away, telling Charity to say it again, louder.

"I said, only barbarians yell at their siblings," Charity shouted, straining to speak, her voice cracking at the end like a frog's croak.

Abbie shook her head. "You'll have to do better than to insult me with your whispers."

"Some help you are, Abbie." Charity pouted. "I need to get this down."

Abbie leaned forward from several feet away. "What's that you say now?"

Charity screamed, "What kind of friend are you?"

Abbie raised her eyebrows before she doubled over in laughter, which then made Charity laugh at herself. When Abbie recovered, she said, "That's much better, dear. But less shrill. You sound like a turkey in distress."

It was out of sheer annoyance that Charity started to use her whole chest to put volume and bass in her voice.

Abbie walked several more feet away over the course of the afternoon as the day turned into evening. She shouted commands until they neared curfew and her throat became hoarse. By the time it was dark, Charity's throat began to ache. But now she knew what she needed to feel and hear from herself to be heard by others. And she had the feeling she would need that more than anything in the months ahead.

That had all been a little less than two years ago, and what a difference a couple of years had made. Charity now stood in New York City's Penn Station, taking in the hurried crowds, men with newspapers under their arms, women scurrying, pulling toddlers along so fast it seemed like their little feet barely touched the ground. A small sign with a weak chain separated the Negro waiting area for the train from everyone else.

Her first time in New York City alone had been interesting indeed, a blend of the familiar social lines she could not cross as a Negro woman and the ones that she was used to transcending whenever she was in public—in Iowa, at home, or elsewhere—in uniform. She was always a bit out of place wherever she was, too striking and impressive to be ignored or blend in.

The sheer number of people, including Negroes, everywhere softened the scrutiny when it landed. The Negroes here were bold or emboldened, perhaps, because they were not in positions of power, but they were everywhere, at the shoeshine, at the barbershop, pushing brooms, dusting clocks, washing clothes, carrying white babies, trailing white women in parasols to shield them from the sun.

Charity felt comfort in numbers that she didn't feel back on post, where even if integration of the officers' school made things feel more normal for the women to converse together, in the real world, like where she sat, the color line was not nearly as perforated. It was a straight, solid boundary.

She kept her eyes on the ground, aware that it probably looked like they were closed but also unsure that anyone was paying her any attention in this great, pulsing humanity around her. Above her head, a giant *V* for Victory beside an enormous American flag; beside the ticket booths, women shaped like pin-up girls selling war bonds. A thin haze of cigar smoke rose above the voices. When she looked up to glance at a clock, two men stared at her evenly from a few feet away.

She tried to return their gaze for a moment, then remembered herself and turned her attention back to the floor.

Others had been watching Charity for as long as she could remember, so she no longer withered under hostile gazes. If the world would watch her so closely, she might as well give them something to see.

"All aboard!" the conductor shouted into the Colored waiting area.

Charity rose to her feet. Protocol for boarding railways in wartime was that uniformed personnel were invited to board first. As a result, Charity stepped forward behind the white male officers, her ticket in one hand, duffel bag in the other.

The loud voice belonged to a stout steward, balding in a haphazard pattern that seemed to have no rhyme or reason. He tried to look above and around Charity, which almost amused her, considering that she was almost six feet tall. As Charity stepped forward, the steward barred her entry, flinging his arm across the door.

"Excuse me, sir," she said, willing to pretend there had been some mistake and he simply did not see her. She spoke firmly and loud enough for not just the steward to hear but the uniformed passengers that were now trying to forge ahead in front of her.

"Uniformed personnel only," the steward repeated, shouting in her face.

"Oh, for God's sake," a loud Southern voice boomed from behind Charity. It sounded like the twangy voice of God to her, deep enough that it thundered. She saw that the voice belonged to the most attractive man she had ever seen, in an Army uniform that designated him as a colonel.

He was well over six feet tall, with bright blue eyes and straw-blond hair. As he made his way from the back of the line, the crowd parted like he was Moses. Charity braced herself for the sea to cave in on them all. She was sure he was about to blame her for causing a scene.

Instead, the colonel turned his fury on the steward. "You did just say all personnel in uniform, so what the hell do you think that is she has on? Get your goddamn hand down from there before I take it down. Right now."

Charity was so shocked she smiled in spite of herself, suddenly able to breathe again. But she was not as surprised as the steward, who looked alarmed but unmoved. "Sir, I mean to say that we are boarding official personnel only. No Negroes are permitted to board before whites. It's the law." The steward's voice was quieter now, trying to pacify the colonel who seemed only to grow more impatient.

"The law! Some decency and respect you're showing for your country. What are we even fighting this damned war for? The likes of so-called Americans like you? Her color doesn't make a damn difference if she's in the same military as me. In fact, I intend for her to eat with me. On this train. Today! That's an order and not a request!"

This last outburst melted whatever resolve remained with the steward, who took the tickets shoved in his face for both the colonel and Charity. She appreciated the intervention, though it felt excessive, a bigger fuss than anyone had ever made over her. The steward stepped aside from the door. Once she was inside, the steward showed her to a table for four. The colonel followed, nodding while standing right beside her. He waited until the steward sulked away before he seated himself opposite of her.

Charity stared at him, her heart beating so fast that she was sure everyone in the dining car—so unaccustomed to such a sight—could hear it.

"I reckon this is more comfortable than all that business outside was, right, Captain?" The shape his mouth made looked more like a sad wince than a smile, as if this particular win made his body hurt. She smiled tightly, unsure of what to say. "I'm Colonel Douglas Richards."

"Captain Charity Edna Adams, sir. Thank you."

"Pleased, I'm sure. There's no need for thanks," Richards said. The silence between them did not last long before he held up one of his long arms and barked, "I'd like someone to come and take our order before I lose my home training altogether."

It was too late for that, Charity thought, but she tried not to show the mixture of confusion and amusement she felt in this man's presence. He ordered for them both—two orders of eggs and toast, along with black coffee and tea, in case that's what the lady wanted. "Bring it while it's hot, too, or so help me, you will be sorry you ever laid eyes on the likes of me and your superiors will never hear the end of it."

Charity had never been defended in quite this way before—and certainly not by a white man. It was a relief, but so unusual that Charity felt uneasy. She wondered what made Richards so fed up with their colliding worlds, the one where he was free to move and shout and tell people what was what when she had no such rights, even if, as he said, they wore the same uniform.

The waitress flew away from them, clearly feeling the fear of God. Charity sat astonished as the colonel continued to go on about "cheap whites" and the irony of it all. He never stopped to ask her what she thought of his opinions, of the food or the service. It was all so lightning fast. She ate in silence, entertained and unnerved.

Richards paid the bill without leaving a tip, the dining car finally quiet enough at the meal's end for Charity to hear her own thoughts. When she was done, he escorted her to her seat, bowed and said, "Godspeed, ma'am," and left. She thought about him for the rest of the trip, especially when she got up and made her way to the Colored car as they approached the Mason-Dixon Line.

On her brief visit home, Charity would encounter the more typical side of Southern whiteness. She had not been home in the months since her promotion. After joining the army and encountering an expansiveness she had never experienced in Columbia, South Carolina, Charity increasingly experienced low-level dread at going home. She often sent regrets by mail, saying she wished she could get away, but that she was too busy. Surely the reverend of the Columbia African Methodist Church and his First Lady, upstanding, learned Negroes, understood her striving. But she couldn't be on the East Coast and not show her face after the excuses had piled up. Edna said as much when she met her at the train. Edna was barely five feet tall in stocking feet, so Charity had to bend down to kiss her mother's beaming soft cheek. Edna reached up to put her arms around her daughter's neck. "Oh, you're a sight for sore eyes."

"I know, Mama. I'm sorry." She was only apologetic in her mother's presence. She sometimes felt that she wasn't entirely sure what exactly she was sorry for, in fact. It was the way Edna looked at her, as if her mother could see every wounding gesture or the imprint of every small or belittling remark. Edna squeezed Charity's cheek gently before grabbing hold of her hand.

"That Abigail is not holding up our agreement, now," Edna said, massaging Charity's hand. Charity's breath became shallow when Abbie's name was in Edna's mouth. But maybe that's just how it was when you cared for someone. Anyone mentioning their name but you caused a kind of jolt to the system. It perplexed Charity and comforted her.

"What secret arrangement did you two make?"

Edna smiled knowingly and patted Charity's hand, letting go to get into the car. "I told her to make sure you kept your figure and remembered to eat, but it seems she's been letting you go to skin and bones."

Charity relaxed. "I'll be sure to let her know you have thoughts about that." Charity was rarely at a loss for words, except when it came to the matter of Abigail Campbell. Maybe it wouldn't always be so, but being at home brought her back to being her awkward teenage self, unable to get away from this place and the way it confined her and confined them. No matter the season—sweltering hot, as it was that summer, or in the dead of winter, the South had few sanctuaries where she felt most like herself.

But her father's church was one such place. When Charity and Edna arrived there, it was filled with Negro men and women in their Sunday finest—large frilly, floppy, brimmed hats in lilac, and tangerine three-piece suits with vests buttoned, and proper, gray handkerchiefs to match the buttons. The energy in the place was sanctified, electric—they had been praising God for prayers already answered, miracles they hadn't seen yet. Deliverance from the evils of the world. If they only knew, Charity thought, that the preacher's daughter was a sinner in her heart.

Rev. E. A. Adams, her tall, broad-chested father, had a voice that carried above their heads and out beyond the open doors of the standing-room-only crowd. When Charity walked into the church beside her mother, he stopped in the middle of his sentence.

"Oh, you'll have to forgive me, now," he started, looking over the top of his glasses. "Some of you may know that my daughter, Charity, is in the women's army. Please join me in welcoming her back home, as Captain Charity Adams."

Around her, the church rumbled with applause—"Y'all can clap, come on," her father encouraged them—and exclamations of "Praise God" and "Amen."

He stretched out his arms, and it all made Charity feel as she usually did in his presence—like a cherished Daddy's girl. The only tension she had with him was the one she shared with her mother—the secret of how and whom she loved. One day, they would have to discuss it. But not today. For now, she let her father and his church see the version of her they knew and loved and could put up on a pedestal. She was the carrier of their big hopes and dreams. She could not let those collapse under her own desires—not all of them. Not yet.

"You're too much, Daddy," Charity said softly.

"Blame your mother for making you so gorgeous and smart you can't help but make a powerful entrance," he said, pulling her away from him with pride. "Lord knows, I had nothing to do with how fine you've turned out to be. I'm so proud of you for embracing this journey. I know there will be many more."

She wondered what he envisioned beyond her travels, so far from South Carolina. But what really made Charity's voice break with tenderness and emotion when she said thank you was the warm sunlight of her father's expectation. His encouragement was a beam, a large floodlight amplifying his certainty of her worth. It made tears of pride well up in her eyes, in part because she wasn't used to him speaking directly from the heart, and certainly not in such a public way.

He put a hand on her shoulder. "Find a spot in the crowd, and I'll head home with you and your mother when we are through."

When the meeting was over, a deacon approached Edna with a low tone. And she nodded solemnly before informing them both of the bad news. "Honey, the Klan is back at the house."

Rev. Adams took off his glasses to clean them even though they were already spotless. He frowned, put them back on. "Are our guns in the car?" Charity noted the irony of being the only member of the military in the church, and the only one among them who wasn't armed.

"A few deacons are going on ahead of you," Edna said. "We'll ride with you with some cars behind us for support."

"Very well," he said. "Let us hope the Lord covers us."

Sitting in the back of the car, her parents with their guns nestled in their laps, Charity felt she should have been ready for the nausea and fear that welled within her as they pulled up to the house. It made her wish that she had learned more about weapons in the WAC, but maybe that wasn't for her to know. How hard would it be to go from handling, cleaning and storing weapons to pulling the trigger?

Wearing the blinding white hoods, a row of several Klansmen stood across the street from their home, quiet and menacing, staring at them like malicious ghosts as Charity and her parents walked into their home. Charity did not sleep, too focused on when they would leave, which wasn't until dawn.

This was just what it meant to live in the South: even if nothing happened when the Klan appeared, the threat was enough to linger, to warn Negroes against getting too comfortable with being free—or thinking themselves citizens, worthy of free movement. Living in Iowa, working with the WAC wasn't perfect by any means, but at least she didn't live constantly worried. She had to be watchful in other ways back at the post, sure. At least there she didn't worry she might lose her life at any moment, the way she feared she might when she was supposed to feel safe in the comfort of home.

FIVE

MARY ALYCE

The world Mary Alyce and white girls like her were born into in the 1940s shaped women's lives in parallel to, or in the shadow of, men's lives. That was especially true in Vermont, in the rural areas where the hard work of planting and harvesting on farms was surpassed only by the loggers and truckers who had paused that work to join the war effort. The radio and newspaper headlines screamed that the war had spread to parts of the world Mary Alyce and her childhood friends, Ethel and Betsy, had never even known about before. An uncle of hers on her mother's side, Joseph, had been writing and sending them letters, sometimes with money but mostly with observations about the Germans, who he referred to the way General Patton did, calling them *Krauts* to be destroyed.

Her mother, Helen, read these missives aloud as she took rare breaks from managing the things that needed tending to in the barn or in the yard or in the kitchen. They shared it all with Mary Alyce's ninety-year-old grandmother, including the notes, which the old woman clicked her tongue at but also smiled to hear. That son of hers was a real piece of work, but at least he was doing something important.

In the old lady's mind, that was what ninety years on earth had taught her. The real measure of a life was to do something of significance, something that only you could do, so that by the time your life ended, you could see what impact you had had in the world.

It was a lot of pressure, Mary Alyce felt, for small-town ladies. But she spent almost half of her girlhood trying to find what that might be for her. She grew up feeling that she was born to a woman and a ghost, as her father had died in a car accident when she was a baby. But whenever Mary Alyce asked further questions about the man she wanted to know but couldn't, Helen changed the subject or her grandmother would encourage her to just leave it be.

It was for this reason that she hoped to marry a man who would never leave her guessing or leave her physically at all, the way her father had by dying. That wasn't to assign fault to the man; because she didn't know him, she could make up any myth or legend about him she wanted. In some versions of the tale, she told herself, and sometimes tried out on Ethel and Betsy, that he had fought in World War I and the car incident happened over there, and he was a decorated, valiant man whose death was a sacrifice for victory.

Ethel would roll her eyes and Betsy elbowed her sharply when she did. They thought Mary Alyce couldn't see exchanges like that, that she wasn't aware of just how much she didn't really belong in their circle since they both had parents at home and a bunch of siblings, which was considered a normal family, unlike hers.

When she was alone, Mary Alyce considered how different she was from her friends in her mind as she shoveled dirt, turning over garden beds. Were her father alive, she might never dream of leaving town. That was what men did, older sons.

On her knees, pulling weeds, she thought that sons and husbands also usually did this dirty work, too. If she would not or could not marry—rare for a pretty, if plain, white girl like herself—finding work and purpose elsewhere would do just fine. Wiping sweat from her face with the back of her hands, she could feel the streaks of dirt she was leaving there. If she at least worked with other women, one might tell her, might reach over and rub the streak off, keep her face clean.

She had been carrying these dreams and hopes around with her for eighteen years when she went to their local post office, to check for mail. Her uncle Joseph's letters rarely reached them anymore because of how busy the post office had become. All the mail carriers had been drafted or went to work in factories, building machines and ships and everything else. So, it fell to Mary Alyce to add a stop at the post office to her regular duties.

It was while on those errands that she saw the poster that would change her life, like a snapshot of the future that showed up one day in the form of an army pin-up girl. The poster showed a woman in a neat, khaki uniform, posed with a hand on one hip and her other hand saluting at her temple. Below her smartly heeled feet, the question "Are you a girl with a Star-Spangled heart?" was followed by a call for women to help with administrative support in the war.

This is it, Mary Alyce thought. Her moment had arrived.

She kept applying for the WAC to herself. She thought it would be as simple as sending in her application and waiting. Since it was considered seditious and unladylike to work out-

side the home, better to tell everyone when she was on her
way there and not a minute before.

So it was with some alarm that she waited weeks for a response, vigilantly and faithfully looking for her fate to be decided by the very same post office, only to come up empty
week after week. One Friday, when Helen volunteered to pick
up the mail while Mary Alyce worked around the house, her
mother came home worried about the official military envelope that bore some resemblance to Joseph's letters, except it
noted on the envelope that a prompt response was needed.

"Mary Alyce, this letter came for you," Helen said, holding
it with both hands. "It was the only thing to pick up. What's
it all about?"

Knowing that she had never been a great liar, nor was she
generally able to conceal anything from her mother, Mary
Alyce still tried to act like she had no idea. She shrugged.
"I'm not sure," she said, and reached for the letter. Helen let
her tug at it before letting go, watching her child, waiting for
her to reveal the letter's contents.

"All right, well, let's see what it says, then," Helen said,
hands fidgeting at her sides.

Mary Alyce was unprepared for the pressure of opening
this letter while her mother watched, even though she knew
she'd eventually have to explain what she'd done. Mary Alyce
ripped open the envelope, harried and palms sweating.

"I applied for the Women's Army Corps," Mary Alyce almost whispered, like a confession, an admission of a long-held
secret, though it had only really been a few weeks.

"The army," Helen said. Her hands stopped moving.
"Whatever for?"

"You know that poster down at the post office…with the
star-spangled…"

"Yes, the girl with not many clothes on. The flag as a heart.

Oh dear, Mary Alyce Dixon. What have you gone and done now?"

Mary Alyce was sweating. Her pulse had picked up, like the sheet of paper was a bodice ripper or some provocative radio program she stumbled upon and wanted to think about all on her own. "They're asking about my education and my work experience. They need me to send it back. That's what I'll do."

"I cannot believe you did this without talking to me, Mary Alyce," Helen said. She started to pace. "I mean, we need to talk about where you can go. And there are your documents they need copies of, and I don't even know the last time I laid hands on your birth certificate."

Mary Alyce looked away from the note to study her mother, whose nervous rambling surprised her. Helen was not a person who kept track of documents. She looked after her mama, her child, her animals, her land. If she had some tending energy leftover, she looked after herself, but she almost never did, so she always looked the same, and sounded the same, day after day: like a woman who dressed in the dark and fooled with her hair to make sure it wasn't in the way; like a woman who physically made herself get in the bed, but hardly slept, so that she always had the sound of exhaustion in her voice, meaning she sounded like a bone-weary woman who did too much.

But Mary Alyce had never heard her mother sound as surprised, almost upset, as she did at that moment. Like the world was aflame because she'd accidentally dropped a match. "I'm sorry, Mama. Of course. But they're not asking for all that yet, so there's no need to worry. I should have told you about the application. But I knew it would make you sad, and I just wanted to try. And now, this," Mary Alyce said, lifting the letter. "You might be worried about finding my papers for no good reason."

Helen chewed at the corner of a nail. "That's what you

want, though? To go off? To be a lady soldier?" She sounded wounded and curious. And Mary Alyce could not remember Helen, or really anybody, asking her what she really wanted. There were things, always, that needed doing—so she did them. Theirs were lives that required focus but not dreams. What they wanted, desired, hoped for—those were luxuries Dixon women could not afford.

"Not to go away, not that. I want to help out. Make more to help you and Nana. See someplace other than this for a while," Mary Alyce said. "Besides, it wouldn't be for long. Surely the war will be over in a few months. It's been dragging on."

The reports they heard and read throughout that spring of 1944 were optimistic that they would defeat Hitler at any moment. The boys in the Pacific were winning under General Patton's command—though they had lost so many men he was now calling in Negro tankers, which some called outrageous. It seemed strange to her that in matters of life and death, keeping the races separate would come up at all, even if she had not met a Negro in her life, since their town was completely white. Still, the Negroes and the women were the last invited to join this effort, and in that, at least, they had something in common.

"I suppose you have a point," Helen said, her hand picking up its nervous twitching. "Well, I'll let it go, since, like you said, we're not likely to be in this thing too much longer."

Relief lifted the tension in the air between them, and Mary Alyce was glad for it. She wrote back that night, telling them she'd made it through public school and could not afford college, and besides, she was working to help out her folks. She was just nineteen, but she had plenty of real work experience. She wanted to use what she thought she knew to help lead them all to victory.

When the time came for her to share the documents, Helen

insisted on sending everything directly to the army address. Mary Alyce admired her mother's ability to change her mind, to be nimble enough to let her go on this noble endeavor. Soon as she was able to, Mary Alyce vowed, she would repay her mother for this kindness.

SIX

JUDY

Monday, 29 April 1944

Judith Washington:
Under Section 1534 granted by the Secretary of War and in
accordance with wartime emergency service duties carried out
by the Women's Army Corps (previously Women's Auxiliary
Army Corps), you are instructed to report to the quartermaster
at Fort Des Moines, Iowa at 0800 hours on 8 May 1944.
Herein are instructions for traveling to the post in Iowa and a
train voucher for your travels.
Captain Oveta Hobby

There were some fifteen thousand women soldiers, and just six
thousand total spots for Negroes. Judy felt lucky to be among
those chosen for the highly competitive positions. When it

was time to head out, Margaret wished her well with tears in her eyes. "You will hear from me just as soon as I can write," Judy promised.

"You better, Judith," Margaret said, squeezing her girl's hand. "You go be great."

This heartwarming encouragement made Judy's heart soar. She carried it with her on the segregated train, seated right next to the hot engine, which made that part of the train noisy and dust-filled. To manage her nerves, she closed her eyes, trying to get some rest.

She woke up from a fitful sleep in the narrow, hazy space filled with smokers, vagabonds and businessmen. A young Negro mother held her cranky baby on her lap, her hand around the girl's full belly like a belt strapping them both in, bouncing the child until she squealed and revealed a gummy smile.

An abundant streak of trees zooming past the window had lulled her to sleep. The first thing she noticed about the world beyond New York was how lush and fertile and spacious it was. The horizon opened up, and blue sky seemed like an invitation to dream.

After several hours, she arrived in Des Moines, Iowa. The train depot was part of a trio of small wooden buildings clustered together. Beyond it was a group of women who looked like they would never be gathered together for any social reason at all. A stout, strong-looking Negro woman in dungarees and a plaid button-down shirt stood with her legs on either side of a thick canvas bag, which rested partially on her feet and partially on the ground.

Another was dressed in a slinky royal blue dress that appeared sewed on, with matching pumps and an oval-shaped trunk.

Judy approached them and asked, "Excuse me, but are you with the women's army?"

The glamorous one, taller than Judy with almond eyes, high cheekbones and a pert mouth gave a friendly nod as the stout one said, "I sure hope so." She offered her hand. "I'm Stacy McFadden."

"And I'm Bernadette Moore. From Chicago," the woman in the blue dress said.

"We were on the train together. I'm from Missouri, St. Louis," Stacy said. "And you?"

"I'm Judy Washington. From New York."

"Ooh." Bernadette swooned. "Harlem? I've read divine things about that place."

"No, the Bronx. But they're not far from each other."

The shoulder pads in Bernadette's dress seemed to sink a little with her disappointment. Judy's hands were sore from Stacy's too-strong handshake, and as she rubbed them, she became aware of the purplish clouds above them. Taking her cue, the other women also glanced up.

"Oh, those clouds look familiar in a bad way," Stacy said. "Hell of a storm coming."

Bernadette sighed, pulling out a square of plastic from a clutch she retrieved from her luggage. Judy wondered if there was anything Bernadette hadn't brought with her to basic training. She simultaneously wondered if she hadn't brought enough. "It's always something, isn't it?"

A boxy army truck arrived a few feet from them, dust from the road stirred up by the movement and flying in their faces. The side had been painted with the phrase Property of the US Army. A plain white sign in the window read Fort Des Moines.

"Finally, the adventure begins," Stacy said, as a stern white man climbed out of the truck.

76

"You must be the Coloreds assigned to the women's army," he started. Bernadette, Judy and Stacy, who were standing close enough together that Bernadette's arm shot out to hold on to Judy as she muttered, "Did he just say that?"

Before Judy could answer, the man snapped, "Fall in!" Dazed still, Bernadette retrieved her hand, and reached up coyly as if raising her hand in a class. Judy was embarrassed on her behalf.

"I said fall in," the officer repeated, his ears getting red.

"Sir, I'm afraid I'm not sure what that means, exactly," Bernadette said in a soft voice.

Instead of responding to her, he gestured to a few white WACs who were standing in a line. They were only slightly less awkward than the Negroes, Judy thought, because who just happened to know military terms?

The officer got close enough to Bernadette for the height difference to be laughably evident. She was a model's height, maybe five-eight or five-nine—with the heels it was hard to tell. From the looks of the officer's boots, he got a slight lift from them, but it still meant that he was staring at her elegant throat and, to look Bernadette in the eyes, he had to tilt his angry face upward. "You just do what the smart ones are doing," he sneered while pointing out the white women officers in a line next to the truck.

"Yes, sir," Bernadette said, smiling flirtatiously. "I'm so glad 'falling in' is not throwing myself on the ground, particularly in *this* dress."

The officer looked startled. "Oh, it's you smart Negroes that I love breaking at boot camp."

Bernadette put her hand to her chest, dismayed. The officer, satisfied that he'd had an impact, finally, turned back to the truck to deliver the new recruits to the Fort Des Moines Training Center.

★ ★ ★

The Fort Des Moines Training Center consisted of a reception area, which doubled as the main building for military officers in charge of the post, and a large square building boasting a huge American flag at the top of a plain brick building facing a roundabout with a victory garden at its center. Behind the reception center was a field and several other buildings: mess halls, dorms, classrooms for basic training, a ropes course for boot camp.

It was the spring of 1944 and, though Negro press leaders in Pittsburgh, New York, Missouri and Chicago had been pressuring the President to let Negro soldiers serve in combat roles overseas as well as further integrate the US military, many Negro soldiers, including Herbert, Judy guessed, were considered inferior fighters. Without word from loved ones overseas, it was hard to know exactly what was going on. Letters were starting to be held up as the giant shipping vessels—which everyone called monsters and could carry weapons, cargo and upward of seven thousand troops—were being sunk, blown up and destroyed by Germans.

But what most impacted the women's futures in ways they could not know was the June 6, 1944, D-Day invasion that led to so many thousands of troops lost on Omaha Beach that it would alter the course of the war. D-Day gutted the number of combat troops on the ground, backing up support operations so Negroes formerly ignored for the job were finally encouraged to join the frontlines of the war.

The sheer number of troops lost meant the war would not end as quickly as military leaders hoped. They needed more troops and fast to liberate other parts of the world from Hitler, to fight back in Italy and Japan. The women would have known more, except all the operations in the US were slowed by the decreased manpower. None more so than the wartime postal service.

Draft-aged men who normally worked as carriers and supervisors were away. The young ones and women who could replace them immediately still needed time to fail on the job, misrouting things and the like. The result was that letters sent from combat zones took months, if they arrived at all, and mail sent overseas, particularly to Europe or England, stacked up slowly in warehouses until the army could find the right officers to sort it out.

Judy, like her new friends Stacy and Bernadette, was ushered to a reception center after leaving the truck, carrying their things close, as if that were the only safety under their control.

"Maybe there's still time to head back," Bernadette said.

"I think you missed your window for departure back at the train," Judy said, also feeling a thorn of doubt.

"I'm certain the window closed before that," Stacy chimed in.

The abrasive officer who drove them was back as they took in the surroundings. A sergeant was beside him now, followed by the woman Judy recognized from the Bronx Slave Market, Charity Adams, who had been promoted after finishing training to Captain. The sergeant frowned at them and ordered them to fall in.

"Coloreds on the right, ladies to the left," he shouted.

Judy felt a flash of anger at his words. Captain Adams stepped to the front of the area that had been designated for them, and after a moment of hesitation, she followed, as did Bernadette and Stacy. Their moods had shifted quickly, from bright and hopeful to tense and upset. They believed they had signed up for a different experience, one available to white woman officers but not them.

The sergeant seemed to have a different set of orders for the white enlisted. Captain Adams cleared her throat, glancing awkwardly at the dark sky as drops began falling in thicker pellets on them. "Ladies, welcome to the Women's Army Corps," she said. "We're Company B, Third Platoon. Everything for Negroes on post is essentially the same as it is where you're from, so I suggest you adjust any expectations. It'll make your training easier understanding that now."

The rain began falling in watery curtains. Judy tried to avoid wiping her face, but she couldn't see anything for the rain in her eyelashes. Bernadette was shaking. Stacy stood perfectly still, drenched, like Captain Adams, who continued to talk, water dripping from the brim of her cap, seeming to float off her shoulders as if she were waterproof.

Judy was impressed by how regal Captain Adams looked in spite of the deluge. Another Negro woman in uniform, with a more pleasant demeanor and a curvier silhouette appeared next to the captain with an umbrella and a wry smile. "Thank you, Lieutenant Campbell," Charity said, opening the umbrella and covering them both as they huddled beneath.

Without knowing she needed permission to talk to her superiors, Judy said in an awe-filled voice, "You don't even seem like the rain has gotten to you at all."

"Private, you are to be spoken to not spoken with, not without permission," Lieutenant Campbell said.

Captain Adams put a hand on the lieutenant's forearm, a gesture that looked both friendly and more...intimate than Judy expected to see between them. "It's OK, Lieutenant. I'll allow it this one time," she said before smiling at Judy with pride and adding, "I drape a towel around my shoulders under my coat, since the sky has a habit of opening up when you recruits make it on post."

Judy's eyes went wide. Adams laughed a hearty hoot at their reaction before she recovered and ordered them to follow her to the Negro barracks. As they set off awkwardly, Lieutenant Campbell offering them another large umbrella, Captain Adams said, "I know the culture seems like a lot right now. But in time, you'll get used to it. You'll see."

Judy should have asked Captain Adams how much time she meant by "in time," because the early days at Fort Des Moines felt like an eternity. Between the military phrases, the callous officers, inspections, classes and the sterile, austere barracks, Judy wondered if she hadn't made a huge mistake. Stacy mocked her from the beginning, over breakfast in the segregated dining hall.

"Aren't you married?" Stacy asked, chewing a roll in what Judy thought was a mannish way. She said she was, but nerves danced in her chest. She could let them know she had a husband, yes, but she was too ashamed to say she had not heard from him now for more than a year.

"Oh, you poor thing," Bernadette said. She had a utility blouse on, with severe shoulder pads, and a black skirt. She had packed even a decent drab outfit with her, which impressed Judy, who was in a navy blue ensemble her mother had made.

Stacy, in a black T-shirt and jeans, shot Bernadette a look. "I only ask because I hear this is what marriage is like. You walk into it with high hopes. But then reality sinks in after the honeymoon."

"Sometimes before, I bet," Bernadette added, patting Judy's arm and smiling. "Not that I would know. I'm twenty-five and am about to be an old maid if I don't get married soon. But I have not found my match."

"I don't doubt you will," Judy said, and she meant it. She was also relieved the conversation had veered away from Herbert so she would not have to lie about having news from him.

Their first stop was the post's clothing warehouse, a giant

shack that still smelled like dust from long ago and was on the edge of the ropes course they'd soon be using for their drills. A no-nonsense quartermaster ran the warehouse, so it was efficient, like all of her clipped, short sentences. But what the quartermaster didn't say is that they had very few properly fitting uniforms for women—there was not enough of anything in those days, but also the army did not count on women ever needing to don uniforms.

Judy thought a proper-size uniform shouldn't even matter, since they were still military outfits. Then she saw the sign: "Clothing Total: $172.34. Deducted from your check in three installments. Cash allowance for underwear: $30. Cash allowance for tennis shoes: $3. Cash allowance for dress pumps: $12★." The asterisk was followed by the sentence in smaller print: "After successful completion of recruit's fifth week."

The math was slightly daunting, but it didn't intimidate Judy nearly as much as acquiring her clothes with Stacy and Bernadette. She was sensing from Stacy, who was inclined to eat anything with her hands, lick her fingers and wipe them on her pants, that her new friend would not be very particular about the fit of her clothing. But Bernadette was exactly the opposite. Merely being around all the plain clothing made Bernadette begin to fidget. She looked more nervous than she had been at the truck.

"What the heck is going on with you?" Stacy bellowed, startling the quartermaster and the junior officers who were helping her with items from the back.

"I'm allergic to ugly clothes," Bernadette hissed, clasping her hands together to keep from scratching herself.

Judy chuckled. "Well, prepare yourself, because there is a lot of ugly headed our way."

At the front of the line, the quartermaster grunted, "Size?"

"Medium, please," Judy answered, expecting to have the

right-sized pile of clothes offered in return. The squat woman reached over to a row of baggy-looking things and put together a pile of thick skirts, mud-brown slips and panties; a small brown leather bag and a stiff-brimmed hat the girls called Hobby Hats—after the WAC director, Colonel Oveta Culp Hobby—on top. Before Judy could voice any questions the woman shouted, "Next!"

Judy wondered why the quartermaster even bothered to ask her size. Stacy and Bernadette were treated the same way. Poor Bernadette looked like she was carrying a sack of manure in her arms. "Are you sure it's not too late to go home?" Bernadette asked in her throaty voice.

"We're sure," Judy and Stacy said at the same time, which made them all laugh on their way back to the barracks to put on the offending attire before drills within the hour. The laughter was an acknowledgment that even if things were not exactly as they wanted them to be, they were together in this new environment, with new clothes to prove it.

Inside the building, bunk beds rose from the cement floor, with faded white bedding and woolen gray blankets folded with precision at the foot of each bed. The screen door was ripped through its center and squeaked on a rusty hinge.

The bunk bed Judy shared with Stacy was one of a set of several anchoring their segregated barracks, several feet from the common dining hall and the classroom building where Captain Adams worked with Lieutenant Campbell. Morning sun caught the light of the brass symbols of Pallas Athene, the Greek goddess of victory and the art of war, which Judy knew from her love of history class.

"That symbol's the fanciest thing about this getup," Stacy observed, pulling out the broad necktie and fiddling with one of her stiff shirts.

Judy pulled on the jacket with its angular shoulders and thick buttons. "These aren't so bad. Just clearly made for men."

"My daddy was right," Bernadette said, looking smart and shapely, even in the boxy uniform. Nothing could make her look less than stunning, even army-issued hand-me-downs. She slipped her feet into the clunky brown leather pumps beside a pair of heavy boots. "I'm not cut out for the sacrifices of war."

Judy giggled at that. "You're hardly suffering."

"Not on the outside," Bernadette answered without missing a beat. "But, darling, these shoes are really breaking my heart."

"It's the bag I can't stand," Stacy complained, holding with both hands the plain leather shoulder bag, which had within it another small brown satchel that they could attach to their suit belts. They all also received ill-fitting winter coats like Adams's. Judy's billowed out over her ankles and brushed the tops of her shoes; the sleeves were too short and left her wrists naked. Judy thought the idea of the uniforms were grand, even if the reality of them was less so.

A bugle sounded, signaling a start to their drills outside in a field near the barracks. With a start, the women abandoned the new clothes they weren't wearing, which they would have plenty of time to contemplate later.

Captain Adams and Lieutenant Campbell stood erect and alert in their uniforms at the front of the field. Lieutenant Campbell was more anxious-looking than the captain, and they stood a few feet from one another. Lieutenant Campbell held a clipboard tightly to her chest, then clutched it to her side, like she was trying to figure out what to do with herself and her body.

Judy looked around at the other hundreds of women around her—all shapes and skin tones, short, tall, eager, afraid. Even on the slave market, she had not encountered this many Negro women in one spot before. Being gathered there with them in this new place, to serve her country, filled her with pride, and she couldn't wait to share the feeling by writing her mother and even Herbert, as hard as it was to think about him and his silence.

"Attention, please," Captain Adams said, sounding to Judy like she was straining to make her voice carry. Lieutenant Campbell nodded in approval and they exchanged looks. "Attention! Fall in!"

The second command made everyone line up quickly in rows the length of the field. The white women officers were behind their much-better barracks on the other side, but the Negro officers had seen them marching and being instructed, so they knew what was expected of them. Learning by watching and doing is what Judy did at home, so she could see that life in the WAC would not be that different from life at home in one important way: no one would teach Negro women what they needed to get ahead. The women would have to figure it out on their own.

As if Captain Adams could hear those thoughts, she announced, "It is my duty to guide you as you undertake this important responsibility and service to your country. I do not need to tell you the stakes are high. If you do not fulfill your duties with the utmost efficiency, poise and determination, it will be an excuse to close the door on Negro women who seek to follow your example for generations to come.

"We do not yet have information about where we will be stationed, but I have it on good authority that our main work will be to help with stateside postal operations to fix the backlog of mail keeping soldiers low, making them more vulnerable to death as they fight. They are in need and awaiting the words of encouragement from home to keep them going. That means your service is crucial to the morale of these soldiers. No mail, no morale. It will be our mantra.

"That said, though you will not bear arms or be trained in utilizing them, you still need to be prepared for the wartime environment. And we need you to have physical, mental and emotional stamina. Our drills and your classroom work will be toward that end."

Captain Adams paused, and Lieutenant Campbell gave her a gentle, approving smile. Judy admired the light between them, the way they seemed to communicate without talking. She had had that once with Herbert, hadn't she?

"'Yes, Captain Adams' is a good response," Lieutenant Campbell announced to them, her voice loud and strong. "Or 'Yes, ma'am, no, ma'am.'"

Stacy rubbed her hands together. Bernadette rolled her eyes. Judy glanced at them, then turned her attention back to Captain Adams. She had not really felt before like she had coconspirators in school or even on the market, besides her mother. But now, in her fellow recruits, she felt she had found a group of friends.

"Now that you have your uniforms, I wanted to inform you that your days will begin with reveille, you will be instructed in drill and military commands and ceremony," Captain Adams continued. "You will embark on a time-honored tradition of learning the ways and formations of the US Army. These traditions have more or less been in place since 1776, commands that have instilled discipline and dignity into the scrambled masses fighting for our independence.

"It's a lot to take in all at once," she continued, her hands clasped behind her as she stood. "But you will be expected to learn it all faster than your white colleagues. You cannot compare your journeys to theirs. They will have more time to learn the material and different opportunities that are not yet available to us, like being deployed to overseas posts, which are still rare for Negroes, especially Negro women who are not nurses.

"Still, we will do as we always have had to do and rise to this occasion," she added. "Do get some rest and settle in for the next eight weeks, which will determine if you have what it takes to help our boys end this war. You are dismissed."

In the afternoon, into the evening, before the final bugle and lights-out, the women quietly unpacked their things and talked about what had brought them to the Women's Army Corps. Judy had not brought much from New York with her. In a way, her home was her people: her mother, Herbert. So unpacking was easy. And she was done first, so she sat with her legs stretched out in front of her on the bed in an L-shape as Stacy placed an assortment of T-shirts and jeans in her storage trunk.

"Do you own a single dress?" Judy asked, eyes cast down. It felt ruder than she'd meant it when she said it aloud.

"Back home, I do," Stacy said, not looking up. A sadness was in her face suddenly, and Judy realized she may have touched a tender part of what Stacy left behind. "We're all farm folks. Dad is very conservative. Likes women to dress the part. Says if I want to be a real race woman, I should be less mannish."

"Ouch," Bernadette said.

"He lost all my brothers to the war," Stacy added. "And I was the last one standing. So, I did what they did and worked the land, tried to help the old man out. But we were always fussing with each other. And when I saw the WAC ad in the newspaper, I thought maybe there would be other girls like me, doing mannish things for the war."

"What did he say to that?" Judy wondered, while she tried

to digest the meaning of losing sons to war. Were they dead? She didn't allow herself to think of any connection between Stacy's brothers and her husband. She would let it be.

Stacy puffed out her chest and drew in her chin, imitating him. "'Only kid who shouldn't be in a uniform, and here you go.' But in his eyes, I could see he understood. It was a sore spot because why wouldn't it be? He even shed a tear when I left. Told me to take good care. To ask for a skirt for once, for my uniform, instead of pants. And what about you, Judy?"

"I came to the WAC looking for better work, since I was cleaning houses with my mom up in the Bronx for way too little pay. A job going nowhere. But we needed the money after my daddy died. Now my husband is over there, to boot," she said, instantly regretting the mention of Herbert.

"Where's he stationed, Judy?" Bernadette asked. Judy felt a slow panic build and she decided she would answer quickly then change the subject.

"The 337th Infantry. He was one of the first to report after Pearl Harbor. But enough about me. Bernadette, you haven't told us anything about yourself," Judy said, trying not to sound in a big hurry to move on. "What brings you to the WAC and its ugly uniforms?"

"I'm like Stacy, I guess…"

"Oh no, you most certainly are not!" Stacy tried her best to look gravely offended, which made them giggle.

"Well, let me rephrase, then. Hold on," Bernadette said, sitting up and pointing her toes, which were painted a bright fire-engine red. "I mean that I heard about the WAC and it felt like maybe the one thing I could do to see other places and be more than what I have been, which is just pretty."

"Not just pretty, honey," Judy said. "You're stunning."

"You're a doll. We're all friends here," Bernadette said, smiling. "No need for me to rub it in."

The lights were flickering in the main area of the barracks, the signal that it was time for them to wind down for sleep. But in true Bernadette fashion, she didn't miss a beat. She simply slinked out of her blouse, skirt and girdle on the discreet side of the bunk away from the window and kept talking. Judy admired that about them all—they could adapt. They would still be themselves while serving in the army. They would have to hold on to that here.

"I have a passion for fashion," she said, striking a pose in a large bonnet and pajamas. "We have a family-run beauty salon at home. My mother studied with Madame C. J. Walker and likes having a dozen jobs. And I love the work, making us as beautiful as we can be, but I have always wanted to see the rest of the world. I know it's a crazy dream, but oh, can you imagine walking the same Paris streets as the glorious Josephine Baker? I can't speak a lick of French, but it would be worth learning, to strut in her footsteps."

"The farthest any Negroes have been in the army is to Fort Huachuca in Tucson, I heard," Stacy said. "But a dream is nice."

"It is," Judy added. "And dreams have a way of sometimes becoming real."

The lights went out then, around the post. They retired to bed, the thoughts of dreams like blankets covering them in the dark.

The women started training the next morning at 0600 hours. They woke to a flurry of sounds, from roosters on the post's victory garden to the bugle blaring reveille. Judy and her two new friends stirred easily, but not without some discomfort and grumbling.

They were assembled once again on the field, to receive

instructions from Captain Adams. They fell in formation at the right side of the field. White recruits were to their left.

"For the next eight weeks, I will train you in military structure, commands and operations with my fellow officers. When I give a command in these initial days, Lieutenant Campbell will demonstrate during our drills. The point of drills are for you to listen closely. Even if you will not be on battlefields and only some of you will be near enemy lines, learning to listen closely could save your lives."

Their training at Fort Des Moines was the only aspect of the Women's Army Corps that was integrated. It surprised Judy to be now in an environment where she was not considered less than or inferior to white women; at least no one said that in words at first. It was her first glimpse of a place where it was possible for a Negro woman to lead things, to be powerful.

Captain Adams laid out the day's schedule quickly, then dismissed them so they could proceed to breakfast, the start of their classes and to change into exercise uniforms for boot camp drills. The days were interesting and dynamic, even while following a strict routine. Judy stumbled a little bit over little things like polishing boots to the perfect shine or misunderstanding the chain of command. But she excelled at inspection, given all that she learned on the Bronx Slave Market.

It did not take long before she came face-to-face with the realities of race at Fort Des Moines. About a month into their training, during a drill to prepare the recruits for possible support-unit ambushes—common in the Italian and French combat zones—white and Negro women alike were issued gas masks.

Tear gas was deployed on the second floor of their classroom building and Lieutenant Campbell instructed them in how to use the masks, adding a caveat: "You have ten minutes to cover your mouths and head outside. You should then be sure to wipe your faces as soon as possible to keep any of the chemical agents from ruining your sight. Fall in!"

Now that they knew what to do, Judy found herself jostling less. She was more confident. She made a beeline down the steps into the fresh air. She could breathe in the mask, but only in a shallow way and really just for the duration of time Lieutenant Campbell gave them. When she lifted the sticky rubber off her head, she gasped.

Rags circulated between recruits. Another Negro private wiped her brow with one and handed it to an indignant-looking white woman. "I need a clean one," the white officer said. "I'm not using the same cloth as them."

In the tense silence that followed, Judy wondered why the woman's declaration was so painful. She thought it was because she had not made room here for the overt bias she experienced at home, even though, there it was, plain as day.

"Just use this one, Jane," another white officer whispered. Jane could hardly see with the sweat spiking her eyelashes, but she settled for her moist forearm. Judy and the others used the cloth closest to them until they were dismissed.

Aside from the frequent drills, boot camp was pretty difficult. She'd had the impression that of the two commanding officers, Lieutenant Campbell was the more lenient. She certainly was less physically intimidating than Captain Adams, though she was heavier. Maybe it was those eyes of hers, light like honey drops, round and curious. Her pressed hair was always pulled back into the same tight bun beneath her cap, prim and buttoned-up.

But on the obstacle course behind the field, Lieutenant Campbell was much more demanding. She barked orders and teased the women who struggled. Judy dreaded catching her attention but knew eventually the day would come. She could not, for example, climb a rope over the twelve-foot wall to save her life.

"That's absurd, Judy," Bernadette said over lunch one day, when they got to talking about what they liked and what they loathed. Easy for Bernadette to say, since she managed to do everything gracefully and elegantly. "If I can do it, and I've done a lick of hard labor in my life, certainly you can."

Stacy sat beside Judy at the mess hall, across from Bernadette. In their first few weeks, someone had the audacity of placing cards on less desirable tables that read Coloreds Only, which Captain Adams discovered and had promptly removed. All the officers self-segregated into the groups they had bonded with. Stacy grabbed at the loose flesh of Judy's upper arm and shook her head. "I'm afraid it's not that absurd," Stacy assessed, dropping her hand.

"Thanks for the vote of support," Judy said, rolling her eyes. "I can run just fine and jumping jacks are okay. It's just climbing that blasted wall that gets me stuck."

"Maybe it's in your mind," Bernadette offered. "You're thinking so much about it your body won't just go."

Judy nodded and bit into her sandwich, grunting her approval. "You may have a point there."

"You may do well to take an etiquette class while we're learning things, though, if you eat while talking, honey," Bernadette teased.

Judy shook her head and finished her food, mulling over facing the brutal wall again. After their meal was done, she marched with the platoon to their spot, to get the drudgery over with. She was going to fail again, she knew. But maybe Bernadette was right and all she needed was the strength of her mind.

"Private Washington, you're up," Lieutenant Campbell said, standing a few feet away from the rope, calling out victims to take their turns. Judy inhaled deeply, studying the thick rope intently before grabbing hold of it with both hands. She kicked herself off the ground and planted her feet on the board. She was focused on one foot then the other, climbing steadily, then pulling herself closer to the top edge. She was halfway up, close to the top, when her feet slipped and she dangled into the air before dropping in defeat, crying out, her face planted into her forearms now.

"It's okay, Judy," Stacy shouted.

"Come on, you were so close!" Bernadette added.

Judy was grateful to have friends in her corner. But she was disappointed in herself, that she couldn't get a simple thing like this right. She needed to successfully finish training to stay in the army. She had fought so hard to do something besides cleaning houses. She had promised her mother she would send money. And she still needed to find Herbert, which would certainly never happen if she didn't make it through boot camp.

"Quiet!" Lieutenant Campbell said to the group that had gathered and completed the task already. Lieutenant Campbell approached Judy on the ground. "Private Washington, collect yourself and try again. I don't associate myself with losers or quitters. They're the same in my mind. Are you a loser?"

"No, ma'am."

"What's that, Private?"

"No, ma'am!"

"That's what I like to hear. Get up over that wall, then. Unless you're a quitter."

"No, lieutenant, I am not," Judy said louder, crawling up from the ground. She wiped her hands on her pants. Her face was flushed, and her body was tired. It was almost as bad as scrubbing floors and windows all day for pennies. But now, she was doing this grueling thing for herself, for her mother.

The rope dug into her hands. She inched and inched, gritting her teeth. Finally, at the top of the wall, she moved close enough to swivel and hook her boot over the edge. A few of the women who'd already made it over looked at her with hopeful eyes, Stacy and Bernadette included. She made it over the side, letting the rope dangle behind her so she could climb down the ladder perched on the other side.

Lieutenant Campbell approached Judy and said, "See there. I knew you had it in you."

Judy smiled back and said, "Thank you, ma'am." She knew she had it in her, too. She just sometimes forgot herself was all.

Lieutenant Campbell dismissed them. Stacy and Bernadette stayed back with Judy to embrace her for sticking with it.

"I shouldn't have doubted you, flabby arms," Stacy said. "You're a trooper."

"What she said," Bernadette added. "Guts like that and we might just make it through this thing."

Judy felt that she couldn't have said it better.

SEVEN

CHARITY

Tuesday, 2 August 1944

Dear Daddy,

*I know it's been a little while since I wrote, but I have been
thinking a lot about you and Mama since my trip home months
ago. I don't know what it was about encountering the Klansmen
this time that bothered me so much, but this last time stayed in
my head. Maybe the difference has been being in a position of
authority here, having a title, so to speak. Even so, there is still
segregation and hatred at Fort Des Moines.*

*Seems to me, thinking about it, praying on it, that groups
like the Klan guard the idea that whites and colored folk were
made so different that we might as well keep our lives on parallel tracks. But everywhere I look on post, I see lives that in-*

tersect. Some officers are curt with me, but I have won a few of them over. Just a few.

It's been a revelation to be around white folks and not feel unsafe. Abbie is still my closest friend here, the one person I can truly confide in. But I can be around white folks who don't prefer my company, and it doesn't mean they want to destroy me or make me feel inferior. I'm just so different from what they have been told to expect in a Negro woman. So they can go be with people they can tolerate. And for the most part, I can do the same.

I wonder if one day every part of society will be like that, segregated or not. It's hard to imagine that, even though it feels like I'm working towards that very thing every day.

Know that I'm thinking of you and Mama.

Love,

Charity

As the summer's end approached and her newest recruits were graduating from basic training, Charity could sense a change coming. One she wasn't at all pleased about. The Omaha Beach massacre in June was an enormous loss for the Allied Forces and was translating to low morale across the military branches.

By August, the sentiment from earlier in the year—that the war could end in '44—was growing quieter all the time. A vocal group of Negro leaders, including a courageous and influential Negro woman named Mary McLeod Bethune, was beginning to help women officers and military officials break down even more barriers than the initial campaigns by the Negro press. The first fights were for Negro soldiers to serve in combat and for Negro women to be allowed in the women's army. Segregation in civilian life was still very much the law of the land, but the wartime needs in all areas of the military forced the government to admit that they would need to make some exceptions in order to win the war.

The initial wins for Bethune, an advisor to Eleanor Roosevelt, and the Negro newspaper publishers were that Negro soldiers now served abroad in the thousands. The battle that Charity and others were still waging was for the chance for Negro women to serve overseas, too. But for now, they were still stuck on domestic soil.

Charity had been mulling over the confines of their stateside service the afternoon Abbie pulled her aside, her face long, looking at an envelope she was holding.

"Edna, you won't like what I've got to say," Abbie started, not making eye contact. Charity felt a little faint, recognizing the official army seal on the envelope. She knew those were orders for Abbie to go elsewhere. But she could not, would not cry about it, certainly not in front of the whole battalion. "My orders are for Fort Oglethorpe. In Georgia."

Charity looked evenly at Abbie, the way her plump cheeks looked highlighted by the sun. There was no angle or light in which she looked less than perfect to Charity, but at that moment, she looked particularly beautiful. Charity wanted to curse her and to kiss her. She wondered if it would have been better to never have met her. She paused and said, "Maybe it's a good sign, Abigail."

"How do you mean?"

"That's where they train officers for overseas posts."

"Only the white officers go overseas, you know that." Abbie was perplexed, understandably suspicious of Charity's reaction, or lack thereof. "Who knows what they'll have me do. Just training Negroes for domestic posts, probably. It can't be more than that. But Charity," Abbie said, stepping closer to her friend, holding on to the envelope with earnest hope.

"You can tell me you're upset. I am, too. I have to leave in three days. We don't have time to spare."

Charity struggled to find the right words. She wanted to say, "Please don't go." Or, "Wait for me. I'll come to you as soon as I can." She wanted to say, "I wish we had more time. I wish we could be married, and no one could take you away from me." But Charity could not muster any words that wouldn't make her voice break. Instead, she said, "Of all places, Georgia?"

Abbie's face crumpled. "You are a piece of work."

Charity tried to grab her arm as Abbie walked away, but she lost her chance when a loud voice yelled, "Excuse me!"

Charity turned around to find what appeared to be a white woman with sandy-blond hair who looked as lost as Charity felt.

"Are you talking to me?" Charity looked at the woman impatiently, glancing behind her at the direction where Abbie had gone. It was too late to make things right. But maybe not. She had a few more days to apologize, to say what she really felt. She would try again.

This woman, though, had horrible timing. "Yes, yes" the woman blurted out. Her arms weren't moving, but she had the demeanor of one who was flailing about. She appeared jumpy and flushed. "I'd like to talk to your superior, if possible. There's been some terrible mistake. I've been assigned to the wrong platoon."

Charity walked closer to the woman, as if to see her more clearly under the bright light affixed to the front of the barracks. It was not unusual for a white recruit to demand something of a superior who happened to be a Negro. But she hadn't seen a white private behave this way before.

"It's quite late," Charity said, though it was just after dusk.

WOMEN OF THE POST

She needed to stall. Her head was starting to ache. "Are you sure this isn't something that can't wait, Private…?"

"Mary Alyce Dixon," the woman replied, her face contorting into discomfort and agitation. "I'm not going to spend a single night sleeping with Coloreds. No, it is certainly not something that can wait."

Charity inhaled sharply and stood up straighter. She was at the end of her patience with this day. And the mention of Coloreds this Mary Alyce could not abide was going to put her right over-the-top. Charity stepped her feet in line with each other and folded her hands at her waist. Her first thought was that this seemed to be a matter above her pay grade.

And then after a deep breath, Charity thought that perhaps it was another opportunity. To show her value, her good wisdom. She turned toward the administrative building where Colonel Barrows's office was and said, "Follow me, Miss Dixon."

EIGHT

MARY ALYCE

From Mary Alyce Dixon to Helen Dixon

Tuesday, 2 August 1944

Mama,
I pray this finds you well and happy. I have not had time to write, really, because we've been doing so much training and figuring out all that will be expected of us, learning the military lingo and schedule. But it is a relief to be here, like I told you it would be. It feels like I have found a good place for myself.

Ethel and Betsy are already thinking about how we can get off post to flirt with the men in town. There are also Negro women officers here, which surprised me. They keep us separate, of course, but still, not the environment I was expecting. Part of being here seems to also mean rising to the occasion.

I will let you know how all of this turns out when I write again. In the meantime, thank you for giving me your blessing.
Love Always,
Mary Alyce

On the walk from the Company B barracks, in the still and humid evening of the Iowa summer, Mary Alyce kept her arms folded. She did not want the women's army to go making a liar out of her, now that she'd written Helen an update saying all was well. But maybe she was naive to think there would be no hiccups and everything would go smoothly.

The weeks of her training with Ethel and Betsy in the First Platoon had been busy but focused. They'd learned everything from the proper makeup to wear with their uniforms to how to take cover during air raids.

That afternoon, she had been pulled out of class by a Sergeant who told her she was to report to the Colored regiment as soon as possible.

"There must be some mistake, sir," she said eagerly.

"No mistake, Private. You are dismissed. Make your way to Company B, behind the field. You're looking for Captain Charity Adams."

It was unbelievable, but she did have to follow orders. Someone would know they were wrong, as soon as they saw her paperwork and application. Maybe Helen had not sent her birth certificate in time.

Trotting behind Charity, Mary Alyce thought about all her time working on the farm, feeling she wasn't living up to her potential. Helen had tried to talk her out of finishing high school. "I need you to keep up with the crops," Helen said wearily. Sixty acres was not a lot, but it was still something.

"But I enjoy school," Mary Alyce said. "Not only that, once I have my diploma, I can look for better-paying work."

Helen wore a look on her face whenever Mary Alyce brought up her ambition. The look said it was a fine thing for her to keep to herself, but a troublesome thing to expose to the world.

Helen bit her lip and changed the subject every single time they fussed with one another about the value of work over school.

"Why not help me out in the kitchen?" Helen would say sweetly, knowing that was one of Mary Alyce's favorite things to do. Even when she was little, she thrilled at wrapping her little arms around a big mixing bowl and lifting it above her head to help Helen. As she grew older, she liked baking Golden Nugget cakes with soft bananas, or mashing together precious meat-and-potato patties to help stretch the meat rations.

As much as Mary Alyce loved to cook, she figured it was studying that could take her somewhere beyond working the land, feeding the chickens, milking their cows. When she had a little free time, she visited the town library with her grandmother Patty, who had only gone to school up until the sixth grade and couldn't read. The saddest part for Mary Alyce about her grandmother was that she had long ago given up on her dream of being a librarian, despite Mary Alyce's efforts to read to her from the books for children.

"I do like the sound of your voice, Mary Alyce," Patty would say, reassuring her with a loving pat on the hand. "You keep reading. You'll be my eyes and ears someday."

Mary Alyce couldn't guess what her grandmother meant by that, but she did what she was told.

When she wasn't sitting with Patty or working the farm, Mary Alyce did everything with Ethel and Betsy, her closest friends since first grade. They played with dolls, swam and imagined growing up to be perfect housewives in Vermont, like their mothers aimed to be. Like the quaint country folk they were, none of them ever mentioned that Ms. Helen was the rare widower who didn't seem to be in any rush to remarry, and she rarely talked about that husband of hers who'd died. All anybody knew, really, was that he was an outsider. And then, he was gone.

Mary Alyce wanted to be gone, too. It's why she was enchanted by that WAC poster, the woman soldier asking about their patriotic hearts. She'd even shared her wild longing and curiosity with Ethel and Betsy, her pale blue eyes aflame.

They went with her to look at it, and because they were young women, they each compared themselves to the woman on the poster, a symbol of one potential future. Mary Alyce felt her eyes were set a little too far apart and her lips were unfashionably full. So maybe she wouldn't be modeling the WAC uniform anytime soon—but she could be a nurse, probably, and travel to the front lines to find one of those soldiers to marry and bring home. She imagined how flattering she would look in a nurse's uniform, which would give her more of a shape than she really had, and the tall handsome fighter pilot she would charm, in his flawless uniform and cap, with his duffel bag slung over one shoulder and her arm tucked in his at their farmhouse door.

"Is it possible to be a patriot in those hideous uniforms?" Ethel asked. It was a typical question from her, the prettiest and vainest of the three. They all agreed on this, and they would have even if all the boys didn't let her skip their penny-pitching lines or buy her smoked turkey legs or offer her huge ice cream cones in the summer. Despite the fact that she also worked her family's farm as much as they did, her hands never seemed to dry out or get dirty.

"Don't forget, we all must make sacrifices for the victory of our boys," Betsy, the smartest of the three, said with a smile.

"That includes giving up any notion of good fashion." Betsy reminded Mary Alyce of her grandmother, or who Patty might have been if she had been allowed to be bookish. She had dark brown hair that fell over her thick glasses. None of them came from money, but she was the poorest in the group. She'd worn hand-me-downs from her elder sisters her whole life and was ready to stop thinking about clothes, or her endless need for better ones, for as long as she could.

"Even with ugly uniforms, I'd say the women's army has more for us than Woodstock. Don't you think?" Mary Alyce had turned away from the poster now to look at them. She wanted them to see what she saw: that their way of life could expand every bit as hers would in the women's army.

Ethel was defensive. "We have all that we need right here. It's quiet and beautiful. Besides, it's what we know."

"But I bet there will be thousands of women training to do their part," Mary Alyce interjected. "It's the opportunity of a lifetime."

Betsy looked at them both and shrugged. "I suppose there's nothing wrong with applying. Not like we have better things to do."

Ethel shook her head. "I like my life here just fine. Those boys over there are doing the Lord's work, but they were called in a way that I'm just not."

"Suit yourself," Mary Alyce said. "I've already applied." But the rejection stung. Betsy, however, timidly plucked an application from the pile. Ethel rolled her eyes at them both. "Well, it wouldn't be suitable for me to be left behind since you two insist on this," she said, and folded her application in thirds.

And now, six months after that exchange, they were finished with basic training. Ethel and Betsy had been assigned to North Africa. Mary Alyce was sure she would be joining them; she'd packed her trunk and was ready to go. Then she was ordered to report to the Negro unit. Which is how she ended up following this Charity woman, which she thought was a nice name for a Negro.

"Wait here," Charity said, as she went inside the back of the barracks where the senior leaders were. Mary Alyce waited patiently at the door. When Charity emerged with the pale and rumpled-looking Lieutenant Colonel Barrows, he rubbed his eyes and said, "What's this all about, after hours?"

He said it like it was her fault she'd been reassigned!

Charity said, "Officer Dixon is confused about why she's been reassigned to our unit, given that we are an all-Negro unit, sir."

The Lieutenant Colonel frowned at Charity, then at Mary Alyce. His voice was soft when he said, "Did you know about the aberration with your paperwork?"

Mary Alyce's heart beat loudly in her chest. She had passed the written and the physical tests without issue. She'd submitted a copy of her high school diploma as evidence of her education. The only other paperwork she could think of was her birth certificate. Helen had said she'd sent it directly to the post. "Did you receive my birth certificate?"

The Lieutenant Colonel grunted. "We'll have to take this up in the morning, Dixon. I don't know the ins and outs of everyone's file. There are thousands of you on this post to think about. Charity, find a bed for her in your quarters. Dixon, follow her orders."

"But it's illegal, isn't it, for a white woman to be sleeping in the same place as Negroes?" Mary Alyce was hoping one last plea could keep her from having to spend a single night with Negroes. She was not opposed to them; she just didn't know any. There were no Negroes in Woodstock, so there was no need for separate libraries, schools or bathrooms. That meant everything she grew up around was for white people by default. It was just how she'd been raised.

"It's an order is what it is," the colonel said before he saluted them both and took his leave.

The women walked silently back to the barracks. Inside, Charity peeked into a room with two bunk beds and invited Mary Alyce to take the empty bed that awaited her. "Just for tonight," Charity whispered.

Mary Alyce tried to blink back tears of disappointment and frustration as Charity left. She looked around at the Negro women sleeping near her. She took off her shoes and her nylons. To top it all off, she didn't even have her things. She'd been in such a rush, and so sure there'd been a mistake. She stretched out on the bed, still in her uniform, and stared at the bed frame above her head.

Her thoughts piled up on one another while crickets and cicadas sang in the night. The whole point of coming here was to find her rightful place in the world. She was like one of those pieces of a puzzle with a little extra paper around the edges that needed to be pulled apart for her to fit into her hometown.

Belonging to First Platoon, Company A with Ethel and Betsy, for the first time, made her feel like she was in the exact right place. They had already had a good time during weekends off, dancing at the soldier's club. Farm-town boys in the Midwest turned out to be just like farm-town boys in Vermont: tall, broad-shouldered and mischievous.

Not many men in town had both avoided the military and marriage; the boys too young for war were doing jobs to support it. In Iowa, many of them worked long hours in a Food for Freedom campaign to produce more beef, pork and dairy to help feed American troops at war.

So when Mary Alyce and the girls of the First Platoon were

sick of preparing for inspections or learning about the right shades of blush to complement their uniforms, they flirted with the few available men. Just the night before, when they received word of new assignments, Mary Alyce had been in the arms of a handsome private cutting his teeth in management as support personnel at Fort Des Moines on his way to the Philippines.

"You're too good to be true," he'd said, then made a face when he looked at the uniform jacket she'd borrowed from Betsy, which was better fitting than her own. "Then I get to thinking about this uniform. What it means."

She tried not to look as startled as she felt. "What's that?"

"A girl should be satisfied to be a mother or a wife, probably both," he said. "A girl in a uniform means she doesn't really want to do any of that."

She wrested her hand from his and stepped back. She looked up into his eyes, frowning. "Don't be ridiculous. I'm just patriotic. I want victory for America, same as you."

He shook his head. "Doll, it's just not natural for us to wear the same kind of clothes."

She was livid, and she stormed away, confused by the interaction and how it made her feel. A uniform was supposed to help her blend in, after all, to make things a bit easier. But she was starting to feel that same out-of-place feeling again. It set her nerves on edge.

Reassignment to the Negro unit without a clear explanation did not help put her at ease. She tried to keep her mind from moving in so many directions at once, and to convince herself all would be well in the morning, when the colonel and the captain realized their mistake. She couldn't imagine making the kind of error they had, but she would be gracious about this little blip as soon as she was back where she belonged.

But in the morning, when Mary Alyce and Charity returned to Lieutenant Colonel Barrows's office, as he had ordered the night before, a single letter would change all that. She had slept perhaps twenty minutes or so and stepped out of the barracks before reveille to not draw attention to herself. As weary as she felt, she was still awake enough to notice Barrows's sideways glance as he handed her a folder with just a single photocopy of her birth certificate inside. She opened it to see her parents' names. Beneath her father's, the letter *C* for Colored.

She stared at the paper in disbelief, a combination of shock and terror. "There must be some mistake," she said, her voice shaking. But even as she said it, a small part of her understood that the only mistake that had been made was her own. She had not asked the right questions of her mother. Who was her father, really? Where was he from, who was his family besides them? Why were there no pictures of him, and why did she never speak of him? She had not had the courage to allow herself to pose these questions, but part of the answer was symbolized in that single letter *C*, which now would mark her path forever.

NINE

JUDY

From Judy to Herbert

Thursday, 4 August 1944

Dearest Herbert,
It's been so long since I heard from you, I suppose I can't even reasonably expect that you'll receive this. But I wanted to tell you for months now that I've joined the Women's Army and passed basic training. It took a grueling number of weeks of trying to get over a tall wall with the help of tough ropes, all while wearing awful clothes and missing home. Missing you.

Oh, but how I wish I could see your face when you read this news! I think you'll be proud of me. I've enclosed a photo of me that the local photographers took. They wanted to know who all these women were, acting like men in uniforms. The way I see it, the more women and men join the Army, the faster you'll make it home.

*I also now have a glimpse at what must be keeping you from
writing. The military does know how to keep a body busy.
Please send just a few lines when you can.*
Love Always,
Judy

Judy worked harder some days in the women's army than she
had on the market, always preparing for a class or memorizing
some part of a drill. The chain of command also took some
getting used to, especially the sneering, scowling commanding officers, offset by the kindnesses of Lieutenant Campbell
before she was reassigned, and now Captain Adams.

Of the Commanding Officers, Judy found herself growing
most fond of Captain Adams. She admired the woman's com-
posure at all times. Though the Captain couldn't have been
much older than her, she had the bearing of a mother. It was
that reserve, maybe, or her authority.

So when Captain Adams pulled her aside to say she had a
request about a delicate matter, Judy was more than willing to
do whatever was asked of her.

"You've met the new private in our company, Mary Alyce
Dixon?" Adams asked.

"Met" was not quite how Judy would describe the lump of
a body in the bunks she'd seen in the barracks. She'd didn't
know what to make of her and hadn't had the time to investigate further. "I've seen her sleeping. Is she unwell?"

"She's stopped eating regularly and has taken to staying in
bed for the foreseeable future," Adams said, pausing. "But it's
a little more complicated than that. It appears that Ms. Dixon's
heritage is Negro, but she didn't know that until she came to
the army. She has lived the first twenty years of her life believing she was a white woman."

Judy gasped. The Captain was not exaggerating when she said the situation was sensitive.

Adams continued, "We've recently learned, thanks to her papers, that her father was Colored. But he died before she could know him. She never knew."

Judy tried to wrap her brain around what Captain Adams was telling her. They had all been sacrificing and giving up things for the war, for the sake of freedom. She could only imagine what it was like to have to abandon being a white woman, if that was a choice Mary Alyce would make. Because what neither of them could know is whether Mary Alyce would decide to leave the army and keep the secret by passing as white for the rest of her life. Judy was not light enough to have the option of making a choice like that, and neither was Captain Adams. But they both understood that society loved and protected white women. It would be tempting for anyone in Mary Alyce's position to at least consider keeping the fact of one's Negro identity to themselves. Who could blame her if she were to run back to her old life with this secret so she could live in peace?

"Please don't repeat what I've told you, but I wanted you to understand her current condition so you can handle things accordingly," Adams added.

"Yes, Captain."

"Please see to it that she has the option of eating her meals, even if she doesn't take it. Perhaps you can offer yourself as a friend. I imagine this is the loneliest time of her life."

"Whatever she needs," Judy replied. She looked toward the barracks and thought about what that ache must be like for Mary Alyce. She could relate to feeling alone, but here she was, feeling sorry for herself about Herbert, and this woman had lost the most valuable part of her being. She would have to learn now, if she chose to live truthfully, to be part of the most invisible, disrespected class in the world.

★ ★ ★

The next morning, after observing Mary Alyce again in bed after everyone left, Judy stayed behind and introduced herself. Being inside was a welcome distraction from the summer heat, which stayed evenly hot all day, often without any cloud cover. Far away, the Allied Forces were liberating Florence. American troops had liberated Guam. And a Negro woman whose name Judy read in the press from time to time, Mary McLeod Bethune, was continuing her efforts to persuade the First Lady, Eleanor Roosevelt, to push her husband to allow the Negro women officers to serve abroad.

Bethune was a member of a small group of influential pioneers that was nicknamed the Black Cabinet; the phrase described advisors to the president regarding Negro communities around the country. Bethune, who led the National Youth Administration and founded a school, was also instrumental in supporting integrated war efforts. She served as special assistant to the secretary of war of the women's army and was responsible for all their abilities to train and serve.

But in their day-to-day lives, Judy and Mary Alyce could only see the narrow slivers of what they were told was possible now. They only had the post and each other and the unknown domestic assignments ahead of them to look forward to.

"You must be Mary Alyce," Judy said.

Mary Alyce did not budge from beneath the white sheet.

"Captain Adams has asked me to help you along, if you're so obliged," Judy said, struggling. It wasn't in her nature to try and make friends, especially not someone who seemed resistant to it. But Mary Alyce didn't respond that first day or the day after.

On the third day, as Mary Alyce's stonewall continued, Judy turned to leave for the mess hall. There, she assembled a small tray of powdered eggs and toast, eating a small plate of her own before taking time to answer the questioning looks of Stacy and Bernadette. Mary Alyce was still turned on her side, facing the window, her eyes focused on the stark, blank sky.

Judy held the tray out, as if to ask Mary Alyce to take it. Mary Alyce emerged from under the sheet then, pushed herself up to lean her head against the bed frame.

"You've got to eat sometime," Judy said.

Mary Alyce looked at Judy with puffy eyes. All she had done for much of those few days was sleep. Her hair was flattened on one side of her head. "What's the point?"

"Food is good. Well, maybe 'good' is an overstatement for this," she said, looking at the powdered eggs. "But you'll need your strength for when you're ready to join us."

Mary Alyce let out a gust of air that was not really a snort or a sigh, but some mixture of both. "*If* I'm ready to join you."

The emphasis on *if* made Judy feel a sense of familiar anger. Mary Alyce's angst summoned the feeling of powerlessness that Judy had felt working on the slave market. For Mary Alyce, discovering she was a Negro woman meant she had become a woman whose main identity was a problem to be solved, fixed or concealed.

While that was precisely what it meant to be a Negro in America, Judy still resented the ability that Mary Alyce had to just give up. She could hear her mother in her head now, telling this girl that this was just the way life was going to be. She couldn't change it, so there was no use wasting time wishing things were any different. Time would be stolen from her now that she was a Negro, like money from her purse. She would just have to learn to go on.

Without thinking, Judy said, "When are you going to be done with this sadness?"

Mary Alyce narrowed her eyes at the noticeable change in Judy's tone. "I suppose it'll take some time. I have no idea,"

Mary Alyce said, shifting onto an elbow. "I've been assigned a counselor. And I'm to meet with the chaplain regularly. But what's it to you? Tired of bringing me food I don't eat?"

Judy crossed her arms. "So, you're going to stay? In the army? With us?"

"I don't suppose I have much choice. I can't avoid this at home any more than I can here. There are no Negroes where I'm from. But there's no way I can hide this. Woodstock is a small place. People write. Everyone will know soon enough."

"So what?" Judy spat. "You think I wouldn't rather sit around and mope about how unfair it is to be a Negro woman all day? It is shocking that you didn't know the truth about your father before you came here. But now you know, and you can't *not* know. So all that's left is for you to decide how you're going to manage. But you can't go on like this, propped up in bed like a scarecrow. And, no, I don't want to keep waiting on you, forced to watch you mourn or whatever it is you're doing, every day."

Mary Alyce turned red in the face and at the tops of her ears. "Well, this is just the problem with you people," she said, forgetting herself. "Leave me be! I never asked for your company anyway."

Judy left in such a fury that, as she walked away, she nearly bumped into Captain Adams. Judy scrambled to salute her and when Adams suggested that she stand at ease, Judy felt her hands still shaking a little from anger. "How is Private Dixon?"

"The same as two days ago," Judy said, feeling that she was responding to a trick question.

Captain Adams stood still, looking expectantly at Judy.

Judy continued, "I don't think she plans to get out of bed. And I'm glad I ran into you because I respectfully request to be relieved of this assignment, to take on something else."

"Something else," Captain Adams repeated slowly. She was silent and staring until Judy clarified.

"I'm grateful for your trust and the assignment. But with all due respect, I just wonder if there isn't a better use of my time."

Captain Adams nodded and said, "I understand it might be frustrating to look after someone who is dealing with so much. But give it a few more days, Private."

It was Judy's turn to stare silently at Captain Adams. She did not know how to explain to Captain Adams that what she thought was wrong with Mary Alyce would not be made right in a matter of days or weeks. Every exchange with her clawed at a tender wound. Mary Alyce expected everyone's lives to stop at her discovery. When Judy's father died and when Herbert left, there had been no such allowance for Judy. Living her whole life as a Negro woman meant that no matter what happened, she was supposed to take it and keep going.

Captain Adams continued. "I've found that the most challenging assignments I've experienced have taught me the most—often lessons in patience and empathy that I might otherwise have missed. You may yet learn something about yourself, as well about Mary Alyce in the days to come. If things have not changed in forty-eight hours, I will relieve you of this duty. Just give it a little more time."

Judy nodded reluctantly, accepting her orders. She saluted the Captain to signal that she understood. Captain Adams gave her an encouraging pat on the shoulder and left.

The evening after Judy's conversation with Captain Adams passed in tense silence. The next morning, Mary Alyce was still in bed when the others rose, but when Judy returned dutifully with breakfast, she found the bed made up and empty. She was so used to seeing Mary Alyce there that she stood with the tray for a moment, looking around. When she glanced out of the window, she saw a composed-looking Mary Alyce—hair combed, uniform neat—talking to two white WAC officers near the mess hall.

"I'll be damned," Judy remarked.

She carried the tray outside and walked around the side of the building to eavesdrop on their conversation without being spotted.

"I would have told you if I'd known," Mary Alyce said. "You have to believe me."

"Now, why would we believe that?" Ethel said, hugging a training binder to her chest. "We should have known the Dixon family had skeletons in its closet. And you've always been so different from us anyway. Right, Betsy?"

Betsy nodded quickly. "It's true. You even have Colored features."

Judy wondered what that girl was talking about, since Mary Alyce didn't look a bit like a Negro. Mary Alyce appeared flushed with shame at the suggestion and also at this fresh rejection from her friends. But what kind of friends were they, anyhow, pointing out what they thought they knew in retrospect? No one needed enemies if these were the kind of girls she called friends.

Judy felt herself getting upset on Mary Alyce's behalf.

"Nothing has to change between us," Mary Alyce said, pleading. "You know my heart. We grew up together! All that's changed is now I know my father was Negro."

"Oh, is *that* all?" Ethel sniffed. "Mary Alyce, *everything* has changed. I've already written home to expose your dreadful lie. There were no Negroes in our town until your father and now you. People need to know Woodstock has been polluted."

Betsy looked at Ethel with surprise, like she'd gone a bridge too far. Ethel widened her eyes at Betsy, who turned back to look at Mary Alyce.

Watching them, Judy remembered Captain Adams's words about learning from difficult assignments. And with that, she felt a rush of compassion for Mary Alyce and her new situation.

"I don't know why I'm surprised. You were always like this," Mary Alyce said, balling up her fists. "An entitled, smug...gossip! I wish I'd never known you!"

Mary Alyce ran back to the Third Platoon, and Judy watched with a heavy heart as her new friend threw herself back into bed. She had the urge to comfort her but decided it might be better for Mary Alyce to be alone.

Throughout her morning classes, Judy could hardly pay attention. Had those awful so-called friends of Mary Alyce sent her back to her lethargic sadness forever? What a shame that would be, after she had gone through the trouble of finally getting out of bed.

At the mess hall over lunch, she sat with Bernadette and Stacy, hardly listening to their banter. She didn't touch her salad. Suddenly, Bernadette waved a perfumed hand in front of her face. "What's got you so quiet? You haven't said a word to us all day."

"Sorry. I've been thinking about Mary Alyce," Judy said

"The white girl?" Stacy said. "I mean, used-to-be white girl?"

Bernadette turned to Stacy. "You do know that you don't have to say everything you think, right?"

"But I want to." Stacy shrugged. "Anyway, what about her?"

"I heard her talking to the white girls from her town. They used to be friends, but they've disowned her."

"Sounds right to me, honey," Bernadette said. "I mean it's awful, but it's what I expect. You know white folks aren't about to change their minds about Negroes just because they knew one by accident."

Judy shook her head. "They were just so cruel to her. For no reason."

"Being Negro is reason enough, girl," Stacy said. "You know that. She'll just have to get used to it."

Judy looked at Stacy and Bernadette. "That's just the thing. I guess for us, it's how it's always been. But now she's got to catch up on not knowing how to be like us for all her life." The idea seemed to sober them. "Anyway, let me go try and give the girl something to eat."

"Good luck," Stacy said. "Remember, if she don't want it, I'll eat it."

Judy smiled for the first time that day as Bernadette shot Stacy a look of disapproval.

With a half sandwich on a plate, Judy approached the barracks solemnly. Mary Alyce was standing in the foyer, arms folded and leaning against the threshold. She glanced at her watch. "I figured you'd quit me like everyone else."

Judy lifted the plate and grinned. "You can't get rid of me that easy."

Mary Alyce took the tray and sat down on a nearby bench. She tore into the sandwich, gobbling it until only crumbs from the crust remained. Judy joined her on the bench between their room and the entrance. The screen door kept out the bugs, but it allowed the infrequent breeze to cool them and add some power to the listlessly spinning ceiling fans above them.

"I heard you, you know," Mary Alyce said, putting the plate aside. "Talking to the Captain."

Judy raised her eyebrows and looked at her hands. She would not apologize for words she meant. "You weren't the only one eavesdropping."

It was Mary Alyce's turn to cast her eyes on her hands. "You mean Ethel and Betsy?"

Judy nodded.

Mary Alyce folded her hands. "I suppose I should feel lucky that this all came out now. I was supposed to join them on their assignment to North Africa. Before all this, I was so set on being a nurse. Something practical, honorable. We wanted to help the boys win the war, of course. But mostly what I wanted was an adventure.

"I wanted to be a more exciting person than I have ever been. And I was so close. And then all of a sudden, I find out I don't even know *what* I am. So now I spend all my time wondering about how I'm supposed to fit those old dreams for that old girl into this new life. But the more I think about it, the more I realize that none of that can happen now."

Judy understood, listening to Mary Alyce and thinking about the conversation she'd had with Ethel and Betsy, that while she couldn't relate to the specifics of Mary Alyce's predicament, she knew what it was to try to reconcile old dreams with a new situation. Maybe what Mary Alyce was facing wasn't so different from being the wife of a man at war, which also made your life into something different than you imagined. You just had to keep hope for the future, despite all the uncertainty.

"I'm sorry," Judy said, finally. "I can't understand exactly how you feel. But it does sound hard."

Something tense that had been on the edge of their words softened in the hot air. Mary Alyce gave Judy a quick nod. They sat silently like that for a little while longer, before the next bell rang, signaling their afternoon classes and drills. Mary Alyce picked up her plate. "I'll take it back this time. Thank you," Mary Alyce said with a faint smile.

"You're welcome," Judy said, feeling a wave of relief and a new respect for Mary Alyce. There was hope for that girl yet.

TEN

JUDY

From Judy to Margaret

Friday, 5 August 1944

Dear Mama,
I have not been as good as I had hoped about making time to write you, but I want to be sure to send some of my pay. Enclosed is thirty dollars. I know I can't tell you what to do with it, but I hope you'll use it to help with whatever is past due and save the rest to last you until I write next. Maybe you can take a day or two off from the Market? I can hear you saying, "And do what?"

The answer is that you can rest.

We don't get much rest here. If one of the commanding officers sees us relaxing or looking like we're enjoying ourselves, they come up with something for us to do pretty fast. We are

all done with basic training, and now the long wait begins to
find out if we will be split up or sent with our new friends to
the same post. There are rumors that we might have to help
support operations dealing with the mail, but nothing has been
settled. The good thing about working around the post is that it
helps time move quickly.

Write soon and let me know how you are.

Love,

Judy

Although she was top of mind for Judy, she purposefully left
Mary Alyce out of her letter. She was still trying to understand the fraught situation herself. She didn't expect her mom
to understand the complicated revelation. Mary Alyce had a
lifetime of adjustments to make. But Judy did, too.

For one, months into her training, the Iowa quiet began
to unsettle her. Whispering breezes and soaring hawks and
wide, open spaces everywhere she looked were so dissimilar
from the rowdy rent parties and bustling crowds that electri-
fied whole city blocks. She even missed the sounds of shouting drunks and screaming couples. The sounds of people and
their humanity made the city sing.

There were nice things about the outdoors, she supposed.
There was a flat beauty to Fort Des Moines, what with its
plush green-and-fuchsia sunsets over wide farmland. The
pretty, quaint aspect of Iowa was just enough to keep her
spirits lifted and buoy them against the long reach of segregation that followed her wherever she went.

On the rare weekend pass they received to enjoy in the
town, when she touched doors or tabletops, even in the segregated sections, or when she obediently went in the back way,
there was always some frog-mouthed white person, a civilian,
staring at her in uniform with contempt while wiping down

her fingerprints. She knew they weren't just trying to clean up behind her. They were trying to erase any trace of her as soon as she arrived.

She considered these things one night after lights-out. She was settled into the top bunk and Stacy was on the bottom. They were both early risers, but it was Stacy who wore a bright pink bonnet with a frilly white band and had taken to blocking out the post lights that streamed in their window with an eye mask she borrowed from Bernadette. Judy liked to stay up with the moon, something she couldn't do while working at the market. Stacy liked to fall asleep as close to lights-out as she could. There was very little that could wake her, once her snore that sounded like a broken whistle started rising and falling, as though she were wheezing in her sleep.

She was wondering where Bernadette was that evening when she heard her familiar voice, slurring and a bit loud from the window. "Private Washington!"

Judy pushed herself up on her elbows to see what Bernadette was getting into. Stacy woke with a start, mid-wheeze, saying, "Shhh!"

But they both looked out at Bernadette in her pajamas, a long nightgown, with the summer uniform jacket draped over her shoulders. She was joined by a few other women, huddled in front of a small hedge just outside the barracks. Another raised a flask with a thin arm.

"How is anybody supposed to get their beauty rest with all this ruckus?" Stacy complained.

Judy found the flashlight she kept in a cranny between the bed frame and the wall, and tucked it in her pajama-top pocket before she climbed down from the bunk. "I think the point is to have some moonshine instead of sleep."

Stacy groaned with disapproval and lifted her eye mask. "Wait, are you gonna leave me here?"

Judy hushed Stacy and motioned with her hand for her bunkmate to follow her before they woke up the entire barracks. "Fine, come on. You going out with that bonnet on?"

"What's wrong with that?"

Judy and Stacy tiptoed out. When they were free and clear of the door, they bounded out into the night to join Bernadette and the other girls. They made their way to a spot on the edge of the post where they built a fire to cut the brief cool of the evening, grateful the army had taught them how. They passed the flask around their little circle as they sat on adjacent thick logs.

Stacy was an instant hit. Her boldness in wearing her bonnet out, even just in the company of other women, gave them all a good laugh. Bernadette, who appeared to have had the most to drink, began by pretending to be Captain Adams.

"Uh, McFadden, you must be aware that the way that you look tonight is, uh, treason of the highest order," Bernadette said, tucking her chin to her chest, which she also stuck out, frowning in the same way Captain Adams often did.

"Yes, ma'am, Big Ma," Stacy responded, using their nickname for Captain Adams, the liquor already starting to make her drowsy. The girls giggled before she hiccupped, which only set them off more.

"I shouldn't tease," Bernadette said, her voice low. Judy marveled at her smooth, dark skin and the delicate, cared-for hands of someone who worked at making people beautiful for a living. Even in the wretched conditions of training, Bernadette's hands looked impeccable, like she'd been walking around with gloves on the whole time. "But seriously. Who knows what that woman goes through, for herself, for us?"

"But she's so stuffy all the time," Stacy complained. "And the way she cuts her eyes at us. Lord. It's just rude."

"Oh, be nice. Her best friend has been shipped down to

Fort Oglethorpe. Lieutenant Campbell kept her happier. And I should hope if we get separated, you'll be a little cross. I would be, anyway." Bernadette sniffed.

There was an awkward silence before Judy said, "I believe they're more than just friends."

Stacy and Bernadette swooned. Stacy said, "Judy Washington! That is the most scandalous gossip I've heard from you yet!"

"Not that there's gossip that's civil, really," Bernadette pointed out.

"Well, the army is not civil, ladies, haven't you figured that out?" Judy asked.

"That much is becoming clear, which is why we're drinking," Bernadette said. The bushes nearby rustled and they fell into silence. "Oh, heavens, are there bears in Iowa?" she asked, clutching the flask.

"It's too warm for bears," Stacy said, looking in the direction of the noise and holding her breath. But it was just Mary Alyce emerging from the brush, looking shy. "Ah, it's the new Negro," Stacy quipped.

"Hush, Stacy," Judy said. Turning to Mary Alyce she said, "You about scared us half to death!"

"I'm sorry," Mary Alyce said. "I thought I heard you all out here, but I wanted to be sure." She looked with curiosity at the flask in Bernadette's hand. "May I have some?"

"Yes, of course," Bernadette said. "But," she said, holding it captive for a moment. "We want to learn a little bit about you before I share. We've seen you in the bed at the barracks. But we don't know too much about you."

That Bernadette was a charmer, Judy thought, but it was too soon. She started to interrupt, but Mary Alyce gave her a look that said she would talk, or at least try.

"That's a fair request. I'm from a little place in Vermont. I came to the WAC to be a nurse, travel the world. And then I found out that I'm not exactly who I thought I was, and Negro women aren't allowed overseas."

Her words hung in the air as Bernadette offered her the moonshine, which Mary Alyce almost finished before she handed it back.

Bernadette looked at her watch and lifted the flask above eye level. "This is almost finished up and it's the last of it. So, a toast to us. Wherever we came from, wherever we end up. May we rise to the occasion that destiny has laid before us with joy and courage."

"Hear! Hear!" Judy said. They stayed up for another couple of hours, exchanging stories about the people and places they'd left behind. Every story and memory shared was a thread that stitched them closer together. They were forming a bond unlike any Judy had experienced with other women, and it felt exhilarating and powerful. When the sun announced its intent to rise, dawn peeking in glowing rays over the horizon, they scrambled back to their barracks, bleary-eyed but energized by their new friends.

ELEVEN

CHARITY

From Captain Charity Adams to Captain Abbie Campbell

Saturday, 6 September 1944

Dearest Abbie,
To say I miss your company here in Iowa is an understatement.
As I and the Company have adjusted to our daily routines and
readied ourselves for our assignment, I know the women also
miss your presence. Even the tomatoes in the Victory Garden
have failed to come in, no doubt protesting your disappearance.

How are you faring in Georgia, anyway? Is it very differ-
ent from home?

Not much has changed here except that the white WACs
come and go, off abroad, while my ladies (rightfully) wonder
what is next for us and whether we will be dispatched together.
There are more than 800 of us now.

As far as I know, I am the highest-ranking Negro in the WAC. It means a lot to me, but I also feel the more I succeed, the more I encounter our superiors who view me as a rare exception, not a rule. And I am not only succeeding for my own sake but for the sake of other Negro women. We have talked before about this, being the first Negroes to achieve rank and being determined not to be the last.

It doesn't seem like progress will come without a fight. Or maybe I am thinking too much. I don't think I told you about my experience with a pair of Military Police when I traveled for my last recruiting trip before you left. It was upsetting and I didn't want to alarm you. I knew you had other things on your mind.

They eyed me in the train station, approached me and disregarded my uniform. No salute. They demanded to see my identification. Said they had never seen a Negro wearing Captain's insignia before. I pulled my notebook and pen out of my purse so quickly they didn't even have a moment to have another thought or ask me something else. Abbie, I wish you could have seen their faces!

I assured them that I was, in fact, a senior officer. Higher ranking than them, which clearly bothered them, but I was also the highest-ranking military in the whole place at the time. I then proceeded to ask them for their names, duty stations and the name of their commanding officer. I assured them I would be following up to report them for their insubordination. And that was the end of that! As upset as I was, it felt good to stand up for myself.

But not an hour later, on the train, a white woman in my car stared so hard it felt like she was trying to bore a hole into my head. The trip takes 25 hours, Abbie! There was no way I would last.

An MP came through the car, and that white woman de-

manded that I be arrested for impersonating an officer. The MP looked over at me before saying to her, "Ma'am, we're here to make sure there's no lawlessness on the train. If I arrest a Captain today, I will not be a Sergeant tomorrow." Then he saluted me and went about his business. It was a bittersweet moment because she stewed even more after that. She wanted a seat elsewhere for the overnight. Everything was full, so we were stuck with each other the whole way!

Anyway, I guess I just miss having you to tell me not to take any of this to heart. It's toughest being the only one. Feeling like the fact of my existence makes some white people and many Negro men uncomfortable. I can hear you reminding me this is not my problem to solve. And I suppose since I never share any of this with anyone, writing to you is the best means I have to vent. Let me know how you are when you get a chance.
With love,
Charity

From Captain Abbie Campbell to Captain Charity Adams

Saturday, 20 September 1944

Dearest Charity,
I miss you, too. Very much.
Fort Oglethorpe is about like home, but with almost every man here outranking me.
I cursed you for mentioning the tomatoes. I wish I had time to garden. You'll think I'm crazy, but I miss Iowa. Mostly the weather, which felt more tolerable than this sticky heat inside these bulky uniforms.
I was tickled by your description of putting those MPs in their place, whether they knew that's where they belonged or not. I

bet you made that stern face that makes a vein pop out of your forehead when you did it, too.

Aside from making me chuckle, your letter made me think of my brother. Everywhere Thomas goes, especially in uniform, someone is trying to push a broom or a bag of garbage at him. And he's one of the country's first Negro medical doctors. Yet, like you, he still has to put up with that.

If it's any consolation, things at Fort Oglethorpe are as raggedy as they were at Boomtown at first, although I'm grateful that my move here offered a promotion to Captain. The only difference is that the girls who arrive here are mostly white and preparing for the overseas Theater of Operations. But there aren't enough of them for what the Army's needs are.

I can't imagine a more backwater part of the country to expose recruits to, but that's obviously above my pay grade. Rumor has it that new assignments for Negro officers are on the way. Charity, we might finally get stationed abroad! I also believe this bodes well for you and me to be reunited…

In any event, do your best to put all that ugliness over your rank and your loneliness to the side. You can always just put what ails you and keeps you from getting a restful night's sleep down somewhere. If you're ready to pick it back up, it'll be waiting for you right where you left it.

You've been chosen for a time such as this, Charity. Don't let the ignorance of others sink your spirit. You've come too far and have too much to do to allow it.

Chin up, sister.

Yours, Always,

Abbie

Charity folded up Abbie's letter and tucked it back into its envelope after savoring it a couple times from her office in Fort Des Moines. She had made her home at this post for two years, steadily progressing in rank and responsibility, and she felt she had little to show for it. Her office was a third of the size of the other officers'. As the only Negro, they couldn't justify a separate building for her, so they gave her a neglected area with a single light bulb at the center of the ceiling and blinds that curved in the center from the nervous peering out of the office's previous occupant.

Charity had waited to read Abbie's words for a day like today, when she was told she was to have a status report ready for Lieutenant Colonel Barrows on the fitness of her company for domestic postal-service supporting operations somewhere stateside. She fumed over the dedicated training they'd focused on, drills and other formalities, only to be literally pushing paper, probably in a segregated town that would likely be just as dangerous for them as being stationed near combat.

Abbie's optimism and hopes were a balm for Charity; they drew her to Abbie. But she had serious doubts the army would post them abroad. Traveling overseas not only would require that the army trusted in the abilities and work of the officers deployed but they were also meant to represent the best of America. By leaving Negroes at home, it sent the signal to the rest of the world that they were not really citizens.

At least that was the message received by Charity, whose entire career was both symbol and duty.

She knew it was a miracle they had even been stationed outside their hometowns. And new orders for the women officers arrived weekly. By contrast, the white WACs headed abroad were more highly regarded than anyone else, even if they would be doing the same kind of work.

Charity wondered if she had risen as far as she could in the army. Lieutenant Colonel Barrows was one of the good ones, meaning he did not try to block her path to success in the WAC. She was, however, annoyed by what she felt were unnecessary reports about the women under her command—if any of them had traveled before beyond the cities where they were born, how they fared under pressure and learned new things under duress. She wanted to tell him that being a Negro in America was the duress, that it was like being in combat daily. Instead, she let herself be inspired by rumors that this line of inquiry would lead to a miracle and they would finally get an assignment worthy of their efforts.

As she prepared her report, she was grateful that, for the moment at least, there wasn't more talk of further segregating the WAC by putting her in charge of all the Negro enlisted. That would mean that she would be solely assigned to Negro units and have little to no contact with her white peers. She wanted nothing to do with that. A segregated unit of Negro women serving in the US made her think of the violent lines drawn by the Klan at home. She understood all too well that segregation was intended to make sure Negroes stayed in their place—whatever that was.

She made herself stop daydreaming about being stationed overseas and focus on her report for Lieutenant Colonel Barrows. It was the only thing she felt like she had any control over.

Two weeks after Abbie's letter, Charity was scheduled to discuss her report with Lieutenant Colonel Barrows. On her way to his office, she spotted him walking from the mess hall, several minutes late for their appointment, which was highly unusual.

She immediately began to panic. Was she being demoted? Had he gotten some awful orders for them? She greeted her ranking officer with a salute and a steady gaze. He returned it and gestured for her to sit. His was the most spacious office in the building, with ceilings large enough for two fans, to give plenty of clearance for the American and Iowa flags that framed his heavy oak desk. It looked like a country club nook compared to hers.

"I have the report you requested, sir," Charity said, presenting the two-page, typed report that had taken her longer than it should have. Abbie liked to tease her for typing with two fingers, but Charity was always sore about it. Lieutenant Colonel Barrows looked surprised and Charity felt a sudden wave of panic. "Right. Well, I have something for you, too. I'm just— Well, hold on," he said walking to the door of his office to duck his head out and say, "She's here!"

The stoic, mean-looking sergeant, Darlene Hicks, had blond ringlets and an uneasy scowl, no matter what was happening around her. Sergeant Hicks came into the room wearing that same grim look, holding the Major insignia: a black band with gold stars affixed to it. Lieutenant Colonel Barrows took them from the sergeant, thanked her and said, "Congratulations, Major Adams," motioning for her to stand, so he could shake her hand.

Charity froze, as she was flooded with emotion. So that's why the commander had been so distracted. She felt a little foolish, but also very moved. He *did* see her efforts and he did believe in her. And she had reason to keep believing in herself now, too, which made her tear up. The recognition of her hard work in the form of a promotion gave her immeasurable pride.

In the next moments, she wished Abbie was there, too. But she would write her as soon as she could hold a pen steady. Her hands trembled at her side as Sergeant Hicks pinned the stars to Charity's uniform.

"Thank you, sir," Charity finally said, dabbing at the corners of her eyes with her hand. "This is quite unexpected. But I will not let you down."

Just when she thought the day's surprises were over, her

commanding officer had more. He excused Hicks, who offered her sincere congratulations before saluting them both and leaving. When she was gone, he asked, "Major, what would you say if I said I wanted you to lead your company in the European Theater?"

It was too much and everything she'd dreamed of. She felt lightheaded. "I would say, sir, that I am ready and willing to do whatever it takes for us to fulfill our mission anywhere in the world."

Lieutenant Colonel Barrows smiled brightly, revealing teeth browned from chewing tobacco. Charity had not actually seen his front teeth before that moment. He was really pleased to give her this assignment, and that moved her even more. "I thought you might say that," he replied. "As much as the war has slowed down our post offices in the US, the European Postal Operation supporting the Allied Forces in Birmingham, England, is in desperate straits.

"In September, we were ordered to hold winter and holiday mail to be redirected home. It seemed the fighting was over, and we would be pulling folks out to bring them home. They reassigned their support staff over there. But then the mail kept coming with no one to look after it as soldiers kept marching all over Europe. Now there's more than a million pieces of mail and parcels stacked up in these warehouses near an old boarding school. The Germans bombed it to hell, so it's not a school anymore. It'll be where you and the women of the Central Postal Battalion will be based while the city recuperates."

Charity listened quietly and attentively, trying to process the orders as Barrows detailed them. She thought of what her father would say—that she didn't need to necessarily know how to conduct every part of the operation. God would guide her through what she did not yet know.

Barrows continued. "You have six months to complete this mission. You will need a second-in-command, or an executive officer."

Charity immediately thought of Abbie, and her recent promotion, which meant that there was a possibility they could be reunited soon. She felt sure Abbie would say yes, if asked, but she still felt nervous.

"If you are successful, it will lead to more assignments for Negro women in the ranks, and not just in the army, but the other branches of the military where Negro women have not yet served. If you fail, the doors of opportunity will stay closed to Negro women for who knows how long.

"The most important thing is those letters," Barrows continued. "They keep soldiers connected to the most significant people in their lives. Their families, their children, their wives and mothers. That keeps them motivated to fight and to remember what they are trying to win victory for. You get them those letters, you inspire them to live and fight another day. Without the mail, morale sinks. This war drags on and on.

"You ship out from Fort Oglethorpe in two weeks' time. You will sail from Camp Shanks, New York, to Scotland, from there to Northern Europe, then travel by train to Birmingham. You will be the 6888th Central Postal Battalion, and the only self-contained unit of Negro women serving in the war. I know you won't let us down. Don't prove me wrong."

"Thank you, sir, for the honor," Charity said, beaming and still processing the enormity of the task.

TWELVE

JUDY

From Judy to Herbert

Friday, 15 October 1944

Dear Herbert,
I wonder if I haven't heard from you because of all the challenges
with the mail. I've learned about those recently because we're
to be stationed in England to help sort a bunch of it. On one
hand, it gives me hope that you're on the move and my letters
to you have merely piled up with many others along the way.

I never imagined I would ever leave The Bronx let alone New
York, and now I'm to be in Europe! The ceilings I've felt my
entire life are lifting in the Army. The confines of what mother
and even I thought were possibilities just keep on expanding.

And I believe you would love my friends here as much as I
do. I'm glad they are on this adventure with me. Mary Alyce

is a long story, but she came from Vermont and didn't discover
she was a Negro until after she enlisted. Bernadette is a glam-
orous beautician from Chicago. Stacy is a quirky farm girl from
Missouri. So it'll be us and 850 Negro women sorting mail
over there.

  And maybe, just maybe, I will also finally find you.

  A girl can hope.

Love,

Judy

Major Adams summoned the Third Platoon to officially announce their assignment, though word had already spread
somehow. She had the authority to officially designate them
on post as a unit, so she called for all of her soldiers to stand
at parade rest for her final speech at Fort Des Moines. The air
was turning crisp, requiring them all to don their fall uniforms, the long-sleeved jackets and skirts with tights.

All lined up and proper, their hair tucked in identical buns
under their caps, Judy saw a notable difference in herself and
her fellow officers from their initial days on post six months
before.

"The eyes of the world will be on us," Major Adams began.
"We are now officially part of the 6888th Central Postal Battalion, and while we will not be directly in a combat zone,
there will be plenty of activity around us with German dive
bombers, air raids and the ongoing invasions of France and
Italy."

The idea of proximity to war suddenly became more real
to Judy. She was thrilled and afraid at once. Bernadette and
Stacy looked shocked, too. Mary Alyce fidgeted.

"Allied soldiers who were handling the post have been reassigned, so the work now falls to us. We have six months to
clear a backlog of a million pieces of mail. This backlog will be

the heart of our activity and will be our work and our world for the foreseeable future.

"Our task is to reunite soldiers at war with their families through this small but significant gesture. To remind them what and whom they're fighting for. If they don't have mail, they don't have morale. If their morale is low, they can't fight and win. No Mail, No Morale is to be our mantra, day and night.

"I don't need to tell you what an extraordinary opportunity this is for us," Major Adams added. "As the only and the first Negro women deployed overseas in a dedicated unit, we cannot fail. The future of Negro women in the military depends on us."

Judy had not intended to be a part of history, but knowing that she was, or that she would be, made her even more proud of her decision to pursue service. Major Adams reminded them that during their travels, domestic and soon across international waters, they would have to represent the women's army through impeccable conduct.

Her eyes grew wide with excitement, pride and wonder during Major Adams's speech. The more she thought about it, the more she was certain her letters to Herbert were part of that backlog. She would be part of the team helping to set them loose.

The air above them crackled with their shared excitement as they were dismissed to pack their bags for the first part of their adventure. It was amazing how much they'd accumulated in a matter of months.

Stacy was the first to finish packing, which should not have surprised Judy one bit. "Bernadette has a mess over there, and I aim to help, I suppose. She's got hat boxes, for heaven's sake."

Judy giggled. "I assume those are not for her uniform caps."

Stacy rolled her eyes and walked past her small suitcase and duffel bag to head out.

At the far end of their barracks, Mary Alyce quietly folded her clothes. The news of their departure had made Mary Alyce withdraw further into herself and it made Judy curious. Mary Alyce sensed Judy's eyes on her and she looked up with a smile that was more like a grimace. "The last time I was on a train, I was white."

Judy nodded as if she understood, even though she knew she couldn't. She paused, searching for the right thing to say that wouldn't be callous. "To tell you the truth, traveling is a nightmare no matter who you are."

It was Mary Alyce's turn to nod without full comprehension. The silence between them was thick with all they weren't saying. Judy turned back to her own things, brimming from their containers.

In Des Moines, over time, they had stopped drawing the hostile stares from the local residents. For several months, Negro officers and recruits had become town fixtures, just part of a new, more modern way of life. Now they would move into new states and spaces, and wouldn't know how welcome they'd be until they arrived.

The same steward who caused a scene for Major Adams when he was embarrassed by Colonel Douglas Richards was still working for the Southern Railway. He had been demoted in the months since that incident and was responsible for boarding on the Colored cars. He let many of the officers go but held up a hand when he saw Mary Alyce.

"You're mixed up with the wrong crowd," he said to her gently. Judy gave Stacy and Bernadette a worried look.

Mary Alyce's cheeks flushed. "No, sir, this is the right place for me. Thank you kindly." She tried to pass him, holding out her ticket.

The steward stepped in front of the door so she couldn't board. "I don't think you understand. There is no intermixing of the races on this train, ma'am."

It was Major Adams's turn to try to communicate the issue to the steward. She made her way to the front of the group, which parted for her easily. He looked at her and grumbled with recognition. "Sir, what's the trouble here?"

He frowned more deeply at Major Adams, it seemed, than he had during their first encounter. "The problem is that you can't have a white woman sitting with all these Negroes."

Major Adams looked at Mary Alyce, who sheepishly looked back at her before digging in her bag for the copy of her birth certificate. It was worn now from her looking at it, double-checking it each time she saw it, to make sure it was still real, that the *C* for Colored still branded her a different woman than before the WAC.

The steward's lips moved when he read, which would be comical if his stubborn ways weren't so inefficient. When he finally saw the evidence, he looked first at Mary Alyce, tilting his head, then shoved the paper back at her before moving out of her way.

"So that's what kind of trip this will be," Judy whispered.

"I'm already tired," Bernadette said.

"You'll need to sleep for sure, then," Stacy said, "because this is only the start."

When it was Judy's turn to board, she searched for Mary Alyce's face, wanting to make sure she was okay. Mary Alyce was seated at the back of the Colored car. Her cheeks looked flushed from fresh tears. Judy considered asking to switch seats with the officer next to her but then thought better of it and found a spot of her own for their journey south.

THIRTEEN

CHARITY

Very little made Charity giddy. As a girl, she was known for being stoic and reserved. The expectations for her to behave and reflect well on her family in the church made it important for her to keep her feelings buried or hidden. But when the officers on the train slept and occupied themselves, she beamed as she let her head lean on the train window. She was on her way back to Abbie, just as she hoped.

She had twelve hours and more to consider how she would ask Abbie to come with them, to help. She was pretty sure that Abbie would say yes, but Abbie could be unpredictable. Her friend, her love, might see through it as a ruse. She wasn't sure it mattered. Besides, it wasn't a total ploy. Abbie was a great leader: helpful, beautiful, an inspiring woman.

Charity could certainly lead the battalion alone, or alongside any second-in-command. But she wanted Abbie. And like everything else in her life, because she wanted her, she knew she would have to go get her.

The central postal unit arrived at the Extended Field Service Battalion Third WAC Training Center at Fort Oglethorpe mid-morning. Charity led them in formation from the train onto the buses to the post. She managed to keep a steady tone until they passed the front gate and she saw Abbie, her perfect legs in the uniform pencil skirt, her waist cinched just so in the jacket. They'd both been promoted, and celebration was in order for both of them, Charity thought, as she bounded from the bus and wrapped Abbie in an uncharacteristically tight, effusive hug.

"Abigail," Charity exhaled softly, like she never expected to see her again.

Abbie was stiff at first, but then she softened and giggled, leaning into Charity. "Major Adams. You're setting an excellent example, as usual," she said.

Charity jerked herself away from Abbie, remembering herself. She saluted her friend, remembering the performance that was required of her now. "Captain Campbell. My apologies."

"Good eye, Major," Abbie said.

"Congratulations, Captain. Look at us."

One of the enlisted, Stacy, cleared her throat, snapping Charity out of her reunion with Abbie. She needed to focus now.

"Attention!" Charity boomed. It was exactly the right volume, just as she and Abbie had practiced so long ago. When the enlisted quieted and stood still, Abbie said, in an equally commanding voice, "Thank you, Major Adams. Ladies of the Central Postal Battalion, it's great to see many of you again. For those of you I have not yet met, I am Captain Abbie Noel Campbell. I will be your guide to this post for the next ten days. Our installation will be your home as you prepare for

your time abroad. Any questions you have, I can answer, or
I will find someone who can get you the answer you need.
Does anyone have any questions for me now?"

It took all of her much-used willpower for Charity not to
ask the one question she most wanted to. The women seemed
eager to go back to chatting with one another. Some of them
had been on field assignments to Arizona, Texas or Oklahoma
and were reunited at the training center for the first time in
months. In addition to the few hundred who came from Fort
Des Moines with Charity, there were hundreds who had been
screened and tested from other places and had not seen each
other since their initial training.

They knew only during their orientation that they would
be deployed where other WACs had been pulled out and—
The best part of all, perhaps, was that it was the tireless
letter-writing campaigns of people like Mary McLeod Bethune and influential editors with the Negro press and the National Association for the Advancement of Colored People,
that had made it possible for the battalion to be formed and
deployed to Europe.

In the days that followed, they were kept busy with drills.
Abbie gave Charity the overview first; she understood how
particular Charity was about being efficient. So over breakfast in the mess hall the morning after their arrival, Abbie
gave her the rundown. But not before she proposed a nickname for the unit.

"I have a comment and some clarifications," Abbie started.

"Good morning to you, too, Captain," Charity grumbled,
still on her first cup of coffee.

"Okay, I'll give you the comment first, then," Abbie said,
making herself comfortable in the chair. "The 6888th Central Postal Battalion is a mouthful. Why not just call them the
Six Triple Eight?"

Charity stirred two scoops of sugar into her black coffee and tapped the spoon on the side. "That does sound…catchy, I suppose. Let me think about it."

Abbie pretended to look offended but saw that her friend was struggling to stay awake, so she dropped it. Charity was grateful and looked at her impatiently to get to the clarifications. On cue, Abbie said, "We'll need to divvy up some of this instruction. Unless you're opposed," Abbie said it more as a statement than a question.

"Is that an order or a request?" Charity raised an eyebrow. She was perking up.

"Are you pulling rank on me, Edna?"

"Quit using your outside voice indoors," Charity complained. "And no, I am most certainly not. I just want to know if you're telling or asking."

"I'm suggesting, but if you want, I'll take all the instruction on. I imagine you've had to shift your thoughts on deployment to the ETO quite a bit, and I know that can be a lot."

Charity nodded and she felt her mouth get dry. It was the sensation she got whenever she was nervous, when she needed to say something vulnerable.

Abbie could sense she was struggling, because Abbie always seemed to know what was happening with her. "Charity, are you going to vomit?"

So that's what she looked like agonizing over this question. It made her mood lighter. Her face changed, her muscles relaxed. "Oh, my word, Abbie. That's not it. I just—well. I might as well just ask you. I need a second-in-command to come with me, to help in Birmingham."

Abbie sat back in her chair, her mouth slightly open. Before she could say anything, Charity continued, "I know you've got a good thing going here, and we've never talked about if you even wanted an overseas post or to work with me again, but…"

"Yes," Abbie said, leaning forward. "Yes, Charity, I would be honored." She put her hand over Charity's on the table. Charity knew she would probably feel the trembling of her hand, and it made Charity feel silly. It was like her heart was beating through her veins, drumming its rhythm all through her skin.

"You didn't even let me get the question out, which is so like you," Charity said, recovering, then smiled. Abbie laughed, patted Charity's hand.

"That's why you want me to go with you, right? To be the real one in charge. Or is there another reason?"

Charity felt all the blood rise to her face. Before she could say anything else, Abbie changed the subject, returned to describing all they would need to do before they were ready to deploy. They both knew the other reason. They could talk about it another time.

Now they needed to sort out the logistics of giving each woman more clothes to wear. They needed to learn how to spot enemy aircraft overhead and enemy ships at sea, how to board the mock ship at the center of the post via cargo nets in the likely event of an attack, what they should say if they were captured by the enemy.

They would need a full day to march through a nearby forest with heavy backpacks for miles to help with their endurance. It was all the training men got, but without them being armed.

When the tenth day came, Charity got a familiar sense of jitters, but she felt prepared for all that was to come. She herself had been a part of the training exercises, so she could fully understand her women as they prepared. It felt like they were all changing in a phenomenal way—that they were poised to become even more of themselves.

In the meantime, Charity had sent official word by telegram to Lieutenant Colonel Barrows saying she had selected Abbie Campbell as her executive officer. When he issued the orders, they were ready to finally set sail.

The port at Camp Shanks, New York, was now a famous one for seeing the enlisted off. Crowds of cheering women and children waving American flags had sent off naval officers and other troops over the past two years. Sometimes those crowds welcomed them back.

But the port was eerily quiet and empty for the Six Triple Eight. Instead, the battalion generated their own excitement led by Charity and Abbie as they boarded the *Ile de France*.

Charity stiffened as they boarded, with Abbie right behind her, stepping as lively as she could.

"Must you be so perky at all times?" Charity muttered.

"You're snippier than usual," Abbie said, smirking. "Why are you walking like you've got a board strapped to your back?"

This time, Charity felt her mouth water. She was nauseous and it wasn't just nerves. She had never been on a boat. But she would not admit seasickness, not now. She swallowed hard and inhaled sharply as she tugged at the bottom of her uniform jacket. "I don't know what you mean, Abbie."

Abbie peered devilishly into Charity's eyes, making her even more resolved to conceal the rising bile. When Abbie put her arm around Charity, she said, "Come on now, let's get you a bag. If we're going to work together, and you're going to lie to me, you're going to need to practice your poker face. I can see in those stubborn eyes of yours that you're going to be sick!"

Charity's eyes watered from the wind. She shrugged Abbie's arm off. "No, I'm not. I just need to find the ladies' room."

Abbie grunted. She patted her stomach. "Guts of steel over here. Just get it out and you'll be fine."

Charity rolled her eyes. She did not have time for Abbie's shenanigans at this moment. She tried to walk normally through the waves of women who felt, to her, like they were walking much too slowly onto the ship.

The boat was a marvel, a modern example of Art Deco set out on the sea. Lena Horne, Rita Hayworth and Cary Grant had all had their tour of the French vessel with its decadent First Class cabins, replete with taffeta, silk and crimson.

The necessities of war required ships like the *Ile* to be stripped of its superfluous touches and elegant cuisine and transformed from being a dream boat into a lean warrior. A dozen women were crammed into previously spacious rooms. They had bare-minimum accommodations for the two-week voyage. Enlisted men—white and Negro—from every branch of the military, with experience serving on warships were housed at the top, charged with escorting the women safely across the sea.

When Charity finally found the bathroom, everything she'd eaten that morning came out of her. She regarded herself in the small oval mirror before she wet her handkerchief and patted herself with the moist cloth. A dream of hers was coming true. She had to set an example for her troops and get ahold of herself.

Abbie encouraged Charity to join some of the women standing on the top deck of the great vessel, the American flag flying high and proudly in the fall breeze as it set sail. Now that she was less nauseous, Charity was able to appreciate that they were making history, that very moment.

"For such a brave woman, you sure are chicken about a little bit of water," Abbie said.

Charity laughed. "You mean on this tiny tugboat taking us to another continent?"

"Your father, mine, our mothers—this is their dream we're living. For us and for them."

The ship captain announced they were leaving the port. Charity stood with them for a while, the sky foggy and gray, like the sun would never rise again. She felt good they were finally headed to a different shore. All she had to do was remember her father's advice to her, to do right.

"I'm headed to the quarters," Charity said to Abbie.

"Suit yourself. You look much improved since you took my counsel, by the way," Abbie said with a twinkle in her beautiful eyes.

Charity began to walk away, but first said, "Abbie, I'm so glad you're here. That you're coming."

Abbie smiled knowingly. "It's a good thing I like you. Otherwise, I'd have turned you down."

FOURTEEN

MARY ALYCE

From Mary Alyce to Helen

Sunday, 1 November 1944

Mother:
*You haven't heard from me in some time, and given how angry
I am with you, it's likely you will not hear from me again any-
time soon.*

*Here I thought you didn't want me in the Army because of
what it would mean for me, but actually what you cared about
was making sure I didn't find out the truth about my father.*

*It makes me wonder if anything you told me about him is
even real! Is it? Because all he is to me now is the man responsible for completely changing my life. But do you know more,
more that would help me understand that side of my family?*

If you do, I sure hope you're ready to tell me. Because I am beside myself. Why wouldn't you just tell me the truth? You have no idea how upset I've been.

This news has changed everything I believed, not just about myself, but also about you. I never thought you would keep a secret from me. I love you, of course, you're my mother. But I don't like you at all right now.

It's the betrayal, the lie that stings, but it's also loss. I left home and instead of finding belonging in this new place and with new people, I actually lost my two best friends! I tried to appeal to Ethel and Betsy, but Ethel said she had already written home to expose me. So the secret is out and there's no use hiding it anymore.

Even though I am still trying hard to think about how and why you made the choice you did, I am still your only daughter. That's why I wrote this and I intend to send it, when I calm down.

Mary Alyce

The first nights on the ship were eerily quiet and uncomfortable: cold, dark with miserable food, limited light and the same stale air circulating in the cabins in which everyone was snugly packed. In their training courses, they had learned that the Atlantic Ocean was an extension of the many other battlefields of World War II in 1942, when, in the first six months, German U-boats—so named for their shape—sank over two hundred Allied merchant marine vessels at the rate of two or three each day.

But at the end of 1944, with cooperation between British and American war strategists, the military had managed to wrest back control of the Atlantic. That was, at least, the story that the US Department of War told in its films to the public, and to its recruits.

Mary Alyce was learning that she could not always trust

what people told her, but she could trust how she felt, and that was a lot of anger.

Compared to the other women on the ship, she felt about as fine as she did when she was on land. A main respite from work on the land and around the house was a nearby lake in Vermont, which gave her some familiarity with how it felt to have water beneath her. She was still shy about standing out among the women, but it was Stacy, emerging from one of the restrooms and wiping her mouth who said, "Aren't you just as calm and collected as you can be? Tell us your secret."

Mary Alyce clenched her teeth at the word *secret*, before taking a beat to process what Stacy had actually asked. "I spent a lot of time in a kayak as a kid."

Judy was nearby, waiting to use the facilities. She clutched her stomach as she wailed, "What in God's name is a kayak?"

"A very small boat," Mary Alyce said, trying not to look amused at Judy's suffering. "Looks like a little paper boat you make—"

"Oh, fine," Judy said, shaking her head. She was turning green now, and just talking about small boats on water was enough to make her feel even more sick.

As much as they could, the women tried to maintain a regular schedule. Stacy remained the early bird and sang a little song to wake them up after her morning routine at 0600 hours: "You gotta get up/You gotta get up/You gotta get up in the morning." They woke, made their beds and ate a bit of breakfast while they watched the waves. They fell asleep to the rumbling of their bags, the clinking of perfume bottles as the ship frequently lurched.

They had been told that, while they could expect long stretches of boredom, they should also stay alert. Given that the country was actively at war with Germany, it was probable that the Axis forces out on the ocean would try to strike. Regardless of the cargo the ship carried, including the women, the clearly American ship would be viewed as a hostile vessel entering European waters, making it vulnerable to attack at any time.

Initially, the women were certain that the concern was all for naught. Mary Alyce couldn't help but think about how excited Ethel and Betsy would have been, making this voyage together. It was possible they'd had a similar journey, she mentioned to Stacy and her new friends as they sat around the cabin they shared with Judy and several other privates. "All the people from our town thought we were such odd women for wanting to go to where the actual fighting is happening," she said. "But I don't see what's so strange about that."

"Well, maybe that's how your town thinks about it for women. It's hard to imagine that any Negroes, let alone Negro women, would want to give more to America than what we already have," Stacy said. "At least that's how my folks took it. But I have military family going back all the way to the Civil War. So they understood. Sort of. They expect men to serve, I guess, because of the draft and all. It was the voluntary part that was harder to explain."

"My daddy said he thought I was crazy when I tried to integrate the beauty school in Chicago," Bernadette said. "Then he heard I applied for this unit and he said 'Oh, you just an onion of crazy. We keep peeling back the layers to get right to the heart of how nuts you are.'" Her family couldn't understand why a girl so pretty would choose frumpy uniforms, bad food and uncomfortable bunks. And the news reports about the women were often mean-spirited. Male reporters wrote that Negro women were being deployed abroad to keep Negro male soldiers from harassing white women. They were expected to be chauffeurs or prostitutes.

"What's so crazy about wanting to be a part of history?"

Stacy said. "I just want to say I helped a little instead of sitting at home hearing about it on the radio or reading about
it in the papers. I know how to work with my hands and my
whole body, but that's not going to save lives or help a soldier
win at war. I want to do something that will actually make a
difference to someone other than the people I'm related to."

"I just needed to get away from home," Judy said, more to
herself than to the group, but they all laughed and nodded with
recognition. "I needed to do something to bring my husband
home faster. And while I'm at it, find out what else I'm made
of. Take a bigger risk."

Just as they were agreeing with her, a loud knock at the
cabin door startled them all. It was a Negro enlisted assigned
to communicate orders from the ranking officers on the ship.
Mary Alyce sensed trouble in the pit of her stomach.

"Privates, I've been instructed to tell you to prepare to hunker down. Spotters on deck have detected German U-boats
beside the convoy. I didn't want you to be caught off guard
or frightened. But you do want to be prepared for enemy fire
or anything else."

Mary Alyce was suddenly less composed. She felt her palms
grow sweaty. They had learned to protect themselves and shelter in place on land, but they'd only had a little training on
how to do so at sea. "What does that mean?" she asked, trying to hide a quake in her voice.

"'Hunker down' means what it sounds like," he said, hurriedly before he disappeared.

"Lots of help *he* is," Judy muttered.

The commotion started then, the women around them
abandoning a card game to find life jackets and looking for
corners. Mary Alyce went about finding her own coat and
a space in which to crouch, but there was none left. A loud
siren and horn went off simultaneously from the upper deck.

Since she didn't have anywhere to fold herself, she went to a nearby circular window to see what all the fuss was about.

"Girl, what are you doing?" Stacy shouted from a crawl space nearly behind a bunk bed.

"I just want to see what's happening—"

"Are you sure you're not really a white girl?" Stacy asked, her voice shrill.

Judy and Bernadette gasped from across the room. "Stacy!"

"Baby, Colored women don't just go looking at death in the mouth, whether you just found out about it or not, that's all I'm saying!" Stacy made a face at the room and jerked her coat tighter around her shoulders.

Mary Alyce was ready to say something in return, when the ship lurched sharply, knocking her down, so that she fell along with several others who had been standing.

The ship was part of a convoy, or at least it had been, and the force of the blast seemed to come from a vessel several knots behind them. She got back up on her feet to look out of the window and saw part of an enemy ship rising from the water to open fire, obscured mostly by the dark sky above them. Lights from the top decks of the vessels illuminated the giant mass, water slipping from its edges.

"My God," Mary Alyce said, turning in a frenzy to find a place to shelter. Yes, they knew a moment like this was possible, but she had believed they would never encounter a real enemy situation. Stacy stretched out her arm and pulled Mary Alyce down next to her.

"The last moments of our lives is a good time as any to come to your senses," Stacy said.

"Don't even joke that way," Judy said, kneeling next to one of the bunk beds.

"Lord, I don't know if I can handle actual guns and bombs,"

Bernadette said. "This is going to be bad for my nerves and probably my skin."

The ship maneuvered sharply again, sending pots and pans crashing down, cosmetics carefully arranged on dressers slid down taking bonnets and barrettes with them. They all crouched in the dark as bombs crackled, barreling loudly against ships behind them, bright yellow flames lighting the black sky.

The men above them were yelling at one another, as the ship seemed to pick up speed, chasing another vessel ahead of it. Mary Alyce was thinking about how comfortable home had been, and why she was still glad to have left it. It was a good thing she hadn't sent her mother that angry letter. She couldn't bear the thought that the last words she might have written to her mother were full of scorn.

It felt like they had been hunkered down with one another for hours when a male private came to the door of their cabin and said, "Everyone all right in here? We're all clear and hours away from our destination," he said.

"What was that terrifying sound?" Mary Alyce asked.

"Torpedo hit the rear vessel, and the blast pushed the rest of the convoy forward. Not to worry, there were no casualties. The ship is lost, but we managed to get the troops onboard, onto our vessel," he said.

"We could have been hit!" Stacy moaned.

"But thank goodness we weren't," Mary Alyce added.

"Happens all the time in open water," the man said before leaving.

"And here I thought a little cruise on the Atlantic was a reward for surviving Iowa," Bernadette quipped.

"That's what you're calling this?" Judy said, incredulous. "A cruise?"

"I'd rather go back to the cornfields if this is what a cruise is like," Mary Alyce grumbled.

It was the first time Judy, Bernadette and Stacy looked at her like she must be okay. When their nervous laughter broke up the tension in the air, she felt her shoulders ease. She was starting to relax, just a little, around these people who looked and sounded so different from her. They had survived the scare of being attacked at sea and shared the same threat to their lives. Now that they had been through something scary together, it felt like they were becoming a unit—a team she had been wanting to be a part of since she joined the WAC.

The *Ile de France* sailed past Ireland to the northern tip of the United Kingdom, the storied shipyards of Glasgow, Scotland. The bank of the Clyde, the main river, appeared from their entry point at the intersection of the Atlantic and the North Sea. This time, when Mary Alyce stared through the cabin window, the three women closest to her joined her, marveling at the tall sheets of steel, enormous cranes before them, the tall steeples of churches dotting the hills.

They disembarked, stretching and weary. The reality of how far they were from home was starting to settle in. The women gathered in a loose formation and set off from the dock where local Allied officers directed them. Around them, men were shouting in Irish accents; metal clanged, hammers tapped at steel.

Mary Alyce was in awe of the scene. The air even smelled different, if not more pleasant, than back home. No one in her family had ever set foot outside Vermont; they had barely made their way beyond the Woodstock County line. Traveling this distance was an expensive endeavor for Americans, and so few had the chance to hear, see and smell the sights of a distant land. She closed her eyes to take it in.

When she opened them, a man in a uniform was standing directly across from the women, staring at her. He wasn't frowning or smiling. His eyes had an open curiosity in them. She returned his gaze for a moment before looking away. The next thing she knew, Judy was standing in front of her in a protective way.

"Why do you suppose he's staring at me that way?" Mary Alyce asked Judy with worry in her eyes.

"Probably like the mix-up we had at the train station," Judy responded. "But maybe if I stand here long enough, he'll move along."

Mary Alyce wanted to know how Judy knew what she didn't—that even here, in this foreign land, that she was an out-of-place oddity, that others would see her with the Negro officers and assume she did not belong—but she was starting to see that much of being Negro had to do with identifying the hostilities that existed but weren't always spoken: unsettling looks, rude stares, mouths crumpled with disgust.

Just as she had decided to put her mind to better thoughts, a screech filled the air. The ground right beside them shook violently with a blast, sending the entire batallion running behind wooden boxes and crates on the dock. She'd barely had a moment to take in the scene that she had fantasized about so much; in her mind, overseas was a peaceful and grand place. This screeching jolt instead made her first memory abroad be intermingled with chaos and confusion.

The adrenaline she'd felt beating in her ears during the U-boat scare was good preparation for this attack. This time, though, there was no cover, no place to hide. Judy pulled her behind boxes with her friends and a few dozen women from the platoon. Major Adams was crouched in front of another dozen officers across from them, shouting, even though Mary Alyce couldn't hear a word she said.

She was noticing how much they stood out in the landscape. Their uniforms and brown faces so separate from the pale longshoremen in their dark, rugged clothes. The bomb smoldered for several minutes as Mary Alyce looked on, watching the billowing smoke turn into wisps of gray before dying out.

Until the buzz bomb landed near them, war had been both distant and theoretical for the new battalion—perhaps most of all for Mary Alyce. War was the stories women like Judy told about their husbands suddenly leaving for the battlefield. It was the occasional news announcement of victory from Roosevelt. But it wasn't real to her, she realized, until the thunder beneath her feet. The terror, the real possibility that she could die landed with that bomb on this new shore.

The poster from her post office back home came to mind. She could prove, now, she was a girl with a star-spangled heart. Except that her heart threatened to burst from her chest.

Allied officers gathered around the bomb, talking to one another before they retrieved it and hauled it off in a wheelbarrow. A sergeant from the ship asked Major Adams for permission to speak before he gave her an update on the event they had just survived and spoke to her for a few minutes before being dismissed.

Major Adams walked to the center of the dock and called the women to attention. "That was an unfriendly welcome from Germany, one of their many aerial assaults," she said. "I was pleased to see that you all remembered how to take cover in an open but narrow space. I understand no injuries have been reported, which is a relief. We are marching now to the train station to head to Birmingham, our final destination."

Stacy grumbled, "About how much bombing would y'all suspect we're going to encounter after this? I'm certain my nerves won't stand up to all this carrying on. I've seen some things working on the farm that would turn your stomach, but bombs are something else."

"They don't call it war for nothing," Judy added.

"I bet if they knew we were Negro women, they wouldn't waste their artillery," Bernadette sniffed.

The startling event had sobered them all, not only Mary Alyce, and after these few words, they marched in silence toward a destination that they had been so excited about until just then. Now they were unsure how to feel, or what would come their way next.

PART . TWO

FIFTEEN

JUDY

From Margaret to Judy

Wednesday, 18 November 1944

Dear Judy,
I write to thank you for the regular money you've been sending.
It's been a help to me as things pick up at the market, what
with families setting up their houses and kitchens to prepare for
Thanksgiving. I guess I was used to your father not being with us
for the holidays, but I feel extra lonesome without you here, too.
    Market work has kept me preoccupied. And since you've been
away (traveling the world!) the city has made a point of setting
up other ways to get relief or find work. There's agencies now set
up to recruit more Negro women into support roles at businesses
in the city. But if I'm cleaning whenever I go, I don't see what
difference it makes as long as it's the same thing. Maybe it's just

*that they don't want the press they got from those ladies you
wrote to at the newspaper who came to the market undercover.*

*The streets are mostly quiet now, but they're getting rough.
What I mean is, the folks left behind from the war are not okay.
We got boys with no fathers trying to care for families like men.
All the economy goes to buy weapons. We keep getting told to
buy war bonds, to save and ration the food. All of it together
makes for a bad situation.*

*They ever tell you when you'll be coming home? It's prob-
ably too soon to know. But I miss you and it's only been a few
months. Next time you write, I want to hear how you passed the
holiday. I decided, I think, to get a turkey, make some greens and
cornbread and have a few women from the market over who have
sons and husbands over there. We shouldn't have to all be alone.*

*Anyway, I'm going on. But I say all this to tell you not to
worry about me. Let me know how you are when you get a
chance—and what y'all are over there eating.*

Love,

Mama

The women enlisted who had been ignored, ogled or worse
in their homeland found tremendous celebration in Britain. It
was almost too much for Judy to take in. When they stepped
off the bus in front of King Edwards School, a private, former boarding school sitting on fifty acres in Edgbaston, just
outside Birmingham, they were welcomed by a thirty-piece,
white-male army band outside its gates playing "Beer Barrel
Polka." The music matched the green scenery, with mountains around them covered with bits of snowcap. The aroma
of the racks of lamb that had been prepared for them in the
too-small mess hall hung in the air.

"All of this, for us?" Judy wondered aloud.

"They must really have been missing that mail, huh?" Mary Alyce smirked.

"I might never go back to the States, this keeps up," Bernadette said. "This is some kind of welcome."

Major Adams and Captain Campbell stood before the crowd, once the jubilant music quieted, to address the women. "We'll let you get your bearings after our long journey," Captain Campbell said. "Your quarters are the two buildings across from the main building. Find a bed, drop your things and meet us in the mess hall."

Judy watched the women scatter toward the tall, slightly worn buildings where their quarters were. Compared to the barracks in Des Moines, the steam-heated, framed buildings promised a bit more luxury than she was expecting from a former boys' school. They'd learned in a briefing about the grounds that several buildings had been torched in 1936. During the war, the chapel and other buildings were defaced in the aftermath of the Birmingham Blitz.

The main building reminded Judy of New York City, except that offices were on one side, rooms for the enlisted on another. It was a multipurpose, multifaceted place. In the center, as she approached, she was surprised to find rows of metal showerheads lining the courtyard.

She would have remembered if they had been warned they'd have to shower outside. She would wait until she saw inside that building before she complained. Stacy would probably tell them she regularly took cold showers for her health. But Mary Alyce and Bernadette would share her alarm.

The sight of a bed was very welcome after so much time in motion, and she stretched out on her bed, in her uniform, after dropping her things on the floor. She ignored the fact that the roof had a hole in it; they would have to patch that later.

A heavy curtain blocked out the foggy natural light. A modest closet was large enough to fit their trunks and duffel bags.

"So, this is why they call it service," Judy remarked, her voice heavy with sleep.

"You can't get enough of being my bunkmate," Stacy said from the bed beside her. "Just admit it."

"Please don't snore as loud as you did back in the States," Judy pleaded with mock seriousness.

In her weariness, Judy ignored the impulse to sweep and tidy up the floor before she rested herself for a few minutes. She thought of her mother's loneliness over the holiday, the odd combination of excitement at being in a new place and sadness over being without Margaret and Herbert. She dozed off and was awakened by machine-gun fire in the distance and warplanes zooming overhead.

"It's just as well," Stacy said, nudging her to get up. "We're due at the welcome feast."

Judy rallied, rising to follow Stacy to the dining hall. Like their uniforms and army life, the decor was bare minimum, made for boys or men, the napkins and tablecloths plain white turned slightly beige from use and age. Their new mess hall had rows of tables to seat most of them, but the overflow officers gathered outside to hear Major Adams's statement about their mission before dinner.

"We made it here, and I salute you for all that you've done to arrive," she began, standing at the front of the middle table, everyone seated. The energy in the room buzzed with excitement and anticipation. Judy saw the Major as their fearless leader. She was a little stodgy at times, but clearly devoted to them and their cause. She had looked out for them, made dreams they didn't dare admit they had become reality.

"Tomorrow, the work begins. We'll see the backlog of mail and the warehouses that hold much of it. We are expected to process fifty to sixty-five thousand pieces of mail daily. Captain Campbell and I will walk you through our strategy for how to tackle it. But tonight, let us celebrate that we made it safely as a unit. We have more to do and further to go, but we have together made it successfully over a very long distance. Cheers," Major Adams said, lifting up a cup of water.

"Bottoms up!" Stacy said grinning.

"We'll need to replace this with real alcohol," Bernadette griped.

"You're ready to drink already?" Mary Alyce said. "It's too early."

"Big Ma would have our heads," Judy added.

"Why do we even call her that?" Mary Alyce asked.

"Who knows?" Judy said back. "It fits though, don't you think?"

Mary Alyce shrugged. "I suppose. Not like I could come up with anything better."

"Me, neither. Herbert has always been the creative one between us," Judy said, realizing she hadn't said his name in some time. Although he hadn't written back to her, her letters still somehow made her feel like she was in conversation with an old friend, even if it was one-sided.

"I wish I were married," Mary Alyce said back. "It must be a comfort to be experiencing the challenges of war together."

Judy's heart beat a little faster. She could, and maybe she even should, confess that she had not heard from him in more than a year. But she didn't want to tell anyone still. She felt sure that being in England would answer the questions she had been living with, now for such a long time. And once she found him, she could pretend this whole stretch of time, her secret and guarded worries, were inconsequential. Blips. Just small moments in a big life.

With Mary Alyce, Judy changed the subject. "Do you feel alone in all that you've been through?"

Mary Alyce looked surprised by the question and hesitated. "Maybe at first, but not now."

Judy put her hand on Mary Alyce's. "Good, because you're not by yourself."

She knew that her friend couldn't know Judy was talking to herself as much as she was talking to Mary Alyce.

The next day, their first morning at their new post, Judy woke before the first light, at 0430. The music from the band, the enemy fire in the distance, all of the noise and commotion had fallen away. It was serene, foggy and cold. She eyed the courtyard showers again from her bed, reluctant to bathe outside. She had a good mind to fill her helmet with water to wash up instead, but maybe there would be something exhilarating about showering outside in late fall weather.

Stacy, who beat Judy there, squealed and cursed.

"I wondered where you were," Judy said, her towel draped over a forearm.

Stacy made a muscle as the stream of frigid water trickled down her body. "It's better than coffee. You'll be fine."

Judy was not so sure. But she decided to just dive in. Two showerheads away from Stacy, she turned the faucet all the way, putting her towel on the hook, along with her nightgown. It was as torturous as she'd imagined, like being showered with tiny ice cubes. She shuddered, lathered a washcloth with soap and quickly powered through so it could be over. When she was done, her teeth were chattering.

"I'm never doing that again," she complained.

"Well, you already know what it's like now. Next time you'll be ready," Stacy said.

Judy felt certain she could never get used to bathing outside like a bird, but it was too early to argue. They had a long first day ahead of them.

She focused on suiting up, her uniform spotless beneath her wool coat. She had felt official when she finished training, and even more so when they were christened the Six Triple Eight. But marching with the battalion in formation through the battle-worn streets of Birmingham, led by Major Adams, made it all real in a different way. She felt herself focused on completing the task they'd been given and excelling, even as the emotional ties of home and family tugged at the pit of her stomach.

They were commanded to stand at ease before a building set off from the road on a dead-end street that looked like an abandoned factory. Judy figured it to be an old clothing warehouse that had been gutted like some of the shirtwaist factories in New York, but this structure was twice that size, maybe three stories. The windows were painted black to protect whomever or whatever was inside from German detection.

Major Adams stopped the women at a small, barren patch of land in front of the building. "I'll warn you to hold your impressions until you've had a good look at what we're dealing with."

Judy glanced at Stacy and Mary Alyce and Bernadette as the women began to file into the cold, cavernous space. A large pile that flowed in every direction—paper, envelopes, crumpled packages—started from a far corner of the building. A mountain of letters and parcels unfurled from the ceiling and reached toward them near the door, which might as well have been a half a mile away. Judy's mouth was flung as wide open as her eyes, and her heart sank.

She had been prepared for hard work, but she was not sure if they could do anything to put a real dent in the enormity of the task. Her fellow officers murmured their same protests. Major Adams held out her hands, asking for them to be quiet.

"Yes, I know it is a daunting amount of mail. But there was a lot of sweat and sacrifice and petitioning to bring you here to fulfill this important mission. And if we do well here, your reputation will follow you and Negro women for generations in the military. If you fail to excel here, you will sever the ties of approximately three million enlisted men from their loved ones. You will snuff out the little bit of home within them that remains.

"I don't have to tell you this is not glamorous work. But the reason we made it here is because you will likely live on. Your name, your legacy, the history of this unit will live on because of what you do here, whether or not you receive that recognition in your lifetime. You will always have yourself and you will always have your service. Any questions?"

Judy's back straightened at Major Adams's words. She had not looked at her service that way before: enlisting for her had been about Herbert and making money for her mother, but it was also about doing something rewarding for herself.

It was not an easy place or time to be in. Right before their arrival, Adolf Hitler had launched a surprise blitzkrieg on Allied Forces in the wooded, ancient forests of Ardennes. The Allied Forces were assembled along a link of the forest that made them appear as a bulge, and Hitler's army was able to easily spot the soldiers and attack. That set the Allied Forces back early in the battle considerably. Nearly one hundred thousand US soldiers were killed in what would later be called the Battle of the Bulge.

Morale was low, and the many messages of love and hope from the home front were needed now more than ever. To make matters worse, the white WACs who had been working alongside local civilians trying to manage the flood of mail from around the world had been sent home or to a different post in the region.

It was clear soldiers wouldn't miss the items they had already survived without. The Central Postal Battalion was meant to prioritize the letters that had the most essential components for building morale back up. From a mother to her son, a letter was a reminder that he was more than just a body with targets on his helmet; he was home to a beating heart that throbbed to a rhythm just like her own. A letter built a bridge between the time it was written and when it would be read. It touched its reader in a way that brought another place directly to his hands.

Before the war, everything was as black-and-white as the lines on stationery. Handwriting was one of the few visuals from back home that could travel to the battlefront, along with pictures of one's beloved and pin-up posters. Most of the time, there was nothing to look at, only endless sound—radio news bulletins, screaming, careening bombs, the cries of the wounded and dying, the weeping of those terrified for their lives. But before the noise, always, was the quiet, steadying force of a written letter.

"Captain Campbell has smartly devised a strategy that we estimate will take several months for us to implement," Major Adams said. "But I will let her take it from here. You will work in eight-hour shifts, six days a week until we have moved all of this mail out of this space," she gestured behind her.

Major Adams nodded sharply at Captain Campbell, who stood forward at one of the work tables that had been set up closer to the door. Folded green plastic chairs were stacked in rows at the borders of the warehouse; old oak desks were placed in ovals around the room with more plain chairs sprayed with white lettering that announced they were property of the US Army.

"Ladies, you meet these items in a chain of custody that has been broken by war," Captain Campbell began. "We'll fix that by having each unit or shift take letters and parcels from the pile and load them into these postal crates, courtesy of the local post offices. In the canvas bags," she said, pointing to forest green bags with cards stapled to their fronts with parts of the alphabet, A through E, F through J, and so on. "You will simply sort the mail alphabetically and place them inside. Another shift will go through the items to determine if any addresses are incomplete or names are missing before the full bags are tied up and officers take the mail to be sorted at the local army postal station by regiments, branches and divisions."

The more she listened to Captain Campbell, the less anxious Judy felt. It would be a lot of work, of course. But they had a plan, and that was certain to help. Judy fiddled with her hands inside the pockets of her coat, as Campbell unfurled a yellowed paper, crinkled and bearing water spots, which described the flow of mail from the army to civilians and back.

"As you can see, the flow of mail between the US and overseas is complex. It's easy for mail to lose its way," Campbell continued.

Judy couldn't make out all parts of the paper from where she stood, but she visualized Captain Campbell's words.

Battle activity on international waters meant standard mail could take up to a month to deliver. Victory Mail, also called V-Mail, took half that time, because it consisted of a one-page, filmed document with a serial number and a space for a censor's stamp of approval so that no compromising details about the war could fall into the wrong hands.

Single sheets of V-Mail stationery had room for about three hundred to six hundred words and were available at five-and-dime stores. The advantage of V-Mail was that the military could track it easily and move it faster, since it weighed less than standard mail.

The process of handling mail from a soldier overseas to loved ones at home added in two steps: a unit censor blacked out operational or tactical details, overly descriptive mentions of maneuvers and other sensitive details before the letter made its way through the APO and the Postal Regulating Station. Then, before the mail was shipped, a post censor checked the same letter to make sure nothing compromising had made it through the first.

All of it went from the US Post Office to a Postal Concentration Center to be sorted, then an Embarkation Army Post Office, where the V-Mail was sent to a V-Mail contractor to photograph the paper and fold up the lighter film into an envelope for it to be shipped via air mail to its corresponding Military Post Office. Ordinary mail and packages were routed to seaports of departure from the United States. From there, everything had to go through a Postal Regulating Station to an Army Post Office, or APO, before it was all sorted at the overseas unit's Regimental and Unit Mail Clerk. After a two-week or month-long journey to the soldier the mail was meant for, he would finally receive what was meant for him, eager to hear those two delightful words: "Mail Call!"

Captain Campbell let them begin their work by saying, "The sooner we get started, the faster we'll finish."

After all the discussion and thinking about it, Judy was somewhat relieved to begin the work. She and Mary Alyce worked at a desk a couple of feet from the mail pile in the corner. Bernadette and Stacy worked beside them.

Judy grabbed one of the mail buckets and filled it with envelopes and packages. The silt from dust and time settled on her fingertips and made her sneeze.

"God bless you," Stacy said. "And God be with us." Stacy passed her and Mary Alyce to get her own pile of mail.

"He might have already left us," said Bernadette, holding the corner of an envelope like a stinky rag.

"It's only the beginning now," Mary Alyce said. "Too early to complain."

"Have you tried sitting in these chairs for more than two minutes?" Bernadette said, gesturing to a creaky metal one.

"That's why they call it work, Bernie, and not paid vacation," Judy said with a huff of laughter.

They all joined her in laughing at that. It was a nice moment as they began to stack alphabetized letters on the tabletops before them.

"Well, what if they are only addressed to *John?*" Judy asked, stumped and searching the envelope on both sides before looking up.

Stacy took the envelope and plopped it on her table. "Goes with the *J*s, maybe?"

"But there must be a million *John*s!" Mary Alyce exclaimed.

Stacy gave her an exasperated look. "There's a joke in there I feel too Christian to make, Mary Alyce."

Bernadette and Judy pretended to clutch the pearls they weren't wearing before the four of them started laughing again.

It wasn't long before their backs and legs got tired as the hours dragged on, making their banter less frequent. They each settled into a quiet focus, clearing up a little space at a time on the floor. This was not so different from cleaning a house, Judy thought as she worked. You couldn't do it all at once. You needed to pace yourself in order to make real progress.

They were a few hours into the first shift when air horns started wailing. Remembering her training, Judy felt her heart start beating wildly as she dropped to shelter under the desk. She didn't wait to see if anyone followed her lead. She heard

Major Adams order them to take cover. Mary Alyce was wide-eyed beside her for a second before Judy made herself take slow, deep breaths and exhaled, her red face losing some of its color.

Instinctively, Judy said, "It's all right." They knew the air horns and sirens signaled German air raids or bomb threats from enemy aircraft. There was a blast from miles away, which was powerful enough, Judy not only heard it but felt a slight tremble of the ground beneath her. What felt like an endless amount of time passed before the all-clear siren sounded and Major Adams gave them permission to come out.

"I guess that boat situation was good practice after all," Mary Alyce said as she stood, smoothing down her pants.

Judy was amused at the surprise she detected in Mary Alyce's voice. "Didn't you pay any attention in class or during drills?"

Mary Alyce shrugged. "Not really. I didn't think a lot of it would apply to me. See how right I was about that."

They returned to their task, and Judy thought that the longer she worked with Mary Alyce, the more she felt she wanted a little space from her. There had been the awkward assignment back in Iowa, their close quarters in Fort Oglethorpe, and of course, her anxiety on the ship and voyage over. Judy was getting distracted, trying to adjust to the new surroundings, to being abroad, to their enormous assignment. She and her friends had been so swept up in making sure that Mary Alyce was okay and settling in that they didn't pay enough attention to their own transition to their new post. It was a lot to carry.

As they wrapped up the first shift, she decided she would ask Major Adams if she could work with another officer—maybe Stacy or Bernadette. She felt a pang of guilt, but she had come to make a living, to do her part and find her husband, not to be consumed by this nervous Nellie from Vermont.

Before their shift began again the next morning, Judy approached the green metal desk at the front of the warehouse where Major Adams shared a space with Captain Campbell. Judy asked, "Permission to speak, Major?"

"Yes, Private Washington. How can I help you?"

Judy hesitated, bit her lip, then forced out, "I'd like to work with someone else, if possible. Mary Alyce—Private Dixon, I mean—is a good person, but I don't think it's good for us to do *everything* together."

Major Adams looked steadily in Judy's eyes, and Judy felt like she was trying to read her soul. She tried not to feel timid or naked for asking for what she needed. "Do you feel strongly about this?"

Judy wondered to herself what she truly had strong feelings about. She just wanted other options.

"I'd like to see what it would be like to work with someone else," Judy said, just before she was startled by a slight sigh behind her. She turned and found Mary Alyce, her face flushed red.

"You wanted to see me, ma'am," Mary Alyce said, staring past Judy.

Judy's heart sank. How long had Mary Alyce been listening?

"I want you and Private Washington to refine the organization system and workflow for the mail so we can get it out the door more quickly," Major Adams said. Judy was annoyed that her request to work with someone else was clearly being denied, and now, she was embarrassed that Mary Alyce also knew she'd made that request.

Major Adams looked at Judy and said, "I understand your preferences, but I know that you and Private Dixon have worked successfully together in the past, and I'd like to keep that momentum going."

Judy did not protest further. She could now tell it was no

use; all complaining would do is hurt Mary Alyce more than she meant to and it would be a sign of insubordination to the major. She saluted her superior right before Major Adams disappeared without another word.

Judy felt horrible. She started to explain, but Mary Alyce cut her off. "You're not so great to work with yourself."

The nerve! "Now, hold on—"

"No, you hold on," Mary Alyce said, a strength and gravity in her voice that Judy hadn't heard before. "I didn't ask you to look after me or treat me like some kind of charity case. You think I don't know the kinds of jokes and things Stacy and Bernadette say about me? All that new-Negro stuff. And you're almost worse. At least they don't behave like you, acting like you have the burden of babysitting me. Truth is, you need a friend, too. Someplace to direct all your nervous energy.

"I might not know all there is to know about how to be Colored, but I'm at least honest. I'm a good human being. Decent. I know better than to talk badly about a fellow officer in front of a major, to make myself bigger than I am because I feel small all the time. Maybe that doesn't make me the belle of the ball around here, but at least I can sleep at night knowing I did the best I could to be a good person. And that's more than I can say for you right now."

Judy was livid. Mary Alyce had the nerve to overreact to what she knew she needed and wanted, which was simply a break from working with her. "You think I'm a bad person because you're not the only officer in the Six Triple Eight I want to work with? I suppose you can think what you want, but you've got a rude wake-up call coming. We are all adults. And I have the right to ask for what would be easier for me. Even if you don't like me for doing it."

Mary Alyce's lips were trembling now, and she looked like she might cry. Judy had hoped for that, actually, to hurt Mary

Alyce in the same way she'd been hurt by her outburst, her utter misunderstanding of Judy's request.

Instead of crying, Mary Alyce said, "You do what you want, Judy. You want to disobey Major Adams's direct orders, go right ahead. I'm going to do what I was told. You might try it sometime." With that, Mary Alyce stormed off after she grabbed a pencil and a scrap of paper, which she stuffed in her coat.

SIXTEEN

MARY ALYCE

The nerve of that Judy Washington, thinking she was some kind of savior to Mary Alyce. It was so careless for her to speak that way about her in front of their superior. If she had been a real friend, she might have broached it with her first. But no one could be trusted to be a friend anymore. The grief of losing Ethel and Betsy was still fresh. Now she added to her heartache and loneliness fury over Judy's insinuation that she had somehow made it Judy's job to translate the Negro experience. The woman had offered herself and Mary Alyce accepted. Maybe that was her mistake.

Writing out her feelings had helped her deal with her anger toward her mother and now she did the same about Judy. She was still letting the letter to her mother sit, but she wanted to know more about her father now and the other side of her family. She had a lot to sort out. On her own.

So before Mary Alyce was abandoned by one more friend or she forced herself to be in Judy's company, she decided she would follow Judy's lead. Mary Alyce would focus on herself.

She rose at first light, shivering in the cooling mornings after her courtyard shower and dressing quickly so she finished breakfast just as Judy and the girls were just getting started. She ate a tough roll with black tea so fast she nearly choked. One of these days, she would see if anything could be done about the awful food.

What these women didn't know, because they had not asked, was that Mary Alyce was used to keeping her own company. She almost preferred it, being an only child on a farm. Judy wasn't the only one who felt, after all these months in close quarters with women from everywhere, that she could use some time with herself and her own thoughts.

There had been no quiet from the time she was assigned to the platoon until they became a battalion shipped across the world. Overnight, she felt that she had gone from being a woman who had some kind of say over her days and a little bit of control over the ways that people should treat her, to a woman who needed to learn again how to speak carefully if she expected others to respond.

Good for Judy, that she had always known the rules for how she should be and what was taboo. Mary Alyce fluctuated between feeling gratitude and confusion about how important it was to remember her place as a Negro woman in the US—especially since, as Judy reminded her, she did have a choice should she decide to pass for white.

Everything in America, in life, made it clear that remembering one's place meant remembering your inferiority to anyone white. The signs, the looks, the treatment—what waited for her back home was now the inferior version of a run-down waiting room, a crowded hospital, a diner's back entrance or a broken water fountain.

Despite this, Mary Alyce was learning that part of becoming Colored had to do with expressing the better version of whatever you felt. If she were irritated or upset, she could only show grace and kindness. If she felt outrage, she had to transform it into powerlessness, wear a look of affection, appear crestfallen. To be a Negro woman meant to cloak your true feelings behind a mask of pleasant, polite acceptance because no one cared if you felt otherwise.

To hear Judy and the others tell it, no one believed in the humanity of a Negro woman—and Mary Alyce, looking at the world through that distorted lens, understood exactly what they meant.

But her favorite holiday, Thanksgiving, was approaching, and she wanted to be grateful. She gave herself permission to throw herself into the work as she never had before. Instead of working the same station as Judy and the ladies, Mary Alyce politely asked another clerk to switch with her, just for a little while. Whatever they could do to break up the monotony of sorting mail into boxes and bags in the dimly lit warehouse, which was so cold many of them wore ski suits to stay warm.

When a third day passed this way, Mary Alyce picked up an extra shift or two. She missed the jokes and observations of her friends. But she still wasn't sure what it even meant to have a friend now and was content enough being on her own.

The glue on the back of many of the envelopes had lost its binding effect, which left them open for inspection before it was time for the WAC to forward them to the censors. This gave Mary Alyce a chance to sneak reads from them. It was a quick cure for her loneliness, and a way to make up for the conversations that had paused for the days that she let stretch into a week.

Dolly,
Nothing has changed since I last wrote. I hope you received my
last letter. I don't know when I'll get the chance to write again.
Let me just tell you how much I love you. What good you've
done being the woman you are.

Even if I don't make it back to see you and kiss you again—
that's what I dream about, hunkered down, smoke in the air
and in my lungs. Know that you are always in my thoughts.

Norma,
Kiss our babies for me. Hold on tight to them. I have no inten-
tion of letting these Germans beat us. But there's no telling what
is coming for us next. Not a single day is promised.

Frank,
We all stopped what we were doing June 6, reading about the
Invasion of France. We keep praying for you. Don't let up.

These emotional letters made her think about home, about
her first days in the WAC, the really good parts of finally
making it to the army. She had been able to share that with
Ethel and Betsy—something to be thankful for. She had been
saving up descriptions of Iowa and their drills and their time
at the officers' club to paint the picture for Helen. But now,
there was no one to send an update to, and she wished she
had someone to write about her situation, about her mom.

Reading the heartfelt words of others in those letters also
gave her more time to think about what a letter meant, the way
it gave you tangible proof that someone loved you enough to
find the time and the materials to write down their thoughts
and feelings about you, their demonstration of affection or love
in sentence form, sent by plane or ship to wherever you were.

Mary Alyce was also, in this season of reconciliation, reconsidering her own letter to Helen, how harsh it was even if it had truths in it. Helen didn't even know she had left the country. Mary Alyce began to wonder if she should write a different letter, one fit to put in the mail. Reading the contents of others' letters made her put her feelings in perspective. Lives were being lost. Her mother was probably worried sick about her. Yes, the deceit about her race was hard to bear. But she was managing.

The next morning, Mary Alyce rose with the other women and met Judy and the girls for breakfast. They had been chatting with a rising energy when she approached and then everyone fell quiet.

"Judy, I'm sorry," Mary Alyce said, like the words had been smoldering on her tongue and she just had to get them out. "I know I've been distant."

"You disappeared, all right," Stacy said.

Judy and Bernadette turned away from Mary Alyce to give Stacy looks. Mary Alyce kept talking. "I've had a hard time and I was overly sensitive to what you said. I took it too personally. You've made it so much easier for me. All of you have, really. And I haven't thanked you properly, but I am grateful. I was never all that well-mannered, to tell you the truth."

Judy stood, holding her tray to her body with her forearm. "I don't accept your apology. I have enough to think about without worrying about how you'll handle something I need to do for myself. So if you don't want to spend time together, that's fine by me." Judy walked away as soon as she was done speaking.

Mary Alyce wanted to cry. She had gathered her courage, and she was sure that her hurt feelings could be at least understood. But when she went to say something else, Bernadette followed Judy, and Stacy followed her. They were not too far from the bin for dirty dishes, and Mary Alyce followed them.

"It's too early for this carrying on," Bernadette complained.

"I really do apologize, Judy," Mary Alyce said to Judy who had emptied her tray and was holding her hands in her pockets and staring. "I overreacted. Time to myself helped me see it."

Judy had no expression on her face, but she was studying Mary Alyce, looking at her like she was trying to figure her out. *Join the club*, Mary Alyce, thought. It felt to her like the whole dining room was waiting for Judy to say something else. Eventually, Judy smiled and shrugged. "That's fair enough," Judy said, holding out her hand in a gesture of reconciliation. "Takes a big woman to admit when she's wrong. But if you abandon me again because I say something you don't like or agree with, I might not be so forgiving."

Mary Alyce shook Judy's hand firmly, relieved. She was holding in her other hand a scrap of paper she'd been using to solve one of the battalion's biggest issues. Judy glanced at the paper curiously. "What's with the chicken scratch?"

Mary Alyce chuckled because she could barely read her own handwriting most of the time. "I'm trying to work out the puzzle of the incomplete addresses and some of the other mail in limbo." They stored everything in locator boxes which were labeled for each unit—and one unit could account for dozens of boxes. But because troops were moving all the time, the battalion couldn't trust the locator cards alone to help them find the right soldiers, especially if they had common first and last names.

"I'm thinking of something like a database," Mary Alyce continued to explain. "My grandma aspired to be a librarian, but she quit going to school in the third grade because my family needed her on the farm. We used to visit the town library and reshelve books. She'd give me the ones that hadn't been put back and I would find their rightful place. So I'm always thinking about categories and the right place and order for things. The mail is the perfect puzzle for that, only on a much bigger scale."

Judy stared at the drawing and asked, "How does your system handle duplicates?"

"I'm not sure yet," Mary Alyce said. "I think we need a list of the regiments and their hometowns to cross-check to make sure we have the right letters for the right people."

"It could take a while for us to get the information we really need to get things moving," Judy said. "Nothing moves fast in the women's army. Especially not out here."

"Well, the good news is that we're not asking for our own benefit but for all the men missing home. You heard Big Ma—no mail, no morale. Maybe we can change how quickly things can get done."

The battalion chipped quietly and tirelessly away at the mountain of mail until its slope grew less and less steep, each woman grabbing what her arms could carry to the rectangular work tables and the stiff chairs. Straining their eyes, they held the letters to the fading lights, tilted and examined small, beat-up boxes with faded brown paper and blotched ink. Every so often, a package or letter was damaged beyond recognition and had to be thrown away.

Meanwhile, the Allied Forces were gaining on the Axis, in France and in Italy, liberating thousands who had been conquered by the Germans. But those heroics had led to even more combat-unit movement, at a pace that made keeping track of a soldier's exact location difficult.

While they waited for the list Mary Alyce mentioned to Judy and that they subsequently requested from Major Adams and Captain Campbell, Mary Alyce worked with her and Stacy to make address cards with names and infantry numbers to help them avoid mixing up men with the same names. When the sorting was mostly done after about a week and a half, a group of the battalion's nosy but rather dull officers were assigned as unit censors to read through the letters—a job relished by the chief censor who slowed all their work down, Second Lieutenant Catherine Landry, who was meant to be the eyes and ears of Major Adams and Captain Campbell when they were otherwise occupied.

Mary Alyce disliked Landry because of how she and other censors added an unnecessary layer of delay to their process, though she was sure Landry was nice enough as a person. They were already behind on the mail backlog when they arrived; adding days for censors to read old mail seemed unnecessary.

Besides, there were just several weeks left in the year, and they had until spring to move these letters. Thanksgiving was in a matter of weeks. The war could not end with these messages still stuck in some English warehouse. Soldiers needed word from their families just as soon as the Central Postal Battalion could get their letters delivered.

Landry was both in charge of the nosy censors, assigned out of their innate preference for tamping down effusiveness in any expression, and addressing logistical concerns that might otherwise escape their commanding officers' notice. It was Landry's doing, for example, that elicited a strong warning from Major Adams early one morning against pilfering the rare salvageable snacks, socks, and money from the open packages.

"It disappoints me," Adams said with her trademark seriousness, "to have to wake up early and remind you that not only is it sinful to steal, but if you are planning to do it, to make sure whatever you take is worth the fines and federal prison time that you may have to incur as a result."

That they had been warned like children struck Mary Alyce

as funny. "That should definitely do the trick," Mary Alyce said to Judy. "I bet the stealing will be solved now."

"I should say so," Judy added, smiling. "Raising Big Ma out of her bed is like raising the dead, and for the trash that's been sitting around here so long, it's not worth the sinning."

It was nice to laugh with her friend again after weeks of repetitive work. Mary Alyce had come to enjoy the feeling of the gritty paper beneath her fingers as she started a pile just like the women around her in their pantsuits and sweaters beneath standard-issue jackets. Dusting off those accumulated words felt like bringing hope back to life.

Even with a good system in place to categorize dozens of packages first by branch, then regiment and post, it took days for them to get more information about the men to whom the letters and packages should be directed. Mail was a funny thing that way: in America, everyone took for granted before the war that the postal service would bring all of the important bills and notices and letters they needed right to their door.

But it took many hands to make the global postal services work—from the Six Triple Eight to prisoners of war captured by Allied soldiers, who helped with grunt work, including lifting the heavy canvas bags to and from trucks. They were scheduled to work this way in shifts for at least a few more months, but although it hadn't been that long, the work sometimes felt endless and taxing. But Mary Alyce kept thinking about the puzzle of her database and making the process more efficient.

The tedious work of sorting misdirected or lost letters gave Mary Alyce the benefit of getting lost in the stories of others instead of being so consumed with her own. The questions she had because she still hadn't written her mother. Handling packages addressed only to *Junior* or *Robert* or *John*, she made up a story about each one. Spinning these tales helped her connect to her humanity. In the letters, life was also distilled to a fine point. There were no questions about intent or sincerity.

"You just always know where you stand with folks in these letters," she said to Judy as they worked in the warehouse.

"That's one way to put it," Judy's eyes moving quickly from Mary Alyce's face to the opened letters. "The other way is to remember that the letters are intended for their loved ones and not strangers, so they feel they can be candid."

Mary Alyce hesitated and blinked hard at Judy before carefully placing one of the letters back into its envelope. "Well, even their private thoughts become the property of the US Army. Besides, we do what the censors do. This is maybe the second or third time someone's read this poor boy's letter."

Judy shrugged. "I suppose. But they get paid to read and censor. You get paid to sort."

Was that all they were doing? Mary Alyce wondered to herself. "Maybe," she said to herself softly.

One rainy morning in mid-November, two weeks before Thanksgiving, Major Adams arrived with a stack of papers she held to her body like a dancer with a hat.

"At ease, ladies," she said upon entering so they wouldn't stop their work with the formalities of salutes. To Judy and Mary Alyce, she said, "I come bearing gifts—master lists, recently updated for the European Theater of Operations, as requested," she said, handing the pages to Mary Alyce, who was overtaken by a rush of excitement. She joyfully whooped with Judy and then threw her arms around Major Adams. Charity, mostly out of surprise from the show of emotion from Mary Alyce, stood straight as a board, which made Mary Alyce remember herself, drop her arms and say, "Oh dear, I'm very sorry, ma'am."

The jubilant mood turned quiet with fear as the battalion

watched for Major Adams's reaction. She looked at them with a blank expression for a beat. Then, for the first time since they'd met her, Major Adams laughed, her mouth falling open. It was a full-throated, bass-filled laugh that surprised Mary Alyce and brought tears to the lieutenant's eyes.

"I've never seen anyone so happy over a pile of paper. Please excuse me," Major Adams said. "Well, what I meant to say, before all the shouting started, was that I certainly hope these documents will make your task that much easier. I will say that this list was not as easy to come by as I would have preferred, but that's the life of a woman, regardless of your rank."

Mary Alyce was relieved at the major's response, and to finally have another part of her puzzle to put together. This would make everything go even faster.

Major Adams took her place at the front of the warehouse with Captain Campbell and called the women to attention. Major Adams said, "Ladies, you have been doing fine work in a short period of time, and with the holiday approaching, I think it's time for you to have a real break. We are on schedule with the backlog, even though there is double the amount of letters than we expected. Because of your hard work, we are in the army's good graces.

"Certainly, that standing doesn't last forever, so we've got to take advantage of it. So I want you all to have your first weekend passes. My only request is that you wait to use them until after Thanksgiving."

Mary Alyce was ecstatic. They would get to be free from their schedules, from their desks for a little while. Away from the dark warehouse. There would also be, out and about, handsome men.

"Before you head out, please remember you are American soldiers in a foreign land," the major continued. "You represent the United States Women's Army Corps. All of the rules of your post apply to your behavior off post and off duty. You will have to live here, at least for the weeks ahead, and whatever you do will become part of who you are in this place. All of that said, I do want you to have a good time."

Mary Alyce found herself clapping, as if she'd just heard a wonderful speech. Her colleagues followed suit. Major Adams smiled at the women and said, "As you were."

SEVENTEEN

JUDY

Nothing made being away from home feel lonelier than the approach of a holiday. The letter from Margaret filled Judy with longing for both the Bronx and for Herbert. When she was working with the mail, she was also keeping an eye out for his name, his regiment. There was too much volume for her to keep track of, and she still had managed to keep the fact she had not heard from him in over a year now to herself.

Before lights-out in their quarters, Judy wondered aloud to Mary Alyce, "Do you think we should plan something for the holiday?"

Mary Alyce seemed to weigh the request for a moment before asking, "You mean, like a Thanksgiving meal?"

Stacy, who Judy thought for sure was asleep, slipped down her eye mask and propped herself up on an elbow. "A feast, you mean. A proper Thanksgiving feast."

"That would be dreamy," Bernadette said.

"But where? The mess hall can't hardly fit all of us," Judy noted. There were other spaces, but they weren't repaired from the bombing. She had been drawn to an old building near where they worked that wasn't used for anything as far as she could tell, but she didn't have the energy or the time to do anything about it.

"We can make it work," Mary Alyce said, her voice getting that I-love-a-good-challenge sound to it. Judy could hear the wheels turning. "We can't all sit with the tables as they're set up now, but we could have it buffet style. Or maybe we can have the shifts come at different times, to stagger it so all of us can eat with the folks we see all the time. Make it feel nice and cozy."

It was an excellent idea, Judy thought. She was picturing in her mind the list to make the feast a reality. Tablecloths and fall decorations she could ask Landry about. And food. The kitchen workers would need some assistance. "Mary Alyce, that's genius. And you like to cook, right?"

"I *love* to cook. But I've never made anything for more than eight hundred people," she said.

"First time for everything," Stacy said, putting her mask back on and turning over on her cot. "Good night."

"You can't encourage the girl and then go back to bed," Bernadette teased. "Aren't you going to help?"

"I did help. I told her she can do it."

Judy chuckled along with Bernadette and Mary Alyce. "Stacy's right, but she also knows we'll volunteer her to work when we actually make the meal."

Stacy groaned. It had been decided. Judy and Mary Alyce dreamed aloud about their ideal Thanksgiving menu: the turkey, the ham, macaroni and cheese, potato salad. Stuffing, sweet potato pie, yams, collard greens.

"I have a confession to make," Mary Alyce said sheepishly.

Judy knew what was coming. She said, "You don't know how to make macaroni and cheese?"

"That," Mary Alyce admitted. "And collard greens, I'm afraid."

"Very easy," Judy answered. "The greens more than the mac and cheese. But that's easy, too. It's just like a cheese-and-noodle casserole."

Mary Alyce tried to imagine it. "With breadcrumbs?"

Judy looked horrified. "Absolutely not. That would be like putting squash cubes at the bottom."

Mary Alyce wrinkled her nose. "Maybe we should do everything else."

"Fine. Heaven help me, I will make the macaroni and cheese. Now let me sleep," Stacy pleaded. "Work on the menu tomorrow. I need my beauty sleep."

Judy and Mary Alyce laughed. They would bookmark their exciting plans for the coming days. Now they had two events to look forward to: Thanksgiving for the battalion and their weekend leave.

Judy and Mary Alyce went the next day to Lieutenant Landry, who was in charge of ordering supplies of all kinds for the unit. Lieutenant Landry said, "I'm not sure if anyone has mentioned it, Privates, but we are still at war. Which means we still ration goods. Especially food. We don't really *do* special orders."

Judy disliked Landry's smug, self-important tone. She knew, too, it was an exaggeration to say the army wasn't making special arrangements. Over in London, Negro officers—men only—had special segregated quarters. They could do things women in the WAC could not. And the women's mission was about hope, inspiration and morale. How could they offer it if they didn't have any for themselves?

"Surely a dinner for the battalion, as a way for the army to express its gratitude to us, is not an imposition," Judy said aloud. "We're not asking for a USO concert. We just want to make a meal and break bread, like we would do at home."

"And I would handle the food operations," Mary Alyce said.

The lieutenant huffed, "This is above my pay grade." Captain Campbell walked past them in the main building, overhearing. Judy turned to her; the timing was a Thanksgiving miracle.

"What's above your pay grade, Landry?" Captain Campbell asked.

"If I may, Captain," Judy said. "We want to have a Thanksgiving meal for the battalion, in three shifts so we can all sit down with our companies for the holiday."

Captain Campbell's facial expression did not change. Judy could see her doing a mental inventory. A flash of recognition let Judy know she understood the challenge of their small mess hall and kitchen. "That's a kind thought," she finally said. "Tricky, though."

"Yes," Judy admitted, "but we only need to have the food ordered and Private Dixon and I will coordinate the rest."

Captain Campbell looked at them evenly. Judy thought she was going to stand there thinking the entire morning. Time was ticking—they only had ten days to put things together. "This is a wonderful idea, Judy. I'll take the matter to Major Adams for final approval, but you have my blessing. Landry, be sure to help these ladies procure what they need. Within reason. No champagne."

"Shoot," Mary Alyce joked. Judy looked at her nervously, but Captain Campbell chuckled softly.

"You can buy your own drinks after Thanksgiving," the captain said.

Even without libations, Judy was certain the feast she had in mind would be a welcome event for the ladies of their battalion on their first major holiday away from their families, probably for the first time in their lives. It would be a rare moment for them to all come together, to name how grateful they were for each other, for the WAC and to be alive in a time of war and uncertainty.

Thanksgiving morning, Bernadette pulled out a gorgeous burnt-orange dress for the occasion. Stacy pressed a blouse to go with her slacks. Mary Alyce wore a dress Helen made for her, with puffy sleeves and full skirt. Judy's dress was also made by her mother: a polka-dot number she wore with red pumps she borrowed from Bernadette.

Judy carried a clipboard with a schedule for the meal prep and serving that she and Mary Alyce had spent hours and hours on, including working with Lieutenant Landry to order from available suppliers willing to send them whatever they had from the European Theater. Instead of collard greens, they had to settle for spinach. Bernadette had to settle for a macaroni and cheese that had only two kinds of cheese, cheddar and Muenster, instead of four or five, as was tradition. Bernadette mixed it and Mary Alyce did the cooking.

"Don't add anything else," Judy warned, micromanaging Mary Alyce.

"I heard you the first time," Mary Alyce said, rolling her eyes. "Don't make me request a different work partner."

"Too soon," Judy shot back, pretending to be hurt.

Standing in the kitchen, Judy's feet were killing her, and she couldn't remember the last time she had slept or sat down.

But there was a feeling coursing through her that was unlike anything she had felt before. Ambition. Purpose. Meaning.

She had been looking for meaningful work and a way to make a difference. Now she finally felt that she had. She had an idea for bringing people together and now it was coming true. It felt like the beginning of something special.

The Allied officers, Military Police, and other support staff who guarded the King Edwards School and helped with various maintenances, decorated the mess hall at Judy's request. Golden-and-auburn paper leaves adorned doors and walls. A paper turkey sat on a table at the entrance to the main mess hall.

As planned, there would be three waves of officers having their Thanksgiving meals. Despite Stacy's grumbling, the four women central to planning ate as part of the last shift. The same army band that had greeted them more than a month ago set up outside the mess hall entrance and played softly, adding to a festive atmosphere.

"You've really done something wonderful," Major Adams said to her as she passed Judy on her way out of the dining hall. "You should be proud."

Judy beamed into the eyes of her exacting commanding officer. "Thank you, Major, for allowing it, and for believing in me."

"Thank you for believing in yourself," Major Adams said.

When it was finally time for her to have a seat at the head of their table, Mary Alyce untied her apron and tossed it ceremoniously over the back of her chair, ready to finally sit after hours of making plates and serving others. Judy thought she hadn't really seen her friend this much in her element, until she heard Mary Alyce kiss her teeth slowly and stand up. She had forgotten something, but it was time for them to eat.

"Where are you going now? We've got to eat, I'm starved," Judy protested.

Mary Alyce waved her off and disappeared hurriedly into the kitchen. She emerged with a bottle of Belgian ale. She lifted it victoriously and Bernadette clapped her hands together in recognition. "She got us booze!"

Judy couldn't help but laugh at Bernadette's eager tone. Stacy found proper glasses for the ale and finally they all sat, almost too tired to eat.

"Before we dig in," Stacy started and Judy held up her hands.

"So help me if you people do not let me have dinner..." Judy said.

Stacy widened her eyes, as if telling Judy to hush. "A toast, to the great idea you had, and all that you and Mary Alyce did to make it real," Stacy insisted. She stopped and smiled, awkwardly, Judy thought, because she was waiting for a joke or some other snide comment, as was Stacy's way. "What? I mean it, Judy. This is special for us," Stacy added, tears forming at the corners of her eyes.

"Oh boy, I put on makeup for you to make me mess it up!" Bernadette sniffled.

It was rituals and traditions like this that Judy loved because they had given her occasion to mark time with the people she loved the most in the world, which now included the friends at her table. These women were starting to feel like sisters she'd never had and hadn't known she needed. Like everything at wartime, celebrations had been scaled back—not just for her or for the WAC officers, but for everyone. Celebrating this moment in time and with gratitude reminded her of what was good and valuable.

"I'm thankful for all of you supporting my idea," she said. "For keeping me company while we are on this adventure.

The work we are doing here is going to help many people who will never know us or our stories. But we'll know, and what a beautiful thing that is. Happy Thanksgiving, family."

Judy raised a glass and they toasted, and then she finally got to savor the food.

EIGHTEEN

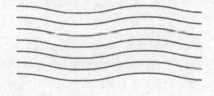

JUDY

A week after their Thanksgiving meal, Judy got a tip from Lieutenant Landry, of all people, that their first stop during their weekend passes should be the Better Beer Pub. It was one of the last bars of its kind in the city's downtown, perched on the corner of a small, cobblestoned street. Several larger businesses and buildings were missing roofs and windows. Entire floors had been reduced to rubble. But the pub, thankfully, remained.

They had marched through downtown, but they had not yet experienced it as civilians. Out of force of habit, Bernadette had begun moving into their formation when Judy put her hand on her friend's arm to stop her. "There will be none of that this evening," Judy said.

Bernadette touched the back of her bun and grinned. "You don't have to tell me twice."

Mary Alyce and Stacy walked directly behind them as they approached the pub. "Are we sure they serve Negroes at this bar? Did anyone ask?" Judy asked.

Judy had not forgotten that the rules of American segregation seemed to apply everywhere. Even though the British were friendly, many of the white military officers brought their American Jim Crow attitudes with them. They sometimes threatened to stop patronizing British businesses that served Negroes.

"Only one way to find out," Judy said, leading the way in.

The pub smelled like baked bread and ale. But the glares from some of their fellow revelers, a mix of civilians and military, carried the same frost as the weather. Just moments after the women arrived, relaxed, glassy-eyed patrons trained their sights on them, cloaking them in silent disapproval. A small cluster of Negro men sat in the far back corner, eyeing them before turning their backs. White WAC officers were clustered at the opposite end of the room. Clearly they would not defy the God of their bigotry, even abroad.

"Seems like we're *allowed* but maybe not *welcome*," Bernadette said, her eyes narrowing.

Spotting the bartender's faint smile, Judy tilted her chin at him as he wiped down the bar.

"Bartender's the only one who matters," she said.

No one would argue with that in a pub.

They seated themselves at an empty table near the edge of the bar. "Well, then, we've waited long enough! Get us some drinks, girl," Bernadette said, pounding the table with her delicate hands.

Judy ordered a round of ale pints for the group. She overheard Mary Alyce asking Bernadette about accessories she liked. It looked like Stacy was taking notes on a napkin underneath the table. They were starting to think about Christmas now, and the whole battalion seemed to be focused on White Rabbit gifts. Mary Alyce and Stacy made a good team, gathering intel, but Judy thought they were wasting their time. Bernadette would be delighted with any gift they got her that was shiny and heartfelt.

As she waited, a tall white man approached. He was also waiting to order, but she felt him giving her furtive glances. When she turned to check, he looked away. But seeing him even with a coy glance confirmed how handsome he was: he had thick, dark, curly brown hair that curved over one side of his head in a perfect, distinguished wave. When he looked elsewhere, she saw his brown eyes were framed by wild lashes that faded to a light brown the farther away from his pupils they grew.

She stared at him a moment too long and saw that a dimple in his right cheek deepened when he smiled. Their eyes met for a moment before he cleared his throat.

"Pardon my staring," he said. "Are you with the postal battalion?"

"I am," she said.

"Pleased to meet you. I'm Bernard Welsh," he answered, like he couldn't wait to tell her his name. "Thank you for your service."

He stuck out his hand, like he had seen Americans greet one another that way and now it was his turn to try. Judy timidly offered her hand, afraid of offending him but too aware of the other white people around them. Bernard seemed to understand her stiff handshake, but she wondered if she imagined that he held her hand a second too long.

"My lady," the bartender was saying, trying to get her attention. She had forgotten to pay him for the drinks.

"I'm so sorry," she said, realizing, and reaching into her purse for the money.

Bernard put his hand up in protest and nearly brushed against her as he moved to put money on the bar. "Please, let me buy you and your friends a round. It's the holidays! And in appreciation for your service. Your name is?"

"Oh! Uh, thank you, sir," she said, her eyes jerking up from her purse. "Judy Washington."

"Thank you, Private Washington, for all you do," Bernard said. He looked like he wanted to say something more, but he didn't. Instead, he set down his money and paused as she collected the beers.

She had never hesitated in her life to say what she felt, but now she found herself grasping for words. It did not seem right to say "You're welcome," nor did silence seem the appropriate response. "Thank you for the drinks" is what she decided on. "Are you also a soldier?" She realized it was a silly thing to ask as soon as she spoke. He wasn't wearing a uniform, after all.

Bernard scoffed. "No, I'm a paperwork sort of gentleman. I help the Allied with logistical matters. And since you're with the postal battalion, you must be stationed at King Edwards now. I might see you there. I sometimes have business at my alma mater," he said, showing off that dimple again.

The idea that Judy might see him again made her stomach move the way it did when she sat atop the Wonder Wheel at Coney Island. Herbert had convinced her that the only way to dispel fear was to look it right in the eye. She thought a rickety Ferris wheel perched right alongside the Atlantic was a bad place to start, but no, he'd insisted, that was why it was so perfect. He'd said that even as she trembled, holding his hand, his calm voice keeping her from completely falling apart as the wheel slowly began to turn toward the street and they were floating.

"Yes, we have been there for more than a month now," Judy

said. "This is our first break from the mail, since, as you know, there's not much that can be done for leisure there on campus."

Bernard's eyebrows furrowed. "Well, maybe not the buildings you've been confined to. But in my day, there were quite a lot of ways to pass the time over at ol' KES," he chirped, a look of nostalgia in his eyes. Remembering himself and her friends, he said, "Oh, we can discuss that some other time, perhaps. Your beer is getting warm."

Judy nodded, looking quickly down at the pints and over at the smirking faces of her friends. She would never hear the end of her chat with a handsome English man at the bar which delayed their drinks. Her face was hot with embarrassment and something else she couldn't quite name. "Yes, well, thanks again, Mr. Welsh."

"The pleasure is mine," he said, tipping an imaginary hat before he turned around to order his own drink.

She nodded, careful to turn her attention to her friends, who leaned in with teasing looks on their faces as they took their drinks.

"Who's your new friend?" Bernadette said with a lilt.

"I wouldn't say we're *friends*," Judy said, perhaps a little too quickly. "His name is Bernard Welsh. He's one of the local Allied contractors."

Mary Alyce eyed the back of his head. "Seems too handsome to be a mere contractor."

Judy remembered her vows to Herbert, even as her attention threatened to follow Mary Alyce's gaze to Bernard's back. Better to distract herself with a change of subject. "I wish we had a bar at King Edwards," she finally said, sipping her beer.

"And a place for us to do our hair," Bernadette chimed in.

"A proper gym for us to play basketball, or something," Stacy added.

Mary Alyce tilted her head at Stacy. "Are you tall enough for basketball?"

Stacy frowned, "You calling me short, Dixon?"

"Sounds like it to me!" Judy said, grateful for a change of subject. "Too bad we can't get you height for Christmas. Besides, it's no use dreaming. Big Ma just signed off on the Thanksgiving celebration. She'll probably tell us to focus and not be distracted from our purpose."

"'No mail, no morale,'" Stacy said with a hint of mockery in her voice.

At least back in Iowa, they had their pick of restaurants and military social clubs, even if many of them were segregated. They could socialize with the occasional US Air Force personnel flying across country on their way to missions in the Pacific Theater of Operations. But in the month since they'd arrived in England, they had been relegated to eating, sleeping and dreaming about that blasted mail backlog. Their calf muscles and shoulders ached from the repetition, the dust and silt settled into their fingernails and hair. Hours stretched into days.

"Maybe we're just sore that we've been without a break for so long," Mary Alyce said, draining her pint. "It's possible this can be our watering hole from here on out. It's not so bad." She finished her thought by looking around. Judy noticed that the crowd was starting to thin out.

And Judy wasn't so sure that the Better Beer Pub was the best place for them to kick back. The air felt tense and divided, the way it did in every segregated place back home. But maybe she was just unaccustomed to sharing social space with white people. That would take some getting used to.

When no one said anything in response to Mary Alyce's cheerful declaration, she slapped the table and said, "I'll take your silence for agreement. Time for another round."

At the bar, a white WAC private with piercing blue eyes approached Mary Alyce as she waited. Judy felt a sinking sensation in her gut, and when the woman spoke to her, Mary Alyce turned red in the face before she spat something out angrily, which made the private step back. Mary Alyce was breathing heavily when she returned to the table with the beer.

"Are you all right, honey? What did that woman say to you?" Judy asked, touching Mary Alyce's hand as she sat down.

"She said the atmosphere would be better without the Negroes stinking it up," Mary Alyce said, her voice still trembling with anger. "I told her I was one of those Negroes that she was talking about and that she should be ashamed to speak about her fellow privates that way."

They were all stunned into silence.

"You're probably right that we should have a place of our own to relax," Mary Alyce continued. "This place will not do."

Judy patted her friend's hand, and they all sipped their beer, the mood sullen. Just when they were beginning to feel like they belonged in the military, and to a cause helpful to America, the reach of racism pulled them back to reality. Back home, they could each find solace from the blunt edges of bigotry by being with their people, in their homes, in the places that welcomed them, even if they had to be set apart by race. They needed to create a place just like that at KES. And because it was a concept so simple and plain to Judy, she had an idea of how to accomplish just that.

NINETEEN

CHARITY

Shortly after the women's first weekend passes, Charity had landed on a gift for Abbie for Christmas. She'd found a brass pin in the shape of a bullhorn. It was small and funny, she thought. Inexpensive and friendly, that was what she was going for. A small token of thanks for all her hard work. Secretly, however, all Charity could think about was mistletoe. Because the only gift she really wanted was to press her lips to Abbie's in some private moment.

And while the thought passed her mind, Abbie walked into her office with an uncharacteristically glum expression.

"That's not exactly a festive look on your face," Charity said, trying to get her to smile. It made Charity feel better when Abbie was in a good mood. But it was not to be. Abbie held out a paper folded in half.

"You won't feel like smiling either once you read this."

Major Adams—
It has come to our attention that your Central Postal Battalion
girls have been seen behaving in a manner unbecoming of officers
in the Women's Army Corps. I intend to see for myself when
I visit there shortly for an overdue inspection. In the meantime,
deal with your officers. Do not let it happen again.
General J. G. Nash

Deal with it and do not let it happen again kept catching her
eye until she folded up the faint yellow paper and placed it
under her palm. She fiddled with her pencil with one hand,
wiggling it and tapping the eraser to the desk. "Some early
Christmas present this is," she muttered to Abbie.

"How can you make a joke at a time like this? We could
be in serious trouble."

Charity sat back in her chair, folded her hands. Abbie was
right; they could be sent home, court-martialed, depending
on the complaint and who it came from. If it involved the in-
termingling of races, the WAC officers higher in the chain
of command could say they were undermining the American
way of life, all while declaring that they were there to support freedom.

She was in a complex position, being a Negro woman in
a position of influence. Her station was supposed to give her
power. But in the US and even in England, real power never
belonged to Negroes, especially not Negro women. All she
could really control was the way things looked to outsiders,
and that wasn't real power, just the optics of it.

"Well, I figure the worst that could happen is we end up
sailing home early," Charity said, finally.

That got Abbie to smile. "That doesn't sound so bad, actually. We could make it home in time for the start of 1945,
maybe?"

JOSHUNDA SANDERS

"It's a date," Charity added.

They shared a brief chuckle, their laughter rising and falling at the same time. When their laughter fell away, Charity started thinking about the line J. G. Nash mentioned about his upcoming inspection.

That Nash had recently been reassigned to the European Theater of Operations, much to Charity's chagrin, was hardly a coincidence. She suspected that no matter how efficient, clean and orderly her women were, inspection would somehow turn up something she needed to improve.

As the US military had begun to integrate more branches of its operations out of pure necessity because so many had died, racial violence against Negro soldiers was on the rise, inside and outside the armed forces. In Texas, a Negro WAC was court-martialed because a local sheriff didn't believe she was a part of the military and accused her of impersonating an officer. Another woman in Arizona was beaten by civilians and barely survived.

The Six Triple Eight had been shielded by most of what other units faced because of where they were located and the fact that they stayed busy—in the weeks since they'd arrived they cleared an average of sixty-five thousand pieces of mail each shift. At the rate they were going, they were ahead of schedule and even with setbacks in combat, Charity estimated they would be done by February.

But first, she needed to figure out how to pass inspection from J. G. Nash, who she knew would try to find every reason to stall their progress. Her mother had always told her that being born tall and stately was a good thing. Being used to having eyes on her primed her for pressure most of the time. "Be so good they can't ignore you," her mother said. "If your excellence doesn't command their attention, your presence will."

In church, at home, doing club work after school—all of it prepared her for the scrutiny of leading a battalion of Negro women, the most underestimated and undervalued members of the US Army. Even as she excelled in most of her officer training and had earned all the bars and stars on her uniform, the tests came frequently, big and small.

Charity viewed Nash's visit as one more of these tests. Knowing the army the way she did, the note was only a few days ahead of the surprise visit. She would have to be more prepared and watchful than usual. She had passed this kind of test before. She would do it again.

General Nash appeared at the warehouse where the women worked at 0700 hours on an icy Wednesday morning in early December. Charity was there early with Abbie, managing the few hundred women on the first shift. General Nash looked smaller than the last time she'd seen him in Fort Des Moines, probably because he was without the Military Police escorts that usually accompanied him.

He walked through the door of the warehouse, his eyes roaming and taking in the women working in their winter gear, a low hum of conversation, bags and boxes of paper on nearly every table. Charity tapped Abbie on the shoulder briefly; she was reading something.

"General Nash, sir," Charity said.

"At ease," he said, slowly, like he didn't mean it. He chewed at a toothpick so aggressively his temples pulsed. "I imagine you've been expecting me?"

"Yes, sir. My women are always ready for inspection."

"I'll be the judge of that," he said.

Within the next fifteen minutes, Charity rang the obnoxious lunchtime bell to signal a break for the first shift. When the women grew quiet, she instructed them to be at ease and informed them that General Nash was there from headquarters for an inspection of their unit.

Some of the women shifted in their seats, but mainly they remained quiet and still until Charity said, "Thank you for the moment you just allowed. As you were."

They went back to work, unfazed.

"It's my understanding that there are hundreds more of you," General Nash said in a huff. "Where are the rest?"

Charity tried to keep the irritation out of her voice. "Sir, we work three different shifts. The other women will start work later tonight and just went to bed."

"Sounds irresponsible to me," he said, starting to walk around the women. He stopped to glare at Judy, and then, with a puzzled look, Mary Alyce. He kept walking, arms folded behind his back, eyes filled with disgust. He stopped near a pile of mail and cleared his throat.

He turned to face Charity. "Well, I can't have this kind of half-hearted representation from the battalion, Major. You need a better plan for inspection, at least, or else I'll find a white first lieutenant looking for opportunity to show you how it should be done."

Shame and anger coursed through Charity. She could feel Abbie willing her to keep her temper, to mind her words, but she was turning over the words he used in her mind, and they twisted like a knife in her gut. In the army, the word *first* in a platoon and often in rank, was reserved for whites. Negro units sometimes got second, third or fourth, but never first. So she wasn't sure if it was the word *white*, *first*, or *first lieutenant* that made it hard to stay neutral.

"Over my dead body, sir," she spat out.

Abbie gasped audibly. Charity shot her a wilting look. Abbie shook her head. It became very quiet in the warehouse. Charity stood taller. She would not yield. She would pass this test.

Nash tilted his head. "What's that now, girl?"

"I said," Charity said, walking closer to him but stopping before she got too close, "Over. My. Dead. Body. Sir."

General Nash was furious. The gall of this girl, thinking she could talk to him like this in a room full of Colored women. She knew that's what he was thinking by his expression and yet she would not be moved.

He stayed where he was. Nash didn't want her to think that because she towered over him, like everyone else, that she had the power to make him feel smaller, but she knew that she did.

"Major, if that's how you want it, that may be how it has to be," he said, and turned on his heels to stomp off.

Charity felt hot in the face but triumphant. Abbie stood proudly beside her. "Are you okay?"

"I feel quite well," Charity responded, and it was true, which surprised her.

"The legend of Big Ma will only grow larger now," Abbie said, smirking. "Big Ma told the little racist general who looked like a toy soldier what was what!"

Charity scoffed, but there was a twinkle in her eye. She knew that was not the last she would hear from General Nash after the inspection, but she let herself grin all the same. As far as she was concerned, she had not only passed the test, she'd aced it.

News of Charity's interaction with General Nash spread as quickly as Abbie suggested it might, making her a modern-day legend for the women. As was the tendency with a new, hot phrase, the refrain of resistance in everyday conversation was "Over my dead body, sir." As was the custom in the Negro oral tradition, her encounter with Nash grew more embellished and outlandish with each telling.

By the time the last few hundred women in the Six Triple

Eight heard the story, Charity had put the man in a head-lock and challenged him to a fist fight outside the warehouse where they all worked—a fight from which he ran scream-ing like a frightened boy.

In her quarters—a relatively spacious room she had to her-self—Charity kneeled to pray in her bonnet and slippers, and chuckled to herself about the scene Nash made. She knew her family would be proud that she had stood up to his bul-lying. But her smile faded as she thought about what would come next.

The women of Six Triple Eight saw in Charity a heroine who shared all their features, to help them remember them-selves and to hold fast to their pride. What they didn't know is that they motivated her, too.

The following week, Charity found a small pocket of time to find a plain gift box for Abbie's pin and a golden ribbon from one of the officers prone to decorating. She had not passed down word of the mysterious complaint to headquar-ters to the Six Triple Eight rank-and-file because she believed her battalion deserved to move freely in England in exchange for all they were doing. It was hard to make a direct correla-tion between getting the letters to their intended soldiers and the improvements on the battlefields, but combat was easing, fewer lives were being lost. More boys were going home. They were part of a system that had been broken but was on the mend, and the women under her command were a big part of that repair.

Charity was in her office with Abbie's gift, looking for scis-sors in her desk to clip the end of a red ribbon when Abbie knocked. Charity clapped a hand over the box, nearly smash-ing it, looking up while she slid it onto her lap.

Abbie came in before she was done fidgeting. "What have you got there, Major?"

"Is that what you came to ask me about, Captain?" Charity asked quickly, bunching up the trailing ribbon and stuffing it all inside the desk drawer. It would obviously have to wait.

Abbie smiled knowingly. "No, ma'am. It appears we begrudgingly passed inspection," she said and handed Charity a telegram.

Major Adams:
While it remains my official opinion that a white woman should be in charge of the battalion, my inspection of the 6888th Central Postal Battalion, limited as it was by the number of WACS available, was satisfactory. We intend to follow up to ensure you can maintain the level of service expected by the US Army.
General J. G. Nash

Charity folded the telegram, annoyed. She had a good mind to crumple it up and throw it away. Instead, she kept it. She tucked it right beside Abbie's gift inside a drawer so that Abbie couldn't see. Then she stood and changed the subject entirely, wanting a moment to think about something more than just the next inspection or complaint, since it felt like it was all she was thinking about lately. "Have you found the proper gift for your CO yet, Abigail?"

"That is confidential, ma'am," Abbie said with a coy smile. "But yes, if you must know. It's quite something. And you? Is a certain Executive Officer to receive something splendid for the holidays?"

Splendid? Charity wondered. She tried not to sigh. Maybe she needed something more than the pin. It was so small. A trinket, really. But Abbie wasn't fussy. She didn't wear makeup or jewelry. There were no rings on her hands, not yet. Thank God.

"Indeed," Charity said.

"Don't sound so enthused," Abbie said, raising an eyebrow. "You look serious all of a sudden. What are you thinking?"

Charity recovered from her rabbit hole of worry for long enough to change the expression on her face. "It's nothing—thank you for the news about Nash. I'll be sure to keep the ladies in line so we can keep the noise down around us."

She sounded more confident than she felt. That was the case with everything all the time for her now: with her superiors in the army and with her choice of gifts.

TWENTY

JUDY

From Margaret to Judy

Saturday, 10 December 1944

Dear Judy,
I hope this gets to you in time for the holiday. Is it as cold there
as it is here? The money you have been sending (thank you)
has given me a chance to take a day off from the market here
and there. I took a trip down to Manhattan to have a look at
the Rockefeller Center tree we love so much. They won't turn
on its lights because of the blackout restrictions here, but it's still
impressive. I may even get myself a small one to decorate.
*   I am getting as used to being on my own as I suppose I can*
get. I like my days off so much it's a wonder that I never tried
before. I guess I never had any reason to try, especially when
your father was alive.

The thing about hard work is that you don't realize how much it's taken out of you until you stop. That one day I slept in instead of getting up with the birds in the morning, I think my body was so relieved that the aches I've had in my knees all these years just eased up and they weren't cracking and talking to me anymore. The city is different, too, when you have a moment to stop and listen to it, to look at the quiet, let it seep in your bones.

When I sit still long enough, the city feels a little like back home. I don't want to get carried away, now. But I think what I mean to say is that your gifts to me have made me see some of what it must be like to be a free woman. They have taught me what money is for, and what good work can change.

Thank you for being the daughter you are. For all that you've given me.

Merry Christmas, Judy.

Love,

Mama

Judy read and reread her mother's letter, astonished by such a significant change in her mother since Judy had started in the army during the summer. Margaret had been so calloused in her spirit about labor that it was moving to Judy to hear her mother refer to the money from the WAC as a gift. She saw it as a way to repay the work ethic, the determination to survive that Margaret had instilled in her by setting an example.

All those early mornings, Ivory soap and coffee and toast in their nostrils. The soft sheen of Vaseline on her mother's elbows and hands, her cheeks glistening. They had worked so hard together, just to survive. To hear that her mother was using the money for relaxation was the best possible outcome.

If she could give that respite to Margaret, she wondered if she could help create the same kind of space for the Six Triple

Eight at King Edwards School. Their work was not as grinding or humiliating as working at the Bronx Slave Market, but it still was hard work. And it was not all their lives were meant to be. Margaret was the one who reminded her this time, instead of the other way around: they deserved rest, fun and joy.

They clearly weren't always welcome off post; if they wanted to travel to London, they could stay in the segregated American Red Cross hotels, but that was too far. What they needed was a space just for them.

She pulled on her coat one frigid Saturday morning. The foggy day was particularly quiet, the sky usually stirred up with warplanes was still and gray above her. The soft grass held frost that crunched beneath her boots as she walked beyond the main building to the old gym building at the back corner of the school's property.

To her left, there was a flurry of activity at the gate. A familiar, wavy-haired man ducked into a car. Her heart stuttered in her chest. Bernard Welsh, she was sure of it. Her stomach felt again like it had on that Ferris wheel, like it was dropping down into her knees. Remembering Herbert made her feel a flash of shame. She turned to the building and crossed her arms.

They needed: a place to lounge and talk, another mess hall, a place for them to have their hair done, and, at the immediate moment, some spot aside from the lobby of the main building for a Christmas party. Judy wanted to throw a party for her battalion family. They could exchange their White Rabbit gifts or whatever they wanted. Drink eggnog (spiked, of course) and get the band back together for a little dancing. Surely the Negro officers off post who had heard they were billeted there would be happy to have invitations.

It was decided. But it was just over two weeks before Christmas. She would have to ask Big Ma for permission. She looked at her watch, the sun breaking through the morning mist. She walked back toward the main building and took her chances walking by the lieutenant's office, which was empty. She had better luck at the mess hall, which was busy for breakfast.

Stacy was working, Bernadette was asleep, and Mary Alyce was talking to another officer, though she waved at Judy as she arrived and Judy waved back. When she spotted Major Adams sitting with Captain Campbell, she approached them both. She needed to ask them about this before she dealt with her growling stomach.

"Good morning, ma'am—permission to speak?"

"Yes. Good morning, Private," Adams said, as she dug into her eggs. "You look like you have big news?"

"Yes, ma'am, good morning," Judy said in a rush of breath. She wasn't winded, just excited. "I have a great idea for us, but I need help."

Major Adams chewed intently, like she was focused on every movement of her teeth. "You've certainly got my attention."

"The main challenge we had at Thanksgiving was seating everyone at the same time. But there's another building we haven't used that has overflow space for the mess hall and another kitchen. It has other areas we need, too, like a space for us to lounge and visit, room for us to make a hair salon."

The major glanced over Judy's shoulder, deep in thought. Then she said, "It's a great idea. You have my full support. With one caveat. We have inspections that appear to pop up suddenly. Which means I have to ensure that every area is to be kept up to code. So be sure that your renovations of that building won't lead to any more confusion. In fact, Captain Campbell will put you in touch with Mr. Bernard Welsh, who oversees new construction here, to ensure everything is as it should be. I can't afford to rile up headquarters in London any more than I have already."

Judy was delighted to have permission to proceed, but the mention of Bernard made her breath catch. She would worry about it later—how to make herself behave like the married woman she was. For now, she was ready to get to work.

TWENTY-ONE

CHARITY

From Rev. E. A. Adams to Charity

Sunday, 12 December 1944

Dear Edna:
I pray you have been as well as can be in the other Birmingham
as I like to call it. Our Advent festivities at the church are not
the same without you, but I know you are mighty busy with all
that is transpiring with the war.

By now, you may know this, but I hear the Rev. Thomas
Butler, an old friend of mine in the A.M.E. church has been
assigned chaplain at your post. Rev. Butler is a bit old-fashioned
and sometimes he can come on a little strong. But his heart is
in the right place.

Please show him as much grace as you can spare as you run
your operations. I know it will not be easy, but please try.

We will be wishing you a Merry Christmas from down this
way throughout the season as we celebrate Jesus' birth. Send us
a line when you can.
Love,
Daddy

Charity tried not to be too angry about Rev. Butler's assignment to the Six Triple Eight because, as her father noted, the
Christmas season was upon them. She could be charitable to
a man of the cloth, even as she resented his presence among
them. The army was giving her one hurdle after another to
leap over—cold weather, backlogs, inspections—and now her
father's friend's supervision to make sure they weren't sinning.

She was too tired to complain or be nervous about what
amounted to a spy who might also pick up on her closeness
to Abbie. Back home and in training, Charity thought she
was good about keeping her emotions concealed. On break
from their daily routines and restrictions on holiday, she was
a little sloppier. It was much easier to stand too close, to touch
Abbie's lower back. It was becoming more difficult for her to
monitor her behavior as it often felt like Abbie was responding, smiling at her just so, teasing slightly.

But the daily operations of the battalion were at full tilt.
Charity was up at 0330 hours, splitting her time between her
tiny office and barracks, barely getting enough sleep, on constant alert for another inspection from Nash.

Charity had last seen Rev. Thomas Butler as a little girl
and was concerned that despite her position and reputation
in the women's army, all he would see is the little girl he used
to know. This thought was reinforced by his cheery, infor-
mal greeting.

"Edna!" he exclaimed, grabbing her and holding her in a

tight hug that left her breathless. "Aren't you a sight for sore eyes?"

"I suppose so, Reverend," Charity said, readjusting her suit jacket, which he'd dislodged.

"I was delighted to hear that your unit had been without a chaplain and that I could be of use to you here," he said.

Charity smiled tightly at him as her hand rested at her side. She didn't think he was needed there at all, and the more time she spent with him, the more she felt that his assignment was a mistake. But clearly that blasted Nash and other superiors felt differently. If they could not find cause to replace her with a white officer, sending a Negro man to report back to them would do. But she would not be disrespectful of her father's colleague. "It was kind of headquarters to send you, to uplift us all with your faith. We are always grateful of any help we can get." It was the closest she could come to engaging him without lying. "Let's get you settled in. Tomorrow, you can lead worship in the auditorium for Sunday service."

The auditorium in the main building was where they held most of their gatherings, even as Judy enlisted the help of others to provide an alternative. Its unfinished, scuffed wood floors were perfect for Sunday sermons and Saturday night jubilees. A small stage at the far end of the space hosted the army band and those aspiring to recreate a WAC band when they needed a few tunes. Any officer not inclined to dance played cards or sat around gossiping.

The night before Reverend Butler's first service, a light above the lectern burned out. Charity took note and would get it fixed come Monday. They would have the light of day anyway, and that would have to do.

"Finally, back to your church roots," Abbie said, helping Charity to arrange chairs around the foot of the stage on Sunday morning.

"I'm in no mood for your smart comments," Charity said. "If you must know, Reverend Butler is a family friend."

"Ooh," Abbie started. "Even better. You must be so thrilled."

"Forget I mentioned it," Charity said.

"I was going to offer to introduce him, but since you know him better than I do..."

"Barely, but yes," Charity said. "I guess I must."

For the hundred or so gathered at the Sunday service, Charity channeled her father with a rousing, bright "Good morning, we have a new visitor joining us. A chaplain for our mighty battalion, the esteemed Rev. Thomas Butler, a family friend, here to deliver sustenance via the good word."

Reverend Butler's smile faded a bit as Charity gestured to him to come to the lectern. He must have been expecting a little more pomp and circumstance, and she had none. When he came, he climbed the short distance to the lectern. He squinted up, slightly, at the burned-out light and frowned. He rustled the paper in his hands, tugged at his collar like he was warm and, finally, turned to smile at them.

"Praise God we are able to gather another morning on God's green earth, Amen?"

"Amen," the crowd responded.

"Amen. Lord, we gather here today to ask you in this season of Advent and waiting to watch over these women. I ask particularly that you do so for their commanding officer, Edna, and her priorities. When the women want to engage in activities that do not serve you, Lord, she made sure that all the lights were working. Now it's time for praising you, but we have to do so in the dark."

Charity had bowed her head and closed her eyes, but at this bogus mention of light and dark, she looked up to train her eyes on the reverend, whose eyes were still closed. She should have heeded her intuition, but it was not too late.

He continued, "Please be a hedge of protection anyway for Edna Adams and all those under her command. Lord, please help her truly see the light, pun intended, and ensure that she sees fit to turn away from the sinful path to serve only you and her country. In Jesus' name we pray, let the church say, Amen," he finished, opening his eyes without looking at Charity, who tried not to fidget as her temper flared. A buzz in the audience made her cheeks hot.

She had a mind to go and arrange for him to leave that very moment, but Abbie, seated beside her, dug her elbow into Charity's ribs. "Not now," Abbie warned.

The choir began singing, and while their voices soothed her, her mind turned back to the conversation she needed to have with Reverend Butler about his future elsewhere.

As soon as the service concluded, Charity turned to Abbie. "Please make sure Reverend Butler reports to my office in five minutes. And have my driver prepared to escort him off premises."

"Yes, ma'am," Abbie said without hesitation.

Fifteen minutes passed between when Charity stomped to her office, reflecting on the best way to fire the reverend in a way that was respectful and organized. When he walked into her tiny office, she said, "Don't bother to sit down, Reverend, because you don't have much time. In one hour, my driver will take you to London. I'm afraid we won't be needing your services."

"Oh, Edna," the reverend said. "I was just carried away by the spirit. I didn't mean anything by it."

Charity took a deep, bracing breath. Some man was always telling her that what she felt wasn't valid, but she had been striving all her life for respect, and it was hard won. The smallest slight, intentional or not, wounded her confidence, and she couldn't manage that on top of everything else she had to contend with.

"Reverend, your saving grace is that my father is fond of you, and I respect you as his colleague," Charity said, straining to keep the fury out of her voice. She had learned from her father, especially, not to tolerate even the slightest show of disrespect in public, because it invited bigger ones. "But putting me down in front of my officers is not something I can abide. I hope you understand. I will see you back in South Carolina, perhaps, and I will let my father know you sent your regards."

The reverend appeared like he was searching for words. As he looked at her, she added, "As I mentioned, you have about an hour before you'll be leaving. Goodbye," she said. Abbie appeared behind the reverend at the door. He muttered goodbye before turning around to gather his things.

TWENTY-TWO

JUDY

Judy, Stacy and Bernadette were tickled at the reverend's swift exit, and he quickly became the talk of their battalion over breakfast the next day. The business with the light bulb and the prayer that sent Big Ma into a tizzy was too delicious to stay quiet about, even as Judy began to busy herself with preparing for the battalion's Christmas celebration, less than two weeks away now.

"You have to admit it was pretty funny that we had good light to sin in and left him in the dark for his long prayer," Stacy said.

"He also managed to look slovenly, even in a uniform," Bernadette pointed out. "Hurt my eyes. And my spirit."

"I rather liked him," Mary Alyce added.

It was Stacy who couldn't do the same. "Mary Alyce, I feel

like you're about to say something only a white girl would say, in five seconds."

Mary Alyce had a tortured look on her face. "He reminded me of the chaplain in Iowa is all. It was the chaplain there, besides Judy, who helped me see that my situation wasn't some unfortunate accident—that maybe it was destiny."

"Don't let these preachers sell you on being a Negro woman as a calling," Stacy said. "They only put it that way because they want you to feel good about giving them all your hard-earned money."

"And cleaning up after white folk," Judy added.

"And making sure you don't go having dreams of your own," Bernadette said.

"Maybe so," Mary Alyce said, unsure.

As the bugle sounded to signal their second shift of the day, the women cleared out, with Judy and Mary Alyce lagging behind. When Judy emptied her tray and situated it on the dirty pile near the door, she touched Mary Alyce's arm. "Don't feel too down about the reverend, okay? I know you've had a lot of friends come and go." Judy wasn't sure how Mary Alyce would take her gesture, but it was worth it to try. Even losing someone who reminded you of someone else could feel disappointing.

Mary Alyce looked surprised. "Thanks, Judy. That means a lot."

Judy gave Mary Alyce's arm a light squeeze. "You'll have plenty of work to keep you busy this afternoon. I'm going over to work on that old building today."

"Skipping your shift to have fun, huh?"

"Hardly," Judy said, although she was looking forward to it. As promised, Captain Campbell had invited Bernard Welsh back to the post. "Well, maybe a little. Remember Mr. Welsh from the Better Beer Pub? The one who bought our drinks?"

Mary Alyce looked at her slyly. "Oh, well, that's...convenient for you, isn't it?"

Yes, that was the word—*convenient*. But also uncomfortable. "It is, Mary Alyce. But you have to swear that you won't tell anyone. I am devoted to my husband, but I don't know. I felt something when I met Bernard."

Mary Alyce leaned closer to Judy and said, "And it seemed he did as well. Judy, just enjoy your time with him. Your secret is safe with me."

The bugle sounded again, meaning that Mary Alyce was late.

"Thank you, Mary Alyce. I'll let you know the details about the new spaces as soon as I know them."

"You better," Mary Alyce called, running to the warehouse.

Armed with a new task and the appointment to meet Bernard at the unused building, Judy let herself take in its potential. A brush of grass hit the top of her boots as she walked the perimeter. It was a modest, one-story building with a cellar and Bernard stood in front of its entrance, turning a white tube in his hands.

"Private Washington," he said in a jolly voice.

"Mr. Welsh. I thought I spotted you just yesterday. Glad you could join us again so soon."

He looked at the ground, searching as if he had dropped something. "Ah, yes. I met with the captain and brought the blueprints she requested." He lifted the tube slightly. "I was also eager to help you with this unique undertaking."

"That's kind of you," Judy said.

"It's nice to be back here. Like in the good old days," he said, the blueprints tucked under his arm, his hands clasped behind his back. The sky was bright blue and there was a crisp breeze, which fluttered through his wavy hair. He was looking at the building, before his eyes met hers. She felt uneasy, then a prickle of something electric. "So many good memories of this place. Have you been inside? There's even a bowling alley."

So that was what was down there, Judy thought. "In the cellar? No, I was afraid to go wandering down there alone. I thought I'd wait until we talked about the project before I did too much more on my own."

"Makes sense." He pulled the blueprints out from under his arm and unfurled them. "Do you mind?" He lifted the left edge of the paper so that she could hold it, which she did.

"Thank you. So here we are," he said, pointing to the edge of the prints, close to his right hand. "Oh, and please do call me Bernard. Mr. Welsh is my father." He chuckled. "But I will call you Private Washington. I want to be respectful."

"Judy is fine," she said, that warmth rising in her cheeks again. He was like the sun, the way he beamed at her. She distracted herself by taking in the small writing on the blueprints.

"Very good, Judy," he said, pausing.

"How much space do we have to work with?" Judy felt suddenly self-conscious and wondered if her inner awkwardness was coming across on the outside. The silence stretched between them.

"Obviously, everything on the bottom here is occupied," he said. "That leaves the other three areas. You have ideas for what they should be?"

"Yes. A beauty salon in the infirmary. An upgrade to the gym, and the kitchen as an extension of our tiny mess hall," Judy said, satisfied that she finally had an easy answer to something.

"A woman who knows what she wants," Bernard said. A dozen thoughts crowded her mind. She kept them there. "How can I best help?"

"We don't have much time, and there's still a lot of mail to get through. I'd like to have everything ready by Christmas."

"Very well," Bernard said. They walked inside and he walked a few paces from the front of the old gym so that he was able to see both the old mess hall and the infirmary. He put his hands in his pockets and said, "For those uses, I don't imagine you'll run into any code or inspection conflicts, which is the reason I'm here. The buildings are all quite structurally sound. But that infirmary never saw a truly sick student in my day," he said, a wry grin on his lips.

"You know that from firsthand experience?"

"I can neither confirm nor deny my false sicknesses," Bernard said. "In any case, for the mess hall, I think I can procure a military discount on food and drinks for you from our friends at the Better Beer Pub."

"Even for us?" Judy said, remembering the mixed reception there.

"Of course. Not all of us share the perspective some backward Americans have about skin color. We only see you as Americans. That was true even for my wife, may she rest."

Of course he had been married. Judy was startled, and she tried to keep from jerking her head to look at him, but she failed.

"Hazel was a Negro," he continued. "We met in France. She lived there as an expatriate from Harlem. Part of the Renaissance there in arts. I knew so little about it, but apparently Langston Hughes, Richard Wright, James Van Der Zee…the list is very long of the Negroes who were writing and taking photographs, making art that defined what it was to be Colored beyond the confines of slavery. They were all children of the South whose families had been a part of the Great Migration. They were now in a generation of Negroes who dis-

228

covered new possibilities for themselves, and new expressions of what it meant to be a Negro."

Judy was impressed: a British white man who knew Negro culture enough to speak intelligently about it. She could hear the respect in his voice. No wonder she felt so comfortable around him, like she could relax.

"Hazel's particular talent was singing. She sang so beautifully, and with such sorrow. That's how we met. I overheard her and when I followed her voice, I knew at once we would marry. I felt when I met her that I had met someone whom I could love. I wonder if there's a word for that—it was almost a premonition."

Listening to Bernard talk about love made Judy realize she had never experienced a love like what he described: an instant, inevitable, electric connection. The difference between that and what she felt for Herbert was the difference between a warm cup of cocoa and the crack of lightning in the sky.

"What happened to her?"

Bernard looked down at the ground. "She was in the wrong place at the wrong time. Killed in enemy fire three weeks after we married."

Judy felt his profound loss, the arbitrary unfairness that his wife would be one of the millions lost to war. "I am so sorry, Bernard."

His eyes were wet, but his tears didn't fall. "Thanks for that. For listening."

Judy was struck by how much more she wanted to learn about this man. What had it felt like to marry a Negro American? What had Hazel been like? But she was also aware that these were not questions a married woman should pose to a widower.

Bernard misread her silent questions and said, "You must be eager to get on."

"Yes, of course," she replied, flustered, the moment between them gone. "But you've been so helpful," she said. "Please let the captain know when you can return. As we get materials for every space, we'll want you back to make sure it's all up to code."

Bernard considered her, looking at her like something precious he'd found, or maybe she was imagining it. "I'm happy I could assist. Yes, I'll certainly follow up with your CO. Best of luck, Judy. Until next time."

She knew it was awkward to wave goodbye from such close proximity, but her arm and hand wagged. She immediately turned and walked fast, then ran, back to the barracks, where she wet her face with a small rag and pressed her hands against a wall to steady herself.

Listening to Bernard talk about Hazel made her realize that something more could be possible between them than she had allowed herself to imagine. But it was still a farfetched fantasy. She was a married woman. And she loved Herbert. She missed him dearly. It took a few moments all the same for her to breathe regularly and allow her pulse to slow, her heartbeat easing with her slowed-down thoughts.

TWENTY-THREE

MARY ALYCE

Winter in Birmingham reminded Mary Alyce of home, her solitary mornings on the farm in Vermont, when she would be up before the sun illuminated the sky. When it was too early to feed the chickens or tend to the cows, she found her peace in the kitchen, warming bread, spreading the strawberry preserves they jarred during the summer over toast, flipping through the tin box of worn index cards, written in her grandmother's ragged script, and thinking about what she could pull together for lunch and dinner that night.

Now that Judy was throwing herself into the building renovation for Christmas and had enlisted Mary Alyce to help her sort out the new mess hall, they had more time together to discuss menus and supplies, to work together on making their home away from home as cozy as it could be. The war was slowing down in the European Theater and was spreading now to Japan and Manila.

The air was cool enough to be more rejuvenating than coffee or tea, brisk but not yet frozen, just as she liked it. She enjoyed the same kind of quiet and solitude as she woke up for an early morning shift at 0400 hours. Everything moved quickly as the women were beginning to make significant headway on clearing the backlog that had seemed so daunting just weeks ago.

As a result, instead of working six days a week, Major Adams said they would reduce their work shifts. An early Christmas present to allow for more leisure. Mary Alyce used the time to come up with a list of gifts to make for her friends—all food related. She wasn't sure it was the most exciting idea, but it was at least reliable. She knew Stacy liked sweets and Bernadette carried hot sauce from home in her purse and Judy would eat breakfast for lunch and dinner if she could. She thought of decadent cookies and quiches, but there was still time to brainstorm while they awaited supplies.

It did take some getting used to working solo on sorting the mail, while Judy focused solely on the building renovation. When she arrived that morning to the work area they usually shared at the warehouse, she found an envelope with the official US Army seal at the center of Judy's table. Mary Alyce looked around her at the other officers to make sure she could slide the letter discreetly to her desk.

The envelope was not sealed, and like the other mail she peeked at, she couldn't help herself. She pulled out its contents—a folded telegram from October 16, 1944.

We deeply regret to inform you that PFC Herbert Washington reporting with the 337th Infantry Battalion has been designated Missing in Action after D-Day operations at Omaha Beach in

June. A notice of this unfortunate circumstance has also been sent to his relatives. Given the amount of time that has passed, PFC Washington is presumed dead at this time. We understand that this is distressing news, but we will certainly share an update with you if one is warranted. Our most sincere and heartfelt condolences to you during this tragic time.

Mary Alyce felt a deep pain in her chest as she refolded the telegram and placed it back in the envelope. She put her palm over her heart and closed her eyes. Then she began to pace, nibbling at the corner of her nails, something her mother had always tried to discourage, but it helped with her anxiety.

Knowing a truth that her friend didn't know yet was one thing. But knowing such a brutal, devastating truth was another. This would change Judy's life and break her heart. Mary Alyce was processing it all when she realized with a start that Stacy had arrived for her shift.

"You look paler than usual, Mary Alyce," Stacy said. "Everything okay?"

It was not. Mary Alyce slid the telegram under a stack of papers. "Oh, sure. Just a sad one, is all."

"They're all sad in one way or the other," Stacy mused. "But you might want to pick up the pace before Landry or somebody sees you over here pacing around and not working."

Mary Alyce dutifully sat down and plastered a smile on her face. "Good thing I've got you to keep me calm and keep me working."

"Don't mention it," Stacy said. "Always happy to help."

Mary Alyce put the telegram in her pocket after Stacy walked away, and began to sort the other letters. She tried to pay attention to the day's tasks, sorting letters in the middle of the alphabet that were at least a year old from their stamps, but her mind kept pulling her back to the letter she had in her pocket. It was a reminder of just how fragile all their lives were.

Mary Alyce felt it best to wait before she told Judy this news, but she was torn about whether that was the right decision. Judy was so excited about the big reveal of the renovated space; it seemed only right to let her have one more Christmas believing her husband was alive and safe. In a couple of weeks, when the flurry of activity would die down, before the New Year, Mary Alyce would tell her. This was news that should wait.

And still, the calculation made her heart hurt. When was a good time to tell your friend her husband had died? This made her reconsider how her mother had kept the news from her about her father. Maybe she couldn't find the right time because there was no right time. Suddenly, she wanted more than anything to talk to her mother.

She looked furtively around for some paper and sat down to write a new letter to her mother.

Friday, 14 December 1944

Dear Mama,
I know it has been some time since you heard from me, and I hope you have not been too worried. I think I understand now why you were hesitant about me leaving Vermont, joining the Women's Army Corps. I was angry at you at first, for keeping my father's true race from me. I have so many questions for you about him, about your relationship, how you two met.

I have been thinking about secrets a lot lately. And I would like to know as much as you can share with me about him. All I know is that his name was Eugene Dixon. But where is he from? What did he do for a living? Where is his family now?

I have more questions than these, but answers to those are a good place as any to start. In the meantime, I have been doing my best to learn my new place in the world with the help of the other Negro women in the 6888th Central Postal Battalion, to which I have been reassigned. It's a bit easier now that we are in England, where we have been stationed for three months now, because we spend most of our time with one another. But I have no idea what life will be like for me when we get back home. We hear news on the radio or by way of other families that Negro vets are being attacked without punishment. The word is that the Nazis have learned a thing or two from Jim Crow laws in America.

But I'm trying not to think too far into the future. Even if we're not on the frontlines of this war, it's clear how fleeting life is, the smell of death in the air, recent news of a friend whose husband is likely dead.

I miss you and grandma. Please give her a kiss for me. Write when you can.

Love,
Mary Alyce

TWENTY-FOUR

JUDY

After her initial meeting with Bernard, Judy reported to Major Adams's office and found Captain Campbell there. Winter light streamed into the office from crisp skies, an unusual respite from the normally fume-filled air. Adams's office smelled like the stacks of paper that had settled onto the fine oak bookshelves and the desk, a musty scent of wood and dust. Major Adams's air of calm confidence further enhanced the place with gravitas.

Captain Campbell held a tube of paper like the blueprints Bernard had. "We were just talking about you, Private," Captain Campbell said. "Mr. Welsh gave us a copy of the plans as a courtesy, even though the project is yours to lead. Did you have a productive meeting?"

Productive was one word for it, she thought. "Yes, I'm working with Mary Alyce and the other ladies in my unit to ensure we have inventory to transform the spaces."

Captain Campbell let out an excited hoot, like an owl, startling both Judy and Major Adams. The women in the rank-and-file clearly weren't the only ones looking forward to the new building.

Major Adams cleared her throat. "This is exciting news. We'd like to have a look for ourselves, since he assured us there should be no compliance issues. Could you do the honors? Is there enough time?"

Judy didn't feel like she had the time to spare, but she also didn't feel like she could say no. "Of course I have time," she lied. And the three of them were off.

Back in the building with her commanding officers, Judy could see the stone and gloomy wooden beams through their eyes, like a hostess preparing for guests. In the kitchen area, when the water ran rusty, Major Adams frowned at her and Captain Campbell. "Mary Alyce will help with this," Judy said apologetically. "Ma'am, may we ask Lieutenant Landry for maintenance officers to fix the plumbing?"

The major nodded and said, "See to it, Captain," and Captain Campbell said she would.

The list for all that needed to be done kept growing longer. In the infirmary, it was an electrical strip so they could heat more than one metal stove for straightening combs and curling irons. That's where Bernadette would run the show.

The edges of the wooden floor in the old gym were chipped and curled as if wild horses had stomped through, kicking up important parts of the earth as they went. Softball and cricket jerseys hung in black frames, like shrouds against the wall. Captain Campbell flicked the lights on, then off again, revealing a loft with weights and exercise contraptions that weren't in much better condition. That would be Stacy's domain.

"I'm impressed by you and the other privates. You seem to have everything you need to make this a success," Major Adams said. As they approached the front of the building again, Judy realized they hadn't yet been to the bowling alley below, and in her nervousness with Bernard, she'd forgotten to ask him to show her.

"Thank you, ma'am. There's one more thing. A bowling alley."

"Oh, we have to see that," Captain Campbell said.

They had to venture down a dark, narrow set of stairs. A single light illuminated the sloping ceiling near the door, and it flickered like a candle on a drafty desk.

The lights below were much stronger once Judy turned them on, as if they were surprised they could still work on their own. Before them was a three-lane bowling alley, with shiny green-and-black bowling balls, holding the glint of new light, and pins that had been standing at attention in their respective lanes for too long. The wall behind them held rows of men's old two-toned shoes.

"Fantastic!" Captain Campbell exclaimed.

"It is, indeed," Major Adams said, her voice soft.

Judy was slightly surprised at Lieutenant Adams's emotion, but she was more surprised at her own. All her life, Judy had been taught to make every act of her body something to be bought or sold. But she had fought to unlearn that lesson by coming here. And she believed in her soul that there was a life beyond work, one that offered her the freedom to find joy. They had worked hard, and they deserved rest and space. It was a downright radical notion for Negro women to claim those things for themselves.

Back at the barracks, Judy shared with her friends that they were cleared to start the update on the new building the next morning. Since the idea emerged at Thanksgiving, Judy had shared her plans for the space and that she would need their help. They'd waited a week for news that Big Ma and Captain Campbell would release them from their mail duties in order to spend the next ten days before Christmas helping Judy with what they liked to call the hospitality building.

Judy volunteered to get them all up to speed on the new building the following morning. After breakfast, they walked to the far edge of the King Edwards School grounds. They were bundled up in their wool coats with scarves at their necks, with sweat suits underneath, with the exception of Bernadette, who wore jeans and flat patent leather shoes.

"We're going to be put to work," Stacy grumbled. "Is that the best you could do?"

"I should ask you the same whenever you're not in your uniform, ma'am," Bernadette said back. "Besides, I was not built for hard labor and I will not start dressing the part today."

Their lighthearted banter turned more serious when they were inside the building. Stacy took one look at the gym and wandered in slowly, her feet kicking at the raggedy edging along the side of the basketball court. "Looks like a bunch of people dropped boulders here on the side. But it's an easy fix. Maybe we can get carpet or benches, at least, so it doesn't look quite as shabby. Why do you want me to oversee the gym?"

"You're the most athletic of us all," Judy said. "You may be the only one of us who has actually touched a basketball."

"Fair point, Washington. Okay, add benches to your list. And no cheating, those supplies don't count as Christmas gifts."

Judy pretended to be hurt as she made a note of the benches they would need. Bernadette's salon needed chairs, mirrors, scissors and combs. The more Judy wrote, the more she began to feel that she might not get everything on the list.

As if she could read Judy's thoughts, Bernadette smiled and said, "Whatever we get we will use just fine and make do. Don't stress too much about it. It's good enough to just have a place for the ladies to get their hair done. And you'll be my first client."

Judy hadn't even thought about her hair in days, caught up as she was in all her planning. "Thanks?"

"No judgment, honey. What about music? Will the powers that be let us get a radio?"

"I can definitely ask."

Judy led them to what would become their second mess hall and found Mary Alyce already standing on a stepladder over the stove, opening up cabinets and blowing dust from the shelves, making Judy cough.

"I see you're already busy in here," Judy said brightly. Mary Alyce startled at the sound of her voice, like she wasn't expecting her, and Judy wondered if she was okay. Mary Alyce had been acting stranger than usual, but she tried to push it out of her mind. When Judy got busy, she sometimes made up distractions that she didn't need and only added to her stress.

"Empty cupboards hurt my soul," Mary Alyce said, and Judy laughed at the melodrama.

"Lawd, how did your fragile spirit make it all the way here to Birmingham?" Bernadette said, fanning herself with a piece of paper for emphasis.

"Hush, Bernie. It's true, I can't stand the thought of going hungry. But I am looking forward to making something and having something to eat other than Spam, I'll say that much."

"I even used to like Spam, to tell you the truth, when it was still new to me. Though you can't really know what all is in it," Stacy said. "We only ate the animals we raised on the farm, nothing in a can. My mother would be outraged."

Judy turned to Stacy and asked, "Well, what do you tell her the army is feeding you?"

"I don't. I make up stories about chicken salad sandwiches. Baguettes and cheese. She has no idea about our day-to-day. I think telling her I was eating canned meat would knock her over and send her sailing this way to fix it."

They all had a good laugh at that. "Maybe we can fix it without her going through the trouble," Judy said. She had her orders and so did they. They would have to work together and fast to make it happen by Christmas.

TWENTY-FIVE

CHARITY

Monday, 16 December 1944

Major Adams:
Authorization expenses that have landed on my desk suggest that some sort of building renovation is underway at King Edwards School. Before I approve a single item, I want a written justification for these extravagances during wartime. Everyone has been asked to cut back and this is particularly troubling given that the 6888th is billeted there temporarily and the length of your assignment has not been determined. You are advised to immediately cease planning adjustments to any facility until I have received written explication for such endeavors.

In the unlikely event that you make a strong case for this money to be spent, I may potentially approve any discretionary funding to be directed to recreation for the girls of the 6888th Battalion.
General J. G. Nash

Charity was looking forward to having a new space for the upcoming holiday. She could already envision the perfect wreath for the door, maybe a string of lights or two. Perhaps just a sprig of mistletoe. She hadn't yet wrapped Abbie's gift because she was still agonizing over whether she should get her something else. But the letter from General Nash made her fume.

First, they were women, not girls. Second, everyone was cutting back, certainly civilians, but they were doing essential work for the troops and they weren't asking for anything more than what the white battalions already had. The 6888th battalion wasn't just a random group of women. They had uprooted their lives, put themselves in harm's way to serve. They had already cut back enough.

But General Nash did have one point. Charity was a rule follower much of the time, and she had instructed her women to operate outside the chain of command. She should have expected a rebuke for doing so, but she was also testing her hard-earned rank. She was authorized to order supplies for her battalion, and requesting additional toiletries, foodstuffs and other essentials surely did not need special permission from her superiors.

She read the order twice as she prepared to begin the day. She had all the justifications she needed to respond in her head, she just had not yet committed them to paper. The letter confirmed for her that, no, she could not operate outside the confines of being a Negro woman, regardless of her rank. There would always be a General Nash to slap down her efforts to exert what little influence she was told she had by the insignia allowed on her uniform.

Charity let the letter and its contents live folded up in her desk for a day. She conducted inspections, checked the mail logs and other operational progress markers with Abbie. They were down to a few thousand letters each shift now, and the backlog kept shrinking.

This habit of deliberation, which carried over from her former life as a math teacher, was particularly helpful for the calculations she had to do in her life. Everything had to be worked out as an equation in her mind before she put pen to paper.

The next day, she started her morning with the following missive.

General Nash:
This letter is in response to your request for "written justification and explication" regarding the ongoing renovation of an old building at King Edwards School where my unit, the 6888th Central Postal Battalion, is currently stationed.

As I am sure you are aware, the 855 enlisted and auxiliary officers under my command are almost done with clearing a significant backlog of 2 million pieces of mail—double what we thought there would be. They have done magnificent work abiding by our mission and charge, "No mail, no morale."

We know tired soldiers cut off from inspirational words from their loved ones are more easily taken by enemies, vulnerable as they are to despair and the miseries of risking their lives at the battlefront. We all work five days a week now, but at the height of our busy time, the women were working seven days a week.

While their contributions in comparison to our frontline troops are modest and in some ways hard to measure, they have nonetheless been tireless and effective implementing a successful system for clearing a massive backlog for the soldiers moving rapidly across the European Theater.

Given their tireless and efficient work, I believe the battalion more than deserves a recreational space for rest and recuperation after the harsh, cold working conditions in which they toil, day

after day in a place far from their homes. If you are willing to pay for weekly travel for the battalion to segregated accommodations in the European Theater instead, I will cease planning the renovation of our building before Christmas.
Very Respectfully,
Major Charity Edna Adams

Four days after Charity sent her letter, each item from Judy's clipboard list arrived in quick succession. Women scurried to help with mirrors and boxes or enlisting Military Police to assist with the bulkier materials needed to mend the gym floor. There were just five days until the Christmas holiday, but she was confident the building would be ready in time.

TWENTY-SIX

JUDY

Judy felt a combination of excitement, self-imposed pressure and fatigue while she and her friends prepared for opening the building on Christmas Eve. There was one snag or another every day—a broken mirror, a chipped cup, food delivery delays, not enough beer, too much bread—it was endless. The only upside of the chaos was that it kept her thoughts away from her first Christmas away from Margaret and another one with Herbert at war.

Her drive to renovate the old building was her way of giving a gift to the battalion, and it was also a gift to herself to create something meaningful and worthwhile. She was also inspired by the power of an idea to spur others into action.

In the lead up to the grand opening, the women agreed they would exchange White Rabbit gifts after Christmas Eve dinner in the new mess hall and the old one so the whole battalion could eat and celebrate at the same time. Mary Alyce had done incredible work, polishing the new place until everything from the table surfaces to the edges of the utensils gleamed.

Christmas Eve morning in Birmingham was as frigid as any Bronx winter morning. Judy could see the warmth of their breath rising in frosty gray clouds as they stood in formation in front of the restored building. She could feel herself standing a little taller than usual with pride.

Major Adams had called them to gather and held a beautiful wreath with a scarlet bow. "Ladies, I won't keep you. This weather is not for speechifying," she said. "But I appreciate that you have worked very hard and you certainly deserve praise and recognition. While I know that hasn't come yet and may never come from the US Army, you should feel proud of the work you've done for our mission here to help the men fighting for our freedom and Private Washington's initiative.

"Some of my favorite memories at Fort Des Moines were created off duty. The most peaceful times of my life in the service were spent bending into the victory garden, buying a dress or two, fixing up my quarters with curtains and the like," she continued.

Judy tried not to show her surprise at the major revealing another side. Bernadette whispered just loud enough for her to hear, "Big Ma is a flesh-and-blood woman after all."

"The point is," Major Adams continued, "I know you've been focused on our goals here. But you should have some fun while you're at it. Not too much fun. But enough. And comfort. Thank you to Captain Campbell and Private Washington for coordinating this space for us to celebrate the holidays together. With that, I'll let her take it away," the major said, shaking Judy's hand, handing her and Captain Campbell the wreath to hang on the door. Judy felt her hands growing numb in the cold and the women of the battalion without gloves were starting to rub their hands together for warmth.

"Thank you, Major Adams and Captain Campbell for letting me run with this idea," Judy began, standing at the door. "Thank you to Mary Alyce, Bernadette and Stacy for their important help. Without them, this wouldn't have been possible."

Judy wanted to say more, but there was no need to go into it right now when it was so cold. She smiled and opened the door wide, inviting everyone in. Bernadette explained the salon schedule and how it would run. Mary Alyce proudly displayed the new mess hall; she'd pulled back the heavy burgundy drapes to let in more light.

The gym, though, was arguably the battalion's most improved space—at least Judy thought so. Benches on the basketball court's sidelines helped cover the erosion, with long mats beneath their legs. Off the side to the entrance, where an announcement board was once placed, Stacy made a small concession stand, with bags of peanuts. Judy whistled low, partly teasing. "Stacy, you put that country in you to good use in here."

Stacy waved Judy off, but she was grinning while she did. "I had a lot of help from Captain Campbell and the girls. We're gonna work off some steam in here."

At the end of the tour, Judy held up a hand as the women of the battalion buzzed with excitement. "Before we all break, we can either exchange our gifts by company or do it after dinner."

"Gifts first!" Major Adams yelled, her voice brimming with excitement, which made everyone laugh, including Captain Campbell.

"Okay, ladies, you heard Big Ma. Find your company, gather your presents and let's have a Merry Christmas," Judy said. She couldn't help but notice as the major awkwardly darted to her office, Captain Campbell pulled from her coat a beautifully wrapped box in matte ruby wrapping paper with a green ribbon.

Judy had been so preoccupied with the building, she hadn't had time to get gifts, with the exception of an apron she had sewn for Mary Alyce during one of their first weekend passes. It was black with a bread-loaf pattern. The women gathered around a full, beautiful Christmas tree at the far end of the gym, and Judy presented the apron to Mary Alyce shyly. "I hope it gets good use."

Mary Alyce unfolded the unwrapped present with glee. "This is so lovely," she said.

"It certainly looks homemade," Stacy said. "With love, of course."

Stacy offered a small box to Bernadette with both hands: a pink faux-pearl compact mirror. Bernadette squealed at it, then smothered Stacy in a hug. Bernadette's gift to Stacy was a sturdy, tortoiseshell-patterned comb. Not far from them, Major Adams and Captain Campbell also exchanged gifts. When Captain Campbell opened the small box, Judy wondered for a moment if it was a ring, though she knew the major would never be so bold. When Captain Campbell lifted a brass pin out of the box, she laughed until tears formed in the corners of her eyes. The pin's significance must be even greater than a diamond. Captain Campbell's gift to Major Adams was an all-weather poncho, which also seemed to move her; it reminded Judy of how the major had been wearing her raincoat, with towels around her shoulders, her first day on post. The gifts friends—sisters—gave each other, practical or not, were offered with such care and genuine love, Judy felt the true spirit of Christmas in the air.

She was about to invite them all to the dining room when Mary Alyce interrupted her. "Last but not least, we did not for-

get a gift—well, two, actually—for our fearless leader, Judy,"
Mary Alyce said. "In honor of your inability to properly scale
the wall during boot camp, we figured you needed a better
helmet. We even signed it. We thought it might give you the
extra courage to get on with it. But if that's too harsh—"

"It's not, she can take it," Stacy said.

"Well, we got you some flowers, too," Mary Alyce added
bashfully.

Her friends' signatures were visible on the Army green
helmet surface, in thick black ink, like love notes scribbled
for eternity. The yellow roses looked untouched by frost and
she wondered how they had even found them in this cli-
mate. Words left her as she teared up. All she could manage
was "Thank you," in a small voice, the sound cracking as
the women came in to hug her. It was the very best feeling,
to combine pride and joy with the celebration of the season.
She let herself feel it fully for once, instead of pushing it away.

The day after Christmas was delightfully lazy, as the women
enjoyed the new building for the first time and Judy took in
the rewards of the hard work she had done with Stacy, Bernadette and Mary Alyce. She felt with Mary Alyce, though,
that something was on her mind. Whenever they had a moment alone together, she seemed sad, like there was something she wanted to say. Judy would ask if she felt like talking
about it and all Mary Alyce would say was that it could wait
until the New Year.

With her mind and time freed up to think more about what
might have happened with her friend, Judy wondered if it
might have to do with her confessing her feelings for Bernard,
even if Mary Alyce had insisted she wouldn't judge. She was
just overthinking, tired from all the organizing and running
around to help with the renovation.

Judy tried to focus instead on the good that had come from her project, which she saw right away: women lingered over their meals a little longer than before. They worked hard as they could to finish up sorting the mail, and with the reward of visiting a salon waiting for them, they seemed better able to focus on finishing their tasks. And now, her friends could enjoy working in the areas of their passions, even if it was during their off hours.

Bernadette proclaimed herself in her element, for one. "I believe this is what they call the best of both worlds," she gushed to Judy. "I get to help others and I get to do the thing I love most in the world."

"You've always been a little too glamorous to be solely confined to the mail," Judy observed.

"Aren't you sweet," Bernadette said, coyly. "And telling the truth."

Mary Alyce was a better cook than they'd all expected. She cooked dishes she grew up with but took requests as well.

"You have come a long way since we found out you were Colored," Stacy said, putting great care into her words for once, so as not to offend. "But this food, Mary Alyce. You cook so well for a white girl!"

Mary Alyce smiled with pride. "I do know my way around a kitchen," she said.

"And that's why we might need to cut you off from the foodstuffs supply, before it becomes impossible to fit in our uniforms," Judy said with a grin.

"That's all the encouragement I need, Washington," Mary Alyce said, winking. "Speaking of encouragement, Bernard should be arriving to see the finished building soon." She lowered her voice. "Captain Campbell invited him by.

"Why don't you meet him in the front?" Mary Alyce said.

"You can have some privacy out there while everyone's distracted."

Judy felt her face get warm again and she squeezed Mary Alyce's forearm. "You're too much."

Mary Alyce gave her a solemn nod as she finished wiping her hands on a dish towel. It was that awkwardness again. "You're welcome."

As Judy made her way from the mess hall to the front entrance, she found Bernard in a chocolate-brown tweed suit. A blue handkerchief in his breast pocket brought out the color in his eyes. He was admiring the court, she saw, before their gazes met.

"Private Washington. This looks much improved indeed."

"We all had a part in it. And thank you for doing yours," she added.

"Ah, the modest ringleader," Bernard said, turning around. "I peeked into the salon and the mess hall. All being used with love already, it appears. Have you had a chance to bowl yet?"

The question surprised her. It was an invitation, of course. "No, not yet."

"Shall we, then? Unless," he paused with a hint of teasing in his eyes, "you're afraid."

"You mean right now? In the middle of the afternoon?" She was stalling because she had no other reason to say no. Her shift was done for the day.

And she was not only one of the most competitive women in the company but also in her family. On the rare occasion she played games, Herbert let her win because her temper soured when she lost, which was roughly half the time. She was only half teasing when she said, "I don't know that we know each other well enough to bowl."

"I knew it," he said with a grin. "You're afraid of a little sport." With that, he trotted easily down the narrow staircase. She was impressed that he knew she would follow him. Her pulse picked up. She had never been able to resist a challenge. Besides, there was no harm in one game, she figured.

"It really is just as I remembered," Bernard said, turning on the overhead lights and looking at her proudly, as if he'd built the alley himself. He was already taking off his shoes and locating his proper size in bowling shoes. "Indulge an old chap, won't you?"

"One game," she said, meeting him at the wall of shoes.

"Rest assured, it will go quickly. It will be painless."

"For whom?" She was still looking for the best-fitting shoes when Bernard stood up and patted his thighs eagerly before choosing a red bowling ball.

"You, of course. I won't forget how kind you were to humor me."

"You sound like my husband," she said, without thinking better of it, relieved that she'd found a pair of the goofy shoes that fit and they could finally get on with it.

"Is that so?" Bernard said, his voice flat now, softer, like air deflating from a tire.

Was that jealousy in his voice? "He lets me win all the time and he thinks I don't know it. Not just bowling, any game—bid whist, checkers. He's always tried to spare my feelings."

"A true gentleman," Bernard observed.

"Yes," Judy said. And, she thought, such a good friend. Her best friend. Talking about Herbert with Bernard was somehow just as natural as talking about him to Stacy or Bernadette. But it should have felt different, shouldn't it? Shouldn't she feel as flustered and passionate speaking of Herbert as she did when she said Bernard's name in hushed whispers to Mary Alyce?

Something more was happening with Bernard, she knew. Something different than what she experienced with Herbert, whose presence in her life—when he had been around—was gentle, easy and soft. It did not shock or ripple through her the way her closeness to Bernard seemed to. They had not touched, had not even really stood that close to one another, and yet, she was changed by Bernard's presence, in spite of herself. In spite of being a married woman.

"Just three rounds, then," Bernard said. He confidently walked to the end of the middle lane to adjust the bowling pins. "Ladies first."

Judy wasn't sure she could focus on the game, and as soon as she stood upright in the center of the middle lane, her eyes darted from the arrows to the ball she cradled close to her chest. She bent her knees, and the bowling ball sailed confidently down the center before clipping three pins on its way into the gutter. She grunted disapproval as Bernard restored the pins to their upright position. She couldn't read the expression on his face as she brushed past him, so lightly. "I suppose I have you to thank for that."

He shrugged, blameless. He stood tall, with his bowling ball propped up beneath his chin, focused before he hurled the ball off-center and produced a flawless strike, all the pins falling into one another with claps that sounded like a round of applause. "Perhaps," he said. "But this next go is our tie-breaker. I believe Herbert would be very proud of you for sticking it out."

How had she been suckered into this? She didn't even want another turn. She was trying to convince herself she didn't care about the game at all and then Bernard had to go bring up Herbert. She was tender from hearing him talk about Herbert as if he knew him. As if he was still in touch, actively present in her life, not just in her mind. Her emotions were all tangled up now, and she sat down to take off her bowling shoes and put her boots back on. "You win," she said.

"Oh, come now," Bernard said, surprised. "Are you quite serious?"

Judy continued untying her laces and pulling off her bowling shoes, more frantically as the seconds passed. "I am. But you won. Congratulations," she said, putting them back on the shelf as she stepped into her work boots and fastened their laces more tightly.

"Very well," Bernard said, looking disappointed. He sank into a seat to take off his bowling shoes. "I see why your husband lets you win."

Judy frowned, offended by Bernard's charm, by his bowling ability, by his incredible allure. "We should go," she said, starting toward the stairs.

If she wasn't so aware that she was falling for him, she would have let herself descend totally into anger—at herself, at him—for feeling for him what she should have felt for Herbert. She had been writing Herbert with no response for more than a year now out of loyalty to their friendship, and she'd come to the WAC to make sure her friend was still living, to somehow ensure he knew she had not forgotten him.

Bernard was trying to speak, but Judy was already halfway up the staircase and onto the gym floor, which creaked under the weight of many gym shoes. Captain Campbell and several enlisted were in their workout clothes, ready for a pickup basketball game. Judy tried not to look alarmed at the captain's appearance. Bernard emerged, his cheeks ruddy and hot, like they had been caught in the middle of something untoward.

"Private Washington, Mr. Welsh," Captain Campbell said. "I'm pleased you made it to see the results of your consult."

"Yes, Captain, thank you for the invitation," Bernard said, clearing his throat. "I had very little to do with the finished product. That was all Private Washington."

Captain Campbell looked at their faces, from Bernard to

Judy and back. "It was certainly a great team effort, and we've all benefitted from it. So, thanks for your part in it."

He nodded quickly and the three were silent as the officers flowed into the gym.

Captain Campbell's eyes followed the officers before she said, "Looks like the game might start without me, but I do hope we didn't interrupt your visit," Captain Campbell said, raising an eyebrow. "We're playing a game of pickup basketball, and if you're familiar with the game, you're welcome to join a team."

Judy thought she heard Bernard gulp before he politely declined. "I should be getting on," Bernard said. "But thank you for the invitation. I hope to take you up on it another time."

"Certainly. Do let us know when you're able to return," Captain Campbell said before taking her leave.

Bernard moved closer to Judy, but there was still an arm's length between them. She was aware suddenly of all the eyes on her. On them.

"Are you quite all right?" Bernard asked, visibly worried. "I'm not sure what I've done, but you seem very upset."

"I'm fine. I just... I can't explain now," Judy said. "I need time. But I'm glad you came. Thanks for the game. And for all your help here. As you can see, the project was a success."

"Yes, it seems like it was. Maybe for everyone but you," he said.

He looked at her again in his knowing way, as if he could see the fervent coursing of blood through her veins. She felt the strongest urge to be closer to him, to be alone with him again in the bowling alley, for longer. "I have to go," Judy said, waving as she fled to the barracks.

TWENTY-SEVEN

MARY ALYCE

From Helen to Mary Alyce

Tuesday, 3 January 1945

My Dear Mary Alyce;
*I received your letter a few weeks ago but am just now finding
the right words to say about it. I knew from the first time you
mentioned the Army that you would learn about your birth certificate and Eugene. At the time, it seemed the easiest way for
you to find out.*

*I see what you mean about it being selfish to keep it from you.
You are right. I didn't want to see the world's ugliness turned
against you for being both colored and a woman. Any woman
gets the world's backside shown to her one way or the other, but
once I knew Eugene, I could only guess what it would be like
to be a woman on top of that.*

And he could pass. So maybe that's important to know. Like you, he was light enough to do that, to choose. Mary Alyce, he was just such a good-looking man. He had a spirit like yours—so gentle and strong at the same time. He watched the world, seemed like, to see where he fit in it, to do what he felt called to do. He decided to pass so that he could get all those chains off his life, and I couldn't blame him for that. It's probably the most human thing to want as much freedom as you can get, as you can afford. And who can afford freedom?

He had passed for long enough in Alabama to know he could try it somewhere else. He worked as a mechanic down there, and he wanted to try fixing vintage cars up in Vermont with some friends. They somehow discovered he was Negro and ditched him when they got to Woodstock.

We met during a snowstorm, and he helped me greatly, even though he had a heck of a time changing a tire in the snow because he'd never seen that much of it before. The only reason he told me who he really was, he said, was because he didn't want to have a lie between us. I loved that about him—he had integrity.

He said he couldn't live with the kind of added pressure that would come with hiding himself from me. And while I wasn't sure how to feel about it at first, I realized I was totally smitten with him. I didn't care nothing about his race, but I was scared everybody else would, so I knew I couldn't say anything.

I never did get to meet his family, but I know he had a younger sister, Agnes. He loved her more than anyone in the world. She's probably still down in Alabama. You might try and see if she could tell you more.

I'm sorry I didn't say what I knew earlier on. But Mary Alyce, what you didn't know helped get you farther in life than anyone in this family has ever gone. Things back here will always be closed to you if you live as a colored woman. And I

think I know my girl well enough to know that you will decide
to be honest—even if it makes your life worse.

But look at you, there on the other side of the world. Hell, I
could never do that. Neither can your grandmother. I hope you
can see the blessing in all this. Maybe it was just plain luck.

But I am sorry again for what I've done. The point was to
do what mothers do, and to set you up to be as successful as you
could be, to do whatever you could to go further than me. From
where I'm sitting, it at least looks like I did that one thing right.
Love,
Mother

Reinvention came slowly at first for Mary Alyce, then all at
once. In the months following her initial fog of confusion,
she sometimes talked to Judy or thought about what all her
options were. Passing would be possible, she knew, when she
went back to America. It might even be preferable, since riots
were targeting Negro veterans. The Negroes coming home
complained among themselves that while victory over fascism felt imminent, the war against racism at home was not.

But what had initially presented itself as the end of the world
had helped her find a renewed passion in the kitchen. Cleav-
ing whole chunks of garlic from the post's victory gardens,
chopping dill, learning how to make béarnaise sauce from an
old cookbook. Learning to nourish herself and her friends this
way helped her take her attention from the distractions of the
many more questions she had about Eugene and his family.
Her family. She could work out in the kitchen the right steps
to take to find his sister, Agnes, whom Helen had mentioned.

She was also trying to figure out when to give Judy the
letter saying Herbert was presumed dead, knowing how it
would tear Judy apart. She had planned to give it to Judy before the New Year began, after the Christmas excitement, but

hadn't worked up the nerve yet. She instead avoided her after the day Bernard came to visit. First, she said she came down with something, so she needed a couple of days to recover. Then, the New Year was arriving and she made herself extra busy with making food and finding drinks for the battalion.

But she couldn't avoid Judy forever, and she knew her friend was on to her strange behavior.

Now that 1945 had arrived, one of the greatest battles of the war so far, in the Ardennes, the Battle of the Bulge, was finally over. The Allied Forces had fought their way into Germany, and the forty-eight divisions distributed along the six hundred miles between the North Sea and Switzerland were battle worn but anticipating victory, finally, after so many months. The mood on post was celebratory as the WAC postal unit began to anticipate orders to return home, thinking Hitler might surrender any day now.

It was nearly the end of January when Judy peeked into the mess hall and found Mary Alyce chopping onions and peppers. "Well, look at who it is! Are you feeling better? I haven't seen you in too long," Judy said.

"You're sweet to ask," Mary Alyce said, looking up quickly, then sliding the vegetables off the cutting board into a big yellow bowl. "I'm better now, less busy. How was your visit with Bernard?"

Judy's smile slid away and she made herself busier than she needed to be, drying off a set of forks. "We bowled a little bit and he won."

"Well, of course. He went to school here, didn't he? Home court advantage and all that."

"I had a feeling and I still said yes," Judy sighed.

"You're smarting from it? Or something else?"

"I could not care less about losing. Well, that's not entirely true. I quit after he got a strike. I had only touched a few of the pins. It was a pretty awful showing, I have to say."

"You sound like you care."

"Yes, but not about the game."

Mary Alyce paused. "Your feelings," she said, a handful of knives still leaking water as she let her hand hover over them. *This might be the time,* she thought as her friend confirmed what she sensed. She could tell Judy now about Herbert, and maybe that would ease the torment.

"I think I'm falling in love," Judy said, finally setting down a dry plate to face her friend. And there it was, in a tone of voice that sounded like Judy just realized it as she spoke, as if she was as surprised as anyone. She had never seen Judy look so forlorn. Maybe that was the look of love unexpressed, unrequited. She put down her dish towel and leaned forward.

"How do you know?" She was asking more out of her own curiosity than anything else. She had never been in love, and she hoped to know the feeling so when it was finally her turn, she could name it.

"I can't think of anything or anyone else," Judy said. "I've been writing to Herbert, all this time." At this, she paused like there was another thought that darkened her expression. "I've written out of loyalty, but when I write to him, when I talk or think about him, I feel the same cozy feeling I do talking about you."

"And with Bernard?"

"It feels like he was sent to me to show me what real love could feel like," Judy said, her voice pained. "There's passion. Excitement. Like he was always supposed to be there, right beside me. Everything feels easy with him. Less...labored. I feel silly."

What Mary Alyce heard in Judy's voice sounded anything but silly, and she told her friend so.

"He just lights me up, you know. But I feel horrible. I don't know what I'll say to Herbert next time I write. Or how I'll manage when I finally hear from him."

Mary Alyce winced. She wasn't doing the right thing holding on to that telegram. Before now, it felt like a kindness. But now Judy felt guilty. And Mary Alyce wasn't sure if telling her about Herbert would make it worse or not. Herbert had been presumed dead before Judy even met Bernard. But there wasn't a definitive answer, so Mary Alyce could not imagine if that would ease some of the shock of losing her best friend or help her welcome feelings for someone else.

"Why are you so quiet?" Judy said.

"You say you feel horrible, but you're beaming," Mary Alyce said carefully, adding a slight smile of her own.

"Well, now I do wish you would have stayed quiet," Judy said, and they both laughed. It was nice to feel the kinship she did with Judy. She had never felt the warm safety of true friendship like this with Ethel or Betsy. "I'm being serious, Mary Alyce. I don't know what I've gotten myself into."

"But there are two of you in the situation. Maybe you can't take all the credit," Mary Alyce noted, taking a breath. This was the moment. She was just going to tell her. "And there's something else that you need to consider—"

Judy suddenly turned to her watch and checked it frantically against the clock. "Shoot! I forgot I told Bernadette I would pick up her shift this afternoon. I've got to run. See you back at the barracks!"

Mary Alyce felt both relief and frustration at Judy leaving her alone with her thoughts, which were all tangled up inside her, trying to sort themselves out. "See you later. Try not to worry too much."

"Easy for you to say," Judy said as she left the mess hall.

Watching Judy leave as she nibbled at her fingernail, Mary Alyce whispered to herself, "You have no idea."

A few days after her conversation with Judy, Mary Alyce used her weekend pass to visit a museum, taking in the photographs of some ruins of some buildings in the streets of London that had been nearly obliterated during a Nazi blitz.

A little boy interrupted her thoughts by pointing and saying, "Look, Mum, an American."

She turned to look at him and then his mother. Of course, in her uniform, she stood out.

His mother pressed his hand down. "Timothy, you mustn't point," she chided, tugging him closer for emphasis, as if to set him back on the proverbial straight and narrow. To Mary Alyce she said, "Pardon him, he's just six. All of us have been so proud to have the women's army in our midst. Would you and some of your colleagues like to join us for supper sometime?"

Mary Alyce turned to look at them both. She had just been thinking about this choice, her mother's words, the opportunities like this that would come where she could either admit her true identity or mask it. There was no moment like the present to try. "Yes, I'm sure they would be delighted. But... I want to be sure that you know that we are Negroes."

The woman peered into her face, tilting her head in disbelief. "You could have fooled me!"

Right, Mary Alyce thought with frustration and impatience. That's why she'd said it. The boy piped up to ask his mother, "What is a Negro?"

"Someone of a different race than you and your mother," Mary Alyce said almost as a reflex as she shrank within herself a bit, worried that she shouldn't have mentioned it. But another aspect of being a Negro woman was that you could not spring your presence on white people who weren't expecting you, not without the risk of violence or death. Mary Alyce viewed these two relatively harmless people as a practice run for what she would encounter later. "We come in all shades, from all over the United States. There are other Negro men and women serving in the Allied Forces, too."

The woman extended her hand to Mary Alyce, looking stunned. Mary Alyce wondered what figures had danced in their minds about Negroes before they met her. One of the women from another company had said one family told her they expected to see her in a headscarf and hand-me-downs, not a US military uniform. "Where are my manners? I'm Daisy, and this here is Timothy. We'd love to have you and your friends over to our home for supper. We don't have much, but it would be our honor to feed you all. We want to thank you for your service."

Mary Alyce offered her hand and said, "I'm Mary Alyce Dixon. And yes, I'd love that," even though she was already beginning to panic. Her first dinner with a family abroad. She felt certain she was going to mess this up and say the wrong thing at least once.

Daisy retrieved a small piece of paper and a pen from her purse and wrote down her address and phone number. "If you can come after your duties tomorrow for supper, it would be our pleasure."

Mary Alyce took the address and invitation back to the barracks just before lights-out, as everyone was winding down for bed. Bernadette was the first to ask, "Does the family know we're with the Negro WAC?"

"Yes, they do. I told them right away," Mary Alyce said, pleased with herself.

"Look at you," Stacy quipped. "You're almost a natural."

"Pay them no mind, Mary Alyce," Judy said. "It's a nice gesture and it'll be good for us to socialize with civilians and not just each other, for a change."

"Oh, we're expected to be social?" Stacy protested.

"Just remember what we've discussed," Judy continued. "Less is more, especially when it comes to questions about what Negro women say and do. Okay?"

Mary Alyce didn't feel sure she understood, but she nodded anyway. It seemed to help Judy to guide her along and she wanted to keep Judy distracted, focused on anything but Herbert and Bernard. Besides, Mary Alyce kept wondering about the look on Daisy's face when she revealed that she was Negro. She kept turning the sound of Daisy's voice at the moment of her invitation over in her mind. Maybe it was the idea of being on display that made her most anxious.

They went to Daisy's modest cottage directly after teatime. Timothy opened the door and stared up at all of them as if they were a constellation and he had only recently become aware of the kinds of miracles one could find in the dark.

"Oh, you were right, Mary Alyce," Daisy exclaimed, staring at the women with the same wide-eyed wonder as her son. "You all are so different looking."

Judy gave Mary Alyce a quizzical look and said, "We'll take that as a compliment, ma'am."

"Yes, please do. You're all lovely in a very exotic way," Daisy chirped. Stacy noticed Bernadette scowl and began to say something until she pinched the top of her shoulder. "Please do have a seat with us in the dining room."

It was clear the family had put together about half of their weekly rations for the meal of shepherd's pie, and everyone in the home received a small scoop of mashed potatoes, sweet peas and a little crumble of meat. Daisy's husband, John, was warm enough but content to let her do all the talking for the family. Mary Alyce made the women a bit of food before they came, so they each ate just a portion.

From Daisy, they learned that the family was the third generation to live in that part of England. "Our families have always lived here, working the land, even when the industrial work started. John is a machinist, and he does technical things I can't begin to explain. Isn't that right, dear?"

At this, John grunted and shook his head. "It's a bore, I'm afraid," he said. "I'd rather hear about the work with the soldiers' mail. That is what you do, right?"

"We do work with the big backlog of mail that was left behind when a bunch of previous soldiers and POWs were sent home or deployed elsewhere," Stacy said. "We are just about done clearing that backlog now, and soon we'll have new orders."

"Or we'll head home," Bernadette said. She sounded eager to get back, so much so that Daisy asked where home was for them all.

"For me, it's Chicago," Bernadette said. "I'm a beautician for the family business. At least I was. Now that I'll be an army veteran, I might try to do something else more significant."

"Keeping us beautiful is pretty important, I'd say," Judy said. "Helps our morale."

Bernadette looked shy. "That's sweet of you to say. But I want to be part of something that lasts a long time, maybe forever. Like a schoolteacher. Or own my own business so I can make enough money to donate to young Negro children's education."

It was a lofty dream, Mary Alyce thought, to want to keep serving in some way after this. She had thought about what she might want to do next. But she was more interested in finding her aunt in Alabama. She would be able to plan her future, she believed, when she knew more about her past.

"Sometimes you help others by helping your own folks," Stacy said. "I know my folks are missing me back in Missouri. They didn't have enough hands on the farm to begin with, but they let me go. Probably because they thought I was too mannish to marry."

"You're just strong is all," Mary Alyce said, feeling defensive of her friend.

"Certainly you are," Daisy said, her voice breathless.

"I miss home, which for me is in New York," Judy said. "But I don't know if I'm ready to go back just yet." Mary Alyce looked at her hands, ashamed to still be keeping the news of Herbert to herself. She sat straight as a reed, noting the difference between her and her friends. She did not miss Woodstock and was not eager to get back. There was no real life waiting for her back there.

Everyone kept chatting over dinner as her mind continued to wander. If she wasn't going home, where *would* she end up? It was a question worth getting lost in for whatever amount of time they had left overseas.

TWENTY-EIGHT

JUDY

The time that remained for the battalion overseas was measured by history unfolding around them, along with fewer letters to move. The silver antiaircraft balloons manned by Negro troops became even more rare sights in the skies above. News of the many dead after D-Day several months ago was followed by one hundred thousand Negro infantrymen who volunteered to bury them with as much dignity as possible— for morale and sanitation—at Omaha Beach. Even menial tasks in the hierarchy of the battlefields like this were dangerous. One only had to look at the Negroes who died working with ammunition in Port Chicago.

And this litany of death, the numbers that seemed to only grow as time passed, worried Judy for Herbert and his silence, but she did not want to write another unanswered letter. She sometimes pulled what she called "a Mary Alyce" and peeked inside letters, read newspaper clippings sent from home months ago with news of strikes, marches and calls for victory. Victory was the mantra and seduction they had all been drawn to. Victory for America, even for those who were fighting for, working for, dying for the country and recognized as only half American, as one soldier put it.

That morning, Mary Alyce was moments late to the warehouse, which was unusual. It had been some time since they worked together on the mail, but the shifts were all realigned for the New Year. They were also awaiting news of their fate, looking forward to hearing what their next assignment might be now that the Allies had liberated Rome.

When Mary Alyce finally arrived at the warehouse, she was biting her lip, looking nervous and holding an envelope in her hand with Judy's name on it. Judy met her friend's eyes, which looked heavy and lidded for lack of sleep. "I have something I need to tell you, Judy."

Nothing good ever came after those words. Judy looked at the envelope, then back at Mary Alyce. "I wondered why you were late," Judy said. She thought to add "and why you've been acting so weird," but she didn't. "It's so unlike you."

Mary Alyce handed Judy the envelope. "It's about Herbert. It's from some time ago. After D-Day. I think it was caught up during our voyage from the US."

The muscles in Judy's face tightened at the mention of Herbert and D-Day. She had, in her mind, kept him separate and apart from the major battles. He lived in her imagination as part of a protected, untouchable unit of valiant soldiers like the Panthers General Patton led in the Pacific or the Tuskegee Airmen who showed those Nazis that the Aryan race was indeed not superior and that Negro men could fly, they could soar. They were majestic.

When he was silent, before this moment, she could keep

him safe in her made-up story. But this delayed news and Mary Alyce's voice, sounding like her throat was a dam with a river of tears pressing at it, threatened that story.

Judy flipped the envelope open, unfolding it nervously. When Judy read the words about Herbert, she found that she couldn't really take them in. *We regret* and *tragic* and *presumed dead*. Words that had been reserved for the sorrow of other wives and mothers and sisters, but that had managed not to reach her. Millions were dead, millions more would die.

Until that moment, holding the telegram, she had been safe. The second time through, maybe the third or fourth time she read it, the words blurred from the swell of tears in her eyes.

"I really am so sorry, Judy," Mary Alyce said.

The tears fell in streams down Judy's cheeks as she relented and sat on the hard floor near their desks. All she could say was "I came all this way to find you, and you were gone before I even got here?"

Mary Alyce was sniffling, wiping her tears with the heels of her hands. Trying to guide Judy up, saying how sorry she was. "I can't imagine how you must be feeling."

It felt like every wound she'd ever had had opened up and like she would never feel love again. "When did you get this?" she asked Mary Alyce.

"Does that matter?"

"You know it does, if you have to ask."

"Right before Christmas."

"Weeks ago?" Judy rose up, wiping her face with her dirty hands, streaking her cheeks.

"You were so busy and happy, Judy. You had the building to finish. And I felt that this could wait. And then afterwards, I wanted you to have some time to enjoy what you did," Mary Alyce said in a rush of words. "I shouldn't have kept it from you. I'm so sorry. I really am."

Judy could not believe that Mary Alyce would keep this to herself for so long. She could not know that Judy had been desperate for any word at all about her husband, because it had been such a long time since she'd heard from him, as Judy had kept that a secret. But he was *her* husband.

She was angry at Mary Alyce for making a choice about her life, her feelings. It was easy to direct her hurt toward Mary Alyce, so she did. "Of course you're sorry. You always are. You always are!" Judy shouted.

Major Adams burst into the warehouse and Judy knew she looked crazy, wild-eyed. That she needed to salute the major like Mary Alyce did, but she was weak now from the shock, from her rage. Something in her had broken and left her deflated, weak.

"What is going on here?" Major Adams demanded, looking from Mary Alyce to Judy. "And what is the meaning of your insubordination this morning?"

Mary Alyce had the wherewithal to stand at attention. And Judy did not, not really, but she managed anyway to follow suit, her lips trembling from another round of tears that were about to give way.

"Permission to respond, ma'am," Mary Alyce said.

"You may, Private Dixon," Major Adams said, still furious and now, impatient.

"Private Washington just received a telegram about her husband being missing in action. They think he died in combat, ma'am," Mary Alyce said.

When Major Adams turned to look at Judy, more tears streamed down her face, cupping her chin. Major Adams took off her cap and sighed. Judy cried, still shaking her head, now her body heaving from the shock and grief.

She wasn't sure what would follow, but she did not expect

the major to look at her with softened eyes. To say, "Oh, Judy. I am so, so sorry."

Instinctively and without regard for the formalities of her position, Major Adams walked toward Judy with open arms, folding them over her. She didn't let up until Judy finally allowed the crying that started somewhere deep within to make its way out.

Once she composed herself, Judy left Mary Alyce and Major Adams and returned to the barracks. She took to the moderately comfortable bed. She understood now how Mary Alyce had decided she might stay there for the rest of her days. The world could go on, if it insisted. She would watch from afar, mourning all she had once planned after being reunited with Herbert.

Grief took energy and left her depleted. All she could do was take in the view from the closest window, to look at a tiny patch of sky above her. Suddenly, too, everything seemed both real and unreal.

Now Mary Alyce was the one to bring meals that Judy had no appetite for. She was still upset at Mary Alyce for waiting to tell her. She had no idea what she would have done with the knowledge before Christmas, before their celebration. But it was still important information she'd had every right to know.

At night, Judy's mind wouldn't rest. During the day, all she wanted to do was stay in bed and cry. This was the shape of her hours for two days, going on three.

Mary Alyce set down a small tray with a soft-boiled egg, toast and a cup of tea on top of a trunk at the foot of the cot. Mary Alyce sat next to Judy on the bed, gently rearranging Judy's pillows to prop her up. Judy let it happen because she wanted someone to take care of her and she did not, for once, want to do it herself. They were quiet with one another until

Mary Alyce, bringing up the two skipped meals from the day before said, "You have to eat something sometime."

"What did you say when I said that to you?" Judy said sleepily, still looking out of the window. How had doing nothing made her so tired?

"I said I can't make my body want what it doesn't," Mary Alyce answered. "But that was different, Judy."

Yes, Judy thought, turning to look at her. That was very different. She was really seeing this Mary Alyce—the new, transformed friend, seeing how confident she was now. In her anger and disappointment, Judy wanted to challenge her. "Was it? Is it?"

Mary Alyce bit her lip. Judy thought she might cry. "Okay, it may not be different. And I know that it's partly my doing for taking my time—"

"It is your fault," Judy muttered, knowing as soon as she said it her words were unfair. The tears were back, stinging her eyes. "Partly."

"Yes, I know. It was wrong to wait. I can see that now, and I'm really so sorry," Mary Alyce said. "You are my closest friend. I want you to know I would never do something to purposefully wound you. I thought I was being kind, letting you have a good holiday after all you've been doing for others, for us. For me. It felt like one way to spare you something hard."

Judy thought of Margaret then. Her mother always said no one could experience any part of life on someone else's behalf. They needed to have the joy and the pain on their own.

"It wasn't right, Mary Alyce," Judy said. "But I think I understand what you intended."

She stopped short of saying she forgave Mary Alyce. It was too soon for that. But she did take the tea. She sipped from the cup, the bitter lukewarm water a salve. She looked at the egg.

"Herbert would have wanted you to go on, Judy. He would have wanted you to mourn him, yes. But he would not want you staying in this bed forever," Mary Alyce added.

It was true. Herbert had been a real friend to her that way, insisting that she embrace life moment to moment. She knew he would not have felt that way about her growing feelings for another man. Her guilt was doubled—deepened by her shame over her attraction to Bernard, sorrow over Herbert's death.

She pushed Bernard out of her mind and tried to focus on memories of her life with Herbert. She wondered how his family would take the news, if they would close the blinds in the Bronx brownstone and place a gold star in the window the way so many families did to mourn dead soldiers.

At least, she thought, they had a way of working through the devastation together with those gold stars. All she had in Birmingham were her memories, her guilt and the telegram that announced that all of it had really been for nothing.

A wave of increased bombing coincided in the following days with new mail to sort from the heavy bags the German prisoners of war carried and dropped off. Every few days, the steady silence of their work was violently interrupted by the loud sirens signaling air raids or bombs dropping in the area, which sent the WACs scrambling until all-clear horns sounded.

Even at the start of 1945, the momentary shock of being distant witnesses to the battles being waged around the globe emerged anew every time. The mail they sorted, the letters that offered comfort and a taste of home was good for the WAC's morale, too. Like civilian wives, sisters and daughters, the women of the battalion had their own stories woven into the war effort.

Some of the posts other WACs served on were still segregated. Notes from husbands reported that commanding officers still treated them as enemies even though they fought for the same side. The men in their lives were joined in misery, the smell of flesh and substandard food and mud caked in their boots and socks. Many of the men in combat left out the gory details in their letters, trying to protect the women from the jagged, harrowing truth of their everyday.

But Judy's news was an example of a different kind of missive, a life-changing one the women understood. News of Herbert's death spread quickly throughout the battalion. Judy knew because the occasional officer from another unit or company would introduce herself or simply say, "I'm praying for you." Suddenly she understood that her sorrow signaled to them that they could be next to receive such news. She was a reminder of how war could devastate you even if you were situated far from the trenches.

The day after Judy bickered with Mary Alyce and told her she needed time by herself, Mary Alyce insisted that she let Stacy and Bernadette spend time with her, console her. They moved quietly and respectfully around her those first days and nights. Eventually, Stacy said, "You are still in the land of the living, baby."

Stacy returned later with fresh flowers and made a ritual of changing their water and cutting their stems when she wasn't covering Judy's shift. Noticing them on the windowsill, Judy said softly, "Some things do live after all, huh, Stacy?"

Stacy held her friend's hand. "We go on. But not without our hearts breaking, Judy. You're allowed at least that."

Judy hugged her friend tight. She felt as fragile as a daisy petal, which Bernadette also sensed when they had some time alone. Bernadette rarely had a break from the salon, but in the days after they all learned about Herbert, she deputized one of her fellow workers to supervise and came to Judy's bedside with a tote bag carrying a brush, a comb and hair grease.

"Since you aren't coming to us, I'll come to you," Bernadette said, lifting the bag slightly and grinning. "How are you holding up, dear?"

"As good as can be expected," Judy said by that time. She spread her hands on the empty space beside her on the bed, which made her remember what it had been like the last time she put her hand on Herbert's back, the strong heft of his muscles against her hand.

"Well, you must be sick of hearing it, honey, but I am truly very sorry," Bernadette said. "I've been thinking about what I would want if I were you. What has helped me in the past. So I came to brush your hair and oil your scalp. To try and ease the hurt a little. If you want, no pressure."

Bernadette's suggestion gave Judy a relief she had not felt since she was a girl of twelve or thirteen, sitting on the floor in the Bronx between her mother's knees, listening to the radio and birdsong outside their fire escape. That was a time before knowing what she couldn't avoid.

"How sweet of you, Bernie," Judy said. "I would like that, since you went through the trouble."

Judy moved to sit between Bernadette's legs on the floor. When Bernadette patted Judy on the shoulder, Judy felt supported and cared for. Something final and easy let itself fall away when she let herself rest under the care of her friend's expert hands. The golden light of the sun fell in a warming stream on Judy's face, leaning to one side then the other letting her heart heal.

TWENTY-NINE

JUDY

The four months that followed felt both slow and fast. As May, 1945, arrived, it was hard to fathom four years of fighting from Saipan to Berlin, Rome and Naples to the Ardennes, the Gothic Line. On mountains, beaches, deserts and in country towns.

She had written Margaret with the news about Herbert, to which Margaret replied with her condolences. "A husband can be an anchor or a weight," she'd said, and it struck Judy as true. And now she was getting used to living in the world mostly untethered.

Work remained an anchor for them in the warehouse. It was afternoon on May 8, 1945, when the doors there opened and Stacy shouted the news. "Hitler is dead! Germany surrendered! The war is over in Europe!" They would call it V-E Day—Victory in Europe.

Judy was finishing processing a stack of envelopes when she

heard, about to head to the mess hall a little early to catch up with Mary Alyce. She felt all at once a soaring happiness that the war in Europe had ended after so long. Good for them, for all the countries really, that Adolf Hitler was no more. But sadness tugged at her because Herbert had not had a chance to see the battle to the end.

As the women cheered and clapped, it was clear that the celebratory mood had spilled into the streets of Birmingham, where civilians and officers alike danced in bliss. Someone had found confetti to toss. Trumpeters did not wait for the rest of the band.

In front of the Better Beer Pub, Mary Alyce, Bernadette and Stacy called to her from beside a group of white WACs. They looked like they were celebrating from down the street. "Come join us!" Mary Alyce said, in front of a tank that had rolled onto the tiny cobblestoned streets. There was an American flag on its front, underscoring the pride they all shared. Then one of the white WACs unfurled a Confederate flag to tack on the back, ruining the moment with a reminder that the victory did not have the same meaning for all of them.

"Better to ignore it," Mary Alyce said to them, her face flat with disappointment.

"I'll drink to that," Bernadette said.

Inside the Better Beer Pub, it looked like the entire 6888th Central Postal Battalion had the same idea for commemorating the day. Looking at the women she had come on this journey with and enjoying the moment they helped make happen filled her with hope and inspiration. It felt like they had come full circle.

Mary Alyce asked the question they were all thinking. "What now? You think we're headed home?" Judy thought she heard a choke of fear in her friend's throat. They ordered pretzels and peanuts with their pints.

"Is that where you're headed after this?" Bernadette asked over the rising din of voices.

Judy wondered for the first time if her answer to the question was the same as it had been almost a year ago now. It had not occurred to her to question whether she would go back to the Bronx, not until the news about Herbert. In subsequent weeks, after the initial letter, an official notice and death certificate arrived at King Edwards School. He was officially gone.

"I hadn't given it much thought," Mary Alyce said.

"Me, either," Stacy said, her mouth full of pretzels.

"Disgusting," Bernadette said, appalled. "You can't go anywhere with those manners. Chew your food."

Stacy waved Bernadette off, then opened her mouth to disgust Bernadette more, which made Judy and Mary Alyce laugh. But now the thought of home had lodged itself in Judy's mind, and she kept pondering it.

"Used to be all I thought about was when I would be home again with Herbert," Judy mused. "I thought he'd be coming with me."

Mary Alyce put her hand on Judy's. "He is, just not how you thought."

That quieted them all for a moment. Then Mary Alyce got up. "We are too somber for the occasion. We need to celebrate as much as we can. We've been working hard. So have all our boys, including the dear, late Herbert Washington. Let's go join the fun, shall we?"

Stacy finally swallowed her mouthful. Bernadette wrinkled her nose and then turned to Mary Alyce. "A perfect idea."

As they went to turn out the door, Judy felt a hand on her arm: Bernard. She startled to see him, but of course he was there. "You did it!" he said cheerfully, focused on her, then raising his glass for everyone. "The victory is yours."

"It wasn't just us," Judy said, her voice smaller than she expected. She had wanted to see him, but not now. Not when she already had so many emotions coursing through her.

"All right, I'll take some credit," Bernard beamed. "Cheers to us."

"Come on, Judy," Mary Alyce said, pulling her along. The look of pain on her face must have confused him, but after all they had been through together, Mary Alyce could sense her friend was uncomfortable.

"Yes, well," Bernard said, his smile fading. "I'll see you over at the school."

She had successfully avoided him since she learned of Herbert's death in January. The feelings were just dormant within her, she realized at the sight of him, at the slight blaze at his touch. She had hoped guilt and grief had made them evaporate, but instead, she was disappointed to feel the strength of them rise. "See you," she said, a little louder, giving him a weak smile and a wave.

Outside the bar, crowds assembled with white handkerchiefs waving in the wind alongside American flags. The tank from earlier had rolled on. Elderly and young citizens alike chanted, "Victory! Victory!" Judy did not join the chant, but the joy was infectious. She also felt deep satisfaction that Hitler was dead, that the boys who put him down had the help of her battalion to see them through. She wished Herbert could have lived to share this triumphant moment with her, but she also felt some relief at no longer having to worry about him.

When the festive day was winding down, before lights-out, the bugle sounded for the women to meet in formation at the front of the main building. It could only be an announcement of what was next for the battalion. Judy marched in silent anticipation beside her friends. She could feel their hopes and fears, and her own, beating in her chest.

"I hope you have enjoyed celebrating the victory that is one we all share," Major Adams said. "Before we left home, I remember telling you the great expectations I had for you and you did not disappoint. Through inconveniences and disappointments, you have been resilient, and as a result, we are being rewarded with a move to Rouen, France. Troops returning home—and those already on their way—need their parcels and letters rerouted to the US.

"Several of your peers have been sent ahead of us to set up our quarters and work spaces. We sail in three days. In the meantime, Captain Campbell and I will work on your shift assignments. Thank you for rising to the occasion and proving our supporters right."

Judy had a mix of emotions in response to the news. She was disappointed they were leaving the place she had put so much work into, and where she'd started to heal. Everything lasted a season, but she had grown attached to the school, to the rapport she built with her friends in this new place. With Bernard.

Mary Alyce said, "This day is full of good news."

"France is supposed to be beautiful. Very chic," said Bernadette.

"We'll need you to move your salon over so we can still be presentable," Stacy said. "Washington, you look like you've seen a ghost."

Judy was stuck on her last thought about Bernard. She did not want to explain. "I'm excited is all," she finally said. "France is the land of Josephine Baker and Langston Hughes and Richard Wright. I can't wait to see it."

"Communists! So exciting," Stacy joked.

"Quit that before you get us all court-martialed," Bernadette said.

"They catch me, I'm certain they'll throw me back," Stacy quipped.

Mary Alyce leaned in to whisper with Judy on their walk back to the barracks. "Are you thinking of Bernard, or are you just tired from the day?"

Judy shook her head, a partial truth. She had mostly moved on to worrying about packing. "He's the last thing on my mind."

Mary Alyce grunted in disbelief. When Judy shot her a look, she raised her hands in a sign of surrender and Judy was satisfied that the matter was dropped. "If you say so," Mary Alyce finally said.

With that, Mary Alyce announced she had to tend to something. She left Judy to sort through her thoughts about Bernard, moving again, and the possibility of leaving him behind.

The days after the announcement of the battalion's reassignment were busy. The women who had been sullen and often preoccupied by their tasks were now giddy and light. The victory in Europe gave them hope for victory in the Pacific. It felt like a barreling locomotive beginning to slow to a stop for long enough for them to take a look at their surroundings and admire their beauty.

The time between their work in England and their future in France gave Judy space to consider how much her life had changed since they'd arrived. With Herbert and her letter writing to him behind her now, her mother was her only living bridge back to the Bronx. But it seemed that Margaret needed her less and less these days. It was what she wanted, but it also made her question what she most wanted to be, not just for her mother, but for herself.

Bernard was a useful distraction, or he had been, from figuring herself out. Maybe he was just meant to cross her path to help with the renovation and nothing more. By the end of the week, with her exchange with Mary Alyce still heavily on her mind, she had almost pushed him totally out of her thoughts when she was summoned to Captain Campbell's office and heard Bernard's voice before she saw him.

She pressed herself into the wall, her thoughts tumbling over each other in her head. She smoothed down the front of her uniform and patted her face, feeling its warmth before she stood in Captain Campbell's doorway, trying not to look as surprised as she felt.

"Ma'am," Judy said to Captain Campbell. "Mr. Welsh."

"At ease, Washington," Captain Campbell said, beaming. "Mr. Welsh came to extend his congratulations for our next assignment. And after your successful collaboration, he wanted to let us know he'll also be in Rouen, should we need to consult with him there."

Despite the fact that the news made her weak and also offered a glimmer of hope, she offered her best tight smile, eyes darting toward Bernard and back to the captain, as if they had conspired to spring this visit and news on her when she had just come to terms that she was unlikely to see him again. "How nice."

Captain Campbell lost a little of the glint in her eyes or maybe Judy was overly sensitive. She wasn't sure if she was meant to thank him or thank them both. All she could think of was that he would be where they were going. And now they were both widowers.

"Rouen is really beautiful this time of year," Bernard said. "A small, old city. A little rundown from the war. But it's beautiful nonetheless."

"What takes you there?" Judy wondered aloud. "Aside from wanting another project with our battalion?"

Bernard did not miss a beat. "I follow the contracts where

they lead. In this case, many of your military colleagues are shipping materials back to the States or to the Pacific Theater. I stand ready to assist with that. And I don't think your battalion will need my services. After all, they have you."

"Very well," Judy said. She looked at her watch, although she knew the captain was aware of her schedule and she didn't have anywhere to be but back in the barracks packing. "If you will excuse me," she said. "I'm not quite prepared for our trip. It's been a pleasure to see you again."

Captain Campbell dismissed her and Judy rushed out. She heard Bernard thank the captain again before he followed behind her fast enough to grab her hand in the narrow hallway.

She whirled around and they looked at each other, their chests rising and falling like they were seeing each other for the first time. She didn't know what else to do but wriggle from his grasp. She walked to the main building's foyer to put more distance between them. Even with a few feet between them, she felt flustered, like her tongue wouldn't obey what her mind told her to say.

She was so bothered by him, like a pebble in her shoe she couldn't find to dump out and give herself relief. She wanted him to hold her, but it felt better to fight, to be annoyed by his confidence and certainty, instead of so obviously, helplessly charmed by it. "What do you mean you follow the contracts where they lead? Is that your only reason for going to Rouen, other than its beauty?"

He was searching her face, trying to figure out her feelings. He showed a hint of his perfect teeth when he smiled. The look he gave her had more words in it than the ones he said. "Beauty is always one of my main motivations." His eyes fixed on hers until she looked away, heat prickling now at her uniform collar. Just then, the guilt that always arose alongside the pleasure of seeing him bubbled up within her. She felt suddenly frivolous, a wave of shame. He moved toward her and she stepped back, like they were in an awkward dance.

"Herbert is dead," she blurted out, like the fact was something too much to hold for one minute longer. "He died before I even got here."

She did not expect the anguish on Bernard's face, but there it was. He looked like he might move close again, but instead he held his hands. "Oh, Judy. How terrible. You must be in such mourning. I'm so sorry to hear this."

Judy was surprised by his genuine sympathy, but she shouldn't have been. She wanted suddenly to tell him that even as she fell apart in her friends' arms, she'd thought of little else but telling him and asking him what it meant for them now. Because she could see the transformation in his face; before she told him the news, his face had looked tense with all the things he wouldn't say. Now his expression relaxed. "How have you been managing?" he asked.

"Barely, if at all," Judy said. Her friends, her mother, they all lifted her spirits and helped keep her whole, she said.

Bernard glanced away, out of the front door. "Losing a spouse prompts a particular kind of mourning. I sometimes wonder if I will ever get over Hazel. I suspect the answer is likely no, but one never knows what life has in store."

It was Judy's turn to hold on to her hands. She didn't know what to say, but his expression was one of anticipation. And then he said, "I have some errands of my own, so I have to go. But I hope I'll see you in Rouen?"

She nodded sharply and then he saluted her languidly. She returned his salute, wondering how they had gotten back to pleasantries. Before he left, he said, "I'll keep you in my thoughts as you mourn. There's nothing anyone can say to make you feel better, so I won't try. Just know that the sadness gets better with time. It eases a bit."

He turned to leave after that, waft of his scent trailing behind him like the ripple of water trailing a boat. Judy wanted to reach for him, to tell him that even though Herbert's death was a stone that rattled around in her stomach and pressed on her chest so that she sometimes felt it hard to breathe, her feelings for Bernard felt like a rescue, a way of lifting the boulder of depression, setting her free from ruminating on what could have been so she could walk freely into what could be.

Back at the barracks, Mary Alyce folded clothes into her trunk. "We do collect a lot in a short period of time," she said. She was folding her beloved apron. "Not that I'm complaining."

"I'll have your head if you complain about your gift," Judy said.

"No one wants that. How did your visit with the captain go?"

"Bernard Welsh was on post," Judy said, gathering her uniform blouses from a dresser drawer to pack. Many of them had been pressed nicely, so the cotton was smooth under her hands. "I told him about Herbert. He gave me his deepest sympathies."

"He's a good man," Mary Alyce said.

"I also learned he'll be in Rouen," Judy said, trying to keep her voice steady.

Mary Alyce beamed and squeezed Judy's shoulder excitedly. "That is good news," she said. And Judy felt it was. The thrill of possibilities stirred inside of her as she continued to pack her trunk.

THIRTY

CHARITY

From Charity Adams to Rev. E. A. Adams

Saturday, 11 May 1945

Dearest Daddy,

I write you with a heavy heart over the death of Franklin Roosevelt. I have never been to so many services or memorials for anyone ever in my life. As the highest-ranking American military officer in Birmingham, I represented the US military at approximately fifteen different ceremonies memorializing him. It was an honor even if it was overwhelming.

I was eager to get back to the battalion because we have been assigned now to assist with closing out American wartime postal operations in the European Theater from Rouen, France. We will work with 200 civilian French postal workers to sort remaining mail routed to the ETO to its proper place. The name may sound familiar to you and Mama from your studies of history, as it is the place where Joan of Arc was burned at the stake.

I haven't had a chance to see much of it yet, but Abbie and I did travel here ahead of the battalion. There is a Renaissance arcade—the city's downtown—with the magnificent gothic Rouen Cathedral, majestic iron spires reaching high into the sky. Abbie and I agreed that our favorite tourist destination was the intricate, gilded astronomical clock, Gros-Horloge.

We will be billeted at Napoleon's former barracks, Caserne Tallandier. It may sound grand, but Daddy, there were no beds for us, so we had to order 900 cots immediately before we all sailed across the English Channel to Le Havre. And when we arrived, we were treated like the second coming of Betty Grable. People shouted at us in French, smiling, trying to kiss us, grabbing at pieces of our uniforms to keep as souvenirs! I lost a shoelace and one of the braids in the melee, but thankfully, no one picked my pockets.

I suspect I will get to see Paris before we are to return home. The idea of coming back fills me with mixed emotions, if I'm honest. I do miss you and Mama, but I am aware that the freedom from prejudices and Jim Crow I have so enjoyed here are not possible still in America.

I also miss home cooked meals. Your sermons on Sunday mornings. The comfort of home. But it feels like soon enough the war will be done, and I may get to stop missing you all so much.
Love,
Charity

From Rev. E. A. Adams to Charity

Saturday, 1 June 1945

Dear Charity:
I was so very proud, as I always am, to hear that you repre-

sented America well at the services for FDR. The whole of the church rocked with sadness over the President's death here. He was not perfect, but at least with the help of First Lady Eleanor, he did move the needle some. Allowing Marian Anderson to sing on the steps of the Lincoln Memorial was a huge moment for all of us. I will never forget that.

Getting another assignment is always a testament to faith in your abilities, so I am also glad to hear that. Your mother and I are very proud of all that you have accomplished, but we also miss you mightily. We look forward to your letters and read them as soon as they arrive. You are there in the trenches so to speak, but reading your words makes us feel as if we are right there with you.

On the matter of Jim Crow, we are not as changed as we would hope. Our country is the same, possibly worse off for the example set by the Nazis. When it comes time for you to come on home, you'll need to be mindful that lots of Negroes have been killed for wearing uniforms in public.

That said, Charity, I want you to keep holding your head up, and focusing on your work. All that you do is so important to help move the war to its end. You can worry about home when you make it back.

I love you,

E. A. Adams

Moving from Birmingham, England, to Rouen triggered Charity's thoughts about the eventual realities of being home. The most pressing conflict she faced was already an ethical conundrum, her least favorite quandary: she was in love with her second-in-command. She had not said those words, had not dared even to admit it to herself. But when she and Abbie traveled ahead of the battalion to take stock of the new castle, like a fortress on a winding side road where they would be for months to come, she'd felt a shift.

Abbie was not changed—she was still a flirt, she still touched Charity's shoulder here and there, or her knee when she was telling a story. It was a discreet intimacy, one that would not have gone unnoticed, maybe, if Abbie was not so aware, as they both needed to be, of eyes watching them closely, judging for perfection.

The vessels for their transport across the Channel were much smaller, so the battalion came in waves, following them. The military jeep that escorted them up to the post pressed their bodies together at every turn. A waft of Abbie's lavender perfume and soap was carried by the breeze. It made Charity lightheaded.

"I wonder if more crowds will greet us at the gate," Abbie said.

"They've been warned off, I'm sure," Charity sniffed. She did not like that some overzealous stranger had part of her uniform. She had paid good, hard-earned money for those braids. And now it was impossible to get it replaced since everything was in short supply.

As they arrived, a group of Negro soldiers awaited them, waving eagerly like they were old friends. There had already been a stack of several messages from her supposed cousins—more strangers—and she rolled her eyes. Little did anyone know that she was already with the officer she wanted to be with every day. Their theatrics were moot.

Abbie waved back, which made Charity jealous enough that she stiffened and moved away from Abbie. Through her teeth, Abbie said, "No harm in being friendly, is there? A smile is not a marriage proposal, Edna."

No, Charity thought, it wasn't a proposal. But it was an invitation. "I'll leave that to you, since it's clear you enjoy flirting with people you don't know."

At this Abbie's smile softened. She looked hurt for a moment, then she put her hands in her lap. "When they aren't being pouty, I enjoy flirting with people I *do* know, too."

Charity fumed for the rest of their short ride, as they were unloaded into their quarters, rooms right across from one another at the center of the ground floor. There were five floors in all, and the sprawling rooms had plenty of space for cots, dressers and trunks. The postal operation was a few feet from them, on the same grounds, which was a nice perk of this assignment.

"Let's have some time to settle on our own," Charity said before she turned into her room.

"A splendid idea," Abbie said, smiling tightly. That was the look she gave Charity when she was annoyed. Now that the moment had passed, Charity wasn't sure her snippiness was even warranted. But it was too late for a do-over. And she did not feel like she should apologize either.

"Very well. I'll knock on your door in an hour," Charity said, and closed the door behind her before Abbie could answer.

It was agony to be so close to Abbie, to spend so much time together, knowing full well that whatever they could be in England and France could not bloom back in South Carolina. Back home loomed over them even as a mood of hopefulness abounded. With Hitler and Mussolini out of the way, the war was almost over. In the Pacific, troops were climbing and conquering Mount Suribachi, capturing Japanese islands and prisoners of war.

But she felt—and sensed others did, too—worn down by the sheer volume of the people who had died. Both in the war and also the Negro veterans who were going home. Many of them were given blue cards as they left active duty, discharges that stripped them of the many benefits for the G.I. Bill, like education and homeownership that so many fought for and deserved. Negroes were five times as likely to be discharged this way compared to white veterans.

She still had the work in front of her to contend with, but she very much wanted to continue to fight in the war against racial injustice and inequity at home. She hoped that going home decorated would set her up for more success, even if she would still have to work twice as hard.

Charity looked at her watch after setting out her shoes, putting away her uniforms and hanging up her jackets. Outside the window of her quarters, she admired the French flag and the American one billowing in the breeze. She heard a knock at the door that could only have been Abbie.

When Charity opened it, Abbie pushed her back gently and pressed her mouth to Charity's. Charity was so surprised she moaned softly, her mouth pursed. She frowned at her automatic response. But as she let herself melt into the softness of Abbie, sweet as an apple, Charity let her lips part, her face relax. She pushed Abbie against the other side of the door, sealing it shut with a gentle click. She put her hands on Abbie's lovely oval face and hungrily kissed her back.

Before that kiss, Charity had been wedded and loyal to her duty. She had tried to hold herself accountable to the highest ideals of ethical conduct. Whatever people could say about her flaws, conflict of interest was not on the list. But the forbidden moment she had wanted for many years had finally come to pass. It was a sinful, delightful dish, like decadent cake slipping lusciously off a fork into her mouth. And now that she had crossed to the other side, she could see the merit of bending some rules, or breaking them. Or forgetting they ever existed.

They stepped apart, barely, a palm's distance between their chests, which rose and fell at the pace of two women recovering from a light jog. "You owe me an apology," Abbie said.

"I'm sorry that I've been silly. And jealous," Charity said immediately.

"You've always been so," Abbie said, putting her hand to her face. "It's rather endearing when it doesn't make me so mad."

"Don't patronize me," Charity said, holding Abbie's wrist lightly. Her voice sounded like a plea. For the first time, she did not care. She would beg Abbie for relief if it might get them out of this conundrum, but she knew it would not. "What will we do now, Abbie? About this?"

Abbie dropped her hand. "We will keep on as we have been. We can think about home when the time comes. But we have come so far. We've done so much. If anyone finds out about us...about this...it will ruin everything. And not just for us, but for the entire battalion. And we can't have that."

As frustrating as the truth was to hear, Charity was relieved that what had rumbled about inside of her had been spoken aloud. She did yearn to be public with her love, which is how she knew it was true and not a prolonged attraction or crush based on old feelings. "But do you love me, Abigail, the way I love you?"

Charity had asked herself this question again and again. Now that they had finally kissed, she could dare to ask.

"I am fond of you, yes," Abbie said. Charity heard pity in her voice and balked.

"Fond of me? Is this why you flirt with men? Because you are fond of me, but you reserve your love for them?" Charity felt dizzy. Which was it?

"It's not that simple, Edna. You know where we are from, we can never be together in a real way," Abbie said. "Our parents expect us to have husbands and children. I already delayed the timeline and broke tradition coming to the WAC. So did you. They would disown us. Reverend Adams would be disgraced. It's impossible."

Charity stepped back. "I didn't ask you about possibility. I asked if you love me or not."

Abbie's chin trembled. "Fine, if you're going to try and force me to say it, the answer is no. I love you as a friend, nothing more. I kissed you because I knew you have been wanting it, and I wanted it too, just to see. But it's not romantic, Edna. It can't be."

The sweetest moment in Charity's life was now the saddest. Her eyes stung with tears, mainly because she could feel the difference between Abbie's words and how she really felt. Why would her best friend lie to her about something so important to them both?

Before her tears could fall, Charity stood up straighter and composed herself. "Very well, Captain Campbell," she said like she was addressing a stranger. "I believe you should go. Please."

They had never had a moment like this, a serious disagreement. Something that felt like a padlocked door with a missing or broken key. But being overseas had prepared them for new feelings, good and devastating. She let herself absorb this blow.

Abbie looked stricken. Charity stepped out of her path and turned her back. Even though Abbie wordlessly accepted the invitation to leave, the shutting of the door behind her still brought new tears to Charity's eyes. She should not have made the mistake of feeling, of letting Abbie lead her on all these years. Now they had to work together despite the awkward mismatch of their hearts.

THIRTY-ONE

MARY ALYCE

Mary Alyce was put in charge of planning their train trip to Paris during their first weekend pass after they got settled in Rouen, even as she found plenty to otherwise occupy her time.

June brought less news from Europe and many more headlines from Japan. After V-E Day, she noted carefully in the clips from the press Stacy shared that it was Negro support units like theirs who were carrying water for everyone else, even though none of the radio news bulletins mentioned the eight hundred Negro Marines in Saipan, their importance in Iwo Jima or the Mariana Islands.

She spent time at the post library, trying to track down American records in Alabama, where her father was from. When Helen sent his last known address and the name of his sister, Agnes, she also said it was information as old as Mary Alyce, so she needed the White Pages to double-check. The droll postal librarian for the ETO was a demure redhead, who said in her clipped, harsh, French-accented voice, "How do you say? There is no…uh, international White Pages."

"But we can find soldiers' infantries and current posts," Mary Alyce said. "Surely we also have a system for finding civilians."

"*Oui.*" The librarian sniffed. "But it is much harder."

"Does that mean you can't try?"

The woman pushed her glasses up her tiny nose. "It does not."

Mary Alyce did not ask how long it would take, but she complained to Judy and the others before lights-out in their new barracks. They had gotten used to sleeping anywhere, and now it was time to adjust to the deep, sturdy cots.

"You need to have a little fun in your life, Mary Alyce," Stacy said. "Not that I'm one to talk. I'm starting to get round around my edges here." She grabbed at her stomach to show off her flab.

"Oh, please," Bernadette complained. "I can't remember the last time I held something other than paper with glue on it. We do need time away, all of us. Let's go to Paris! It's not far."

"This weekend," Judy added. "You can pick where we go. But we have to see the Eiffel Tower. The Louvre. And maybe you can find some other places. You can use the library for something other than family research."

They were right—they always were—it made her feel better immediately to consider some time away from the battalion and their new routine.

"It's a date," she said brightly.

They set out on a Saturday morning right after breakfast with a military jeep delivering them to the rail station, which planted them in the middle of Paris. It was an elegant, lived-in place, the Eiffel Tower rising from the City of Light like a sentinel. Stacy brought a camera and snapped a photo of Mary Alyce, Judy and Bernadette in front of the Arc de Triomphe. Stacy managed to ask a kind stranger to take a picture of the four of them together. As they all posed, Mary Alyce considered how impossible it felt for all of them before, to be standing in such a glamorous place. But here they were.

Each marveled at something different. For Mary Alyce it was the busy streets, the luscious sounds of the French language, the smell of baguettes and coffee and cinnamon. Judy kept talking about getting to the blasted Eiffel Tower, but Mary Alyce had made it their last stop before returning to the post.

Bernadette spun through the Louvre the way she acquired hat boxes she foisted on Stacy, who as usual, grumbled but also obliged.

"To the Eiffel Tower, then," Judy said, making Stacy roll her eyes.

"Are there seats there?" Stacy said. "For obvious reasons."

"I can carry my own things, if you insist," Bernadette said.

"But then Stacy wouldn't have anything to complain about," Mary Alyce said.

"Touché," Stacy said. "It's the only French I know."

They all laughed. Mary Alyce's stomach gurgled hungrily, so she suggested they stop at a café on their way to the Eiffel Tower. They sat outside, admiring the flowy, flowery dresses the Parisian women wore, the smart, streamlined suits. Everyone appeared to be thin, though she marveled at how much butter and cheese filled every dish. Between bites of a brie and strawberry jam baguette, Mary Alyce said, "I'll miss this."

Judy grunted approval, her mouth full of *croque monsieur*. When she finished chewing, she said, "I wish I could bring you all back to New York with me."

"What if we don't want to go?" Stacy said.

"You are certainly uninvited," Bernadette said.

"It was just a question," Stacy said. "Seriously, though, I'll miss you all, too. But I also miss the farm. We've worked hard and everything, but there's nothing like getting my hands really dirty and helping my folks."

"Finally, something we agree on," Bernadette said. "Well, the helping-my-folks part. Not the dirt. Ew."

"We know, glamour queen," Stacy said, rolling her eyes.

"I'm not sure I can go back," Mary Alyce said, surprising herself. She didn't have a plan for where else to go, or what she would do when she got there. But now she understood that her life was meant to be unusual, that she was meant to see both sides of the color line to help others. Knowing the why behind her experience, or suspecting it, was good enough for her, without knowing exactly how.

THIRTY-TWO

JUDY

From Margaret to Judy

Saturday, 23 June 1945

Dear Judy,
I was excited to get your last letter with postage from France.
What an adventure you have been on, moving about from one
place to the other.

I have news I think you'll find exciting, but I don't know
how I feel about it, honestly. The slave markets have been of-
ficially shut down. One day, I went early and white women
were handing out leaflets about agencies and fair labor. Said
the city needed to give us better options. Next thing I know,
I'm out on Simpson Street another day and somebody put up a
sign on the wall where we used to lean and sit. "No Soliciting.
No Day Work. Fine $75." I heard on the radio that it is now

officially against the law for anybody to pay us those sad wages from before, a dollar or a two a day. All that work goes through the agencies now, so we get fair money for our time.

Who knew anybody would stand up for us after all? It made me think about what you were trying to tell me before you left for the WAC, about having opportunities and possibilities. It made me see that things can change, people can change. You know how you can know a thing but it's not until it really un-folds in front of you that you can believe it? That's how I felt about looking at work in a different way.

I guess I need to wrap this up now that I'm rambling on. But I just wanted to say that I know I have not been the easiest on you, especially when it came to the market and your feelings about it. I'm sorry if I ever made you feel that I didn't want the very best for you, and for you to not have to struggle along like me. I thank you for not holding it against me, for being a good daughter.
I love you,
Mama

From Judy to Margaret

Tuesday, 3 July 1945

Dear Mama:
I was so pleased to get your letter and to learn that the terrible slave market is finally closed. Fair work should earn fair pay, so I liked hearing that's underway in the city, too.

Thank you for understanding what I was going towards when I came to the WAC. Time apart has helped us understand each other. Distance has also really helped me see life in the Bronx better. The miracle of writing letters for me has been that they have made me explain even better what I really mean.

I can see how your life and work have been shaped by so much that you didn't decide. The idea that a Negro woman would have a choice for the kind of work she would do, and that she would be paid well enough for it—that must be a lot to take in. To imagine I would have enough pay leftover to give to you must have been more, still. But I was never after my own glory or proving any kind of point to anybody but myself. You didn't say that, and I don't think you mean any of that, but I just want that to be clear. I only ever wanted to see what else was possible. And now that I have, I worry all the time about what things will be like when the war is over. If I will have to shrink back into the life that I crawled out of before.

Thank you for the news. I am so glad you have more ease, and that the slave market is over.

Love,

Judy

The truth was, Judy had not successfully found ease of her own, at least not in the form of a hobby. Like her mother, she did not like a lot of downtime. When Herbert was alive and they were a young couple, she spent her free time with him, doing what he liked and keeping their house. She'd learned that from her mother and father—it was how a woman should be.

So as soon as she was free of the market and enlisted, she found that she struggled a bit to learn herself and what she liked outside of working for or caring for others. And she was surprised to find that she didn't really know. Making things to benefit others was fun for her, but that was not like Mary Alyce in the kitchen or Bernadette in a salon. She did not know her particular talent yet, and she wished she knew how to find it. She also wanted to practice relaxing and having fun. Embracing downtime. How ironic her mother had gotten to it first.

The immediate gratification and sense of importance she felt as part of the battalion was seductive to Judy. In Rouen, the French civilians with whom the women of the postal battalion worked seemed to share her drive. They took a no-nonsense approach to the much smaller backlog of about three hundred thousand pieces of mail. One of them was Bernard's doppelgänger, and early on in their time there, when she saw him, her breath caught, thinking about their awkward farewell in Birmingham weeks ago. Neither had promised to write or had made an invitation. But she'd secretly hoped he would reach out, to let her know where he was, to check on her and the battalion.

Everyone in her battalion eased into their new surroundings. The train ride between Rouen and Paris was just under an hour and a half, and Mary Alyce could not get enough of the culinary delights in the cities and everywhere in between. Captain Campbell and Stacy found ex-patriates and civilians to join a basketball league that sometimes took them to Germany. Ever the adventurer, Bernadette did not slow down, even if the women in her unit were reluctant to follow her on her regular countryside jaunts. She easily made friends with women from other companies and traveled with them.

"You all need to get away from the barracks and see the rest of the sights," Bernadette encouraged them. "A few of us are taking a car trip through the countryside this weekend. Come on with us?"

Judy loved Bernadette's wanderlust, but she didn't know if she trusted the driving skills of those other women she hung out with. The winding roads tangled around mountains in a way that made Judy queasy. "I'll pass, but I know you'll have a good time." Mary Alyce and Stacy turned her down, too.

Bernadette gave them all a suit-yourself shrug and was off, a tangerine summer scarf leaving her signature lilac scent behind her.

Judy was more interested with the rich history of Rouen—it was also the most physically beautiful place she'd ever seen or dreamed about. The lush hills rose in subtle slopes above the Seine. Richard the Lionheart rested in the Rouen Cathedral. It was the kind of place where she felt she could discover something new about the past, and possibly, about herself.

And after a month and a half of being there, she was surprised to discover something else: it felt like a place where she could stay. The revelation startled her as much as it also opened a portal to a host of ideas. Now she had a choice of where she could live out the rest of her life, if she wanted one.

The epiphany came with a good omen: a note from Bernard, tucked into her mail slot in their new work area. He wanted to meet for tea at a café near the Renaissance arcade downtown. He was far from a hobby or a pastime, but he would be a good distraction. She took great care with her makeup, with dabbing some of the perfume Mary Alyce gifted her from Paris behind her ears—a floral but faint scent. The French maids who resented that the American Negroes could afford such a luxury and, after the war, they could not, diluted their perfume with water.

She felt heady and cloaked in something elegant nonetheless, though she wore only her plain summer uniform dress as she walked along the rue du Cordier in the bright light of midday. She looked curiously at the many galleries dotting every corner, displaying textiles and paintings through spotless, delicate glass panes. Every park, or square, carried the name of some important man and the steel lacework on the buildings that had remained after the many iterations of war there represented great symbols of resilience.

It was a quality Judy admired in a town but the essence of that character was in stark contrast to her memories of the Bronx. Growing up shaped by the Great Depression, vagabonds and derelicts heaved trash from windows so frequently, you couldn't just walk peacefully down the street. Few things were on display for the sheer purpose of delight. Her parents had bristled at how crammed together and dingy everything was when they arrived. Margaret saw it as an invitation to make their apartment that much more inviting, just as Judy had done in Birmingham with that old building. One's home could be a refuge and sanctuary in opposition to the place where it was located.

And now she wanted to be settled within herself. She wondered if she could find that here, and was thinking of that when Bernard stood from the café table to greet her, kissed her lightly on both cheeks and smiled softly at her. "Private Washington, I'm glad you could make it." He gestured for her to sit.

"How could I resist the invitation?" She sank down onto the chair, eyes meeting his. The light in the town gave him an added glow, or maybe she had simply missed him.

Bernard looked solemn. "You might say no. With good reason."

That was fair, she said. "But I thought you were an optimist." She was not; this they both knew. Only she kept her pessimism to herself. It was obvious, if only to her, that she wanted to turn away from him and this place, to return to at least a more recognizable version of herself. But seeing him now, she knew it was too late.

"Pragmatist, mostly," he said, his gaze traveling toward the bend in the Seine that curved inland toward them. "Hazel was a fan of the river. She said it was shaped in an unruly way. We walked this area together, in our rare free time. I'm happy

306

to say it was a place where people mainly ignored our differences. There are so many people, so many other things to see. Of course, she noticed the occasional stare, but I never did. I was too focused on her."

Judy liked being in a place he associated with Hazel, sipping tea. "Did you have many favorite places here?"

He turned his gaze on her, and she felt heat rise to her face. His attractiveness always felt like a penetrating force that surprised her each time, even though she was always aware of it. His handsomeness was relentless. "Anywhere I was with her became my favorite place," Bernard said. "I called you here because I have not felt that way since Hazel died. So it has taken some time for me to notice that feeling again. To understand that it comes because of how I feel when I'm with you, to understand that the nerves I feel, the way my palms sweat when I'm near you—well, Judy. I'm afraid I have a rather inconvenient confession."

At this last phrase, the mention of emotions she already felt, already knew, he leaned in so that in the midst of the noisy cars and people around them, it felt like they had privacy. The familiar heat rising to her face was accompanied now by moist palms. It was a relief to have finally heard from him that what she sensed was real, and to say, herself, what she had buried in her heart.

"It's not so inconvenient for me, if you're wondering," she said, feeling bold. "I had been wanting to tell you something similar. I have feelings for you, too. I just don't know what to do about them. I don't know what it means for me. For us."

Bernard leaned back in his chair then, as if she had gently pushed his shoulders. His lips stretched into a lopsided smile, just considering her. She wondered if he was remembering each time she had awkwardly stared at him while he was explaining something at the King Edwards School, or how flustered and jumpy she was in his presence.

After a moment, Bernard leaned toward her with tender consideration, reaching his hand through the clear path between their teacups and saucers. She wiped her palms over the thighs of her uniform skirt before letting Bernard's slightly calloused hands fold over her own. "Well, the good news, Judy, is that we don't have to decide what this means today. But I do want you to think about requesting to stay over here when your service with the battalion is over."

Judy raised her eyebrows. "Stay here? With you?"

"Yes, of course," he said. "But take the time you need to decide."

As much as she wanted to say yes to him at that moment, she was worried that it was too much of a risk. What if she gave up everything at home, and she and Bernard turned out to be an awful match? What would her friends in the battalion, besides Mary Alyce, think?

"Okay," she said, clearly shocked.

"Don't sound so thrilled," Bernard said, looking concerned. "Again, don't rush. Take the time you need. I will wait for you. However long it takes."

With a slow nod, Judy let herself enjoy how comfortable, how easy it felt for her hands to be surrounded by his. While it was true that they didn't have to decide what to do right at that moment, Judy couldn't help but feel a shift. She had thought she understood the shape of her life before then, the circle that she would complete, leaving the Bronx, going to the women's army, going home. But Bernard and his affection, welcome as it was, presented a different outcome—one she hadn't imagined. She would have to explain it to Margaret, to hope and pray that her mother would understand. When her mother flashed into her mind, she squeezed Bernard's hand a little tighter, and set thoughts of Margaret aside. She would worry about what to say to her mother later and enjoy this moment with Bernard.

THIRTY-THREE

CHARITY

Charity was more restless than usual. In Japan, early August 1945, US atomic bombs dropped in Hiroshima and Nagasaki and killed more than two hundred and ten thousand people combined—a toll the military would only learn in the months to come. The radio reports and newsreels sounded giddy at the prospect of these being final blows in the years-long war. Oddly, it was the news of the devastation of the atomic bombs that had created an icebreaker for Charity and Abbie to make up, to heal their tense rift, at least in a temporary way. Abbie had gone to Charity's room across the hall after lights-out, uncharacteristically shaken and flustered after hearing the news and wanting to talk about when they might receive orders to return home.

Charity had her own concerns, though she kept them to herself. She had felt snubbed by Abbie but decided to drop the matter—stuffed it in a box behind her heart so she could get on with their last push of mail as they awaited news of re-assignment or return. But avoiding sharing her real feelings with her best friend and second-in-command was no small task. So when Abbie knocked this time in the dark, she answered cautiously, but she was also worried.

"Are you unwell?" Charity asked with concern.

"I must be," Abbie said. "I can't sleep. Every time I close my eyes, I see dead children and civilians."

Charity paused, still standing in the doorway and blocking the path into her room. Abbie looked disheveled and distraught. She hadn't even bothered with a bonnet.

"Edna," Abbie said with an anxious whisper. "Are you really not going to let me in?"

Charity shook her head slightly, more of a reflex, as she moved out of the way. She must have looked as dazed as she felt. "Sorry," Charity mumbled.

So much for her strong feelings and convictions about sticking to curfew. She was almost ashamed she hadn't stood firmer ground against breaking the rule that officers should not be in one another's quarters, socializing, once lights were out. But she couldn't stand to see Abbie this way. She made her sit down on the bed and then sat a ruler's length away from her, stiff as a board. "What have you been listening to that's got you so upset?"

"That's just it, I haven't been listening to much lately," Abbie said. She ran her hands over her face, like she needed to bathe the frustration away. "You know I've been meaning to tell you that you're doing it again."

A lump of anxiety lodged in Charity's throat. This was the moment she feared. Confrontation. But she was sitting far enough from Abbie. She was not flirting. "What do you mean?" Charity asked.

"The mumbling. From training. I can barely hear you most of the time," Abbie said, smiling enough that her eyes softened. "Do you suppose it happens when you're afraid?"

Charity tried not to laugh in spite of herself, but she couldn't help it. She had seen a great many things in herself shift, but the mumble always came back to haunt her. She had not made an emotional connection between her feelings and her volume, but it made the most sense. "You've changed the subject," she said.

Abbie paused. "The women in my family sometimes talk about having the gift of foresight. Premonitions. And I'm worried that someone in our unit might be in trouble."

Charity was not inclined to talk hoodoo and visions with Abbie, but she didn't want to dismiss her either. "Well, we still have work to complete here and I need you rested. If what you've been unnerved by is in our future, we won't know until it happens. There's nothing to be done."

Abbie tilted her head. "That's true, actually. I hadn't thought of it that way."

Charity nodded, proud. Then they sat in awkward silence before Charity patted her legs, clapping herself on the thighs before walking to the door with Abbie so close behind her she could feel Abbie's breath on her neck. Charity turned around and their mouths were close enough to embrace when Abbie moved her face, whispering, "Thank you," in a voice that sounded like an apology.

Charity could not get back to sleep after that, and she would not admit that Abbie's late-night visit was the reason. She tossed and turned all night instead of getting up and doing something else. By the time she was able to focus, the sun was up and the morning bugle sounded. She finally got out of bed and got dressed.

★ ★ ★

In her groggy state, over coffee that had not kicked in yet, Charity was approached by two somber Military Police in the mess hall. After their salutes, the taller one said, "Major, we have some sad news you need to know." He waited for her to gesture for him to go ahead, which she did with a fearful nod, thinking of Abbie's warning.

News you did not want to hear or believe had a way of sounding distorted. The words about *Bernadette Moore, car crash on a country road* and *two other casualties* made some sense, but the impact was dulled. It felt like she had been dunked underwater.

"Ma'am, you will need to write to the next of kin to let them know as soon as possible, and then break the news to your officers," the voice continued. And as always, when she had a task to complete, Charity snapped back into focus and into action.

"Will you have the addresses for my Executive Officer to provide when the letters are prepared?" Charity said, looking up to see Abbie with her hand over her mouth, like she was going to be sick. Charity stepped closer to her, to try and console her before she dismissed the MPs.

"Charity, those are the women that woke me up."

"There's such thing as coincidence, Abbie," Charity said, but she did feel the timing was uncanny. On the other hand, they were in a war zone and death was just a part of what came with war. "We have to tell their families. As soon as you have their addresses, let me know. I'll write them right away."

Abbie signaled that she would, and Charity went to her office to write the hardest telegram she'd ever had to write.

Monday, 6 September 1945

To the family and loved ones of Private First Class Bernadette Moore:

In accordance with US Security and Armed Forces procedure, it is my unfortunate duty to inform you that your daughter Pvt. FC Bernadette Moore was one of three members of the 6888th Central Postal Battalion who died in a vehicle accident during an authorized social trip during a weekend pass. Pvt. Moore was a beloved pillar of our community, and she will be deeply missed. Like her colleagues and sisters, Pvt. Moore will be among the first American women buried with military honors at the military cemetery in Normandy. Please do not hesitate to write to me or my Executive Officer, Captain Abigail Campbell, should you have additional questions or concerns.

My deepest and most sincere condolences to you and your family,
Major Charity Edna Adams

The news was devastating because of its arbitrary nature and its unfairness. Maybe the MP had given her more details and she just couldn't remember. But she could picture them jubilant on the countryside, immersed and maybe distracted by conversation. She could only imagine the driver taking a moment to nod, to look over her shoulder, missing the oncoming car when it was about to swerve into the jeep, sending them all over the side of a steep hill onto merciless boulders below.

As she finished the final letter in her office, she took a moment to reflect on the best way to tell the entire battalion so that they learned the news from her and Abbie first, before rumors began or they heard from an MP.

That afternoon, Charity called the battalion to formation, in the expansive courtyard in front of their quarters. It was a perfect, late-summer day, with no clouds or planes above them, just endless blue.

"I am deeply saddened to share the news that Privates First-Class Bernadette Moore, Mary Bankston and Mary Barlow died in a terrible jeep accident off post last night," she said.

The officers' shock rose in a wave of gasps, and voices whispering loudly. Stacy, one of her most stoic officers, began to sob from the shock. Judy and Mary Alyce were beside her, tears on their faces too, as they held each other.

Charity felt an overwhelming feeling that she had never felt weigh down her shoulders. Her chest was tight. She wanted to throw herself into Abbie's arms and let her tears flow, too. Her grief was compounded by the fact that as prepared as she was for other things, she had not prepared for the reality of losing her officers. The women in her battalion had not expected to die near the battlefront. It had felt improbable, because it was.

Quiet murmurs and sobs rippled through the rows of women. Charity continued, "I don't know if there are any right words at this hour. What I have been thinking and praying about since I got the news is how very special every one of you is to our mission, how precious our moments with one another are and have been. We will begin to make funeral arrangements for them tomorrow. Please take the rest of the afternoon and we'll start our operations again in the morning. You are dismissed."

Tears in her eyes, despite her best efforts not to cry, dropped onto her cheeks as she tried to blink them away. She later ordered the Military Police to fly the American flag at half-staff for the remainder of the week.

Back at her office, she found Abbie leaning against her desk, a handkerchief in her hands, eyes puffy from crying. "You spoke clearly. Loudly. From the heart out there, Edna."

"I had no choice," Charity said. She stared quietly at Abbie and added, "Your premonition was correct."

Abbie nodded. "I was hoping it would not be so."

There was another heavy silence between them. The deaths of their sisters was not something anyone wanted.

"I've asked the companies and units to gather women with mortuary experience to help us prepare the women for burial," Abbie said, her voice breaking.

"Good thinking, Captain."

Abbie moved from the edge of the desk and stepped toward Charity. "All this sadness has given me some time to think, too."

"Whatever about?"

"Charity, don't be that way. Not now."

"Abigail," Charity snapped. "It has been a very taxing day and there is much to be done. Tell me what you want to say or I'll have to ask you to leave."

"I do love you, you know," Abigail said, standing very still, her chest high, her eyes bright. "I love you and you don't believe it because I lied to us both, because I'm afraid. But it is love anyway."

Charity was stunned. She walked to her desk, trying to move around Abbie, who stood in her path.

Abbie took Charity's hand. "I mean it. I am sorry I'm so afraid to be myself. To let you be yourself. But I need you. I choose you. I just needed some time to gather my courage and admit it. I did not want to say any of this until I felt sure I could do something about it."

"It's the perfectly wrong time," Charity said, impatient and relieved. She felt both grateful and irritated Abbie had chosen this moment to declare herself. What about all the back-and-forth? "How can I trust or believe you after all this time?"

Abbie closed the distance between them and pressed her lips

to Charity's. The heat, the waiting, her emotions all gathered to melt any remaining resistance away. Even if she wanted to pull away this time, if out of spite she wanted to show Abbie what it felt like to have your love rejected, placed into limbo, her primal response, her lizard brain bolted her feet to the ground. She could not move. She surrendered to the kiss and when Abbie stopped, she flung herself into Abbie's arms and finally let her tears flow.

"I know," Abbie said, comforting her and rubbing her back. "Let it all out. It's okay. You're safe. You're safe with me."

The entire battalion was invited to the funeral service at the massive Normandy American Cemetery in Colleville-sur-Mer. Officers had pooled their money to help pay for extra flowers. Charity was moved by the way Private Moore's unit volunteered to style her, saying that returning the favor was the least they could do for their friend.

The day was overcast and breezy. Half of the battalion stood and the other half sat. They all wore their dress uniforms with black armbands. The short service began with a benediction, then Charity spoke briefly, better now that she had emptied herself out, bawling with Abbie. Now she could be the pillar of strength they all needed her to be, instead of breaking down in public.

"I won't stay up here long, but I wanted to tell you that I am as shocked by the death of our fellow officers as you are," Charity said, careful to project and watching Abbie for any cues that she might need to be louder. "Support units are the spine of the war effort. Because we do a job that is invisible and does not take place on the battlefield does not mean what we do isn't difficult or dangerous. The deaths of these women, our sisters, are proof of that. The end of our duty is near, though theirs came far too soon. I appreciate all of you for showing up to send them to their true homes in heaven."

The funeral offered a few moments of reflection from those closest to the women in their companies. After colleagues of Privates Bankston and Barlow finished, Judy approached the podium with a small sheet of paper, which shook as she folded it up without looking at it.

"Bernadette—we called her Bernie—was the most elegant woman the majority of us will ever meet," Judy started quietly. She smiled. "She had so many things in her trunk and brought hat boxes to training camp. She was a lovely, bubbly, talented woman, who generously helped us when we looked crazy and ragged.

"As poised and polished as she was, even in uniform," Judy looked nervously at Charity at this honest description, and Charity smiled in agreement, "she had an inner light that just never stopped radiating and drawing people to her. I'll miss the warmth and the strength of that light. Bernie made everybody feel that it was shining just for them. And when you have to be in the dark after having a friend like that, it feels like the world has lost a really important soul. So, here's to Bernie, to the Marys. Here's to us, carrying forward their legacies of goodness and becoming our own lights in this dark world."

Charity was emotional again, and she was also very proud of Judy, who she always saw as her best recruit. Judy was proof that even when Charity wasn't sure about their overall impact, she could still do good.

THIRTY-FOUR

JUDY

The layers of loss from Bernadette to Herbert reached Judy in a deep place. It wasn't just that she would miss Bernadette's elegance, that tenderness she had felt being attended to, but that Bernadette had been part of the trio of people that helped her grieve Herbert. Losing friends, old and new, put her own life in perspective. Would she be a light in the darkness? And would it be here or at home?

Judy felt in the weeks following the funeral a new sense of urgency to answer these questions. The warm, friendly feelings she had had for Herbert had launched her on this journey, across the ocean, only for her to land in Bernard's arms. She had been waffling enough on deciding what to do about the heat she felt with him. There was no time to waste anymore. She wanted to build another life with him. It was hard to imagine not being in the Bronx, because the dream of her homecoming had always involved going back.

But now she had new dreams. It would not be a perfect place to land. France and England did not have the same Jim Crow restrictions as the United States, but white American soldiers had left the mark of their ugly thoughts about women in the WAC with their peers abroad. And she was a Negro, so even more inferior in their minds. Like any other place on earth, being overseas wouldn't keep people from staring at Judy, especially if she was going to be in public with a white man.

But Bernard's gaze was the only one that really mattered to her now. As she imagined a future for herself, and with whom, she knew it was with him, in this place. She sent word to him asking to see him in a few days.

"You've been quiet lately," Stacy mused one afternoon during their mail shift. Compared to the first giant backlog the battalion cleared in Birmingham, the dwindling piles of mail they had to sort was insignificant. That was why dozens of civilian officers had been reassigned to other postal units, and Company A of the Central Postal Battalion had been given their orders to sail back home in two weeks. Orders disbanding the rest of the battalion would be coming to them any day now.

"There hasn't been much to say. But I suppose I've been a little down. Missing Bernadette," Judy said.

"I miss her, too. Every day," Stacy said, looking mournful.

"You've lost some muscle without any of her shopping bags to carry around," Judy said.

Stacy laughed. "Yeah, and it doesn't help that there's no real mail to sort. Our great adventure is almost over. I feel worse for the wear, I'll tell you that."

"I think that's how we all feel," Judy confessed, looking up from a small stack of letters.

"You're stuck with me for life, you know that, right?" Stacy said, her voice catching.

"Well, that goes both ways, McFadden. Don't you go making me cry while I'm working. I'll mess up the ink on these letters," Judy said.

"What in the world is happening over here? What are all these tears about?" Mary Alyce demanded.

"We were just saying how much we're going to miss each other," Judy said when she recovered.

"Speak for yourselves," Mary Alyce said drily.

"Oh, I'll miss you most of all," Judy said.

"What kind of bunkmate picks favorites?" Stacy demanded.

"The kind who thinks you sleep like a banshee."

"Low blow, Judy. I won't dignify that with a response. But let's just say that just because you look dainty doesn't mean you snore like a lady."

Judy's mouth flew open. "What! I do not snore."

Stacy shook her head solemnly. "I'm afraid that's not the truth."

Judy laughed a little more at her serious tone. Now the tears she wiped from the corners of her eyes were from her laughter. She could get used to the feeling of being with the people she loved most, feeling happy and free. She just had to take the first step in that direction.

Days after the news of their pending departure, Judy met Bernard at the Port of Rouen, the site of deliveries of artillery and supplies during the war, textiles and other merchant needs before and after. He was helping to assess damage to the stretch of the Seine coastline due to Allied Forces bombing and to come up with an estimate for city officials to repair the now lazily trafficked place. The wide river arc snaked its way through the country's northernmost countryside before it emptied out into the English Channel and the Atlantic Ocean.

Standing at the shore, Judy followed the water and the shipping containers in white and blue dotting her side of the water until the distant towers of lighthouses and rows of homes became hills and tree bluffs. The toll of the bell from the Cathedral signaled that it was just after noon.

Bernard joined her without a word, touching one of her hands, which made her jump before she turned to him, relaxing. He looked surprised that she was startled at first, but then, his eyebrows settled. They were still new to each other this way, as more than friends. She fumbled with her own hands to hold his own. "I'm glad you were able to get away."

"Not that there's much to get away from, now. Work's almost complete," Judy said, looking at him, searching his eyes. "A few hundred women have been sent home already."

Bernard grunted his understanding, rocked back and forth on his heels. "And your company?"

"No word, yet. I would have told you," Judy said. Now her stomach was in knots.

"Have you thought about what I asked?" Maybe she imagined the anxiety in his voice. Her own impatience with herself might have been what was in her ears.

She had not said anything so consequential since she married her best friend, not even when she made an oath to the women's army to serve to the best of her abilities, at home and abroad. "I wanted to meet with you because I plan to stay."

The air felt lighter, like a pressure valve had been building up, ready to burst before her admission. She had been afraid and excited on the trip over, all the nights between their last conversation and now. Even Bernard opened his mouth to speak, with a slight smirk that suggested he was going to make a wise remark. But the moment was more important to him than that, and she could see him letting out a breath he had been holding longer than she could guess. "In France, you mean?"

"Wherever you are," Judy said, letting him take her hand, and squeeze it. "I'll remain wherever you are."

"Well, Officer Washington, that's quite a relief," he said, taking her other hand. Before he said another word, he knelt on the ground and looked up at her. "Because I would love for you to be my wife."

Judy felt dizzy at first, like the ground was moving beneath her boots. "Get up from there. I can't believe this," she said, thinking he had to be joking.

"Believe it. Believe me," he said, a ring in a red velvet box open now in his hand revealing a beautiful diamond ring. "I can't give this to you until you say yes, I'm afraid. And I have problems with my knees from cricket—"

"Yes! Yes, yes, I will marry you," Judy said, grinning and letting him pull her to him as he stood again. A few passersby clapped for them as he slipped the ring on her finger. It was settled. She was going to be a wife again, this time, abroad.

She inhaled his musky cologne, like a swimmer taking in the air she needed. He was looking at her again, with his startling blue eyes and mess of lashes, as if he saw every possibility for their days ahead together. When he pressed his lips to hers, they were both trembling gently for the moment. She had to sip in another breath again, to remember she was on land and not in the water. She could breathe.

"I'll need to get back, to tell the others," she said finally.

"You're already trying to leave me and we're not even newlyweds," Bernard said with a pout.

"The sooner you let me leave, the sooner I can return," she said with a giddy smile.

"You, too, are a pragmatist," he said, pulling away from

her, still holding her hand. "That's such a nice ring, if I do say so myself."

She laughed and swatted him before kissing him on both cheeks. It was delightful to express her affection openly, without fear or guilt. "It is nice. I will give you a full report of my friends' reactions when they see it and hear our good news."

"Very well, Private Washington. Until next time," he said, beaming.

They would never have to say goodbye, now, Judy thought. And she turned to head back to post.

Like many first kisses, her first embrace with Bernard lingered on her lips until she was alone with just the memory of him. In the days that followed, the women received news that the remaining companies of the battalion were to return back to the United States by the end of January 1946, and they would be debriefed ahead of their return, or in Judy's case, if they intended to end their service while remaining in the European Theater.

Judy wrote to her mother with her heart racing, her hands a little unsteady.

Friday, 20 November 1945

Dear Mama:
It's hard to believe another holiday season finds us apart, but I know you must have plans to celebrate properly. This is the kind of news I wish we could share in person or on the phone, but I'm excited to tell you I have met someone over here, Bernard Welsh. He's an Englishman who was a great colleague to me in Birmingham, who has also become the man I love, and now, we are planning to be wed. I was already wondering what it would be like to make a home here, where there are some ob-

stacles for Negro women, but not as many as back home, and then he proposed.

It feels like fate has intervened here. The future I came to the WAC expecting to live has shifted to be an even greater adventure. Of course, within days of his proposal, we received orders to head home.

I've been afraid to write this letter, feeling the way I have about Bernard and also thinking about you on your own in the Bronx. It's made me so happy to read your letters and to see that you have found a way to have a living wage along with dignity and a measure of peace, too. My biggest worry is that you'll feel I betrayed you by choosing a man over what I initially intended, which was to come back and continue to help around the house. But I still plan to send money to assist and, eventually, I will have enough to come back and visit. Maybe you can even come see us.

It feels like there is still so much here to explore and discover. I will keep you posted on it all. Merry Christmas, Mama. I love you and I miss you. I hope you'll understand.

Always your baby girl,

Love,

Judy

THIRTY-FIVE

CHARITY

From Charity to E. A. Adams

Saturday, 13 January 1946

Dear Daddy:
I write with the bittersweet news that I am finally coming home.
The only bitterness is from leaving behind the wonderful officers
and saying farewell to Abbie. At the end of the month, I return
with the remaining officers of the Six Triple Eight battalion.

I am very proud of all we accomplished over here. Very few
people believed that Negro women had anything to offer the war
effort. But it has been edifying to see how knowing we were
playing even a small part in helping our boys' morale has led to
victory here and in Japan. I would have never dreamed that I
could be a part of such an outfit, but what a blessing it has been.

I am nervous about returning home, even if I expect the voy-

age to be less anxiety-producing than the journey here. I also wonder about how much has changed in the almost four years that I've been gone. I can hear you telling me that it's the South, and only so much can change there. I can't wait to see for myself.

I will see you very soon.
Love Always,
Charity

Charity held the cable from the European Theater of Operations headquarters Abbie handed her, with the official orders to disband the unit and the details of their journey home. The blood felt like it was draining from her face. The pallor made Abbie say, "Come on, Major. It's not a death sentence. We've been expecting these orders for several months."

Charity eyed her friend. Abbie looked as composed as ever, not a stitch of her uniform out of place, or a wily curl ruining her professional look. "Maybe you've been waiting for it for that long." In a softer tone, she added, "Don't you think it is a sentence in a way? For us?"

"Mmm," Abbie said. "It will just be an adjustment. It'll be different back home because we're different."

There were the daily routines, the kind of work, where they would live and those kinds of details to work out. Would she and Abbie try to live as openly as they could together abroad in the South? Charity could not imagine the possibility in South Carolina. But maybe they could go north. To Ohio. Where they could start over. Be more anonymous.

"Did you leave already?" Abbie said, correctly sensing that Charity was lost in her thoughts.

"In a way," Charity said. "I'll say more later when I have a plan." Right then, she needed to focus on preparing hundreds of officers for a final sea voyage. "In the meantime, let's inform the ladies we have our orders."

"Yes, ma'am," Abbie said, saluting.

News always changed the atmosphere, and this time was no different. They had been operating in limbo touched by grief and celebration over the war's end. She remembered how overwhelming it was to arrive at King Edwards School, and how the battalion pressed through its fear, buzzing with purpose. They danced until they sweated out the fine hairdos at Bernadette's salon in the renovated gym. They chattered like schoolgirls, calling her Big Ma, thinking she didn't know it was their nickname for her—it gave her a thrill—telling each other about how she told off that funny little chaplain and that small bigot General J. G. Nash.

They had packed in a lot of life in the months they had been stationed abroad. And Abbie was right—it was time to go. The people who continued to write to her with requests and demands did not seem to think so, however. And between beginning to pack up her things, she opened the few envelopes on her desk. She read a missive from headquarters about returning protocol and quickly put it aside. The other two were more unusual: a first-class stamped envelope from Mary McLeod Bethune's organization, the National Council of Negro Women.

"That went more smoothly than planned," Abbie said, returning to the office as Charity was trying to figure out what she was looking at in the mail before her. "Whatever is the matter? You scared of a couple of envelopes now?"

Charity sucked her teeth. She sounded bewildered when she said, "Girl, just sit down and let me see what this is."

Abbie sat. "It's too soon to quit following your orders, but I'll have you know I'm tired anyway."

Charity opened the smaller envelope and read it aloud. "We are pleased to inform you that you have been promoted to lieutenant colonel." Charity looked over the top of the letter with the shock she felt as Abbie squealed.

"Why aren't you squealing, too?"

"I'm stunned," Charity said.

Abbie stood up and put her hands on her hips. "Are you really surprised or do you think saying that will make me think you're humble?"

"I beg your pardon. I am the most humble woman you know."

"I don't want to argue about this," Abbie said, shaking her head. "You're a goddamn lieutenant colonel. The only woman ranked higher than you is Director Oveta Hobby!"

"And all the other lieutenant colonels who are white," Charity said.

"I was going to come over there to congratulate you with a celebratory kiss," Abbie said, pretending to sulk. "But I can see you intend to ruin the moment."

"And you took the Lord's name in vain, so it dulled the moment already," Charity said, trying to stay serious but cracking a smile. Abbie moved to the other side of the desk to hug Charity anyway, pressing her nose to Charity's. "Congratulations, ma'am."

Charity blushed and let herself relax with Abbie. "Thank you."

Abbie nuzzled with Charity for a moment before she pulled away to pick up the larger envelope. "Now, this looks like a big deal, too. Open it!"

Charity handed Abbie the letter opener. "Could you?"

"I do a lot of things as your Executive Officer, but you want me opening your mail?"

Charity squeezed Abbie around the waist and deployed her best puppy dog eyes.

"Fine. But only because we're leaving," Abbie said, opening the letter with a perfectly even flourish. "Oh, Charity," she said, pulling out the document inside. It was a scroll from the National Council of Negro Women, thanking her for her leadership and service to the country.

Charity was speechless. She let tears pool in her eyes as she read the scroll, signed by Ms. Bethune herself and Abbie patted her on the back. She felt honored she had been called to lead and had answered. But she also felt it was their combined talents—hers, Abbie's and the battalion's—that helped her with these distinctions, nothing she had done on her own.

The day after she learned of their unit's closure and her promotion, General J. G. Nash paid her a visit from Brussels, where he'd been stationed. Just as he had before, when he had suggested that a white officer should be in charge of the battalion and she told him it would happen over her dead body, the general arrived in a limousine and without any notice. This time, however, his Military Police escorts stayed in the car. He alone offered Charity a hearty, smart salute. She returned it, respectfully, though she was still on guard for whatever mean thing he might say now.

"Colonel," General J. G. Nash said in his loud, abrasive bark. "I came to offer an apology. I learned a lot from you, not just about Negroes but also about dignity and integrity. What you did with your battalion and unit has truly been a remarkable service to our country. If I thought I would ever see you again, I would never say this to you. But I do apologize for my behavior in the past. I wish you nothing but continued success."

He didn't give her a chance to respond, which was just as well, because she couldn't put a sentence together in that moment. What a surprise, to hear from a man like that that she had changed his mind, simply through doing her work, and doing it well. She wondered if he knew that he had paid her one of the greatest compliments of her life.

The battalion traveled in a fleet of military buses to the Port of Rouen where they were to set sail on the *Queen Mary*. Her first recruit, Judy, met them at the dock to see them off in the foggy morning. Charity saw Judy standing close to Bernard Welsh, their hands in each other's. Judy had made it clear that she intended to stay abroad and marry him. It inspired Charity that Judy had found what appeared to be real love.

The officers carried their duffel bags and trunks, wearing their thick winter uniforms and coats, their faces ruddy from the wind and cold, their features barely visible in the early morning fog. Charity sent Abbie to corral the women to board the ship as she approached Judy, who was already embracing Mary Alyce and Stacy.

"You may not want to see another envelope after all this," Stacy said, her arms around Judy. "But if you don't write me, I'll have to come find you and no one wants that."

"Of course, I'll write to you, silly," Judy said.

"It's not a threat," Stacy added, stepping away. "It's a warning, Washington."

Mary Alyce agreed, eyes wet. She flung herself at her friend next, and when they hugged tightly, Judy closed her eyes to let tears stream down her cheeks. "Write me too, please. I want to hear every detail. The wedding. The food!"

They laughed through their tears at the emphasis on food and Charity was tickled to overhear it. "I suppose now that you've gotten so much practice, I can't convince you stay over here and give me cooking lessons?" Judy said, coyly.

Mary Alyce pulled away from Judy, wiping her face and looking at her friend quietly for a moment. "I wouldn't have made it through this without you. I can never repay you for what a friend you've been to me. Thank you."

They squeezed hands, then let go. When Stacy and Mary Alyce turned to head toward the ship, they acknowledged Charity with salutes, and Judy did the same. Charity stepped forward, her voice heavy with emotion. "Well, I certainly never expected I would meet you in New York and bid you farewell in France, Private," Charity said, fondness in her eyes.

Judy looked at the dock, then at the ship. She was taking it all in, every moment. "I expected it even less than you," she replied.

"Private Washington, I'm proud of you and the woman you've become. I know your mother is as well. Rightly so. Keep your courage. Don't forget what you've accomplished. In spite of so much," Charity said.

"Thank you, ma'am."

Charity pulled Judy into a brief, tight hug, patting her on the back before the swell of emotion in her chest made itself visible in tears, like her subordinates. That would not do, not even as they prepared to leave. Charity quickly whisked away her tears and saluted Judy. Judy wiped her face with the back of her hand and returned the salute one last time before Charity walked away.

On the ship, Charity was in charge of dozens of white women nurses returning home in addition to the remaining five hundred women in her battalion. She assumed they had been informed that she was a Negro. It was only when she addressed them all from the top deck, as the captain prepared to set sail, that she realized she was mistaken.

"Any questions, ladies?" Charity asked, hoping they understood the question as rhetorical.

A white woman called out, "I don't want to be under the command of a Negro."

"Honestly?" Abbie said, her voice loud. "You will show respect to Lieutenant Colonel Adams. She is the highest-ranking officer on this vessel, and we all have to answer to her."

"I don't *have* to do anything," the woman huffed.

"I knew we wouldn't get back to the States without a hitch," Stacy said, rolling her eyes.

Charity thanked Abbie for her intervention, but she felt her patience begin to thin. "Captain Campbell is absolutely right. I will remind you that I am in charge of you—*all* of you— until we return to New York. Negro or no, I am the senior ranking officer among you. If that troubles you so much, you can make different arrangements under which to sail home. You have seventeen minutes to get off the ship. In exactly eighteen minutes, this ship will set sail for the United States with or without you."

This ultimatum was met with a quiet buzz from the women surrounding the defiant one who had protested. Charity meant every word of it and that much was evident. She glanced at her watch in a way that dared any of the women with the audacity to challenge her command to move a muscle unless they wanted to be shamed even further.

Moments later, the white male captain of the ship appeared and reiterated her command. "Ladies, in case there is any additional confusion, Lieutenant Colonel Adams is in charge of everyone here. And now you have thirteen minutes left if you'd like to disembark."

Talking continued, but no one made a move to leave. And with the resignation of at least one adamant white woman, they all began their homecoming voyage to Fort Dix, New Jersey.

The rest of the journey home was without incident. They

had heard stories in letters and on the radio of the jubilant crowds with signs saying "Welcome Home," sometimes spelled out in the landscape shrubs. For the boys coming home from war, cities were aflutter with ticker tape parades, sailors embracing pretty girls and fathers shooting their guns with glee into azalea bushes. The men were met with tears and applause everywhere they went.

But for the women, the docks were barren in comparison, as though they had arrived on a very late cruise ship. There were a few "Welcome Home" signs that hovered above the small clusters of parents, sisters, friends and husbands there to reunite with their loved ones.

Charity had no expectations for fanfare on the docks or back in Columbia. They may have changed from serving overseas, but America had not. She did not need to go home to see that clearly.

When the women had gone, and it was just Charity and Abbie waiting for an MP to drive them to the train station, Abbie said, "Well, it looks like we're on the last leg of our mission, Lieutenant Colonel."

"It doesn't have to be," Charity said.

"Should I ask what you mean, or are you going to tell me?"

"I mean we don't have to go back, Abbie. Let's go north. To Ohio. We can live there, work. We can make our lives there together," Charity said, one word more frantic than the next.

Abbie looked shocked. She folded her arms and laughed. "You've always got a strategy cooking up there, huh? I should have known."

Charity felt desperate for Abbie to answer. She had finally figured out what more she wanted, besides success, rank and service. She wanted to live out her final days with this spunky, smart, beautiful captain. All she needed was for Abbie to say yes. "Just say you'll come with me."

"Stubborn as a country mule," Abbie said, dropping her arms. The MP jeep arrived and soldiers loaded their bags in the back. "Let's go home first and then we'll talk about when we can leave."

Charity could have kissed her right then. Instead, she grabbed Abbie's hand and squeezed it tight. "I like the sound of that, Captain."

The good feeling stayed with her all the way to the train station and even on the train back to South Carolina, where she and Abbie encountered the same kind of sneers and looks they'd gotten when they first put on their uniforms. The difference now was that she and Abbie were together. Their love was a shield, a force field that protected her from taking in the hatred of others.

Stepping off the train with her bags, with Abbie next to her, Charity narrowly avoided the spittle of an officer who spit so close to her some of it landed on her otherwise pristine shoes. Abbie started to say something to the man and Charity gripped her wrist to stop her.

"Release me," Abbie said, pulling her hand away.

Their train had arrived ahead of schedule, so their families had not yet arrived. "So this is goodbye, then. For now."

"I prefer 'see you later,'" Charity said. "Sounds less permanent."

Abbie's parents showed up first, honking, spilling out of their car with bright eyes and warm smiles to sweep her up. "See you later, Edna. We'll talk again soon. I promise," Abbie sad, giving her a quick hug, too brief for Charity, but nothing else could be done.

"See you later, Abbie," Charity said, her heart sinking as it beat rapidly, a flurry of emotions coursing through her. She waved at Abbie and her family and watched them take her away with her things. Then waited until her father pulled up with Deacon Hurley before they drove away.

When Rev. E. A. Adams got out of the car, he beamed with pride, pausing to just take her in. "Look at you, baby girl. God has surely blessed us today, bringing you home looking like an angel."

She dropped her things and melted into her father's arms. It was still a place where she felt comforted, almost complete and entirely safe. "Thank you, Daddy. You know just what to say."

"Your mother has trained me well," he said softly.

"You are quite a sight, Miss Charity," Deacon Hurley echoed. "Welcome home."

They rode under a magenta sky in tense silence. Columbia was still a sundown town, and they needed to hurry her home, away from danger.

The next day, her mother surprised her with an afternoon gathering, complete with a cake and a dozen family friends who brought gifts and well-wishes. She felt herself begin to relax a little more, moment by moment. She tried not to miss Abbie, but she couldn't help it.

She tried to focus on riding high on the generous welcome home, but she knew that after almost five years away, it would take time to get used to the slow pace of civilian life. She already missed the challenges and the pleasures of leading a large command. She was considering about what her next job would be, whether she wanted to go on to finish school. Where in Ohio she and Abbie might stay.

She was starting to doubt her instincts when, nights after all the celebrating, the smell of something smoldering awakened them all. In her old house, she heard her father's heavy footfall as he rushed to get his shotgun, the muffled sound of her mother warning him to just be careful. Charity approached the window as her father warned her to stay away, but it was too late: a cross burrowed into her family's front yard was aflame. The orange blaze flickered against her resolute face.

THIRTY-SIX

MARY ALYCE

When Mary Alyce returned to Woodstock, her mother picked her up from the train station in a borrowed truck from a neighbor. The first thing Mary Alyce noticed was how much smaller everything seemed—the roads, the stores, even her mother felt part of this tiny, closed-in life.

"Mary Alyce, honey, you've made it back," Helen said, looking as girlish as Mary Alyce had ever seen her, her hair in a ponytail sweeping the side of her neck, the skin around her eyes crinkling. She almost gasped from the tight hug her mother gave her.

"I did," Mary Alyce said, catching her breath. "It's good to be home. It's good to see you."

She said those things because she knew her mother wanted to hear them. Because they were easy things to say; they cost her nothing to offer, at least she didn't think they did. But she was also nervously filling the air between them with words to fend off a confrontation that had started on paper, with the matter of her birth certificate. Mary Alyce was trying to meet a twenty-year-old silence with her anxiety.

"I know I said it in those letters, but I'm sorry I didn't say anything to you about Eugene sooner," Helen said. "Feels like I will spend the rest of my days apologizing for what I didn't do or say about him, but it's worth it if it means you'll forgive me."

"I think I understand, Mama. And I accept your apology," Mary Alyce said. "One is enough. You can stop there."

A look Mary Alyce couldn't read crossed Helen's face and she made herself busy trying to load Mary Alyce's luggage into the bed of the truck by herself. She struggled with the heavy trunk until Mary Alyce helped her heave it into the flatbed.

"It might be too soon to say that, dear," her mother said, closing the door to the back of the truck and walking to the driver's side. Before Mary Alyce could ask what Helen meant, her mother said, "Folks in town have been acting different since the WACs came home. Edith and Betsy sure did spread the word about us, about you. I had to lie to borrow this truck, since no one wants anything to do with a Colored in their truck. I received a stern talking-to at church, about the sinful mixing of the races."

Mary Alyce tried not to show her shock at her worst fear for coming home being real. But she wanted to hear all of it so she knew what she was about to face. "And Grandma?"

Her mother started the truck. "We fought after one of her little friends gossiped about you in her knitting circle. Saying I was irresponsible and selfish. She says she's too old to leave her land, but if she could, she'd put us both out. So, we barely talk."

Mary Alyce could feel her heart get heavy in her chest. She

could not care less about the residents of Woodstock. She had made real friends in the women's army.

But she had not prepared herself for the rejection of her grandmother, who, for days after she returned home, looked at Mary Alyce like she was a stranger. She allowed her to kiss her on the cheek but didn't smile the way she used to. Tenderness and motherly affection was no longer available to this Negro Mary Alyce, her grandmother seemed to say. It was harder to bear than Mary Alyce could have imagined.

A version of this stony silence followed her everywhere like a cloud: to the market, to the post office, to the library. At the latter, the town librarian pulled her aside and said, "Legally, we need a separate library for Coloreds. But I'll let you come in here as long as you don't go causing any trouble."

It was trouble, however, that Mary Alyce most wanted to make. But not here in Vermont. She would have to leave soon. This life would never do.

She smiled sweetly. "That's a terrific way to thank me for my service, and I do appreciate it," she said, walking to a table with an envelope filled with information about her next stop: Birmingham, Alabama, where Agnes, her father's sister, still lived. Mary Alyce had enough savings to live anywhere for a time before she had to worry about work. She did not want to stay in a place like this, where she was tolerated and only barely. She wanted to be celebrated. She hoped she could find that in Alabama, since it was not possible in Vermont.

After a full month of trying to reacclimate to life with Helen and her now muted-by-racism grandmother, Mary Alyce packed a duffel bag and left a short note for Helen.

Mama:
Thank you for making space for me to come home. I found too

*much is different for me to feel like I can live the way I want to
here. I'm headed to Alabama to meet Daddy's kin. I will write
again soon. Please don't be upset.*
I love you,
Mary Alyce

She added Agnes's home address to the bottom and started
her journey south. Wearing her uniform, she felt similar to
the first time she left Woodstock, except this time leaving her
house felt like a permanent goodbye.

In Birmingham, Mary Alyce found a nice boarding room
in a house for Colored women, though the woman she met
with almost redirected her elsewhere. Instead of being surprised by her confusion, Mary Alyce only nodded and gently
corrected, then took her bags to her room.

The next day, Mary Alyce called on Agnes Dixon wondering now why she was so determined to present herself to her
aunt. Maybe it was because she was hoping to find that sense
of belonging with her family that she found with the ladies of
the Central Postal Battalion. Her sense of home had changed.
She found it was now only with other Negro women.

And maybe that was why she chose to wear the uniform.
The experience was over, but she still had the clothes to prove
it was real.

Agnes lived in a modest single-story house framed by two
spindly trees stripped bare by winter. Dingy rattles littered the
low porch, and a rocking chair in need of new paint swayed a
little when Mary Alyce stepped on the creaking wood.

Before she knocked, she heard children squealing and crying. It sounded like they were crawling up the walls inside of
the house. Mary Alyce knocked too softly at first, then with
a little more gumption. The curtains at one of the windows

jerked open and a thin woman with hazel eyes that looked ready to cut whoever was disturbing her peace frowned out at Mary Alyce.

"Y'all hush, there's some white lady at the door," Mary Alyce heard her say. "Y'all done called the law on me?"

There was a hush, the sound of a sweet little voice protesting, "No, no." Mary Alyce stifled a laugh as she leaned in a little to hear more.

She was still leaning when Agnes yanked the door open. She was wiry and brown, like her hair. Wisps leaped from her forehead like they were trying to get away from the rest of her hair, which was mostly in a slicked-back bun at the nape of her neck.

"Good morning, ma'am," Agnes said, tugging at her faded floral housecoat, which matched the powder blue slippers on her tiny feet.

"Good morning," Mary Alyce said back. "I'm looking for an Agnes Dixon. Is that you?"

"Depends on why you looking for her."

"I'm her niece. Eugene Dixon's daughter."

Agnes blinked hard and winced like the sun was in her eyes, but the day was cloudy. "Ma'am?"

"Eugene Dixon. He married my mother, Helen, up in Woodstock, Vermont, and died before I had a chance to know him."

Agnes's eyes went big. She opened the door wider. One of the children said something and she said hush, now, she wasn't going anywhere. The nice lady on the porch wasn't the law.

Agnes stepped out on the porch, and Mary Alyce stepped back. They stood there, eye to eye, for a moment, Agnes looking into Mary Alyce's face like it was full of small print she needed to read carefully.

"Well, I'll be," Agnes finally said. "Had to look close, but you sure are Gene's baby. Just brighter. But what're you doing here in uniform and all? Girl, I thought you was the law come to put me in jail over these bad-ass children."

"I was in the women's army. Helping with the mail."

Agnes nodded, mouth open. She grunted—approval or dismay, it wasn't clear— and then pulled Mary Alyce into a full body hug. Agnes was tiny but she was strong, and her warmth seeped through Mary Alyce's clothes and brought tears to her eyes. She had never been held like that by her mother or her grandmother, not once. She had never known that she needed to be held just that way until that moment.

A loud crash inside the house startled them both—it sounded like a pot fell off a shelf and landed on the floor. Agnes pulled herself away from Mary Alyce and put a hand on her face as the children squealed and hooted and hollered that somebody was going to get in trouble. "I'm glad you ain't who I thought you was. You might as well come on in and meet your cousins before I kill them all."

Mary Alyce put her hand on top of Agnes's and smiled. "That sounds lovely." Agnes returned the smile, opened the door and proceeded to yell at whomever was in there playing in her kitchen, saying that she was going to find a switch and tear up their hide. Mary Alyce felt right at home as she followed Agnes inside.

EPILOGUE

From Abigail Noel Campbell, in Wilberforce, Ohio, to Judy Welsh outside Paris, France

Monday, 1 November 2002

Dearest Judy:
It has been some time. I hope you have been faring well since our last reunion, which was such a delight for Charity and me to attend, even as age has started to take its toll on all of us in one way or another. It's supposed to be a surprise, but we are planning a special 85th birthday celebration for her, and we have been collecting stories to capture a little of her big legacy. Not many people know about how she went to work in Cleveland after we left the service as a registration officer to process veteran's requests for G.I. and education funding.

You know Big Ma—she convinced me it was a worthy cause and of course, she was right. But we saw pretty quickly it was something of a lost cause. And she wanted to be out of the US so we went back abroad, to Zurich. She studied German and analytical psychology (of all things) before we came on back home. She was not going to let anybody or anything keep her from the country she loved, not even her own disappointment in things.

I'm not sure how many more birthdays we'll get, but while I can still see and write well enough to ask, I thought I'd try out this modern postal situation in the States. I'd love to hear the latest about you and your friends and how life has turned out for all of you after crossing paths with the incomparable Lieutenant Colonel.

Please do let me know and thank you in advance for making this a special treat for her.
Love Always,
Abbie.

Thursday, 17 November 2002

Captain Campbell:
What a delight to hear from you. A decade is a good long while to wait for an update, but I am so pleased to hear that you and the Lieutenant Colonel have made what sounds like a peaceful life for yourselves in Ohio and other places around the world.

The more time passes, the more I think that my year and a half with the Six Triple Eight was the richest most surprising time in my life. Not only because that's where I found my beloved Bernard, who is still just as busy as ever (despite being much older than myself!). There were just a few things, as you know, a Negro could be back then. Now, we can be anything. Charity Adams was the first Black woman to show me what was possible.

She did the same for all of us, I think. Stacy McFadden, my bunkmate, tried going back home to help her family on the farm near St. Louis, but she couldn't get G.I. benefits and ended up doing factory work. Even though she kept coming up against barriers and excuses, she kept fighting for what she was owed until finally they got sick of her and let her have her benefits.

Mary Alyce did the same thing—she tried going back to Vermont, but she felt more at home in the South. She ended up being a fighter, too. She devoted her whole life to the Civil Rights Movement as a Freedom Rider. She told me at the reunion before last—the one you and the Lieutenant Colonel couldn't make—that after all she had seen, she knew she had to do something instead of just thinking about it all the time.

As for me, I went to the WAC when Big Ma recruited me because I knew I wouldn't make anything of my life if I stayed. It was different for my mother, who passed away a few years ago, after working as a domestic for most of her life. Later, she became a labor organizer to help others. Bernard and I were so pleased at the arc of her life, but no one more than me.

So I would say to Big Ma in celebration of her 85th birthday that her influence and legacy rippled out not only to those of us lucky to have been under her command but also to everyone in our lives.

We all found ways to mirror her contributions to America, even when our country never gave us back all that we gave it. It's a shame that it takes going other places to help us see how to transform into who we are really meant to be.

I could go on and on, as you can probably tell. This is a lot of information, a lot of life to try and put into words. But maybe we are all always trying to fit our lives on the page in one way or another.

Please wish Big Ma the happiest of birthdays from the Welshes.

Yours truly,
Judith Welsh

★ ★ ★ ★ ★

ACKNOWLEDGEMENTS

About a decade ago, as my mother was dying and I was trying to cope with anticipatory grief, I woke up in the middle of the night thinking about the woman who would reveal herself to me over time as Judy Washington, one of the heroines of this story. The story would change significantly over time, but she was dressed in her husband's clothes and she needed to leave soon.

After ten separate years of applying to Hedgebrook, an incredible writing residency, and failing to get in, I found respite there in 2017, as the US and other parts of the world looked to be sliding back into fascism. While I was in that beautiful place, I read about Alyce Dixon, a 108-year-old veteran of the 6888th Central Postal Battalion and suddenly I knew where Judy was rushing off to.

So this novel and adventure was born at Hedgebrook, to whom I owe a special debt of gratitude for reminding me of how powerful it is to write not only in a tradition but also in community with other powerful women envisioning new, different worlds and recovering lost pasts.

Thank you to Lieutenant Charity Edna Adams Earley for her leadership of the 855 Black women of the 6888th Central Postal Battalion and for recounting her early life with such clear-eyed detail. Special thanks to the Foundation for Women Warriors for screening a documentary about the Six Triple Eight online during the pandemic, which helped me flesh out aspects of this work significantly.

I am deeply indebted to my communities in the Bronx, Austin, Washington, D.C., and New Jersey who have supported this idea and championed it since before I realized I was even writing it. Thank you very much to Anna Vodicka and Frank Bergon, my writing soul mates who lovingly read early versions of this book and made me see it more clearly.

No one was more instrumental to the refining and shaping of the core of the book than my unflappable, wise and talented literary agent, Elisabeth Weed, who is as sharp and insightful as she is witty. Elisabeth, thank you is not really enough to express my gratitude. I feel so honored that we found one another. Many thanks to Julie Barer at The Book Group for connecting us, and for all that every member of your team does to further the work of authors.

Working with Laura Brown on the novel has been a dream, and her edits brought the emotion and love that I felt out more clearly in sentences where I was still being too far from the soul of my characters. Thank you, Laura, for seeing my story, and what was not yet written, so that I could put it on the page.

Thank you so much to Jerri Gallagher, for affirming and seeing my story, for polishing and correcting my willy-nilly imaginative military hierarchies and helping me further bring this book of mine closer to what I dreamed it could be.

I proudly work in a tradition of phenomenal, dedicated writers, scholars and thinkers that is composed mostly of Black women and men, though not entirely: James Baldwin, Audre Lorde, Paul Robeson, Octavia Butler, Pat Barker, Gloria Naylor, Toni Morrison, Ntozake Shange, Alice Walker, Evelyn C. White, Joanne Bealy, Jacqueline Woodson, Isabel

Wilkerson, Elizabeth Alexander, Bernice McFadden, Saidiya Hartman, Gwendolyn Brooks and Nikki Giovanni and many more names that I grew up admiring, like Gloria Anzaldua and Cherrie Moraga and Judy Blume, who taught me how to be, how to move, and the kind of writer I hoped to become. Thank you for helping me to be brave. Thank you for teaching me to dream on the page. Thank you for making me and a book like this possible.

I am eternally grateful to my family for their constant support and encouragement, along with my beloved communities in the Bronx who make it possible for me to write and stretch and win.

Last but never least, I want to acknowledge my mother, Marguerite Sandoval, for the grueling, thankless work she had to do to survive in spite of her many challenges. I want to acknowledge my grandmothers, who faced the same lack of options as the women before them, but still thrived and gleamed and shone.

WOMEN OF THE POST

JOSHUNDA SANDERS

Reader's Guide

PARK ROW
BOOKS

"Somewhere in England, Maj. Charity E. Adams,...and Capt. Abbie N. Campbell,...inspect the first contingent of Negro members of the Women's Army Corps assigned to overseas service." Courtesy: National Archives Local Identifier: 111-SC-200791; National Archives Identifier: 531249.

AUTHOR NOTE

This photograph was one of the first images that led to what would become a five-year obsession with writing about the lives of Black women veterans who served in the US military during World War II, especially the women of the 6888th Central Postal Battalion, who are the heroines of this book.

If I were pressed to describe in detail how I feel about war, I might have to call myself a pacifist given my love of peace, and my dedication to a non-violent mindfulness practice. At the same time, I've learned, partially through writing *Women of the Post*, that my legacy and work in the world has to do with recovering American stories of beauty, resilience and grit as reflected especially in the lives of Black women that have for too long gone undiscovered and untold.

It is with this in mind that I began to learn, for the first time in a serious way, about the relationship of the US armed forces to Black women. Nothing in any of my education—in New York and Pennsylvania public schools, in Catholic and Jesuit schools, at Vassar College or the University of Texas at Austin—ever mentioned the possibility that General Harriet Tubman did more than free slaves; that she was, in fact, one of the first Black women the US military enlisted to assist with Civil War efforts. The same, of course, is true, as it relates to the trailblazing Lieutenant Colonel Charity Edna Adams Earley.

The story of American veterans has always skewed white and male. While things have started to change somewhat with books like Matthew F. Delmont's important reference for me, *Half American*, among others, we still know too little about Black women's contributions during World War II. It was of critical importance to me while writing this novel to do my small part to begin to change that. I was enamored of the 6888th as soon as I learned about them, and the nuanced significance of their behind-the-scenes role in improving morale for soldiers on the frontlines by ensuring that they heard from their loved ones in America, regardless of where they were serving in the world.

Much of the particular challenge of writing this book came from having to piece together how Black women of the Central Postal Battalion would have felt, what they would have done, how they would have coped with their unique experiences and purviews, since only a few of them have been interviewed and only Lieutenant Adams Earley wrote a memoir, *One Woman's Army*, which was a valuable resource for me. This account deviates significantly in some key ways from the actual events of her life, but I'll get to that in a moment.

It was through searching through the abundant stories about white male veterans and their experience in World War II, followed by more extensive looks at Black men, then white women that I was able to augment the few critical texts that exist solely about the 6888th but has so much to attend to by being seminal that it does not position nor locate them in these histories and narratives about the great people who contributed to World War II.

I had never given this much thought until, in 2017, I happened to read the obituary for Alyce Dixon, who died in 2016 at age 108. She was believed to be one of the oldest female veterans in America. One of a few surviving members of the 6888th Central Postal Battalion. At 16, her obituary said, she changed the spelling of her name to Alyce because of a picture show she saw featuring Alyce Mills—"She lived life on her own terms from that day forward."

I was a total fan of this woman, but I also had so many questions, and also a little bit of fury. I had never known that Black women served in World War II in any capacity. (A note about language here: the nomenclature for referring to African Americans in the 1930s and 40s was Negro/Negroes, which is why I opted to use that term in the text, though it is outdated now, so for the purposes of this note, I'll use Black.)

I think I vaguely sensed that Black women had served in some capacity in the Great War, possibly as nurses, but I certainly did not know there was a unit of 855 of them from all over the country who would become the only self-contained unit of Black women to serve overseas in the 1940s, with the main goal of clearing a backlog of millions of pieces of mail to soldiers marching on Normandy. Their efforts were meant to boost soldiers' morale as the war dragged on longer than expected on several different fronts. Seeing the women lined up, Charity Adams and Abbie Campbell standing in the front, has captivated me ever since, and led me to try and do justice to their stories in a more comprehensive way.

With my background in journalism, I immediately searched for as much as I could find about these Black women soldiers. At first, I considered trying to track down those still living and interviewing survivors, but time and money constraints gave me pause. Luckily, I discovered Elizabeth Collins, whose 2017 Defense Media Activity post, "Sorting the Mail, Blazing A Trail" led me to so many other sources.

I owe her a tremendous debt. From there, I read The Library of Congress' Veterans History transcripts, the New York Public Library and the Schomburg's digital archives, Darlene Clark Hine's indispensable encyclopedia volumes, *Black Women in America*, and finally watched a screening of "The Six Triple Eight" documentary hosted by the Foundation for Women Warriors during the summer of 2020.

While Charity Adams, Abigail Campbell and Mary Alyce Dixon are based on real people, I fictionalized the main protagonist, Judy Washington, along with her husband, Herbert, and her mother, Margaret. The members of the battalion, including Bernadette and Stacy, are completely made-up composites; though three women enlisted did actually die in a car accident while the women were stationed in Rouen.

I felt that we needed these characters to contextualize the time period. It was also fun to imagine what the lives and stakes of these officers who joined the 6888th might have been like, while also rooting them in history.

Margaret and her husband James followed the trajectory of some six million Black people who were a part of The Great Migration from the fraught, racist and dangerous post-Reconstruction South to Northern, Midwestern and Western cities. They came seeking increased opportunities in the 1920s, but when the Depression hit, they found themselves in a new place with fewer options. As rough as the Great Depression was for everyone, it was doubly hard for Black workers. That context is important because Margaret, understandably, does not believe that the world will be more forgiving for her or her daughter in the North. Her life has shown her too much to believe in Judy's optimism.

I wanted to set Judy up as an optimist compared to her mother's way of thinking and to show her nearly lose it while working at the Bronx Slave Market. On street corners in the Bronx near major thoroughfares starting in the 1930s, "slave marts" popped up where white housewives could find cheap domestic labor. Famed activist and SNCC mentor Ella Baker teamed up with journalist Marvel Cooke to write a two-part exposé about the markets; they went undercover to write about what they called the Paper Bag Brigade—women who waited patiently on benches and crates with bags holding their cleaning gloves and clothes so that they could be exploited by housewives who, because of federal legislation barring immigrants from European countries who would have been their preferred live-in help, needed Black women to clean their houses to keep up middle-class appearances.

Judy's early experiences on the Bronx Slave Market led her to embrace applying for the Women's Army Corps. While also fictionalized, I used details from Cooke and Baker's articles as well the revelatory scholarship I read in Vanessa H. May's *Unprotected Labor: Household Workers, Politics and Middle-Class Reform in New York, 1870-1940*. To the best of my knowledge, no one else has fictionalized the Slave Market and this unfortunate real-life endeavor.

The Library of Congress has such rich archives and oral testimonies of folks who lived in the Bronx in the 1930s and 1940s that helped me understand more deeply what my beloved borough was like during the Great Depression. There was such a dearth of opportunity that the WACs became a dream and the only salvation.

My details about the Women's Army Corps, were influenced by the narratives Lt. Col. Charity Adams Earley shares in her memoir along with texts like *To Serve My Country, To Serve My Race: The Story of the Only African American WACs Stationed Overseas during World War II* by Brenda L. Moore. Charity only briefly, almost casually, mentions the German U-boats that made their voyage to Birmingham, England, less than pleasant, along with the bomb that met the women at the dock in Scotland. Watching the seven-part Ken Burns and Lynn Novick PBS miniseries, "The War," and reading a bit about soldiers' experiences during WWII—including in the book *Sheer Misery: Soldiers in Battle in WWII* by Mary Louise Roberts—helped me flesh out a little of what most of the women must have been feeling as war continued around and near them. Robert Child's *Immortal Valor* was another very helpful resource, although for the sake of the plot, the timeline of actual World War II events and the WAC's service in Europe are not perfectly aligned, and I took some creative liberties for the sake of the narrative arcs of each character.

Of the WAC officers and leaders in the novel, only Charity Adams and Abbie Noel Campbell are based on real officers enlisted in the 6888th leaders/officers. Some events I've fictionalized in the book are elaborations of stories Earley mentions in passing in her memoir, including the white Southern officer who curses out the racist conductor at the train station, the Reverend/chaplain who quickly found himself fired and her infamous declaration to an officer who outranked her that he would see her replaced by a white woman, "Over my dead body, sir," which reinforced her status as an icon and legend among the women who reported to her, if not beyond. The car accident in which three officers died is real, but Bernadette is a made-up composite character, and was not one of the three. The dust-up from white officers who questioned Charity's authority as the ranking officer on the trip home is also, unfortunately, based on a true story.

The relationship between Charity and Abbie is fictionalized, and serves as a tribute to something Moore mentions in greater detail in her book, which is a more sociological, academic take: as frightening as it must have been for these Black women, who had never before been given any indication that it would be possible for them to live and work abroad, while also making money, they also found themselves suddenly with a level of personal freedom and power that would naturally translate for those of them who were queer to also feel more free to express their love for one another. I know that there were real romances forged at that time between women, but I understand why we may never know the full, inspiring, beautiful details of those relationships. Allowing Charity and Abbie to have this romance is one way of imagining how that love might have looked and felt. These are women who defied all manner of social norms by coming to leadership in the way they did, subverting norms for women's work and stature in society; in reality, Lt. Col. Charity Earley married a man and remained so until the end of her life in January 2002.

The scenario in which Mary Alyce finds herself is based on a true story of an officer, but her name has been changed, some of her circumstances and characteristics imagined. The spelling of her name is my tribute to the late Ms. Dixon. Otherwise, everything about Mary Alyce—from her relationship to her Vermont friends and to her mother and her eventual connection with an aunt on her father's side— was purely fictional, inspired by a few lines in Earley's memoir in which she discusses the recruit who discovered she was Black when she came to report for duty.

I learned a great deal more about World War II than I ever knew before, helped, in part, by the Ken Burns and Lynn Novick PBS Documentary, "The War," along with military sources and historical sites online, including that of the US Army. The imagined details of where Black women fit in the context of American history with respect to World War II are all imagined, since their stories are missing from most documentation of the period.

It's important to note that I took some significant liberties with the timelines, and the 6888th travels and service do not necessarily match up exactly with actual WWII events because of the plot development I needed to reflect their journeys. A good example of this, which historical fiction experts and readers with good knowledge of the war will note, is the timing of the Battle of the Bulge in the book, which happened after the battalion's arrival in Edgbaston, not before, as I wrote in the novel. Changing the timing of events felt important to underscore the context of the war in relationship to the women's service. They were also far more free to travel about in this novel than they might have been in 1944 and 1945; especially because while I reference a number of places in Rouen and Paris where I imagined they would have loved to visit, both cities were heavily bombed and damaged during WWII—and rail lines were completely destroyed—so they likely would not have been able to visit them in reality. There was significant destruction and deprivation, along with significant travel restrictions, so these passages are likely highly exaggerated versions of group outings and bonding moments for the actual women of the 6888th Battalion. Judy and others move around relatively freely, but as enlisted members of the military, their movement would have been more restricted. The same is true about Judy's decisions/autonomy to return to the US or stay in France; she would have needed to be formally discharged with permission from her commanding officer/the WAC leadership before saying yes or no to Bernard or anything else.

Finally, not only was the US military not even really racially integrated—Black men were permitted to serve in small numbers and often they were not permitted to carry weapons; neither were the women—but the military didn't really know what to do with women. This makes sense given gender roles and norms at the time. First, the Women's Army was meant to be Auxiliary and merely for support—switchboard operations, for example. But the longer the war went on, the more men died, the more people were needed to do more things. So the military dropped the Auxiliary part, which made room for the WAC to be born, and for women to start deploying all over the world.

The ultimate point of Judy's trip abroad, her adventures with the Central Postal Battalion, the mentorship of a woman who, then, must have been like a unicorn, is to underscore how much fight it takes in the human spirit to live out the promises of freedom and meritocracy that have become a part of what it means to be American. You need even more of that fight, that heart, the farther you are away from the traditional image or symbolism for what being a real, proud American looks like. *Women of the Post* had all of that fight and heart— and so much more— based on everything I've learned about the women of the 6888th Central Postal Battalion. I did my best to try to convey just a little bit of that in these pages.

1. The story begins with Judy and her mother, Margaret, working in the Bronx Slave Market, a true to life urban slave market where Black women were exploited by white women for domestic labor. Before reading, did you know about the Bronx Slave Market? Why do you think the author included this piece of US history in the beginning of the novel?

2. When Captain Charity Adams asks Judy to be supportive of Mary Alyce after the latter discovers her father was Black, Adams says, "I've found that the most challenging assignments I've experienced have taught me the most—often lessons in patience and empathy that I might otherwise have missed." Can you think of a time in your own life where this advice has rung true?

3. There are many strong, complex female characters in *Women of the Post*. Who was your favorite character, and why?

4. Letters are an important motif throughout the story, and the novel both starts and ends with a letter. Why do you

think that's the case? What do you think letters symbolize in *Women of the Post* and how do they impact the characters' lives?

5. After Mary Alyce gives Judy the letter regarding Herbert's presumed death, Judy reflects on what her mother, Margaret, had always told her: "No one could experience any part of life on someone else's behalf. They needed to have the joy and the pain on their own." Do you agree with this? What would you have done in Mary Alyce's shoes?

6. In your opinion, which character in the novel showed the most personal growth and why?

7. After serving in the 6888th Postal Battalion, many of the women are unable/unwilling to return to the life they had before serving. Consider one of the central characters and discuss how their perception of "home" transformed throughout the novel.

8. There are various portrayals of "love" shown throughout the novel—platonic love, romantic love, patriotic love, and familial love. Considering these different forms of love, which relationship(s) were your favorite, and why?

9. At the end of the novel, in her letter to Abigail Campbell, Judy writes, "Maybe we are all always trying to fit our lives on the page in one way or another." What do you think she means by this? How does it relate to the story at large?